THE MAN OF THE HOUR

HE CLASPED HER TIGHTLY, WHILE THEY COMFORTED EACH OTHER

Page 476

THE
MAN OF THE HOUR

By

OCTAVE THANET

Author of

Stories of a Western Town, The Missionary Sheriff
A Book of True Lovers, etc.

French, Alice

WITH ILLUSTRATIONS BY
LUCIUS WOLCOTT HITCHCOCK

INDIANAPOLIS
THE BOBBS-MERRILL COMPANY
PUBLISHERS

PS
1717
m35

PRESS OF
BRAUNWORTH & CO.
BOOKBINDERS AND PRINTERS
BROOKLYN, N. Y.

TO THE MEMORY OF

R. T. F.

WORKINGMAN AND GENTLEMAN

CONTENTS

BOOK I

JOHNNY-IVAN

BOOK II

IVAN

BOOK III

JOHN

"Spirits of old that bore me
    And set me, meek of mind,
Between great deeds before me,
    And deeds as great behind,

Knowing Humanity my star,
    As forth of old I ride,
O help me wear with every scar
    Honor at eventide!"

THE MAN OF THE HOUR

Book I

JOHNNY-IVAN

THE MAN OF THE HOUR

CHAPTER I

PEGGY

In the early eighties Fairport considered herself a city; but she was, in fact, an overgrown, delightful town sprawling among the low hills of the Mississippi Valley.

Near enough the town's origin still to distinguish its outlines, but remote enough to idealize them, the old settlers were a power, and could be found of a sunny afternoon at Luke Darrell's livery stable, busy with the apotheosis of the days when they shot quail before breakfast; true brotherly love prevailed among men; and the river was the highway of commerce.

Despite the pioneers' lamentations, Fairport was a kindly town, where every one went to the High School before his lot in life gave him college or work for his daily bread; and old acquaintance was not forgot. Like most middle-western towns, also, obscure though they may be, it was touched by all the great issues of the world. This, indeed, is the sig-

3

nificant trait of western life; to feel vividly things which concern not the petty affairs of the individual, but the welfare of the commonwealth or the race.

This breadth of sympathy and of vision is the poetry of the Westerner's material and laborious life, redeeming his crudity, his vanity and his often brutal energy. Fairport, because of it, was thoroughly western; its humor and its generosity also were western; but at first glance it seemed singularly unlike the typical town of its section. It was rich; it was conservative, almost slow moving in some directions; it was not bustling or breezy or lightsomely braggart; it never had a "boom." In the early eighties the down-town streets must have worn an idyllic air, paved with soft lime macadam, disturbed by no harsher noise than the rattle of farm-wagons or the occasional whistle and rumble of a train, and scarcely darkened by the two- and three-story shops. There was green grass a-plenty as well as trees about the yellow jail and the red brick court-house, rearing its Corinthian pillars above a little flock of justice-seekers or attorneys, who were used to tilt their pine arm-chairs (polished smooth by occupancy) while they leisurely awaited a moment of strong enough interest to draw them back to the court-room.

Dwelling-houses dotted the hillsides. Fairport contained some brick houses, ample and of a pleasant homeliness, built by southern settlers after the St. Louis fashion, with steep roofs and a stay-wall between the chimneys, which perched on the gable peaks like miniature barbicans; and there were a

few grandiose Georgian mansions. Of these the
Winslow house caught the eye most quickly.

It was a big pile, with the lofty portico which our
great-grandfathers loved. Its fluted Corinthian pillars and garlanded pediment shone white through
the trees; below, the flowering terraces stepped
down to the soft greenery of orchard and pasture;
above, the house was backed by wooded hills.
"Atherton's Folly" the Fairport people had named
the place; for the house was built by the first mayor
of the town (Atherton, not Fairport, then), a
man of vast schemes that had discounted the future
too lavishly; wherefore he came to grief. His own
downfall he could have borne, being a stanch and
stout fighter; but the town was crippled a while
by the crash, and this broke his heart; he only
lived a few months after his failure. For years the
house stood empty, gray and haggard with neglect,
while time charred and twisted its shingles. Finally, Winslow, the plow manufacturer, bought the
estate for a song; and it began a new career of prosperity, as Overlook.

That was fourteen years ago, in the late sixties;
now, in 1881, a little smiling pale boy played in the
gardens and fed the pigeons. If he were pale, he
was not languid; his dark eyes sparkled and his
thick curls danced in the wind with his running;
and his nurse grumbled to her companions, "Oh,
yes, Yonny-Ivan, he's good-tempered, but if he
git one his naughty times—my crachus, he get
arms an' legs so stiff as iron!" Sometimes a stout
man of fifty, whose black eyebrows looked the
blacker for his graying hair, would pace at the little

fellow's side. Often his thick brows were bent, but always a finger hung downward for the little hand. Sometimes a slender and beautiful woman would walk with the boy, bending a lovely dark head and often stooping to give him a quick caress. Whoever his companion chanced to be, the servants would glance after the pair curiously. Every one in Fairport knew that the Winslows were not a happy pair and that their differences ran high over their only child. His very name hinted their combats. His Russian mother called him "Ivan," or Vanya,* his American father "Johnny"; while the servants fell upon the just compromise of "Johnny-Ivan."

Johnny-Ivan knew nothing of the disputes between his mother, whom he adored, and his father, whom he respected and very cordially liked. His beaming little face reflected only sunshine.

Now, when Johnny-Ivan and the writer are first keeping company together, he is nine years old, so big that he can almost dress himself, wears his knickerbockers attached to his shoulders by suspenders the small image of his father's, and has come to hate his babyish big collars. Only a month before, he had a more carking grief in his curls, at which the boys of the Patch used to jeer; but, after deep consideration, he surrendered to an impulsive moment and snipped them off himself. Thereby came his first movement of comradeship toward his father; his mother had almost wept and he had been reduced to black, sticky depths of re-

* Russian diminutive of Ivan.

morse in consequence; but his father had smiled all over his face.

"I like the looks of you, Johnny; the Mickies were right; curls belong to girls and babies, not to big boys," said he.

"But mamma feels awful!" Johnny-Ivan's conscience forced out of him.

"Oh, naturally; Aunty will tell you it was dreadfully naughty of you, too; but they're ladies; they don't know how men feel; you and I are men."

Johnny-Ivan gravely wagged his little cropped head. Here was a father worth having!

He almost told him about the new book which he had discovered in the library,—almost, not quite; confidence is a frail plant in children, needing tedious nurture and tendance ere it flower. Johnny-Ivan went away, silently, to his new treasure. An hour later his mother discovered him on the floor, both elbows propped on the leaves of a huge folio. He answered her query about the book with a matter of fact, "Richard Three."

"Who wrote it?" said she, amused.

"Shak-es-pary," spelled the reader.

"*Mon Dieu!* do you understand it?"

"Not *everything*," confessed the little boy, "but I like it awful much! it's all full of kings and queens and fightings." Johnny-Ivan kept a martial soul.

Yet on this day, the first day you and I see Johnny-Ivan, his ardor for brave doings has brought humiliation upon him. Really it has been responsible for his first quarrel with his first comrade; and he is standing on the Winslow side of the high fence dividing the Overlook property from the Winter place, pressing a dismal little face against the pickets. His eyes are dark with wistfulness; his heart is full of woe.

Hilma, his nurse, has run up to him, having loitered so long over her lace-making and been so intent upon her linen wheels that she did not note his vanishing; wherefore it is only after a hunt through the stables, the chicken houses and the garden that she has caught a glimpse of his blue blouse and white collar, and appeared before him breathless, in the natural ill-humor of a person who has been frightened.

"Yonny-Ivan," cried Hilma, "you is worse as a rat to run 'way. I tell you' mummer. Wot you doing here?"

"Nothing," muttered Johnny-Ivan, scowling.

"I bet you looking for Peggy. And you was looking for Peggy, yesterday, too, wasn't you? And didn't she go by yoost upturnin' her nose at you!"

No response beyond a wriggle of pain and impatience. Relentlessly the inquisitor turned the screws again.

"Wasn't you here, day before too,—twicet? and she tossed her red head at you. And didn't you take over your new little spade and your red pail and your best necktie, you *naughty* boy? I donno vot you' mummer say—"

"Oh, mamma don't mind,"—the boy shrugged himself out of some reminiscent attentions to his cravat,—"mamma letted me give the red one to a poor little boy on the street."

Hilma put her own opinion into Swedish, getting back to her auditor, however, with the English addition: "Well, you' popper *he* mind!"

"Anyhow, Peggy didn't take them," sighed the boy.

"Vot you do to Peggy make her so mad?"

The boy only squeezed his slim body closer to the pickets.

Hilma, seating herself, took out an interminable piece of lace to begin her crocheting. "Vell, anyhow, sie a mean little copperhead," said Hilma artfully.

The boy, as she expected, fired at once. "No, she ain't, neither; I madded her first."

"Oh, you did,—vot you do?"

"I—I *bited* her," confessed the little boy, with a deep flush of shame.

"Oh my! Ain't you de bad boy, sometime! *I helige verlden!* I guess you come to git hanged for dot ter'ble temper you got sometime, Yonny-Ivan! An' sie ain't do notings to mad you?"

The boy looked miserable; even when one is only nine and doesn't so much as know the word by sight, one may have foregleams of chivalry; Johnny-Ivan hated to cast a reflection on Peggy, whom he had wronged and before whom he would willingly abase himself; at the same time, it was ghastly to have Hilma think that there was no palliation for his shameful behavior, which, like the sins of later years, somehow loomed up so much bigger and blacker and uglier when confessed than when only remembered. After a second of anguish, he stammered out his compromise.

"She didn't *do* nothin'. She just said things."

"Vot tings?" Hilma would not be denied.

"Well, she said—she said I wouldn't be no good in a Blood Feud."

"Vot's a Blood Feud?"

"Why, don't you know? Those things they have down South; when somebody shoots your grandfather and your father shoots him and his son shoots you—like that. Peggy's father's uncle got killed that way, right in the street in Memphis, opposite the park where the squirrels play."

Hilma grunted a comprehension far from approval. "I hope you *don't* be," she remarked, while her head wagged gloomily over her lace, "but I don't be so *sure*."

Johnny-Ivan brightened; it was evident that it had wrung his soul to be considered so ignominiously peaceful. He opened his heart a little wider.

"It was only because, you know, a boy on the Patch, he sassed Peggy and said her papa was a old rebel and ought to be hanged, and she had red hair, and I fought him and hit him and he rolled over the bank. It was there in Winters', you know, where the broke glass tumblers and tin cans are in the ravine; and he didn't have no shoes on, and he cut his foot on a piece of glass and it was bleeding awful, and so I run down to help him and said I'd go for the doctor, for I didn't know maybe he'd bleed to deff or have the locker-jaw,—you can't tell, mammy says, if you run a rusty nail in you, but you'll git locker-jaw; that's just like she says. But Peggy said you can't bleed to deff from cutting your toe, nohow, and it was glass and not rusty nails; and anyhow he was our foe and I was pusserlanimous and ornery to go and—and—what I did."

"Vot did you done?" Hilma's face expressed no human interest and she counted in Swedish between her questions, yet dimly Johnny-Ivan was aware of sympathy. Nevertheless, he hung his head in shame, as he confessed: "I tied his foot up in my hangkerchif."

"Was it one you' new vuns?" Hilma asked very sternly.

"No, Hilma, truly it wasn't. It was one of my real old ones."

"Humph! It yoost *happen* dot way. You take you' new vuns, yoost so quick. But Peggy didn't done right."

"Oh, yes, she did, Hilma, that's the way you got to do if you're quality and live down South!" said Johnny-Ivan. His eyes lightened and he smiled. "Maybe she'll speak to me *to-day!*" he cried. Hilma could see that his lips quivered with excitement, and his little fingers gripped the pickets more tightly.

"Dot's sie now, ain't it?" said Hilma, "koomin' down drive." There before them, just glimmering past the clump of lilacs on the turn of the drive, was Peggy, herself; Peggy, in her new white leghorn hat with the flowered ribbon and her mother's red parasol shimmering above the hat. Her white frock was dainty-fresh and ruffled bravely; nor did it in the least abate the impressiveness of the tiny dame that she held her splendid sun protector at the wrong angle. The boy caught his breath with the beauty of her.

"My! don't the sun make her hair red!" said Hilma.

Stepping daintily over the dusty road, her dazzling head well in the air, Miss approached. She was taller than the boy—by good right, being two years older; thus she could lower her eyelids in his direction. The little fellow bent quickly and fished a basket from out the long grass,—an enticing basket with a load of figs.

"I got some figs for you, Peggy!" cried he; he tried to make his voice bold and careless.

Not the slightest sign of hearing was vouchsafed by the haughty damsel; she looked past the peace-offering and the little arms which held it, to Hilma's stolid front.

"Good evening, Hilma," she cried with affable sweetness, and passed on.

"*Tantæne*—" well, we all know Virgil's moan, cruelty comes to women early. Peggy did not cast a glance at the little figure or the wistful eyes and the mouth which would tremble in spite of him. He began to whistle.

"Well, if sie ain't up-stuck!" cried Hilma.

"It's just keeping her word; she said she'd never speak to me again," explained Johnny-Ivan; "she's got to keep her word, you know,"—then, choking back a shake in his voice and quite forgetting his logic: "Maybe she'll speak to me *to-morrow!*" he cried hopefully.

Now, as it happened, Peggy the ruthless felt what seemed to her degrading twinges of pity; besides, Johnny, although so much younger and, of course, babyish, was nicer to play with than anybody else; he made believe better than anybody, and on the donkey as Sir Lancelot charging on the paynim foe, or with his father's cane as Ivan the Terrible, he was perfectly splendid; Peggy, like many another proud heart, wasn't anywhere near the height of hauteur that she assumed; but she was in the chains of her own will—there, again like many another.

"I *said* I wouldn't speak to him again *to save his life;* and I won't!" determined Peggy, shutting her teeth and walking hard on her heels, such was her determination and stress of soul. She did not notice the two men, who had been raking the grass, drop their rakes and gesticulate. Neither did she get anything from them save a shout—they were too far away for articulate words. But she did hear a pounding thump behind her, and a horrible hoarse bellow. She flung a startled glance around the handle of the red parasol. She was a fearless little creature; but it wasn't in flesh and blood not to be terrified by the great horned mass, with its glaring eyes, bounding down the grassy slope, straight at *her!* Her single wild sweep of the landscape told her that the men were too far to help, and the fence was a wall of bristling pickets! But that same vision of terror had shown Johnny-Ivan frantically tugging at the pickets and crying out at Hilma's unready motions: "Hurry! hurry! knock 'em with the big stone! Peggy! here! *here!*"

Instinctively she ran for the opening in the fence. She felt the hot dust of the brute's onset; her heart pounded in her breast as her feet flashed across the road. Suddenly a form leaped before her; the parasol was wrenched from her hand and made a crimson splash through the air.

"Get down! get down! Crawl through! Pull her, Hilma!" She knew Johnny-Ivan's sweet high pipe, shrill now with intensity. She obeyed; but in the very act of kneeling, her wits righted themselves, and she snatched Johnny's blue shoulder and thrust it at Hilma. Before the boy could resist— if he had thought of any such action—a strong hand pulled him through the gap and returned swiftly for the same service to Peggy. Peggy's skirts, sad to say, caught on one of the loosened nails; but Hilma, usually so severe on the careless treatment of clothes, never slackened her mighty grasp. Rending, tearing, bruising, scratching, Peggy was pulled through the fence. On the safe side, she caught her breath; her eyes glued to the whirling cloud of dust streaked with red and the huge dun shape impelling the cloud.

"Oh! look at mamma's pah'sol!" wailed Peggy. "Silas is just stomping and tearing it all to frazzles! An' I didn't ask for it neither, Mymy! mymy! won't mammy chastise me! she'll be fahly rarin' an' chargin'!" Her clouded face cleared in a second. "I reckon that Silas would be doing me that same way wasn't it fo' you t'rowing the pah'sol at him, Jo'nivan."

Johnny-Ivan blushed proudly, finding no expression save a feeble grin.

There are weak natures that might have been disconcerted by such a situation: having a scorned ex-friend risk his life to rescue them from danger. Peggy was not one of these; she felt that she had

been relieved of her rash vow in a thoroughly cred-
itable manner, and rejoiced without dissimulation.

"Jo'nivan," said she, in a dignified tone, "you
done—I mean you *have* saved my life; of co'se I
was obliged to thank you; and so I *had* to speak to
you; and once I broke my word, why—why, I am
just naturally *obliged* to be going on speaking to
you. Hadn't it been for that I reckon I couldn't
ever in this world, again, have pahted lips with
you!"

"But you *did* speak to me, Peggy!" Johnny-Ivan
interrupted in some trepidation; "it's all broked
now!"

"Of co'se it is; that's what I say; so, now—I beg
you' pahdon, Jo'nivan."

"Oh-h!" breathed Johnny-Ivan, deeply embarrassed.

"Don't say, *'Oh!'* say: 'No gentleman could ask
more, sah!'"

Johnny-Ivan readily repeated the words, and
with equal readiness, when prompted, apologized
for the original cause of offense.

"Now le's make up," said Peggy with a sigh of
relief. "Say, Hilma, can't you mend my frock? and
my leg's bleeding, too; but you better leave that;
mammy won't be so mad if she sees I been hurt.
Say, Jo'nivan, wasn't there a basket of figs?"

CHAPTER II

THE HOUSE OF WINSLOW

"Josiah Curwen Winslow was born in Merfield, Massachusetts, April 1, 1830, eighth in descent from the Pilgrim Father, Governor Edward Winslow. Through his mother (Miss Lydia Ann Curwen), our distinguished fellow citizen claims descent from the first families of Salem and the noblest stock of the Puritans." The writer quotes from the biography in a massive and expensive volume entitled *Prominent Citizens of Winfield County, Iowa.* The book is the bulkier that it includes not only the prominent citizens, but any gentleman of the county willing to be thus enshrined in the hearts of his countrymen, at the publishers' price. With a grim smile Winslow signed a check and pushed it across the desk, midway in the agent's glib exordium.

"Awful trash!" he muttered to himself whenever he remembered, "but never mind, maybe Johnny'll like it! and perhaps Olga'll see that there are other folks with ancestors besides the Galitsuins." As a matter of fact, no one could set less value on ancestry than Mrs. Winslow, who was of the new order of thinkers in Russia, and was proud of simplifying herself. Nevertheless, it was imbedded in her hus-

16

band's soul that she scorned him and his friends as
bourgeoisie, because once that unlucky word had
slipped off her tongue. The occasion was an out-
burst of her indignation over the absurd social
distinctions in America, where she had dreamed
all men were brothers, and found them harder in their contempt of the poor than Russian
boyars. But Josiah made small account of her
mood; the word scorched him. That same day he
despatched a clever young art student of Boston to
Plymouth to secure large oil copies of his ancestors'
portraits which deck the walls of the town's little
Temple of Fame. This is how the pensive Pilgrim
scholar, Governor Josiah, came to hang in the
Winslow library, side by side with his choleric
father, the second governor, and the portly, white-
wigged and red-coated general who won a poetic
infamy by obeying orders.

"When the Galitsuins were crawling on all fours
before your dirty Tartar khans," remarked Winslow frequently, in imaginary interviews with his
princess—which never came off—"my ancestors
were ruling free men!"

Few people (among the few was not his wife)
quite appreciated that Josiah possessed that which
every great man of affairs must possess, whether his
affair be with war, art, manufactures or business,
namely, imagination. In the first part of his life, this
concerned itself with piling up money. As a boy, the
only son of a poor New England minister in a with-
ering parish, he dreamed of a great fortune. He
went West to make it; he lived on crackers and
chipped beef; he was often cold, he was generally

hungry; but he was never discouraged. He was sure of himself; no surer after he became Winter's partner than when he was Winter's clerk. Before the war his success was beginning; even in the sixties he was a rich man; the war made him far richer. His great factories could not turn out plows and sulky-rakes fast enough for the teeming soil's demands. Winter died, and his widow became partner in his stead; but there was no halt in the vast onward sweep of a great industry. Already, Winslow had come to be the soul of it all. It occupied his imagination; it almost contented his heart. At this period he was the master of Overlook, his mother and his only surviving sister living with him. He was proud of his mother; he loved his sister; and—he had the Old Colony Plow Works.

Madam Winslow was born a Curwen. She was a stately dame to whose high aquiline features a "front" of raven hair and a white tulle turban lent a really ducal air. Seeing her enthroned behind the old silver and china, with a deferential black man at her elbow, one found it hard to realize that in her early widowhood, when the children were young, she had not only washed the breakfast dishes and made the puddings herself, but, with little Si's assistance, had put down carpets, mended furniture and painted woodwork. The daughter was less impressive; a pretty, gentle, softly humorous creature, who filled her peaceful days with lessons in everything taught by wandering teachers, from the languages to embroidery.

Madam Winslow's sudden death came like a thunderbolt to both sister and brother. The year

following her death Josiah met the Princess Olga
Galitsuin. The meeting happened during his trip to
Russia, where he went to introduce the famous
Winslow chilled plows, now known from whitest
Siberia to darkest Africa. The plows have been
turning the Russian furrows ever since; so far as
business goes, the visit was a tremendous success;
but Winslow's imagination was kinder to him in
business than in love. He admired his princess as
blindly and humbly as a raw country lad admires
the first beautiful summer visitor who flings him a
smile. She was the daughter of a noble and ancient family. Her own branch was not rich, but
they had a property sufficient to maintain their
state in the country if not at court, and Winslow
could hardly believe his good fortune when his
suit was accepted by the head of the family, with
most flattering promptitude. Not until long afterward did he come to understand the reason.
On her part, the princess told him frankly that he
offered her escape from a life which she hated and
an odious marriage. She confessed (with an
adorable blush) that she admired him more than
any man she had ever seen except Krapotkin, who
was a saint and a patriot, not a lover. Perhaps—
yes, sometime, she would love him.

Such a confession impressed Josiah as the most
entrancing mood of a woman beginning to feel the
power of her own heart; he was touched by her honesty; his soul was on its knees before her purity and
her truthfulness. No doubt Olga was sincere; her
fancy had been kindled by the American's devotion,
his generosity, and the kind of calm power which

she felt in the man, added to the glamour about his nationality prevailing among Russian liberals at that time. She was as disposed to dower her lover with splendid virtues as he was to lavish all a woman's possibilities of charm upon her. The nuptials came off, quietly, but with no lack of proper pomp and state; none, at least, obvious to a stranger like the bridegroom. Olga's parents were dead, but her half-brother and two sisters were present to welcome Josiah, saying all the proper and graceful things expected of the moment; and the bridegroom expressed his grateful happiness in a shower of gifts which Prince Platen (the brother) chose for him. He felt no misgivings save as to his own unworthiness.

In fine, the hard-headed, daring, silent man of business was in a golden dream. But the first jarring note came, soon. One day, on their wedding journey, his wife gave away a priceless sable coat to a beggar. "But the man was cold, dear boy," she pleaded, opening her charming eyes wider; "oh, bitter cold—and he was from Little Russia. Can we not buy another?"

Josiah gasped; did she have any idea how much money such a cloak was worth?

No, a great deal, no doubt, but—smiling and pulling his ear—she had plenty more wraps, she wouldn't miss it. He tried to explain; she listened with plaintive attention. At last, her eyes slowly brimmed with tears.

"Do you, too, feel money is more than human beings? I thought you Americans were brothers, all alike free and equal and kind to each other." She

said the words in a level tone, and those lustrous wet
eyes were searching him.

"How long do you think we should have any
money to spend if we gave to every beggar?" he
protested; but he felt the helplessness of the moderate man before the fanatic and the child.

"Ought we to have money to spend or only money
to give?" she wondered, then she tried to smooth
out the perplexed wrinkles on his frowning face.
"Ah, dear boy," (she always called him thus, running the words together, although her English, in
general, was singularly pure and fluent), "ah, dear
boy, I ask too much of you. I can not expect you to
simplify yourself in a moment, if you *are* an American. I shall be patient." She had the air of forgiving him, he could not help thinking, and began a
lively anecdote of her morning. She had never been
more charming; he was in love; he tried to forget.

"She is an angel, but she is a child, too," he reassured himself; "she doesn't understand life, only
that hothouse in Russia. When I get her safe in
Fairport she will be all right."

Fairport, good, honest, western town, opened its
eyes wide at the exquisite toilets, the amazing
speeches and the bewildering habits of this exotic.
She took her breakfast in bed and gave her cook
music lessons. She never returned her formal visits; but she called often at a few houses of a morning or an evening, in any toilet which she happened
to be wearing, whether a dinner gown or a morning
wrapper. She discarded the beautiful moquette velvet
carpets which poor Miss Winslow had gone twice
to Chicago to select, replacing them by hard-

wood floors waxed up to a gloss that caused distressing accidents to several friendly visitors, and covered with dingy old rugs, some of them not even whole, at least very plainly darned. She filled the house with workmen who did awesome things to Madam Winslow's treasures. There was tufted yellow satin on the "big parlor" walls and not a pillowsham in the house. She made the whole town welcome to her samovar of an afternoon; and Serge Vassy—so Fairport abbreviated Vassilovitch—a Russian who lived on the Patch and was an inefficient mason when he wasn't an efficient drunkard, might be seen touching elbows with Judge Rockford who had tried him for murder. There was not much doubt in any one's mind concerning Serge's guilt, but the affair happened in a saloon brawl, with all the witnesses drunk and contradicting one another; whereby legal ethics, more merciful to criminals than to honest men, gave Serge the benefit of the doubt; hence he escaped. Judge Rockford almost dropped his tea-cup when his near-sighted gaze finally focused Serge's identity. He never smiled again at Mrs. Winslow's teas.

"She's a very pretty woman," said the judge; "very charming, very cultivated, but if Winslow ever wants her sent to the lunatic asylum let him come to *me*."

There was always a piquant story afloat regarding the household at Overlook—especially after Miss Winslow married and went away. While she stayed, she was an unobtrusive influence for peace. She kept the house. She was not a housewife of renown like her mother, still, as Mrs. Winter said

dryly, she did have sweeping and baking days and
expected the beds to be made before dinner, while
Princess Olga didn't so much as know bread was
raised by yeast.

But there was an arsenal on the island in the
river, opposite Fairport; there were officers in the
arsenal; and, when Johnny was five, one of these
men of war bore the peaceful little lady away. Since
then, Overlook was become a topic more picturesque
than ever at the Fairport "tea parties." The cook
ran the house until, after a battle royal, the waitress
deposed her and sent her to the police court, the
constable having been summoned and a search having disclosed Mrs. Winslow's opal bracelet under
the sink and her string of pearls in the baking-
powder. At the time, Johnny was barely convalescent from scarlet fever, and Josiah Winslow was being patient and gentle with his wife. He took an
inventory of her jewels and only gulped when he
discovered that a sapphire ring, her second best
watch, two bracelets, an emerald necklace and a
diamond brooch were missing.

As the years and irritations went on he was not
always so patient. The love that he never ceased
to feel for his wife could not restrain his swelling
irritation, always; it did restrain it often; but anger
is like nitroglycerin: it explodes with none the less
violence that it has been frozen. These two, who
had hoped to be lovers, grew more and more unhappy, and the child who might have united them
became the prize of combat.

Yet after Fairport had laughed, criticized and
sorrowfully pitied, it invariably paid its tribute: the

Princess Olga was charming. Her beauty, her wit, her lovely graciousness conquered every one. Her neighbor, Mrs. Winter, was a cold woman; but she grew to love the Russian. With the double-headed discretion of a very wise and rather selfish person, she adventured tentative efforts after some manner of conciliation between the two natures. She even tried her hand at the conversion of Olga. Once she said: "But your serfs are free, free as our niggers; why do you go plotting and conspiring with disgusting people who don't take baths?"

"It is one of the most expensive things in the world to keep clean, my dear friend," Olga would retort, "and not all nihilists are dirty."

"Most of them," said Mrs. Winter. "I took the trouble to get Pisemeki's *Troubled Sea* and Goncharof's *Abyss;* and upon my word, a more obnoxious, vaporing, bragging, bloody, futile, sickening lot of creatures I never read about."

"They are vile books! And the French translation is bad. Oh, most horrid! I know these people."

"Are you a member of the Society?" asked Mrs. Winter, smiling, but a chill took her at the sudden hardening of Olga's face.

"*Nu.* Of course not," she answered, and changed the subject.

"She is lying," decided Mrs. Winter. The thought did not deter her, it only caused her to be more guarded. But she was too shrewd to flatter herself that she made much impression.

Josiah came to share her doubts. He came to apprehend that his wife's nature was not to be gaged by his Anglo-Saxon standards. It was not only that she had the insatiable yearning for the secrets of life which belongs to the Slav, heritage from his Asiatic progenitors, and the relentless following of logic to its end, whatever or however terrible such end may be; it was not only her blind and passionate absorption in her social faiths which might lead her any lengths; there was always, also, the uncertainty of her oriental nature,—its mystery; he knew that she had a conscience to which she was as faithful as any Puritan can be to his; but her conscience was unfathomable. Equally beyond any plummet of his were the transitions from her soft Russian indolence to violent energy; and her gentle sweetness of manner might be banished by a frenzy of emotional revolt and despair.

He could not understand his wife. And, little by little, his love retreated before the irritation of defeat and the humiliation of constant repulse. He began to suspect that she had carried her social principles so far that her own people were content to give her to any honorable man who would take her out of Europe. The mysterious facility of his courtship unraveled itself. Like as not Olga had joined one of the innumerable secret revolutionary societies which had sprung up in Russia during Alexander's reign. In fact, Prince Platen Galitsuin, the head of her branch of the family, admitted as much when Josiah had been last in Russia, on a much-importuned visit in Johnny-Ivan's sixth year.

"My sister is adorable," said he, smiling, "and we are so glad to have had this opportunity to see her; but may I, as your brother who is grateful to you,

hint that we would better have our family gather-
ings in Paris rather than in Russia—oh, no harm
has been done! Olga, thanks to you, is saved from
being a conspirator; but the indiscretions of a noble
but ill-guided heart sometimes last in their effects
after the causes are removed. One takes—so I am
told—very tremendous oaths and vows, and my
sister is of a devoutness, although she has renounced
the orthodox religion. Frankly, my dear Winslow,
I would keep her away from Russia, no matter how
earnestly she may beg you to take her there; these
snakes crawl in everywhere and they might ask impossible things of her."

Winslow's face assumed the impassive mask it
wore when he was making a big contract. Not by the
twitch of an eyelid did he reveal a harsh disgust
mounting in his heart.

"I suppose," said he meditatively, between puffs,
"that Olga was mixed up with this damn stuff,
seven years ago."

"We have feared so—since," admitted the prince
diplomatically.

"You were trying to marry her then, were you
not," Winslow asked, "to an old Russian—one of
the Ivaslofs—then wouldn't she have stayed in
Russia?"

"No, he was a great traveler—that was his chief
recommendation; he would have mostly lived in
Paris; but that was before we had the honor to consider your proposal. I assure you we were delighted
that our dear Olga should prefer you; and little
Vanya has won all our hearts. Did you know what
the grand duke said yesterday?"

"Did he see him?" said Winslow dryly, but he felt his anger cooling.

"Yes, talked with the child, who behaved charmingly; and the grand duke said, 'Russian and Anglo-Saxon,—you have two great races in you, little one, you should go far!'"

In spite of himself the father could not swallow his smile; he expanded a little.

"A noble Russian race, true enough," said he, "and I can tell you, Platen, the Winslows and the Curwens are as long in America and have had as much influence in their country as the Galitsuins have had in yours."

"I do not doubt it, my dear Josiah," returned Platen suavely, "and now about Michael; my sister wants to take him. I suspect if he doesn't go to America, he may take a less agreeable trip; however, I understand there will be no objections to his choosing your country; I'm told by some of our all-knowing fellows that your climate has moderated my sister's views very noticeably. 'Michael'—this was said to me privately—'Michael Michaelaivitch is not bad-hearted, he has been led astray and he will do well in America; in Russia he will only be lost!'"

"I've promised Olga to take him, but I don't half like the notion; he strikes me as amiable and faithful; but there is never any telling when one of your mild-mannered, sleepy peasants will take a scythe and mow your head off, because his infernal third section has considered you obnoxious!"

"Oh, I think you can trust Mishka, and it will be a pleasure for Olga to talk Russian; you know she couldn't take her maid, before."

Winslow went away from the interview (his last with Platen, for they were just leaving the country) smiling grimly. "To think of those damn smooth cusses doing me that way!" he muttered; "and I thought myself so smart to win a beautiful princess, a bald-headed old plow-maker like me, who has made every dollar he has, himself. You're a dunderheaded old fool, Si Winslow! All they wanted was a cart to carry off their dynamite bomb. And all Olga wanted was *escape!*" But he showed neither anger nor discomfiture to Platen. "This ain't the first bad bargain you've made in your life," he told himself, "and it shan't be the first you whined over. But they nor Olga shall get Johnny."

The only visible result of his discoveries was an interest in his own ancestors. Formerly he had been jocosely indifferent to his mother's tales of Winslows and Curwens and Winthrops and Danforths and their greatness in their world; now he perceived that he had believed them and been proud of them all the time. He would give Johnny as good account of his American ancestors as Michael could of his Russian. Josiah's imagination undertook a new job.

He sent an order to a Boston correspondent for histories and books about the Winslows and the Curwens, with the result that he found a bulky box of books awaiting him on his return to Fairport.

He attacked his information in a characteristic way. He didn't dive into it unskilfully and flounder among the torrents of dates and names; he simply asked different people who would be a good person to detach facts from books.

"I think Emma Hopkins, if she were willing,

could do better than any one else; but she would not like to take the pay." So Mrs. Winter pronounced. Winslow spoke to Hopkins, the superintendent of his shop and just taken into partnership.

"Let my little girl do it," said Hopkins, "she's looking up those things all the time—why, she's traced me back to Stephen Hopkins who came over in the Mayflower"—he grinned a little sheepishly, but Winslow looked pleased.

"I always knew you came of good stock, Billy," said he. He was only too glad to accept Miss Emma's services if—he stumbled a little over the compensation, but he thought he picked himself up neatly with, "She can give it to her pet charity, you know, if she won't buy a breastpin with it."

"Give it to thunder," growled Hopkins. "I guess I know who pulled me out of the rut and believed in my inventions; and if you won't let my daughter be a little useful—first chance I get—why, I'll—I'll— I'll *quit* you!"

Hopkins secured his point. Emma did the work (it was more work than Winslow had realized) and she presented the results in a few weeks. The facts were arranged in the neatest and most lucid form, they were devoid of the slightest girlish struggle for literary style, but they did not slight a man or a deed; and they related the Winslow Tory plots and the brutal part played by the old colonial general in Acadia, as minutely and frankly as the services of Edward or Josiah. Josiah's own hardships began when hers ended; he set to work nightly to learn by heart a portion of the chronicles, and he kept his memory green by relating the doughty deeds of the

Kenelms and Edwards and Josiahs to the little wide-
eyed listener whom he took on drives. So Johnny
was told how Edward was the friend of Cromwell
who was not a king but greater, and how Josiah
stamped out the witchcraft fever, and how General
John fought bravely for his king.

"I guess my stories are not so nice as mamma's?"
fished Josiah once, artfully. To which the polite
child responded: "Oh, I don't know; they are *both*
so nice and so different I can't tell which is nicer."

"And are Michael's stories nicer than either of
ours?" said Josiah, with the little compression of
his lips not quite a smile, which looked so odd sometimes repeated on Johnny-Ivan's delicate features.

"They are nice, too," answered the little boy
diplomatically.

Michael Michaelaivitch had become the coachman
at Overlook. Michael was a big, fair man whose
thick yellow hair was cut straight around his head,
and who smiled when he did not want to answer
questions. He was a past master of narration.
Many an afternoon did Johnny-Ivan sit enthralled
in the harness room, while Michael's hands polished
the silver of the best harness, and Michael's tongue
blazoned the past magnificence of the Galitsuins.
But the ex-serf was always careful to tag a disap-
proving addendum to his unctuous eloquence.

"But you understand, *gospodi*, those vick-ed days,
vick-ed days—*ekh-khe-khe! Nu s bogom!*" Certainly some of the stories dealt with wicked days,
those, for instance which told of Ivan the Terrible.
Unpleasantly suggestive, also, were those about
Leteoseka and his bag for the capture of naughty

children. Nevertheless Johnny-Ivan loved the
shudder of them, and he loved the dreary, yet im-
aginative legends of Russian folk-lore; how Baba-
Yago, the ogress, lives on the edge of the forest in a
house turning like a weather-cock with every wind;
how Mikula Silianinovitch, the "Good Laborer,"
toils for others while they sleep, and can be heard
a day's journey away, striking up the stones of
the furrows with his great plowshare; most thrilling of all, how the mythical Kaler swam the Gulf
of Finland, when the spirits of the North burned
up his vessel with their hot breath, and how
forthwith he builded him a ship of silver which
could not be burned. Johnny was always demanding the Variag rovers, especially Kaler.

Yet with all his fascinations Kaler was not so dear
to Johnny-Ivan as one of his father's heroes, his
very own ancestor, whose portrait hung in the library, where the little boy saw it many times a day.
The subject was that Josiah Winslow, son of Edward, who ruled the colony of Plymouth through
the witchcraft madness, and shrewdly headed off
the contagion by fining the first bewitched man ten
pounds for maliciously maligning his neighbors and
bringing evil ways into the colony. The dark and
beautiful face, with the thought in its pensive eyes
and the delicate, faint smile, bore little enough hint
that it belonged to a progenitor of Josiah of Fairport, who was sturdy and cold of mien and had a
well-fed, enduring countenance and keen, gray eyes.
But Johnny-Ivan's brows and large brown eyes and
sensitive mouth were enough like the Puritan scholar's to have belonged to his own son.

Probably Josiah did not fully realize his own success in awakening his son's imagination. There was such a gulf between his son's and his own childhood, where the din and strain of a hand-to-hand fight with poverty had crowded out idle reveries or romance and kept a boy's wits intent on material things, that he felt like a blind man fumbling in his child's soul. He had no light of experience to guide him. At times he was as puzzled about his son as about his wife. Doggedly he plodded through visible and outward facts, trailing after some inward and spiritual cause, precisely as he would have investigated the signs of the market or his competitors' schemes.

It was before the Russian trip that Olga's fever of humanity was diverted to the people whom her husband employed. She went on a personal tour of investigation among their homes, an arduous and tedious matter at this period, since the homes were scattered and the Fairport ways miry, so that often she was forced to leave her carriage and go afoot in the mud. It was also thankless, the men at the Plow Works being independent, self-respecting American citizens who had no desire to be helped, and an active repugnance to being patronized. Nothing came of her tenders except the scarlet fever for Johnny-Ivan. It was brought back to him from a little girl just convalescent, held by the Princess Olga while she listened sympathetically to the mother's tirade against a cruel and ignorant foreman in the foundry, who had "pets." The little girl's case was very light; not so Johnny-Ivan's. In wrath, Josiah demanded a quarantine and no visits to unknown households. To his surprise, his wife did not rebel.

In truth, at this time, her whole nature was concentrated on her child's peril. Nurses were not to be obtained easily, nor were those at hand skilful. Day and night Olga watched over her boy. She obeyed the doctor with such implicit faithfulness and understanding, she had such keenness of observation, such cheerfulness (before the patient) and such self-control, that a cynical man of medicine and the world never afterward ceased to be her admirer. Josiah himself, with a grinding pain, felt his own stunned and battered love stir again in his heart. Meanwhile Olga hardly seemed conscious that her husband existed. So soon as Johnny-Ivan was convalescent, she made his state the unanswerable pretext to keep him with her. Josiah would watch on the wide portico for his little son, pacing up and down, or would sit in his library, the door open, on the chance of catching him as if by accident when he came by, and proposing a drive or a walk.

The house was too far out of town for informal neighborly visits such as Fairport has always delighted to pay, passers-by halting on the way, neighbors "dropping in," as the kindly phrase has it. The Winters to the right, the Lossings to the left, would sometimes pull the great gong-like bell of the front door, or cronies, by appointment, would drive under the elms to take dinner with Winslow. But there were many lonely hours for the husband and wife; lonelier, it may be, for him than for her. After her efforts at comradeship or charity had been thwarted among Winslow's people; after he had refused to build a hospital and a free bath, and she had lost both her rubbers in the mud, going for personal intercession for a workman to one of Winslow's foremen who refused her appeal, and aired a strong sense of injury, the next morning, to the superintendent,—she found a welcome for her largess and her sympathy among a few of her own people, settled on the common below Overlook. The quarter was known as the "Patch." The Patch had no fine houses and very few comfortable ones. It was dusty in summer and miry in winter. Drainage and sewage were left to the mercy of God and did not seem to find it, since the Patch was the home of diphtheria at a time when diphtheria was more dreaded than typhoid. If the Patch garbage overflowed the inefficient shelter of back yards, occasionally there would be a bonfire, exciting false hopes in town that the whole Patch might be swept away; but, in general, what stray cats and dogs and fowls could not devour was left to the weather.

On the Patch lived Serge Vassilovitch, in the overflowing family of his sister. His sister's husband was not a patriot and reformer like Serge; he was merely a peaceful vender of old iron, rags and bottles, whose sole quarrel with the police was that he would keep his wares piled in the alley. There were, however, several comrades of Serge's own household of political faith, who had listened to emigration sirens and come to a land where all men were to be like brothers and welcome the new lovers of liberty with outstretched hands full of money. They expected free lands, compassion and admiration; they found an unconcerned multitude who demanded as hard work from other people as they were willing to give themselves. It were a pitiful story, did any exile dreamer who has come to our shores write it fully—this malicious comedy of trust and disillusion—the dream of Utopia and the reality of the same old human nature in the same old ruthless grapple with nature and its kind.

Olga, who had been through all the acts, could understand the bewildered disappointment of her countrymen. They did not suspect her motives nor were they indignant at her pity. With them she felt at home. By degrees, she came to spend much time in the Patch. She took Johnny-Ivan with her.

"After diphtheria, I suppose, *this* time," grunted Josiah. Then he was sorry, but pride and helplessness to explain himself held him mute.

"I will not take Vanya anywhere unless I know it is safe," promised Olga, who had changed color.

"Thank you," said Josiah, but in no thankful tone, as he turned on his heel.

About this time came the trip to Russia. It was after their return that Mrs. Winslow began to receive a large number of letters all from across the seas. These letters bore not a Russian but a Swiss stamp. Josiah knew perfectly the hand of the prince and of Olga's two sisters leading blameless lives, according to Russian police standards. The letters' chirography belonged to none of them. Nevertheless, he kept silence; his only token of interest was his despatching Tim instead of Michael for the mail. Josiah pondered. Nor were his ponderings without results of many sorts.

CHAPTER III

THE GOLDEN AGE

The Fairport mothers sometimes looked at Johnny-Ivan with a pity which (had he perceived it) would have bewildered him.

"Poor little lonesome chap!" said they. Really, however, Johnny-Ivan was not lonesome—not even before Peggy came; of course after she came he was as contented as a child could be. Besides his own resources, which were considerable, owing to an imagination of power and the healthy energy of his years which finds joy in any exercise, there were four people whom he loved.

Paramount was his mother. He worshiped his mother. As a rule, children have no acute perception of human beauty; but Johnny-Ivan loved the sight of his mother as he loved the sunset or the flowers or the waving grass. Dimly he realized that her charming figure in its invariable white of a morning, summer or winter, and its flashing jewels and rich, soft, shimmering stuffs of an evening, was something of a quality more delicate and precious than belonged to the other ladies who came to the house. Merely to be in her presence was a deep and exquisite content. He would nestle against her soft skirts by the hour, like a happy little dog, while she read or wrote or embroidered or played on the grand piano in the hall. He would patter by her side on her long walks until his tiny legs wabbled under him and his face was pale with fatigue, and, with caressing Russian diminutives, she would turn remorsefully to clasp him in her arms and make him sit down to rest.

"Oh, I'm all right," Johnny-Ivan would swagger; "I could *run* if I wanted to."

He invested her with every attribute of splendor or loveliness. Once he broke out: "Mamma, I wisht you was a queen!" His mother laughed, but very tenderly. "In Russia I was a princess once," she said. Johnny caught his breath: "Oh, *let's* go back and you be a princess again!"

"No, dear. It is wrong that there should be princesses or queens or any such people. They only oppress the poor. They have no right to have their beautiful palaces and live in luxury while the poor people toil for them, who haven't even black bread enough to eat."

Johnny-Ivan's sigh was weighted with disappointment. "I s'pose not," he acquiesced sorrowfully. But he offered his own compromise in his evening petitions. Every evening he said his prayers, taught him by the cook, who was of the Roman Catholic faith, amended by Hilma, a stanch Lutheran, and audited, as it were, by his father, who went regularly to the Episcopal church of a Sunday, carrying Johnny. Josiah Winslow had not gone to church before his marriage, and his later church-going was a most unexpected result of matrimony, since Mrs. Winslow never attended any church whatever. She smoked her cigarettes peacefully at home and read

Russian pamphlets. Nevertheless he did go, and his little son stayed to Sunday-school, and said his prayers at night at his mother's knee, while she listened, thinking her own thoughts.

This night he added a private postscript to his customary punctilious intercessions for "papa and mamma and Peggy and Aunty Winter and all my dear friends and relations and Michael and Hilma and Lena and Nora Halloran and Teresa and the woman who comes to wash (I forgot her name) and Tim and Jerry and all papa's men at the works and the president of the United States and Father O'Brien and all those in authority." He made a slight pause, then said reverently: "And please God, don't let there be any princes or kings or princesses to *oriss* the poor; but if they've *got* to be some, please let mamma be one of them!"

All times near his mother were lovely, so lovely that did he hear his nurse call: "Your mamma, sie want you, Yonny-Ivan!" he would even leave off helping Michael curry the horses, without a pang, and race to the tortures of Hilma's Swedish movement cure; yet these were truly formidable, because Hilma always washed *up*, with a torturing assault on the nose; she also used a strong lather of suds which no tightest shutting of a boy's eyes could oppose.

"Well, den, you don' git so dirty, I don' must wash you mit soap!" was her stern retort if the sufferer whimpered. It shows, therefore, the strength of his mother's attraction that Johnny-Ivan should dare all the terrors of the toilet to reach her side.

On the whole, the least pleasant times with mamma were at the piano, where she never played pretty songs, like Peggy's, for instance, about the Suwanee River and her old Kentucky home and Nellie, who was a lady; but awful, queer music that sounded like the wind moaning or lost children hollering and crying in the woods, and made a boy feel bad. It wasn't quite so pleasant, either, when she sat having a "reverie" and he must not disturb her, and her beautiful black eyebrows would knit and her lip would curl and she would mutter strange words in Russian. But soon she would shake her head and smile; and like as not there would follow the very most charming times of all, because mamma, too, could tell lovely stories.

Some exalted the ancient valor of the warriors of her line. Others there were of her own girlhood, of the lonely steppes and battles with wolves and wild races over the snow in sleighs drawn by three horses. But the secret stories were the best of all. They were about patriots, about "our people."

Very early, Olga had interested her boy in the Russian political struggles. He was an ardent nihilist conspirator in kilts; and his journeys to the Patch with his mother were fraught with thrilling excitement. The Russian visit was a little disturbing. The aunts and uncles and cousins were so nice, so kind and generous! Yet these delightful people did not love free Russia. This was perplexing. However, it made amends that Mishka, who was even nicer than Uncle Platen or Cousin Saska, Mishka belonged to the patriots. He was proud of the confidence reposed in him by his mother and Michael, and swore (on a sword stuck in the ground) never to repeat any word told him.

The ceremony came off out by the summer-house; and the sword of the ritual was his father's, handed down from a stiff old Tory, who might well have turned in his grave at such misusage. Johnny remembered, always, the swelling of his heart as he laid his scrap of a hand on the big hilt, and the uplifted, strange expression of Michael's face.

"He is one of us, Olga Ivanovna," said Michael. He spoke in a new solemn voice. But *maman* clasped Johnny so close he felt her heart beat; he was stirred by an indescribable contagion of excitement.

"Not that, Michael, not that!" she cried, "he is too young; and he is an American. But he is old enough to keep a secret, the greatest of secrets!"

"*Oui, maman,*" said Johnny-Ivan, "cross my heart!" He crossed himself on his tiny shoulder. "I won't tell even Peggy—if you say so!"

"Not even Peggy," said his mother firmly; and she added, averting her eyes, "not even papa; it's our secret, because we are Russians. Papa is American and he wouldn't understand!"

Were the truth known, Johnny felt it a harder strain to keep from telling Peggy than his father. He did not feel so well acquainted with his father. He always put him in the second place of honor, officially. "I love mamma, papa, you, Michael and Aunty Winter," he used to say to Peggy; nevertheless, he experienced a vague constraint in his father's presence. And a few days after the rite on the lawn something happened which, slight though it was of itself, deepened this feeling to a sorrowful degree.

Winslow had taught his boy to drive; naturally, so soon as the small John could turn the corner without upsetting the buggy, he yearned to drive alone. He was sure that he only needed the opportunity to convince the elders of his skill; and he often pictured to himself his father's surprise and pleasure if only such a chance came. The chance did come, and Johnny seized it, but not with exhilaration; rather out of a fine sense of duty. Thus did it befall: The cow-barn, back in the big pasture, caught fire from an irresponsible cigarette, smoked by one of the princess' pensioners. Michael was over at the stable proper when the alarm was given, just taking out Mr. Winslow's buggy and the big gray. He sped away over the hill with Tim and the stable-boy, first hitching the horse to the post in front of the stable.

Johnny knew his father ought to have the horse —hadn't he heard him cautioning Michael to fetch it in "at three, sharp," because he had an important engagement and must drive over the bridge?—and yet here was Mishka off to the fire! Johnny-Ivan didn't blame him; he was longing to get into the smoke himself, and help take the cows out (he was sure he knew just the way); but how was papa to keep his engagement! He recalled a conversation with his father regarding engagements, which had impressed him deeply as to their stern sacredness. His mother was not at home; already he had discovered the inadequate workings of Hilma's mind in emergencies; Johnny-Ivan felt that he must act! With a somber backward glance at the clouds of white and dun drifting over the trees, he stood on his short tiptoes and untied the horse; this accomplished, he climbed into the buggy over the wheel—not risking the complicated manœuver of turning the horse from the ground—and drove away.

The first difficulty lay in wait at the gate. It was a gate supposed to work itself; you drove on to an iron spring and the weight of the wagon made the spring work a lever and swing the gate open; when you went out you drove over another spring, which neatly closed the gate behind you! Nothing could be more convenient—if the gate worked. It did not work for Johnny's feather weight. He found his wheel poised upon the unyielding steel and a motionless wall of iron and wood before the horse's nose. There was nothing for it but to descend, open the gate and lead Romeo, the horse, through the gateway. Unhappily, Romeo was an animal of opinions; he gazed upon the small figure tugging at the gate and tossed his head in huge contempt when Johnny would have caught the rein; probably he concluded that so small a human being did not know the secret of hurting a horse's mouth to force him to go wherever the hurter willed; slowly, sedately, he ambled off the drive on to the grassy hill and began to nibble the dead grass.

Johnny-Ivan took in the situation and made up his mind, which, though young, was masterful; he did not try to lead the rebel; he knew better after that one jerk of the head; he simply climbed into the buggy again, climbed out on the thills, fished up the reins and hauled up Romeo's head. Why Romeo submitted no one knows; he may have had a sense of humor; submit he did and Johnny in triumph drove forth out of the gate. He did not attempt to close it; he could not trust Romeo enough for that feat; instead, he drove down the road until he met a boy, whom he asked in his politest manner to close the gate for him. Alas! it was the boy who had once called Peggy Rutherford a "red-headed copperhead" and been tumbled down the ravine on to the tin cans,—the same boy whose wounded toe Johnny-Ivan had bound in his handkerchief for Peggy's scorning. This youngster, by rights, should have had a tincture of gratitude in his resentment; but it was plain his was a base, unknightly nature; in other words, he was "mean," for he made a vulgar gesture with his thumb on his nose, and bawled to Johnny-Ivan that cows would run in and "tromp up the garden." He said he saw them coming. Johnny was minded to descend and fight the boy again; but distrust of Romeo chained him to his seat. So he told the boy he was smart, wasn't he? and held on his way.

The next footman to whom he appealed was a man. "Shet it yourself!" growled the man; he was in a hurry. Johnny-Ivan's brow began to show a deep line; but he hailed the third passer-by, this time a girl. The girl owned a pleasant face; very likely her nature was of equal pleasantness, but she talked no English and Johnny spoke no German; hence the colloquy was barren of result. He drove on, thinking deeply. The end of this mental exercise was his proffering the next comer, a very freckled little boy, the sumptuous bribe of a knife with three blades; one (admitted the honest Johnny-Ivan) a little broken, just the point off, if he would go shut the gate. Thus did Johnny take his first step into the mercenary mire of the world—with entire success; for the boy sped to the gate, knife in hand, and swung it safe with a vigorous click.

"It was an awful nice knife," sighed Johnny; but directly he smiled. "I bet he'll have a good time with that knife! I bet *he* never had such a nice knife before," thought Johnny-Ivan happily.

The journey was uneventful; he, or Romeo, made the passage through the most crowded street of Fairport, and drew up at the office door without so much as the graze of a wheel. Wouldn't his father be pleased!

But his father frowned; where was Michael? he demanded.

Johnny-Ivan explained: Michael was putting out the fire in the cows' barn; he knew his father had an engagement; so he drove in, himself.

Mr. Winslow's black eyebrows knitted, nor did they smooth until his questions had gathered the whole story. Then Johnny heard him mutter, low: "Well, you are *my* son as well as your mother's; go off half-cock, but manage to hit, somehow." Johnny-Ivan was not quite sure whether he should consider this praise or reproof; and an uncomfortable choke in his throat had succeeded the pleasant glow of anticipation. "I thought you'd like me coming in," he said; "you said maybe I'd learn to drive all myself; and I did; and besides, it was your *engagement;* you had to go, you said."

"That's all right; but I could have kept my engagement with another buggy—didn't I tell you never to get in without Michael?"

"But Michael wasn't there!"

"Then you shouldn't have got in; I didn't tell you to drive me; I told Michael. Johnny, it will save you a lot of trouble if you learn, right now, not to mind other folks' business unless they ask you, or you've got to, to protect yourself." Johnny's face fell. "You might have broken the buggy or killed the horse, or maybe killed yourself. You don't know how to drive well enough. Remember, I mean what I say. You are never to get into the buggy and drive without my permission again. Do you understand?"

"Yes, sir," mumbled Johnny-Ivan, very subdued now, his heart swelling with a painful sense of failure and injustice. He had wanted to help papa, and only been scolded for it; it wasn't fair. He had never thought of his father as a severe man before; nor was he in the least afraid of him; but to-day an unacknowledged assent to others' reason for dread was working in his childish mind, like the germ of a disease. And an incident on the way home gave the germ a chance to grow. Mr. Winslow drove to the grocery, where the family supplies were bought— he had long ago discovered that his peace of mind, at table, was best secured by attending to the providing himself. While the grocer was writing the order on his pad, Johnny-Ivan studied the sights of the street.

Opposite the store a cottage of the older days still kept its place and its teaspoonful of yard, although long since the neighbors of its kind had given way to brick blocks. Something strange had happened In this cottage. Not a fire, for there was not a sign of smoke or water; yet behold, on the sidewalk all the humble plenishing of the household! There they were: bedsteads, bureaus, a ragged quilt, a red-cushioned rocking-chair, a baby's cradle, some poor straw-ticks, a table heaped with earthenware and gaudy, cheap dishes, a little broken red wagon, the toy of some child; not flung in the reckless mass of fright and hasty moving, but arranged with orderly economy of space, close to the curbing. Yet one could perceive that it was for no ordinary flitting these goods seemed to wait. A flushed and disheveled woman was weeping on her apron, behind the rampart of bedsteads; two very dirty little children rocked and howled in the rocking-chair; and a thick-set, baffled-looking man, with his head down between his shoulders and his hands in his pockets, stood on the edge of the sidewalk and opposed laconic murmurs to a sobbing stream of reproach.

Johnny-Ivan's curiosity and sympathy increased every second. Now and then poignant phrases smote his ear: "Six childer, God have mercy on me! and me man that should wurrk for thim, a misfortunate drunkard! . . . I ain't seen a well day for three year! 'Tis crippled I am wid the misery in me bones. . . . No, I don't drink, and shame to yous for the question! You don't know how to trate a lady, nohow! There's me poor old mither's rockin'-chair—Oh, bless God she ain't alive to see this day! . . . I don't know where we'll go; the neighbors is harder'n stones of the strate. Oh, I can't go to the poor'us! Me wid six childer. . . . Oh, he's gone, he's left me! He blacked me eye.

. . . An' if I *did* throw the flat-iron at him 'twas to save me life an' that old cat, Teresa MacInarney . . . Oh, 'tis a bloody lie. . . . I don't care if the judge did fine me! I scratched her in silf-de-fense—I ain't got a livin' cint in this wurld—'Twill kill me! 'Twill *kill* me! Oh—! Oh!"

Johnny-Ivan was too innocent to detect the squalid truth under this tragic action; the woman's sobs wrung his heart.

"Oh, papa, what is it? Can't we help her?" he cried. He saw that both the grocer and his clerk were grinning; they were cruel.

His father, too, compressed his lips in irony if not in humor. "What is it?" begged Johnny-Ivan.

"Why, just an eviction," said Winslow; "they wouldn't pay their rent and they've been turned out."

"But where will they go, papa? Have they got any other house?"

"Oh, I guess they'll find a place. That's all, Mr. Black, good morning." Winslow, who was driving, couldn't see it; but Johnny-Ivan got his head back over his shoulder for a last glance; the grocer and his clerk were exchanging grins again.

"Can't you give the poor woman some money, papa?" said he.

"I've done all that's necessary, Johnny," said his father.

"She's running after us now, papa—look! *look!*"

In fact, she was making a staggering dash after the buggy which, had she been sober, she might have recognized before.

Winslow gave Romeo a sharp clip with the whip;

he never turned his head. "Oh, papa, she wants us to stop!"

"Can't you see"—Winslow began the sentence in a testy tone, but as he looked down at the innocent little face he stopped short; he couldn't tell the child the truth.

The woman's shrill outcry beat up through the rattle of wheels: "Oh, Mr. Winslow! Mr. Winslow! For God's sake, don't turn me out on the street, Mr. Winslow! I'll pay you, if you'll only give me time—" Here the stout man caught up with her and could be seen soothing her with mingled cajolery and threats, while Romeo swung round the corner, out of sight.

Johnny-Ivan's face had paled; he was stricken dumb by his knowledge. It was his father, *his* father, who was doing this terrible thing! At once he was indignant and frightened. Some instinct warned him that he could do nothing by entreaty. He would tell his mother; *she* would help the poor woman. One single eye-blink he stole at his father's stern face. He wished he knew what he was thinking. It was rather a pity that he couldn't know, since Winslow's comment ran as follows: "What an idiot I was to go to Black's. Forgot. I know that I told Holcomb to serve the writ, first pleasant day. There's the woman fighting and drinking and beating those poor children and the neighbors complaining—but I didn't want to tell Johnny that! He knows nothing about such things. I hope he didn't take in what she was hollering, damn her! Holcomb's got money to quiet her; why didn't he?" Aloud he said: "You don't need to worry about those children, Johnny; that officer will see to them. He'll see to the mother, too."

"Yes, sir," replied Johnny-Ivan, with a child's superficial, misleading docility.

But he carried the episode straight to his mother, who was as moved as he could wish, and promised to see about it and help the poor woman.

"Papa'll do what's right, when he knows the truth," she assured Johnny-Ivan; and later, having hunted up the woman and paid for the cartage of her goods to a new domicile (in the Patch), she told her son that the neighbors had told lies about the woman to papa. There the incident closed. The impression remained. Johnny-Ivan was not quite so much at ease with his father; he did not admire him with such an unbounded trust. There was a shadowy fear which had never been before. Of nights, when he slept poorly, possibly on account of the cook's remarkable choice of dainties for a child's digestion, he would weary his head over problems not good for his youth. He wondered why there are poor people. One day he brought his puzzle to his mother, who only sighed: "There are many cruel and greedy people in the world; they want all the luxuries and they are not willing to give their luxuries to let the poor people have plain bread." Later, after much thought, he asked his father, who looked at him sharply through his glasses, saying: "Well, son, I am afraid you will be older than I am before you understand that; you see, you treat any poor people you meet decently, and don't worry about it; there aren't many poor people in Fairport."

"There's a very poor family down on the Patch,"

said Johnny—he thought he wouldn't begin at once
with the evicted family, but try less obnoxious suf-
ferers first—"there's a little boy big's me; can I give
him my coat?"

"No, nor anything else without asking. I'll see
he has a coat if he needs it. What's his name?"

"Serge Rodin."

"That hound's nephew? You keep away from
them, Johnny; they are bad people, very bad. Mind
you don't go near them."

Johnny was silent; his father took him on his knee
and gave him a simple, adapted-to-youth version of
nihilists and their dynamic ways; he was troubled
by the child's unresponsive attention. He asked no
questions; all his comment was an obedient, "No,
sir, I won't go!" making no sign of emotion over the
atrocities of bombs and bomb-throwers. Winslow
put him off his knee; and Johnny caught a mutter:
"I believe she's begun."

Johnny was glad to be free to run to his mother.
Winslow's harangue was repeated with a child's
literalness, the tale ending, "And I didn't say a
word, mamma, like you said I never was to; I suppose I might to *papa,* but I didn't; he don't know,
mamma; you'll have to tell him. He thinks our nice
nihilists are wicked. He's been told lies, I guess,
just like he was 'bout Mrs. Wiggins."

His mother kissed him. "That's my own brave
boy who can be trusted! Don't tell *any one, galubchik;* and if your papa wants you not to see Serge,
all very well; don't you go; *I* will get Serge what he
needs."

But the sorrows of the poor and the wrongs of the

misunderstood nihilists could only disturb a healthy child in passing; Johnny-Ivan was too busy with his own crowded interests to be puzzled or saddened long. Besides his father and his mother, there were two other very dear friends of his in Fairport before Peggy came. There was Mishka, who was almost as splendid as Kaler. He was so strong he could wrestle with the colt and throw the colt. He never got cross; he was always smiling and pleasant and willing to let a boy ride behind him when he went after the cows. He used to be good to the horses. He would say, in Russian, "Forward, my little pigeons!" so much nicer than "G'lang," or "Getup." Also he played on the harmonica and sang *Down the Little Mother Volga* and other beautiful Russian songs; and he called Johnny *gospodi*—Sir. Johnny loved Michael.

There was still another person of deep importance in his little world whom he loved. Not Serge Vassilovitch, although his mother had told him that Serge was a patriot and had been to Siberia; he respected Serge deeply, but somehow he couldn't quite love him; he used to scowl and curse so much, and the waft of whisky, always heralding his presence, made Johnny's nose wrinkle. He admired her, but he had no more ardent feeling for his nurse, Hilma, whose character was very firm and who exacted obedience by methods which Johnny was too honorable to carry to his natural protectors, but which he disliked excessively. The new cook was a truly superior woman; he liked the other maids; and the gardener and Timothy Doolan and Fritz, the stable-boy, all were kind, delightful, accomplished persons. Still he did not precisely love them; they weren't like mamma and papa.

But he did love Aunty Winter. She lived all by herself in a beautiful big house, as big as Overlook; and she always gave a boy something nice to eat. Likewise he enjoyed her conversation. "She seems such a sprightly lady," he confided to his mother, in his little old-fashioned phraseology.

Aunty Winter never had reveries; but all "grown-ups" appeared to have some difficulties of approach. In Aunty Winter's case the blight on real enjoyment of her conversation came from solitaire. So often when Johnny called she would be busy with her cards spread before her, playing a most difficult game of solitaire, called Penelope's Web. Later, when he was older and not so happy, she taught him the game. She used to say that Johnny Winslow was the only being she knew (herself excepted) who ever succeeded in conquering Penelope's Web three times in one evening. "In consequence," said Mrs. Winter, with a curious little uplifting of her beautiful eyebrows, which all her friends knew as a kind of ironic parenthesis around her marks of enthusiasm, "when Hopkins dies I shall vote all my stock to make him the next president of the Old Colony!"

If Johnny admired Mrs. Winter, he had company a plenty. She was used to admiration, having been a Southern belle before the war, a belle in Washington during the sixties, and a very handsome woman ever since.

Her age, at this time, was nearer fifty than forty; but she looked a good ten years younger; her erect, slim little figure moved as lightly as a girl's; her brilliant hazel eyes were undimmed by even a transient screen of glass; and her white teeth flashed over her own or any one's else wit with a youthful vivacity.

Fairport admired Mrs. Winter almost with abandon: it quoted her epigrams, which shone the more that the West is less given to epigram than to humor, wherefore she had few rivals; it laughed itself into tears over her mimicries; it praised her housekeeping and her lavish entertainments; it accepted her loyally for its social leader. Yet there was always, deep down, an uneasy distrust. She was very good-natured, but she "made fun" of people. And the gifted imitator of Luke Darrell driving a horse trade; or of old lady Carlisle, who was deaf as a post, but insisted on conversing at funerals, might make the auditors of one joyous hour the subjects of another. So there was a reserve in Fairport's affection, although none in either its admiration or its obedience.

Little did Johnny reck of any coldness or any malice in his kind friend. He was proud to help her deal her pretty pasteboards (the reversion of which fell to him until Peggy's arrival, and fell often, as Mrs. Winter was squeamish about the slippery freshness of her cards), and with her ivory ruler he would range the eight ranks of the solitaire scheme in rectangular accuracy; or he would patiently deal out an exact replica of her own problem in order that if her first handling of the clues should fail, she might try over again.

"You are a very useful little trick!" said Mrs. Winter, "and you have your father's dogged patience. Let us hope you won't fasten on to any foolish purpose, for it will be no joke getting you to loose your hold!"

Mrs. Winter acted the First Lady of the Wardrobe, as well as many another amiable rôle, toward the little boy. It was she who designed those suits of cotton or wool so nicely suited to the occasion that one would know that they must have originated in the mind of a woman of tact. They were pretty yet comfortable, whereas the Princess Olga could think of nothing but a toilet of state, blue velvet and Irish point and a sash a boy couldn't run in—if he did, it would trip him! She was very glad to accept her friend's kind offices. Nor did these stop at sailor suits and pea-jackets and leather leggings; Mrs. Winter had a pair of fine eyes, always on scout duty for loose buttons or rents. Hilma was kept on a wire edge of efficiency in regard to stockings by the slippers which Mrs. Winter was unexpectedly forcing on her small visitor if his feet looked wet or he "didn't seem quite comfortable in those shoes." One could never tell when stockings might be inspected; therefore, if the lace suffered, stockings must be kept darned.

The result was that the friends of the family were rather bewildered by the good estate of Johnny's clothes; but Mrs. Winter and the Winslows kept the secret to themselves. Johnny, least of all, considered the First Lady of the Wardrobe's services in this line; but he was too grateful to her on many other counts to miss one. And when all is said, she was nice enough in herself; and then, she was Peggy's great-aunt.

With Peggy's coming, life grew even more interesting. Peggy had visited Mrs. Winter the summer
before, because there was yellow fever in Memphis,
where the Rutherfords lived; and this spring they
came again, because Mrs. Winter was lonesome.
Peggy's mother was with her; she was sick, and she
used to lie on the sofa and write letters every day,
on a block, to Peggy's papa. · Peggy's papa was
a doctor, and he wasn't in the least afraid of yellow fever or anything else on earth. Peggy said
so. Once a man had tried to shoot him,—he promised he'd shoot him on sight; and they all sent word
that the man was waiting on the sidewalk; they
wanted Doctor Rutherford to run out the back way;
he was just eating his dinner; he wasn't feazed—
a mite; he grabbed up the carving knife and went
jumping down the steps, hollering, "Where's he
at?" and when the man with the gun saw him coming he just lit out so fast he tumbled down and lost
his gun. Doctor Rutherford had it now. Oh, he
was a mighty brave man! So was Peggy brave;
she could take a toad right up in her hand; she
killed a garter-snake with a stick; she never had a
light burning in her room at night; down South, on
her uncle's plantation, she used to ride horseback,
and she had a little gun of her own and shot birds,
and she pulled Johnny-Ivan's tooth out with a
string by tying the string to the door-knob and
slamming the door. It didn't hurt so awful much;
he didn't cry. But he cried when he, himself, pulled
out a real big back tooth of Peggy's the same way.
Poor Johnny hated to do the brutal deed; but he
was determined to show Peggy (this was shortly

after their reconciliation) that he would be useful in a Blood Feud; and here was a chance to display the coveted hardness of heart. He grabbed the knob (Peggy, herself, had adjusted the string with a fine air of callous indifference); he shut his eyes tight and swung the door with frenzied energy. But when Peggy's muffled moan drove his eyes open, the spectacle of mingled blood and woe on her beloved countenance overcame his hardihood; he wept aloud. Peggy laughed at him; she declared she *wasn't* hurt.

"But you—you—squealed!" sobbed Johnny-Ivan; "it sounded just like the piggy, when Tim took him away to be killed."

"I *didn't* squeal," denied Peggy with heightened color, "and you're a cry-baby! No, you ain't," she instantly corrected; "you never made a sound when I pulled your tooth; and I *didn't* squeal, but I reckon I did kinder grunt. It was so sudden."

Thus was peace restored, and so effectually that Peggy told Johnny she should *choose* him to avenge her, if any one should murder her in a Blood Feud.

Besides being so brave and so gifted, Peggy (although this mattered very little to Johnny-Ivan) was the prettiest girl in town. Her hair wasn't at all red, really; it was only a beautiful bright color, like the copper boiler in the kitchen; and she could wrinkle her forehead and make her whole scalp move up and down as if her hair were a cap. Johnny-Ivan often begged her to show him how to do this entrancing feat; but she said it was a "conjure trick," and she couldn't tell. Any one can see how absorbing Peggy's society must be.

In this wise did Johnny-Ivan grow up, lonely but not lonesome, taught by the careless but not unkindly tongue of his father's domestics, finding, by the magic of a child's alchemy, gold in everything, and being a loving and happy child, although his father and his mother had little happiness and less love in their relations.

CHAPTER IV

THE FAIRPORT ART MUSEUM

After the war was over, the Middle West addressed itself to Culture. Perhaps the husbands and brothers and fathers might still be busy making money; but the women of the West, whose energies and emotions had been mightily roused, found life a little tame when there were no more sanitary commissions, no more great fairs or little fairs for the soldiers, no more intense emotions over printed sheets. Then it was that the Woman's Club lifted a modest finger at the passing car of progress, and unobtrusively boarded it.

Fairport was conservative, as always, but she had no mind to be left behind in the march of feminine fashion. She did not rush to extremes, but she had women's clubs in 1881. The chief of these were The Ladies' Literary Club and the Spinsters' Alliance. Both clubs tackled the same great themes of ethics and art, and allotted a winter to the literature of a nation, except in the case of Greek and Roman literatures, which were not considered able to occupy a whole winter apiece, so they were studied in company. The club possessed a proper complement of officers, and their meetings went from house to house. They were conducted with artless simplicity, in a pleasant, conversational manner, but with due regard to polite forms; and only at a moment of excitement was the chair addressed by her Christian name.

Naturally, the women's clubs were deeply stirred by the first great World's Fair in America. But the whole West was moved. It turned to art with a joyous ardor, the excited happiness of a child that finds a new beauty in the world. Why had we not thought of the artistic regeneration of our sordid life before? Never mind, we would make amends for lost time by spending more money! In very truth the years following the Centennial witnessed an extraordinary awakening of worship of beauty, almost religious in its fervor. Passionate pilgrims ransacked Europe and the Orient; a prodigal horde of their captives, objects of luxury and of art, surged into galleries and museums and households. No cold critical taste weeded out these adorable aliens. The worst and the best conquered, together. Our architecture, our furniture, our household surroundings were metamorphosed as by enchantment. And the feature of mark in it all was the unparalleled diffusion of the new faith. Not the great cities only; the towns, the villages, the hamlets, caught fire.

Of course, Fairport went to Philadelphia; and Fairport was converted. It followed, at once, that the women's clubs of the place should serve most zealously at the altar; and nothing could be more inevitable than that in course of time there should be a concrete manifestation of zeal. Hence the memorable Art Museum, the fame of which to this day

will revive, when there is a meeting of the solid
and gray-haired matrons who were the light-footed
girls of the Alliance, and the talk falls on the old
times.

The art collection would give its admirers shivers
to-day, but it excited only happy complacency then.
The mood of the hour was not critical. The homes
of the Fairport gentry held innumerable oil
copies of the great masters of different degrees of
merit, which they loaned secure of welcome; with
them came family treasures so long held in reverence
that their artistic value (coldly considered) had
been lost to comparison, and the gems of accomplished amateurs who painted flowers on china cups,
or of rising young artists who had not as yet risen
beyond the circle of trusting friends in town.

In general, the donors' expectation of gratitude
was justified, but even so early as 1881 there were
limits to artistic credulity; and some offerings drove
the club president, Miss Claudia Loraine, and the
club secretary, Miss Emma Hopkins, to "the coal
hole." This was a wee closet under the stairs, where
the coal scuttles were ranged, until they should fare
forth to replenish the "base burners" which warmed
the Museum home. In real life the name of the
Museum's lodgings was Harness Block, and Mr.
Harness had proffered the cause of art two empty
stores, formerly a fish market and a grocery. As
there was no private office (only a wire cage), when
Miss Hopkins felt the need of frank speech she signaled Claudia to the coal hole.

She was closeted with her thus on the morning
of the second day. The subject of the conference

was the last assault on the nerves of the committee, perpetrated by the Miller twins—not in person, but with their china. The china, itself, had the outward semblance of ordinary blue earthenware of a cheap grade; but the Miller twins were convinced (on the testimony of their dear old minister, who never told a lie in his life, and who had heard the Millers' grandmother say—and everybody knows that *she* was a saint on earth, and she was ninety years old at the time, and would she be likely to lie almost on her dying bed? You might call it her dying bed, averred Miss Miller, since she was bedridden for two years before her death, on that same old four-poster bedstead which belonged to her mother, and at last died on it) that the blue ware had been the property of George the Third, had been sold and was on board the ship with the tea which was rifled in Boston Harbor. They had insisted in pasting these royal claims upon the china in the blackest and neatest lettering. The awkward fact that earthenware does not usually grace a royal board, or that the saintly old grandmother mixed up dates and persons in a wonderful way during her latter days, made no difference to her loyal descendants. Each platter with the black chipping betraying plainly its lowly origin, each tea-cup mended with cement, bore the paper-claim pasted securely upon it.

"It took us a whole afternoon," said Miss Tina Miller, "but it's *so* precious and there might be other blue ware and it *might* get mixed—you'll insure it, Miss Hopkins? not that money could replace such things, but, at least"—Miss Tina Miller always left her sentences in the air, seemingly too diffident to complete them, once the auditors were assured of their import.

The Millers kept a tiny little house on a tiny little income; but gave of all they had to give, themselves, without stint. They were public-spirited women if Fairport ever held any such. Although they had neither brothers nor cousins to go to the war, they had picked lint and made bandages and trudged with subscription papers and scrimped for weeks to have money to spend at the patriotic fairs. In consequence they were deeply respected, so respected that it was simply impossible to refuse their unselfish offering of their dearest god.

"I think it just *noble* of you," said Miss Tina. "Sister and I felt we *must* help; so we brought the King George china and a little pencil head our sister Euphrosyne did. The one who died, you know. I'm sorry all your—art things—aren't in yet. No, I can't come to-morrow; I shall be very busy—sister may come—*thank* you."

Both the keen young listeners knew why Miss Tina could not come; it was neither more nor less than the admission fee.

"But I'll take care of that," said Emma to Claudia in the coal hole. "Elly is going to give her and Miss Ally each a season ticket."

"Then we're *in* for the King George china!" groaned Claudia softly.

"We are," said Emma. "I've put it in a good but not too good a place, and Mr. Winslow is inspecting it now."

"And he *knows* about china; he's sent lovely things," mourned Claudia.

"Oh, well, he knows about the Miller girls, too," said Emma, smiling; "I think he'll forgive us."

"You'd better go explain," urged Claudia, "and throw in that landscape with the cow that seems to have five legs and belongs to Mr. Harness. Perhaps he'll forgive that, too."

Emma went,—she was an amiable girl. She was not pretty like her sister, Mrs. Raimund, who had married the great railway man and was a power in Chicago society; but there was something in the radiant neatness and good humor of the plain sister which made her pleasant to look upon.

Winslow's mouth and eyes relaxed at her greeting, and he smiled over her official quotation of the Millers' claims.

"King George's table? H'mn; which table, second or third?" His eyes twinkled at Emma, whose own eyes twinkled back.

"They're awfully good women," said she, in a kind of compunction.

"None better," said he.

As he passed on, with his little son at his side, she thought: "He isn't nearly so grim as I used to think."

Mrs. Winslow and Mrs. Winter were a few paces behind. They halted before the china, which Mrs. Winter examined; but Mrs. Winslow's weary eyes lingered hardly a moment before they found some other object on which to rest and leave as briefly.

"It is to be hoped this priceless relic won't be damaged in any way," said Mrs. Winter. "Still"— she bent confidentially toward Emma—"if such a calamity should occur, I know a shop in Chicago where you can get plenty more for three dollars and ninety-nine cents."

"I hope nothing will happen to it," said Emma, with stolid reticence.

Mrs. Winslow had not listened, her listless face had been transformed; it was illumined now by the loveliest of smiles; she half put out her hand as a little boy snuggled up to her silken skirts, with a laugh.

"Papa letted me come," he said gaily, "and Peggy's here, too,—there!"

Peggy was attired with great care, her long red curls were shining and her eyes sparkled.

Immediately both children were immersed in the beauties of a collection of rejected models which had been obtained from the patent office, and which, surely, were the most diverting toys imaginable.

"Poor things, to them they *are* most valuable!" sighed Mrs. Winslow. She was making conversation about the Miller china; but Johnny-Ivan and Peggy not unreasonably conceived that she spoke of the beautiful churns and hayraking wagons and cars and wheeled chairs and the like marvels which Miss Hopkins was amiably explaining for them.

"The least chip would be irreparable, I suppose," continued Mrs. Winter, "thousands couldn't pay if one were broken!"

"Imagine the feelings of the custodian," said Emma. "I'm in a tremble all the time."

"I pity you," said Mrs. Winter, as the two ladies passed on to Mrs. Winter's great-grandmother's blue and white embroidered bedspread.

"Oh, Peggy, *do* be careful!" whispered Johnny-

Ivan; Peggy was sending a velocipede in dizzy circles round the counter.

Now fate had ordered that at this critical instant the children should be unguarded. Miss Hopkins had stepped aside at the call of an agitated lady who had lost one of her art treasures in carriage; for the moment, there was no one near save a freckled boy in shabby overalls, who eyed the toys wistfully from afar. He was the same little boy whom Johnny-Ivan had bribed with a jack-knife to close the gate a few weeks before; and he was in the Museum to help his mother, the scrub-woman of the store.

Peggy grew more pleased with her play. The velocipede described wider and wider gyrations with accelerating speed; its keen buzz swelled on the air.

"It'll hit somepin!" warned Johnny-Ivan in an access of fear.

But Peggy's soul was dauntless to recklessness. "No, it won't," she flung back. Her shining head was between Johnny and the whirling wheels. He thought a most particularly beautiful little swinging gate in peril and tried to swerve the flying thing; how it happened, neither of the children knew; there was a smash, a crash, and gate and velocipede lay in splinters under a bronze bust. The glass of the show-case was etched with a sinister gray line.

"*Now* look what you've done!" exclaimed Peggy, with the natural irritation of disaster. "Oh, my!" squeaked the shabby little boy, "won't you catch it!" Peggy's anger was swallowed up in fright and sympathy; she pushed Johnny-Ivan ahead of her. "That

Miss Hopkins is looking," cried she, "get behind
these folks down the aisle!"

She propelled the little boy out of the immediate
neighborhood of the calamity; she forced a wicked,
deceitful smile (alas! guile comes easy to her sex)
and pointed out things to him, whispering, "Look
pleasant! Don't be so scared! They'll never know
we did it!" Already she was shouldering her share
in crime, with a woman's willingness; she said "we"
quite unconsciously; but she added (and this was
of direct volition) : "*I* did it more'n you; you were
just trying to keep the nasty thing straight; I was a
heap more to blame. Anyhow, I guess it ain't so
awful bad. Just those wooden things!"

Johnny-Ivan shook a tragic head; even his lips
had gone bluish-white. "She said thousands
wouldn't repair the damage," moaned he.

"You can't make me believe those mean little
wooden tricks are worth any thousand dollars!"
volleyed Peggy; nevertheless, her heart beat faster,
—grown people are so queer. "Are you sure she
meant *them?* Maybe it was those things in the next
glass case, they're her own things! They're some
kind of Chinese china and cost a heap." Peggy's
sturdy womanly wits were rising from the shock.

"And the show-case is broked!" sniffed Johnny-
Ivan, gulping down a sob.

"It ain't broke, it's only cracked; 'sides, it was
cracked a right smart befo'!"

"But this was a new place—I know, 'cause I cut
my finger on the other, scraping it over."

"Well, anyhow, I reckon it didn't be much value,"
Peggy insisted.

"I saw that young lady come back,"—Johnny-Ivan had switched on to a new track leading to grisly possibilities—"maybe *she'll* find it!"

"Well, we're gone, all right."

"That little boy isn't."

Peggy gave an unprincipled giggle. "Maybe she'll think it was *him*."

"Then we *got* to tell," moaned Johnny.

"No, we ain't. He'll run off and so she won't ask him questions."

"But she'll *think* it's him. It'll be mean."

"No it won't."

"It's mean to have somebody else take your blame or your punishment; mamma said so."

The small casuist was too discreet to attack Johnny's oracle; she only pouted her pretty lips and quibbled:

"'Tain't mean if the people who get blamed are mean themselves—like him. I don't care *how* blamed he gets; I wouldn't care if he got licked."

But Johnny's conscience was not so elastic. "I don't care, either," he protested. "I—I wouldn't care if he was *deaded*"—anxious to propitiate—"but it would be mean just the same. I got to tell papa, Peggy, I truly have."

Peggy grew very cross. "You are just the foolest, obsternatist little boy I ever did see," she grumbled; "you're a plumb idiot! I'd like to slap you! Your papa'll be awful mad."

Johnny-Ivan essayed an indifferent mien, but his eyes were miserable.

"Say, Jo'nivan,"—her voice sank to a whisper that curdled his blood—"were you ever spanked?"

"Only Hilma sorter kinder—not really *spanking,* you know," confessed Johnny with a toss of his head. "I just made faces at her; I didn't cry!" he bragged.

"Never your mamma or your papa?"

"Course not," said Johnny with a haughty air; but, "Peggy," he said very low, "were you—did—"

"Oh, my, yes! Mammy did when I was little. I'm too big now."

"I'm too big, too, now, ain't I?"

"I don't know," said Peggy. "Wulf Greiner was licked by teacher, and he's thirteen. It's whether it's mighty bad, you know."

Johnny-Ivan caught his breath and his legs shook under him; the horror of his father's "licking" him came over him cold; it was not the pain; he had never minded Hilma's sturdy blows and he had let Michael cut a splinter out of his thumb with a pocket-knife, and never whimpered; it was the ignominy, the unknown terror of his father's wrath that loomed awful to him. As he looked down the crowded room and suddenly beheld Winslow's face bent gravely over Miss Hopkins, who was talking earnestly, he could hardly move his feet. Yet he had no thought of wavering. "I *got* to tell," he said, and walked as fast as he could, with his white face, straight to the group.

Winslow looked down and saw the two children; any one could discover the signals of calamity in their faces: Peggy's a fine scarlet and Johnny-Ivan's grayish-white.

"What's the matter, Johnny?" asked Winslow.

Johnny's eyelids were glued tight—just as they

were when he pulled Peggy's tooth—he blurted everything out breathlessly: "I've done something *awful,* papa! It'll cost thousands of dollars."

Emma Hopkins had considered Winslow an unattractive man, of a harsh visage, but now, as he looked at his little son, she changed her mind.

"What did you do, son?" said he quietly; his hand found Johnny's brown curls and lay on them a second.

"He didn't do it, really; it was *me,*" Peggy broke in, too agitated for grammar. "I was playing with the little tricks on the table, the models, sah, and I was making the v'losipid run round and he was 'fraid I'd break it; but *I* did it, really, sah."

"And the model fell on to something valuable? I see."

"But he wasn't playing with it, he was only trying to keep me from breaking—"

"Well, young lady, you two are evidently in the same boat; but you aren't a bit sneaky, either of you. Let's see the wreckage; I suppose you got into trouble because you wanted to see how things worked, and Johnny, as usual, couldn't keep out of other folks' hot water. Where's the ruin?"

"The show-case is broked, too," said Johnny-Ivan in a woeful, small voice.

"But it was cracked before," interjected Peggy.

Winslow looked at her with a little twist. "That's a comfort," said he, "and you have horse sense, my little Southerner. I guess you didn't either of you mean any harm——"

"Indeed, no, sah, and Johnny was just as good; never touched a thing——"

"But you see your intentions didn't protect you. Distrust good intentions, my dears; look out for the possible consequences. However, I think there is one person to blame you haven't mentioned, and that is one Josiah C. Winslow, who let two such giddy young persons explore by themselves. Contributory negligence is proved; and said Winslow will pay the bill and not kick."

So saying, he took Peggy's warm, chubby little fingers in one of his big white hands and Johnny-Ivan's cold little palm in the other, and nodded a farewell to Emma. Emma watched him; she did not realize how vividly more than one emotion was painted on her usually placid face, any more than she was aware of Olga Winslow's dark eyes.

"I don't know why, but I dislike that girl," said Olga to Mrs. Winter.

"Emma Hopkins? I shouldn't have said she had enough distinction about her to be disliked; she always seemed to me like apple dumplings, wholesome, but not intoxicating. You can't get up any ardent feelings about them! Now, Mrs. Raimund—"

"Mrs. Raimund"—Olga waved her hands impatiently in a foreign gesture—"she has a kind of beauty, but she bores one, she is so shallow. Now this young woman—she's *deep*. And I do not like her. I will tell you," she added directly. "I know whom she resembles. Oh, immensely! It is my husband,—it is Mr. Winslow. I never understood him; she would never be at a loss. They are cut out of the same piece of cloth."

"I never saw any resemblance,"—began Mrs. Winter, a little amused, a little embarrassed.

"MAMMA, I WISHT YOU WAS A QUEEN!"   *Page 37*

"Nor I until to-day. But—do you believe in pre-sentiments?"

"Not a bit," replied Mrs. Winter cheerfully.

"Me, I do believe. Well, *chérie,* I feel that young woman will have, some day, everything I love best, yes. So I—I hate her!"

"You talk as if you thought she would marry your husband."

"Some day she will. But she shall not have Ivan."

"My dear friend, this is—well, you are not talking sense!"

"No? But you will see it. Ugh! it bothers me; let us look at these strange artistic moods of our town. Was there ever anything cruder! You Americans think you can buy anything. Art isn't bought, it grows. The redeeming grace of an aristocracy is its—ah, what shall I say?—its heritage of beauty, luxury, splendor. Our daily life at home doesn't put on these things, they are a veritable part of it. Here, why, you are like an Indian in breech-clout and a dress-coat, your pomp is so incongruous, so assumed."

"Yet—you say you revolt from your own country's manner of living, for all it's so refined."

"*Nu.* We pay too high a price for repose and refinement. We are unconscious vampires, whose luxury and taste are drawn out of the veins of the poor starved, stunted mujiks. That is why my heart went forth to you Americans—until I knew you. I thought you were free, free in your souls, not only just free to sell your votes. I thought you loved your poor brothers and there was a chance for the poor-est—"

"There is," said Mrs. Winter dryly, "if he is willing to work and has brains. Just look at your own husband; he has made every dollar of his millions."

"Ah, but look you! he *has* brains and—he can be cruel, he can push the weaker aside. Even in Russia a man with those qualities can win money and a place. *Bozhe moi!** Does it not seem absurd to have believed that Americans, the most brutally relentless of all races but only the English, to have believed that *they* would love and help the weak? Yet I believed it. Ah, can't you see the only valid reason, the only living excuse for a democracy is that it should share with the humblest? A democracy must be crude and chaotic; it can't have the leisure and the serenity to be beautiful; but there is a beauty of the spirit that is greater; kindness and sincerity and truth and courage: they are the most beautiful of all! Do you think if I had found my dreams true, and you were trying to deck the bare homes of the poor with these *bibelots,* I should find anything of the ridiculous! Me, I should be on my knees to you! Nor would there be so much to ridicule; the worst art is born of pretense—I speak your language so poorly. I can't explain myself!"

"You speak English beautifully, my dear child," said Mrs. Winter, "our real language—well, I don't know whether you can speak it or understand it, either; and there's the trouble—why, Jo'nivan, how long have you been walking behind us?"

---

* Great Heavens! dear me !—a common Russian exclamation.

"Ever so long," answered Johnny-Ivan calmly; "but mamma says I mustn't int'rupt. Papa says I should tell you there's some nice *itchings* up stairs."

"Now, I wonder," thought Mrs. Winter, who was an astute personage and did not share the almost universal confidence in the deafness of children and one's neighbors in street-cars. "I do wonder how much of her ravings that poor little chap heard; he wouldn't understand the last part; but the first was plain English."

In point of fact, Johnny-Ivan had heard every word, but the futile effort to comprehend the last sentences had made him doubt his own interpretation of the words before. Nevertheless, he was to ponder on them often; and they were to have a more clinging influence on his future than even Mrs. Winter could forebode.

CHAPTER V

A MESSAGE FROM RUSSIA

On the morning after his misfortune at the Art Exhibition, Johnny-Ivan was racing over the lawn, filled with an exhilaration compound of a number of pleasant happenings. For one thing his "aunty" had come on a visit the evening before. In most families there is one aunty and several aunts. Sometimes, when there is a single aunt, she is not an aunty. Sometimes, also, the aunty to one child in a family is merely Aunt Helen or Anna to another. The aunty may be designated as the reigning aunt, the head of the order. Johnny-Ivan possessed several aunts, his Aunt Wanda, his Aunt Marie, his Aunt Clara, and he was decorously fond of them all; but only Mrs. Burney, his father's sister, was aunty, and aunty would be here for two weeks. She had brought him candy, a five-dollar gold piece and a wonderful fireman's suit with helmet and breastplate, in which he intended presently to dazzle Peggy. It was another delightful thing that Peggy was coming over for the whole day. Then, under all, wasn't it spring with the feel of spring in the air, if not yet the tints of spring in the trees! Altogether, Johnny-Ivan sang and shouted for the joy of living that morning.

By consequence he smiled with great friendliness at a small, well-freckled boy, whom he encountered crossing the lawn. This boy carried a tin pail. It was a battered pail of the haggard gray which ancient tin will acquire, and it was mended with a string.

"Say," hailed Johnny-Ivan, "who'd you want?"

The boy dug his bare heel into the soft turf and scowled at his little questioner. Instantly Johnny recognized him. It was the boy to whom he had given his knife, the boy who had jeered at him in the Art Gallery.

"Hello!" cried Johnny, in a different tone.

"Didn't you git a lickin', yestiddy?" said the boy.

He regarded this sally as a masterpiece of irony; and his sullen face relaxed.

Johnny-Ivan laughed. "Course not!"—he tossed his head easily—"papa paid 'em. I told all about it. I wasn't going to have you blamed." Johnny-Ivan was not above bragging about his virtue; in fact, the right to brag is one of the precious rewards of virtue to his age.

"*I* run away; they couldn't have cotched me," said the boy.

"You couldn't run'd away from the p'liceman! He'd catched you."

"Naw, he wouldn't. I kin beat the engine. Say, didn't your pa lick you when you got home?"

"Naw,"—Johnny-Ivan essayed an imitation, not in irony but in admiration of the other boy's accent—"my papa never licked me in my life."

The boy eyed him a minute, hammering a bare heel into the soft sod; his cynical air melted. "Say," said he, "it must be bully to have a sure 'nuff pa like that!"

"Haven't you got any papa?" said Johnny, his eyes wide.

"Naw, he's dead. I just got a step. My real father, he was a awful nice man. On the river. This one he ain't nothin', jes loafs an' bums an' licks us!"

"Does he lick you?"

"Me an' ma, too. _I_ don't mind. But I'm goin' to kill him fur lickin' ma, sometime."

Johnny-Ivan stared at the boy's flushing cheeks and knitted brow; and his own cheek reddened.

"I _would_," said he firmly; "that's what Kaler'd do. You could stick him with my knife. It's awful sharp."

The other did not receive this fiery counsel with enthusiasm. Often, the onlooker is of more desperate mood than the actor.

"He'd git the knife away and then he'd murder me sure'n shootin'," he muttered. "Lots of times, I have made up my mind to run away."

"Why don't you?"

"Only there's ma. He's so mean he'd take it out on her. Oncet he was lickin' her with a hard wood stick, and I jumped on him and bit him."

"Oh my!" gasped Johnny-Ivan, "what'd he do?"

"He bust my head open," answered the boy with somber pride, "and I didn't know nothin'. They called the police on us, that time, and he got thirty days. We'd a reel good time w'ile he was in jail; we painted the kitchen. Ma kep' every cent she got from scrubbing. But he come back; and it was bad's ever."

"Why don't you and your mother both run off?"
asked Johnny.

"It takes money," answered the boy; "ma, she
did save a little money, but she had to spend it all
buryin' baby."

"Did your baby die?"

"Dipthery? Yes. He was mean to her when she
was sick 'cause she cried. Ma said she'd never forgive him. I guess she'd run fast 'nuff if we'd got
the price."

Johnny was breathing quickly. Here was something like the stories. "*I* got some money," he cried,
"my aunty gave me a five-dollar gold piece and I
got it here—in my pocket—see!"

His hand had dived into his pocket and was out
again with the coin glittering in the palm. He
pressed it upon the astonished lad. "You take it,
and run quick!" he cried; "somebody's calling me.
Mind you run!"

Not pausing for an answer, he sped like a deer
back to the lawn and his father.

The freckled boy, after a second, put the coin inside his cheek and ran as swiftly in the opposite direction.

Johnny-Ivan's head was so full of the interview
that he almost bumped into a man, at that moment
mounting the steps where Mr. Winslow awaited his
son.

The man wore a red shirt. He had thick black
hair. Johnny-Ivan shied just in time; and, as he
sprang aside, he was aware of a paper waving in a
dirty hand. He recognized Serge Vassilovitch.
Serge it was, revealed rather than disguised by

liquor, swinging the open sheet and bellowing aloud: "Where is the barina? Where is Olga Ivanovna?"

Winslow, who had a copy of the same paper in his hand and whose face was unusually stern, took two strides toward the Russian. In the hall behind appeared Hilma and Abbie, the new waitress.

"What do you want at the front door?" demanded Winslow, the blood mounting to his brow. No one of the servants had ever seen him in a passion before; James, the gardener, Michael, Tim, Hilma, Abbie, the waitress, all stared at him; but Serge stood his ground and shrieked in Russian that the tyrant was removed!

"Get out of these grounds, you murderer and tool of murderers!" bawled Josiah. "If I see your dirty face here again I'll set the dogs on you!"

Serge, whose legs had begun to wabble, swung his arms and cursed in thick but voluble Russian. "Get out of here!" Winslow repeated. His tone had sunk; he thrust his hand into the bosom of his coat; something menacing in his gesture and more menacing in his eye pierced Serge's thick wits: he submitted to Michael, who whispered in his ear and led him away. The audience was dazed. Tim, alone, ventured comment.

"Is it true thim nahilists have blowed the legs aff the poor sezar of Rooshy?" said he.

The reply came through Winslow's set teeth. "That is just exactly what the damn idiotic assassins have done; and, if they only knew it, kept Russia out of a constitution for a generation, damn them! I'd like to see the whole batch swing!" The last word might not have been the last, had not Wins-

low seen his sister and his wife coming down the
stairway, and tried to put on his usual composed indifference of manner. But there remained the indefinable throb of emotion in the air; and Mrs.
Burney knew her brother.

"What has happened, Si?" she asked in a low
tone.

"The nihilists have assassinated the czar," said
Josiah; "good morning, Olga, would you like the
Gazette?" As he spoke he offered the paper to his
wife. She turned pale.

"What madness!" she muttered. "Oh, my poor
country!"

"I hope now, Olga," said he gravely, "we have
seen the last of Serge and of some others. You perceive what such methods come to."

She made him no answer. In silence they walked
together through the wide hall into the dining-room,
Johnny-Ivan following unnoticed, while their servants exchanged significant glances. The breakfast
passed off in apparent amity, mostly promoted by
Mrs. Burney, who was interested in the Art Exhibition, the weather, the Winslow summer plans,
everything in sight except Russia. Josiah read the
paper as he ate, hurling horrid details of the tragedy
at the others between mouthfuls, oblivious of
Johnny's glowing eyes or Mrs. Burney's pacific diversions. Olga smiled and patted her sister-in-law's
hand; not a word of sympathy or argument did she
offer her husband. But Johnny-Ivan's excitement
grew; it pulled him out of his chair and on to his
father's knee, where he could see the ghastly head-
lines for himself.

"Well, Johnny, let us men go off with the newspaper," proposed his father, "and leave mamma and aunty to talk of the show."

Olga found them together, half an hour later. Johnny was talking; she heard a single sentence. "No, papa, they're not bad cruel men. I guess the czar must have sent their friends to Siberia and that was the trouble."

Olga could not catch the answer in her husband's deeper tones, but she caught every word of the child's sweet, high pipe.

"Yes, papa. I'm awful sorry for the poor czar, if he *was* bad!"

She did not listen further; she went back to the house, to her own little parlor, where she waited for her boy. Her first horror was breaking under the onset of her instinct to defend her party and her friends. She resented this attack on a child's heart, forgetting that she had attacked it, herself.

When the little fellow came, she smoothed his dark curls, fondly murmuring soft Russian diminutives in his ear, and it was as if by accident she asked finally: "What was papa telling you?"

Johnny-Ivan blushed. "I guess I can't tell," said he. His head was bent, so he did not see her cold smile as she answered:

"Not if you promised not. But you didn't tell all those secrets *we* have, either?"

"Not one, *maman*, not *one;* I shutted my mouf *tight,* and I didn't even breathe." Here he suited the action to the word.

She smiled again. "He is mine," she was thinking, "most of all he is mine!"

However, the father had his own grounds for encouragement. That afternoon he strolled down to a corner of his garden where the asparagus bed in summer would make a mass of graceful greenery; now it was only a square of freshly turned black earth. On the edge a spot of clear turf was shaded by a tall and richly spreading elm which had been planted by Atherton's own hands; and Atherton himself had shaped the rustic seat beneath its greenery. To one side, a cluster of flowering almond trees and Paris japonicas used to flower in masses of crimson and pink for the April sun. That March day no bright color tinted the shrubs; but the grass was greening, the tree twigs were faintly red and an odor of earth and springtime exhaled from the newly turned clods. The place was the children's favorite playground; and now Peggy and Johnny were there, playing a game which so deeply engaged them that Winslow captured the seat behind the japonicas, unobserved. He watched them, at once aware this was a game out of the common. No ordinary play could demand such high toilets.

Peggy was decked in a gold embroidered robe (erstwhile a piano cover); the white silk handkerchief crowning her bright tresses was gathered into folds by Mrs. Winslow's opal and diamond brooch and further enriched by the chandelier chains, and a pompon from a small red feather duster. She bore a wand of white wreathed with yellow ribbon; her mien was of solemnest grandeur. Johnny was no less resplendent, wearing his fireman's helmet, a Roman sash of his mother's and a splendid cuirass made of two tin steamer covers attached to his person and each other by gold and white curtain cords. He brandished the Winslow sword and he was pale with emotion. "Let the Russian army approach the bier!" commanded Peggy, waving her wand. The Russian army stiffened and stalked up to a wheel-barrow covered with an American flag, beneath which could plainly be discerned the outlines of a doll.

"I'm sorry we didn't have a Russian flag," regretted the army as it surveyed the wheelbarrow.

"Well, you-all wouldn't take my Confederit flag," retorted the mistress of ceremonies; "it's a flag, that's the main thing." She elevated her tones: "Let the Russian nobility and clergy approach!" In response, she moved with dignity to the other side.

"Now the Royal Family!" She fell back to draw out a large handkerchief (one of Winslow's own) and bury her face in its folds while she tottered up to the bier. The army was visibly affected. Its agitation, in fact, was so great that it only opened its mouth at the next call: "Ambassadahs and ministahs of the penitenchary!" Suddenly came the low but stern command: "*Gimme* my wreath!" whereat the army scrambled under the wheelbarrow and emerged with a wreath of artificial roses, much past their bloom, apologizing, "It dropped off the wheelbarrow."

"It ain't a barrah, it's a *beah!*" said Peggy, with the same hushed severity, then aloud: "Ambassa-dahs, you-all approach! Down in front! the ambassadahs are approachin'!"

Majestically, the ambassadors and ministers plenipotentiary strode to the bier. Their gorgeous head laid the wreath on the flag; his tones swelled sonorously: "We bring this votive wreath in token of the grief and condolence of all nations. The deceased was a good and great man and it is an awful shame how he was killed, for he was basely murdered by cruel villins and traitahs."

The army fidgeted in an unmartial manner. "You're so many *things,*" it complained; "and I ain't nothing but the army."

"Well, you didn't want to p'nounce the funeral 'rashun, you wouldn't call the nihilists 'nuff names—"

"But I let you behead the worst one—"

"You wouldn't let me behead 'em all. They'd ought to be."

"Well, one's enough, 'cause he's the worst one; the others just did it to please *him.* Besides"—there was triumph in the little boy's tone; he felt that he could justify his reprehensible softness of heart— "besides, we'd lose the dolls!"

"Whose dolls are they?" was the haughty and irrefutable reply.

"I know they're yours, but don't *you* hate to cut your dolls' heads off?"

"Not when it's right and your juty," declaimed Peggy with an heroic air. She waved her hand at the bier. "That's Annabel Lee," said she, "turned into a man; and he's got Annabel's stockings on— her w'ite silk stockings."

"Oh, Peggy!" cried Johnny-Ivan, appalled at this Spartan sacrifice, "your best doll!" But instantly his brow cleared. "You—we could *un*bury him after a while, you know!" he suggested.

"No," said Peggy firmly, "I ain't no Injun gifter!"

"But—I don't think it's fair to Annabel Lee," ventured Johnny.

Unluckily, at this interesting turn of the drama, a powerful sneeze caught and strangled the spectator; he fought it in vain; it exploded with a prodigious reverberation. Both the children jumped; nothing remained for the eavesdropper but to come forward.

"I'm sorry I interrupted your game," he said. "I'm going off now, and, see here, little girl, I'd unbury the czar; I think he'd like it, and make him over into Annabel Lee."

"Yes, sah, we will," said Peggy, in her politest manner.

Josiah took his way homeward rather slowly; in truth he would have been glad to see the play out; he was curious regarding the fate of the condemned nihilist; so curious that he questioned Johnny-Ivan.

"We exercutid him," replied the little boy solemnly; "he paid the penalty of his crime; we cutted his head off." Johnny's grandiloquence was always artless; it came from simple trust in the language of his books; his face was full of tragedy, dashed with pride.

"Who was the executioner?"

"Peggy. She had the hatchet; and she dipped the head in red paint and held it up and hollered: 'Thus perish all traitors.'"

"And you cried?"

"No, sir; I didn't even shut my eyes; I played the Russian hymn on the comb, 'cause I was the band."

"Can you play a tune?"

"Not ezackly, but if you hold your mouf close to the comb and sorter sing the words it sounds like a tune. Peggy can do it beautiful; she played soon's she got done waving the head."

"So you had a very exciting time and enjoyed it?"

"I guess so," said Johnny-Ivan; but there was some doubt in his tone.

"Poor little chap!" thought Winslow, "you need an almighty lot of hardening. How am I going to give it to you?"

Not seeing his path clear, he presented Johnny with a silver quarter and told him never to borrow the ancestral sword again.

"Mamma let me have it," said Johnny.

"And let Peggy have the brooch, too, I dare say."

"Yes, sir. Peggy took awful good care of it. We gave it right back."

"Did mamma know what it was for?"

"No, sir. I thought Peggy would tell her what for, but she didn't; she just said for a game, and mamma said, 'Cela m'est égal, chérie!' So she took it."

It was rather surprising, although very delightful to have his father, of whose mood in regard to the disposal of portable property Johnny-Ivan was never quite secure, take these revelations with nothing harsher than his odd widening of his lips, and immediately produce another quarter for Peggy.

"I think, Johnny," said Josiah Winslow, "when you grow up, you'd better marry Peggy. She'll be a help to you in a good many ways."

"Oh, I'm *going to*," said Johnny-Ivan.

CHAPTER VI

AS GALLEY SLAVES, NOT COMRADES

The great trouble with Peggy was Girls! Girls were always tagging after Peggy. One warm afternoon two of the most obnoxious of the tribe came to Hazelhurst and they all went off together and had "sekruts." Johnny-Ivan was told to go find out whether Milly, Mrs. Winter's cook, would open her heart to the extent of freshly-baked ginger-snaps and root beer. He accomplished his mission, one not to his liking, for Milly always embraced him and gave him a perspiring kiss of approbation for being such a "sweet, pretty little boy"—Johnny, himself, all the while, intent on conspiracies and combats and a blood-stained career of reformation of the world— and then, when he had honorably repaid the future beneficence by reciting *Barbara Frietchie*,—after all this strenuous self-sacrifice, the perfidious Girls had run away! And he couldn't find them. He plodded homeward, wanting very much to cry, but he knew that boys didn't cry; so he whistled instead, and, in a little space, became so interested, planning a "sekrut" of his own about the ginger-snaps, that he grew quite cheerful. By the time he reached his favorite little crotch of shrubs on the lawn, just below the porch, he was laughing. The weeks had crept on into late April. The tulips were up and the yellow jonquils gilded the flower beds on the lawn which James had mowed smooth with the new lawn-mower until it was like green velvet, athwart which the sun sent shafts of emerald blaze. The trees, in their lovely faint etching which was not yet foliage, or their red softness of bough and twig presaging the leafing, rose all along the slopes below the terraces where the house stood, and lower still, the little city with its shining church spires, its thin red blocks and its multitude of softly graying house-roofs, spread along the shining river.

For the first time in his life Johnny-Ivan looked on a landscape with a definite sense that it gave him pleasure. Even the Patch was glorified by the morning and the spring. Its ungracious outlines melted into formless, reticent blurs of brown and gray; its card-house roofs were broken by the trees; and there were great splashes of white and pink amid the bronzes of cottonwood and crab-apple trees.

Johnny-Ivan nestled in his corner, very warm and tired with running. He felt rather than heard the twitter of the robins and the shrill call of the blue jay on the capital of the column; his eyelids dropped and immediately he dozed.

When he awoke it was with an indescribable sensation of shock and discomfort. Two people were talking on the piazza. They could not see him; but he could see them, and he could hear them distinctly. They were his father and mother—and they were quarreling! Now, whatever their alienation, the father and mother of Johnny had never permitted him to witness their disputes. He felt his whole little world reel about him when the two people who could do no wrong lashed each other with bitter voices.

What they said was unintelligible to him, and often afterward as he rehearsed the scene and groped through his memory for the dimly recalled sentences, he never could entirely comprehend them. But his sickness of heart was as real as if he understood.

Winslow was walking up and down the piazza, smoking. Mrs. Winslow sat in an easy chair, nor did she ever rise. Her voice kept its musical, foreign inflections and never but once was it ruffled.

The first words which broke into her son's comprehension were: "If you are so dissatisfied with me and I give you so much sorrow, why not let me go away? I am willing to go; I want to go."

"You want to go?" Winslow's heavy black brows were knit.

She drew a long shuddering breath. "I can't bear it any longer," she said; "if I don't go I shall kill myself. Take your choice."

"I guess not," said he (while Johnny's heart contracted with terror); "what are you driving at, Olga? Try to talk plain sense, for once; I've long since ceased to hope you would ever care for me and be a wife to me as other men's wives are. I don't even ask you to keep the house decent; I shut my teeth and let the girls throw the sweepings out of the window, and when they break all the cut glass I get some pressed glass that won't break so easy. I don't bother you. I don't expect you even to return the calls my friends have made you, or to see them

when they take the trouble to come here. I don't
see that you are suffering, particularly. You have
your own rooms, your own allowance to fool away
on damn scoundrels, who make all the trouble they
can for me. All I ask is that you are civil to me before Johnny and that you don't disgrace me openly.
Anything else you want I'm willing to try to
meet—"

"Will you let me go away—to France, to Switzerland?"

"That would be nonsense; you'd find yourself
mixed up with your villainous crowd of assassins.
I will go with you, next fall—"

She began to laugh, very softly. "Thanks, but—
we should be too much together for the comfort of
either of us. Josiah, let me go, go entirely. The play
is played out; we haven't a thought in common—"

"That may be, but we have a child. There's
Johnny."

"I have borne it so long because of Ivan. I can't
bear it any longer. Do you guess, you Americans,
how appalling is your life? I thought this was a
land where all our poor Russian dreams, that we are
so willing to die for, came true. And—you are not
so free—really—as we. I weary myself to death of
this odious *bourgeoisie*, this intolerable, narrow ex-
istence which is all a fight for money—crushing,
crowding, strangling each other. These women,
your friends, they think of nothing but their toilets
and their houses and oppressing their poor servants
—it gets on my nerves until I want to scream! And
you, too! You do not understand—anything! What
is life to me, is folly, madness to you. Life must

mean something; it must have a secret; I have sought for it in your scheme of living and I can not find it; you only busy yourself with the husks of life, the clothes, the houses, the power your money gives you; for you, that is all; and work, struggle, the conquering and trampling on weaker creatures, that gives you your happiness. To me such triumph is intolerable. It is against my nature. Why should we go on, not comrades, only galley slaves? Oh, Josiah, *let* me go!"

Winslow drove his hands deeper into his pockets and his mouth hardened. The breathless little creature, watching, was terror-stricken; he began to crawl out, with a vague notion of protecting his mother. Only his father did not move; he couldn't hurt her unless he moved.

"You're polite to ask me. I wonder you haven't bolted," said he, not even looking at her.

"But there was Vanya," she said. "I couldn't go without Vanya." Johnny-Ivan caught his breath.

His father answered in a harsh tone: "You certainly won't go *with* him. I mean to do the fair thing by you, Olga; if I've made mistakes, they were mistakes, not intentional cruelty. It isn't fair to me to take Johnny away from me, but let that go; the main point is, it isn't fair to Johnny, either; you don't know how to bring up a child properly. I'm not willing to let you have him."

In a tumult of feeling, Johnny beheld his mother spring to her feet, flinging her beautiful arms upward, her cheeks afire, her calm voice breaking. The anguished sweetness of it wrung his heart, as she cried: "But I am his mother! And I love him

—ah, *mon Dieu, mon Dieu,* how I love him, my golden one! But you don't understand that. Understand this, then: I *will* have him!"

"Stay here, like a decent woman, and have him, then," scoffed Winslow. "Do try to see things as they are, Olga. You're not trampled on,—you are a very much indulged woman. You have a handsome house that you could make handsomer if you would only buy things and see that your maids dusted them. You may be tired of your husband, but he doesn't ask any more of you than your coachman does. You've got a nice little chap for a son that you aren't tired of—yet."

"Do you think I ever shall tire of him?"

"I don't know. You soulful, questioning-every-thing sort of folks do get tired of everything in the long run. Never mind; I only want to say that I shan't under any circumstances let you take Johnny away. I think, myself, he'd better go off somewhere to school—"

"Josiah! That little child!"

"He's little, and I don't want to send him, but it might be best; you have been letting him see that hound of a Vassil—"

"Why are you so bitter against that poor man? I heard—I don't want to believe it—that you set the dogs on him Thursday night."

"I certainly did. He was skulking about the chicken-house, and I set Rube on him; and the patriot ran. I think Rube got one bite out of his leg; at least he got some of his trousers. Oh, he's a sweet nature's nobleman! I changed Rube to another kennel, and just as well. I found a chunk of meat loaded with strychnine in his old kennel this morning. Threw it in, I suppose, and ran. And last week there was a bundle of trash soaked in kerosene found —by Tim, not Michael—in the stable. You have nice friends, Olga."

"That was wrong. That was cruel, I admit it," said Mrs. Winslow—Johnny thought how noble she was; and his instinctive dislike of Serge was strengthened—"but he *had* provocation, Josiah. Treat a man like a brute and he will take a brute's revenge."

Winslow made no answer; he had turned his face in the direction of the city and was listening.

"Fire bells," he exclaimed, "and there goes our whistle! Olga,"—he turned with a different expression, "we can finish this talk some other time. I'm a little anxious about that fire. It's our district. I'm going in to try the new telephone. Big thing, those telephones, if they work as well as they seem likely to do. Last week I should have had to send a man to town; but I can find out now in two seconds."

Mrs. Winslow did not turn her head; if he could dismiss the situation so cavalierly, she could not; but Johnny's thoughts were diverted as if a hand had swung them round; for the quiet air was suddenly throbbing with a confusion of bells and whistles. The noise had spread from its corner of origin into all quarters of the city; and Johnny, looking in a familiar direction, saw a thick black column of smoke puff up over the roofs.

His mother's back was turned to him. He ran up to her and clung to her soft gray skirts. Whatever he had felt was swept away, for the moment,

by a new and overpowering excitement. Fire is
often the secret terror of a sensitive child. He never
talks about it, because sensitive children are reticent
to the point of sin; but it is his constant, darkling
attendant. Never did Johnny hear fire bells at night
that he didn't sit up in bed with his heart beating
wildly, listening with all his ears until he could be
certain that it wasn't his father's factory; after that,
with a genuine but not distressing pity for the poor
people who were burning up, he would go to sleep
again. Very likely he would say his artless prayer:
"O God, please put the fire out, even if they are bad
people," and sleep the more readily for this shifting of the burden.

Fire by daylight wasn't so bad; and Peggy really
liked it, she said; and he did like to go to a fire with
her and Michael. Once they helped carry things
out; that was grand! But, of course, there was the
suspense until the fire was surely not papa's factory.

This time—"O, mamma, it looks right on the
street—papa's street," he whispered.

"Why, so it does," said mamma. But she didn't
seem in the least frightened; she even smiled a little;
at least her upper lip curled.

"Listen!" exclaimed Johnny-Ivan, "papa's telephoning."

They both listened and both heard. "You all
right, Hopkins?—Is it bad?—H'mn, yes. I'll be
down. Shut all the windows. Turn off the naphtha
tanks!" The instrument went back with a click and
the bell rang dismissal, for the first telephones were
more formal and leisurely,—one did not have one's
signals automatized for him.

In a second there was a furious clang on the stable bell.

"Oh, papa's works are afire; they're burning up! Oh, mamma! Oh, mamma!" screamed Johnny-Ivan, his panic let loose for once. But his mother's hand was on his shoulder soothing him.

"That's not being a brave boy!" she said; "be quiet, Ivan, or I shall be ashamed of my son of whom I used to be so proud."

The words were the strongest tonic to the sensitive little heart on which they fell. Johnny-Ivan bit a sob in two and straightened himself; before she guessed his intention he had darted across the lawn and run like a hare around the house. The stable yard was all motion and excitement. Tim was buckling straps on one side of the horse, Michael on the other, and his father was already seated in the buggy gathering up the reins.

"Good as the fire department, boys," praised Winslow quietly; "let her go! Michael, get the gate open!"

"Papa! papa! lemme go, too!" shouted Johnny-Ivan; but Winslow shook his head.

"No place for boys," he called. Johnny-Ivan, wasting no time in entreaty, which would be lost on the air, made for the first gate. He outstripped Michael and swung it back.

"Please let me go, papa!" he shouted, "to hold the horse! I don't weigh so much as Michael. *Please* take me!"

He thought his father's answer didn't come quite so quickly as before, but it came: "Can't risk you, son, but I'll telephone you how we get on!"

The next instant there was dust all about them, and only the dark green wheels twinkling through. "He might have let me," thought the little boy; "it wasn't a bit risky; Romeo wouldn't run!" He felt mightily aggrieved, and the resentment which had been rising all through the hearing of his parents' dispute burned more hotly. Papa *wasn't* nice to mamma, and he wasn't nice to him, Johnny; he was *mean!* Yet there grew a gleam of comfort; papa was going to telephone to *him* about the fire. Johnny-Ivan stationed himself by the telephone. There he stayed and waited. He waited what seemed to him a long time before the bell rang. It was hard to wait, because there was the fire to see outside, and every one in the household, as well as Mrs. Winter, Mrs. Rutherford and Peggy, had gathered to look. He could hear their exclamations: "The smoke's awfully black!" . . . "I don't think it's any blacker!" . . . "But it *is*, *mon amie, regarde!*" . . . "Aw-w! ain't it too bad!" . . . "*I helige verlden!*" . . . "Look at the blaze!" . . . "There's the fire sure enough. What's the matter with the department?" . . . "Aw, 'tis manny a good man's losin' his job this day; an' a good man his money!" . . . "Mamma, the fire's going down! It is! it is!" . . . "But look at the smoke!" . . . "Oh, ain't it too bad!" . . . "How it's pouring out! Jist *pouring!*"

Yet Johnny, although every nerve was tingling, clenching his tiny fist in his impatience, stuck to his telephone, even when Peggy's clear tones clove the din outside. "Oh, Jo'nivan, come on out!"

"I can't," he called back; "papa's going to telephone me!"

"But you can hear the bell out here!"

"I know, but I can't keep papa waiting."

As he stood—on a chair to obtain a better reach of the instrument—he could hear louder sighs and exclamations from the maids and the men. The fire must be gaining. But at this moment the bell rang. "Yes, papa," he cried before he got the receiver to his ear. "Hello! You, Johnny?"—the voice came to him mixed with a dozen sounds, dulled into echoes, shouts, the wash of water and the roar of a crowd. "Fire's under control. Tell mamma."

"Hurrah!" cried Johnny, "did you—was anybody hurted?" But no answer came, and Johnny-Ivan finally replaced the black horn and sauntered out on the lawn, feeling himself the bearer of great news. Straight to his mother he went with it.

"That's nice," she said quietly.

"Upon my word," cried Mrs. Winter, "you take these excitements coolly, Olga. I don't think I, myself, take on much; but *you* are a Stoic!"

The Princess Olga sighed. "There are worse things than fires in a factory, where no one is likely to be hurt," said she.

Meanwhile the other minor members of the group were disappearing to attend to their vocations or to gossip more freely together, as the case might be. Johnny-Ivan and Peggy departed to get a new Oliver Optic book, which had just been given to Peggy. There was a boy in that book who wasn't afraid of anything on earth. Yesterday Johnny-Ivan had been keen for the adventurous Richard's perils, but to-day his imaginary world did not entice him; he was full of an uneasy excitement. Moreover, his thoughts kept harking back to the scene of the morning.

"Peggy," he said, "do grown-ups ever quarrel? I mean grown-ups that are married."

"Why, of co'se, certainly," returned the worldly-wise Peggy; "I've heard mammy and Uncle Dari, myself. Mammy's *terrible* when she's r'arin' and chargin'; she called Uncle Dari a heap of bad names—"

"Don't she love him any more?"

"Why, cert'y she does; she's just petted on him; she'd bake all night for him. But—why, ev'rybody gets mad, sometimes. You get mad with *me*."

"That's so," Johnny-Ivan agreed with a long sigh of relief; he turned the talk on to the fire.

His father came back at noon. He was in a strange good humor. Johnny-Ivan couldn't understand his laughter and jokes at the table; he was too young to know the intoxication of struggle and victory.

"Those firemen"—Winslow talked to Johnny, rather than at Mrs. Winslow's languid politeness—"they were fooling when I got there—afraid of the naphtha; they'd a notion it was going to explode, although Hopkins turned it off, and it wasn't any more danger than a chicken! Hopkins and I took some hose into the shop, ourselves, and our own men ran right after us. Luke Darrell was there, happy's a boy to be at a fire again; he went, too. Then the chief got his head at last and got a line into the windows, and all was over in five minutes."

"You did it, papa; you, yourself?" cried Johnny.

"I myself," laughed Winslow, "and it has ruined one good suit of clothes, or I miss my guess." The words were accompanied by a furtive eye-flash at his wife's languid face. Possibly in his hot mood of excitement he fancied that she would realize, at least, that her husband was a man, even rejoice a little that he should have saved his property; it is so hard to comprehend how what moves one's own being profoundly can fall on another's soul as resultless as firebrands on a snowbank. But Mrs. Winslow inclined her head with a formal courtesy more chilling than indifference, saying, as if to a stranger: "I hope you are not very tired;" and Winslow's boyish gaiety fell off like a mask. He smiled again, however, at Johnny's cry: "You're just like a general, papa, leading your troops into battle!"

"Humph! not so bad as that, Johnny, but I was certainly under fire. And that reminds me, Olga," —this time the smile was his grim, straight line of the mouth—"I know how the fire happened."

"Was it an *indecendary* fire, papa?" inquired Johnny, who read the newspapers and never hesitated to charge on a word familiar to his eyes, whether his ears had ever heard it or not.

"*Ce n'est pas exactement juste, Vanya,*" began Mrs. Winslow in gentle correction, with a foreigner's polite seriousness; she always made any suggestions of reproof in French, which Johnny-Ivan spoke as fluently as English. Winslow grinned, and Johnny flushed.

"Yes, it was," said Winslow; "our old friend,

Serge Vassy, was the incendiary. The tyrannical hand of the law has already fallen upon him. He was seen going into the lumber room with something under his arm. And they found the wreck of a nice bomb there, after the fire was out. You see, the fire didn't quite work to order. Serge hadn't counted on a shift of wind; he expected the whole shed would be burned and his pretty plaything with it, but—it wasn't. I guess we've got a clear case."

Now at last he had roused his wife; the red rushed into Mrs. Winslow's cheeks. She did not look at her husband as she said: "Didn't you set the dogs on the man? His revenge is just as brutal."

"Well, perhaps. And mine, now, will not be brutal, but effectual, for I shall have Serge sent up for ten years, anyhow; and I have bought the Patch and am going to build a branch factory with decent houses for the people working there."

"And the poor creatures on the place now?"

"They will have to skedaddle."

"What will they do? Where will they go?"

"Be a nuisance somewhere else, I suppose. Not under our eyes, however."

"I don't suppose you care. You would get the police and drag out their poor bits of furniture and beds and the little children and old people—"

"They won't need dragging. They'll go and poison some other place. It's a pity they can't be dumped in the river, the whole pestilential, cutthroat outfit. Johnny, what do you think about Serge? Shall we have Peggy chop off his head, by proxy?"

"No, sir," said Johnny, in a singularly subdued

tone; "but I think he's wicked; he ought to go to prison."

"Quite right. He will, too. It's almost worth the fire to get that damned—that assassin out of the way. Well, I guess, now I've had a bath and clean clothes and something to eat, I'll be getting back."

He rumpled Johnny-Ivan's hair in passing, and hurried out, quite unconscious of the effect of his last news about the Patch.

"Mamma, what does papa mean?" said Johnny-Ivan.

"He meant," said Mrs. Winslow slowly, "that he has bought all those poor people's homes and he will turn them out."

"But—maybe they want to go, mamma!" Johnny-Ivan was trying to defend his father, who had been so brave at the fire, but he had a sickening light on the situation coming from a never-forgotten picture of furniture piled on the street, a shrieking woman and weeping children.

"Would *you* want to go out with all you have in the world and no place to put it?"

"Can't they rent some nicer place? The houses *are* awfully tumbly and dirty, mamma, for a fact. Some of them don't have any paper, but only just newspapers. Can't they rent some of the nice houses papa's going to build?"

"They haven't any money. Papa'll charge money!"

"But not if he knowed for sure they didn't have any money."

Mrs. Winslow's lip curled; she looked as she had looked that morning.

"Yes, Ivan, papa never lets poor people have things for nothing. And he is angry at the Patch because Serge lives there. He will turn out Serge's brother-in-law, so Serge never can live there again."

"But the baby is sick."

"He won't care for that. Perhaps it will kill the baby. He doesn't care." Never before had she criticized her husband to her child; she felt a cruel joy as she flung off this last fetter of her marriage.

"And old Mrs. Kelly, mamma? *she* can't be moved! She's been in bed for seventeen years; when the Rodins' woodshed was afire she wouldn't let 'em move her; she just wouldn't! She grabbed the bedtick and held on; she said she'd better die of the smoke than the moving, and she'd lived long enough to be tired of this world anyhow, now she'd no more comfort of smoking, 'cause it hurted her. No, mamma, she can't be moved. It's unpossible. *I'll* tell papa and he'll see."

"He will not care," returned the princess, "but come, Vanya, I have much to say to you. Not here; in the summer-house."

CHAPTER VII

IN WAR YOU MAY

The summer-house was so thickly shaded with vines, woodbine, clematis and wistaria, that it kept cool and dim through the hottest summer glare, a property most desirable in the Middle West, where the July and August suns know all the tricks of the tropics. It was built of unhewn logs, but ceiled and floored within; and it was set midway on the hill. Above, the tall elms and maples dappled the clean hillside with their shade; below, a dense undergrowth of brambles, saplings and wild raspberry and blackberry bushes transformed the coppice into a jungle.

A single footpath was kept mowed; but often, running along it, Johnny-Ivan's heart had jumped at a sinuous flash of green and brown across the tangle. The birds nested high above danger from the stable cats, which hunted, in gleeful savagery, through the thicket, their wild grace, as they leaped and glided, proclaiming their origin. Orioles, thrushes and robins found here a refuge from the sparrow banditti, which clung to the haunts of men, where corn and crumbs were to be had for the stealing. Blue jays took their dominion of terror, plundering nests at will; but they were fewer, hence more merciful. So the woodland was full of singing birds, and the flaming head of the wood-pecker tapped on the bark, adding its tiny drum to the forest concert. So long the squirrels had been left unmolested that they would come to be fed out of Johnny's hand; the quails hopped after crumbs almost at his feet. Of a summer night the air would seem to throb with the multitudinous whir of happy creeping and flying things. Then the princess would come, with her little lover, to sing her Russian songs in the moonlight.

She did not dream that there was always a silent, frowning guardian within reach, should there ever be need. Winslow kept these vigils to himself.

Sometimes she would talk instead of sing, voicing the dreams and longings of a passionate mystic who could not interpret her own soul, yet tried to solve the riddle of the universe. But Johnny-Ivan accepted all in reverence. Nothing is impossible or preposterous to a child. Universal love seems to him natural as his mother's tenderness; and God is only a more distant and powerful friend.

Johnny loved the little summer-house; he never spoke of the talks there; they were one of the secrets shared with his mother. He had been glad when the spring grew mild enough to allow again the visits which winter had forbidden. There was only the beginning of greenery on the soft dark boughs of the deciduous trees; but the conifers, the firs and the cedars held their somber bronze over winter, the orange and vermilion blooms of the maples struck a brilliant note of color amid the drabs and browns, and the spring sunshine flooded everything.

The little boy ran gaily along the path, between walls of dead vines and shrubs and thorny brush-wood. He carried his Oliver Optic in his hand to read in case his mother should have to go to speak to any one; for very often of late "our people" seemed to come to speak to mamma.

The princess, on her part, was unusually silent. She sat down on the rustic chair by the table, and he took a stool at her feet, his dark curls pressing against her knee. She had brought her cross-stitch work, but the gay silks lay untouched on the linen as she sat with clasped hands and dreamy eyes.

All at once a shadow fell over her white skirts to lie long and black over Johnny-Ivan's page. He looked up. Serge Vassilovitch had made the shadow; but never had Johnny-Ivan seen a Serge like this. He was perfectly sober, pale and anxious-looking, and the hands which he stretched forth were trembling. Drops of sweat stood under the black locks matted on his forehead.

"Barina, you are our fathers and mothers!" he murmured. He said something more in Russian. Johnny-Ivan could not understand the words, but the tone was entreating. His speech came panting, as if the speaker were spent with running.

Mrs. Winslow hesitated. She answered very low. At once the man flung himself on his knees before her, clutching her dress and stammering broken sentences while his eyeballs rolled up at her in an agony of pleading.

She drew a long sigh. "I can not refuse," she said in English, "but how?—wait!"

He, too, sighed, but his was a sigh of relief. He

scrambled to his feet. All this time he had not so much as glanced at Johnny-Ivan; yet it was to Johnny Mrs. Winslow turned; then Serge's big eyes devoured the pale, little, attentive face.

"Ivan," said Mrs. Winslow, in French, "do you remember the oath you swore on the sword?"

A lump swelled in Johnny-Ivan's throat as he answered: "Yes, mamma."

"Little son, the time is come for you keep it. Do you trust *me?*"

"Yes, mamma," said Johnny-Ivan.

She changed her tongue to English, perhaps for Serge's better comprehension. "Do exactly as I say —exactly. Afterward I will explain. Now, time is too precious. Serge belongs to *us*. We must protect him. They'd kill him if they caught him. They caught him, but he got away; he—he hurt one of them and they will hang him if they catch him—"

"A—a—i! yes!" mumbled Serge, moistening his dry lips.

"I can't help him escape, but you can; *you,* my darling little son, have the life of a man in your hands."

Serge's shadow wavered as if Serge had shuddered; the shadow was all that touched Johnny's vision, for his big eyes were glued to his mother's face.

"Get Serge under the chair and put the afghan over him—get under, Serge—quick!"

An incoherent murmur came from Serge. Mrs. Winslow replied imperiously: "It is the only way. They suspect me at every turn. You *must!* Michael will fetch food and money, later. Now—" she lapsed into Russian, speaking rapidly and with a vehemence that cowed the fugitive. Submissive as a dog, he moved at the beckoning of her jeweled white hand, cramping his long legs under the rustic chair which Mrs. Winslow shielded by an afghan, ere she motioned Johnny into the chair and disposed his feet on a pile of sofa pillows.

"*So*," she approved, "*très bien!* Now, attend! Dearest child! you must be brave and wise. The officers will come here. They will ask questions. Perhaps they will ask if any one has come here. You will say, 'Only mamma.' 'Where has she gone?' 'She has gone to the stables.' You will ask them, politely, to come in. Should they come, there is the bench where they can sit. But do not fear! They will not come."

"Mamma," said Johnny-Ivan, "am I to say *nobody* came?"

"Yes, Ivan. Nobody. It is like in war, you know. In war you may say things not true."

"Yes, mamma. I am to fool the officers because Serge belongs to us."

"You are all right!" growled the man under the chair.

"Then I will go. Remember, I said I was going to the stables."

"I will remember, mamma."

He watched her figure dwindle along the dim path until the narrow way twisted sidewise and it was lost in the gray shadows. When his eyes gave over their search they fell upon the book, which he had retained mechanically. It was not a difficult part to read the pages. Already he was taking on his rôle, his heart beating faster, lest unseen eyes should have stolen up to peer through the trees.

"*Batyushka moi*—"* the voice was meek.

"Shut up!" commanded Johnny-Ivan, "somebody'll hear you."

Although he was obeying his mother and meant to obey her and was keeping his oath, all of which was very great and exciting, just like knights in a book, he had not quite lost his repugnance to the man; only now it was smothered by pity. "I'll take care of you all right," he added. He felt very old and grand, also very scared; but, of course, that wasn't to be admitted. The minutes crept on. The fingers shifting the leaves of the book were fairly steady. Maybe the officers wouldn't come. Still, if they didn't it wouldn't make so much of a story for Peggy. He wasn't sure that he didn't wish they would come; but like a dash of cold water came the afterthought, *this* story he couldn't tell Peggy. Then, he was quite certain he hoped that the policemen wouldn't come. He hoped in vain. First, some of the twigs crackled; next, a branch broke; then a stifled voice called: "Be careful, now, he's got the gun still!" This was quickly followed by a loud shout:

"Hands up!" Three tanned and anxious faces peered into the doorway, three pistols were leveled at Johnny-Ivan's curly black head.

He rose involuntarily. "What—t's the matter?" he quavered. He wasn't afraid, but it was so sudden; and, somehow, he had lost his breath.

*My little father.

"Good Lord, it's only a kid!" cried the first man; "drop your guns!"

The pistols slanted lower; the men looked at the little figure and the peaceful summer-house; they smiled rather sheepishly, but the leader resumed his official sternness.

"Who are *you?* Mr. Winslow's boy?"

"Yes, sir," said Johnny-Ivan.

"Wasn't any one else here?"

"No, sir"—he had never told a lie before in his life, but he told it quite easily, admiring himself—"only mamma was here."

"Where is your mamma?"

"She's gone to the stable. She just went a little while ago. She said she'd be right back. Did you want mamma? Won't you come in?"

The men whispered together.

"We're losing time," called the leader, "let's watch the stable. He'd try for a horse. Say, Johnny Winslow, we're out after the man who set your father's works afire. He was caught and shot officer McNamara, who's like to die. Did you see anything of him? It's Serge Vassy—"

"I know," said Johnny-Ivan, "papa telled me about him." He grew a shade paler.

"Did you see him anywhere in the woods?"

"No, sir."

"If you do see him, run after us—at the barn, will you?"

"Yes, sir," said Johnny-Ivan.

The bluecoats withdrew from the doorway.

Johnny-Ivan heard the crunch of heavy boots through the thicket. He went to the door, and as

he stood there he became aware that his heart was
beating so fast that it hurt him. Recalling his false-
hoods, he wondered fearfully if he could be going
to drop dead like wicked Ananias. But he had no
smallest thought of confession.

"It's like it is in war," he comforted himself,
"you *got* to in war. 'Sides, it's only to the cops, all
the boys tell stories to the cops! They ain't like your
folks!"

"Are they gone, *gospodi*?"*—a hoarse whisper
came to him. In some subtle wise it irritated him;
here he was doing all these wicked things for a murderer. He had seen McNamara once, at a circus,
and he helped him up to a seat. "Jump! my little
man!" he had said. "Well, you *are* a jumper!"—
when Johnny-Ivan had nimbly vaulted on to the
seat, which was a splendid place where you could
see 'way down to the horses' feet!—and he had
laughed such a nice, loud laugh. Now to have to
help his murderer off was pretty hard.

"You keep quiet!" commanded the boy sternly,
in a whisper; "you stay right here and draw your
foots in. I hear somebody coming." There *was*
some one coming. He came from the south by the
cow-path, some one who knew the wood. He came
rapidly, making so little noise that only Johnny-Ivan,
whose ears were of the very keenest, could have
been warned; but in a moment he turned from the
cow-path and broke, snapping and crushing the
underbrush, through the thicket, to the right. And
it was papa!

*Sir.

Johnny-Ivan showed no emotion. "Why, papa!" he exclaimed with mild surprise.

Papa was hatless; he had torn his coat on the briers and scratched his face; little flecks of blood showed on his cheek amid the gray short whiskers; he was breathing hard, like Serge, and he looked angry—oh, but he looked angry!

His eyes flashed over the dusky summer-house; lucky Serge's boot was safe under cover!

"Who's been here, Johnny?" said papa.

"The coppers, papa, the p'lice. They're after Serge—"

"I know. He's been seen in this wood. Did you see him?"

"No, papa." It was said. It *had* to be said. It was like in war. Johnny-Ivan shut his little teeth firmly.

"Where's mamma? Was she here?"

"She went to the stable. She told me to stay—"

"Ah-h!" papa interrupted, "when?"

"Just before the p'lice—"

"Did she hear any whistle or anything?"—papa wouldn't give you a chance to finish your sentence at all.

"No, sir, I don't think—"

"But the blue jays?"

"They're always whistling."

Only a second papa hesitated, then he turned to Johnny-Ivan. "Come with me," he said.

"But mamma told me—"

"Mamma didn't know the danger you're in. If that devil found you in the wood alone—he's due to swing anyhow; and he'd strike me through you.

Come, we'll go to the stables together. Go on ahead, Johnny, run ahead, I'm coming."

Johnny-Ivan had never been so perplexed in his life. To leave his charge when mamma had told him to stay—but it would be sure discovery for Serge if he didn't go. Reluctantly he edged out of the door; on the threshold he ventured a further protest: "Mamma might come back, and he might hurt mamma—"

"Oh, mamma's safe, he wouldn't hurt mamma. Be *quick*, Johnny."

Johnny-Ivan ran out obediently; he ran a little space and halted, transfixed by his father's stern, quiet voice:

"Now, *you!* Come out of that with your hands up, or I'll begin firing. I saw you move that afghan. Out with you!"

The afghan fell in a heap as Serge crawled out. His revolver shook in his hand.

"Drop it!" said Winslow. It was strangest of all to Johnny-Ivan how quietly papa spoke. Serge looked a second into the shining barrel; he picked himself up.

"You got the drop on me," said he sullenly.

"I congratulate you on your mastery of American idiom, Mr. Vassy," said Winslow, "I *have*. Stand up. Now, Johnny, run to the stable and fetch the policemen. Hurry quick, for if you don't I shall shoot Serge, because he'll try to escape. *I* don't mind; but he may. Hurry!"

"Please don't shoot Serge, papa!" pleaded Johnny; "he was there all the time, and he never hurted me."

His queer smile widened Winslow's mouth; not in the least a pleasant smile; nor was his voice pleasant. "Then hurry back with the police, Johnny," he said, *"hurry!"*

Johnny-Ivan shot a single glance at Serge; it was to ask for orders.

"Guess, yes, you hurry," said Serge; his hands were uncomfortable in the air; he looked shrunken and scared, and his dirty, pale face was miserable.

Johnny sped away like the wind.

As he raced stableward, his mind worked faster than his feet. The only chance to save Serge was mamma; if he could only tell mamma first! But outside of the stable he encountered the leader of the policemen and mamma. There was no help for it. He blurted it out in a sentence: "Papa's caught Serge; he says to hurry—they're at the summerhouse."

"By hell!" swore the policeman joyously; "come on, boys!"

He called over his shoulder as he pelted over the grass, the others hard on his heels:

"Best take the little boy into the house, ma'am! Boys, have your barkers ready. We've got him; but he's desperate!"

At last Johnny-Ivan could tell his mother, choking piteously over his last words: "I did try, mamma, but papa's so dreffle smart, and—and—Serge was 'fraid of papa!"

"I don't wonder, Vanya," said Mrs. Winslow, smiling sadly, "so am I. But—it isn't hopeless for Serge yet, even if he gets to jail."

"He's a dreffle wicked man, mamma, but I don't

want him hanged. I telled papa a lie, too. I guess he knows it, too."

"Never mind, darling, it was to save life. I'm not excusing poor Serge. He was wicked. It's all a terrible puzzle, Ivan. Come, let us go back to the house, my poor little son."

CHAPTER VIII

ST. LUKE'S

There was a scrap of dialogue very popular at this period in Fairport:

"Have you been to church?"

"No, I went to St. Luke's."

And should the speaker's wife reprove him, he could answer: "Well, what shall I call him? his name's St. Luke."

St. Luke Darrell was indeed the lawful name which the owner of Fairport's best appointed livery stable still signed to legal documents, although Luke Darrell was on his neat black sign. He himself was a tall, thin man who was clean-shaven in a time of luxuriant beards or mustaches. He had a gentle voice and soothing manner, very successful with customers and horses. He was fond of black alpaca coats and white ties for summer, and in some respects he was as austere in morals as in costume. He never swore; he drank only in the presence of ladies (because he was sure, so he explained, that if he made that a rule he should never exceed moderation); he was the devoted husband of one wife, and the excellent father of two children, and there were two things of which he used to boast: "I've never in my life," said Luke, inflating his chest with a modest man's self-respect, "I've never been fooled in a horse trade, and I've never fooled anybody else."

No one in Fairport doubted the absolute accuracy of this vaunt. We all knew Luke was as honest as he was shrewd; in consequence he bought horses for most of the county and eventually for the government.

This unparalleled, almost bizarre honesty—when one considers how the companionship of that noble animal, the horse, appears to debauch the consciences of even the godly themselves, when they come to barter him—was considered Luke's right to his name. Luke attended church regularly—by proxy; that is, he sent his wife and his contribution. He himself looked over the books at the office, and talked with his visitors. Gradually the custom grew up for men to gather, of a Sunday morning, in Luke Darrell's ample office, which was warm in winter and cool with western and southern breezes in summer. There, on comfortably tilted chairs, in an easy masculine undress of shirt-sleeves, Luke and his friends would discuss the highest themes. This is not saying that they did not relax into that natural and casual gossip suggested by the turns of conversation; but Luke always gave a philosophic or moral twist to the most trivial episodes. The horseman did his own thinking and expressed his thoughts as one who, like John Knox, feared not the face of man. If his similes and apologues made free with Heaven and earth and if his thought itself was audacious, at least there was never a taint, anywhere, of cruelty or of coarseness. He did offend the straight-laced by his remark, one Sunday: "Lots of orthodox ministers have a sight more John Milton than Jesus Christ in their preaching, which is queer, seeing that while some folks doubt about Jesus Christ being inspired, everybody knows for sure John Milton wasn't." But he made amends when a certain famous clerical heretic came on the carpet. Said he : "If the council don't put that feller out for heresy they ought to put him out for foolishness. If a man's outgrown his church's cloth why don't he clear out to another gospel shop where he can get a bigger suit? I say, if you're playing a game and don't like the rules, *quit!* It's better'n trying to kill the umpire !"

On the afternoon succeeding the Winslow fire, Luke was in his office with Jack Rand, the blacksmith, and young Miles Standish, who was learning the wagon business across the river.

Luke's office gave on the street. It was painted a light blue as to walls, with oaken woodwork, and was professionally decorated with pictures of famous trotters, from Flora Temple to the equine idols of the day, Dexter and Goldsmith Maid. There was also a large lithograph of Alexis II, a horse of no mean record, the glory of Luke's own stable. No woman's drawing-room could be kept with more rigid neatness than Darrell's office; a neatness extending to the stable where the hose was sloshing on the cement floor day and night, and brass and silver winked in the sunshine.

Darrell sat at ease by his desk, his eyes examining the immaculate row of top buggies in the carriage-room beyond, his tongue discoursing on the public beneficence of the Art Museum.

"We got to have *some* interest besides making money," said Darrell. "War's over now, and the colored brother's got a lot more than was coming to him, properly, and the public gaze is naturally squinting round to find a new claim. The Philadelphia show has stirred up the whole country. We're all after Art, now."

"We would better be after good taste," interjected young Standish, who was waiting for his horse and buggy.

"Humph! Taste—what is taste?"

"Yes, that's it. What *is* it?" echoed the blacksmith, who was a man of sensibility but few words, and commonly acted as a kind of Greek chorus to Luke.

"What's your idea, Luke?" said Standish—every one called Darrell by his Christian name, a familiarity implying affection rather than light esteem, in his case; he was simply a man whom no one could regard formally—"what do *you* make out of it?"

"Not much. All I'm sure of is that mighty little of it's inherited; none of it's made; the big majority's just contaged, like the measles. That's why these expositions are so useful. Most anybody can *catch* things. Why, *I* don't know no more 'bout china than a horse; but after I'd looked over that lot of truck Mr. Winslow sent, I went home and got my wife to give away our big china figgers for the mantel-piece, and I got a set of china with blue onions on it and not a mite of gilt. 'Mazing thing was, she was right with me; she'd been there, too. And she was at the world's fair with me. There was a show!"

"I don't see how you saw very much of it, Luke. I heard you were only one day in Philadelphia."

"Well, I *wasn't* there long enough to take the machinery to pieces, but I could see it all right. Ain't that the telephone?"

"I'll answer it, Luke," said the obliging Tom. "I know how." The others admired Rand boldly taking down the receiver. "Hello! Who wants twenty-seven?" called Rand in a clear, loud voice. Instantly he plucked off his hat and unconsciously assumed a courteous expression, for man was new to the telephone in the early eighties, and could not quite realize his protections. Rand said "Yes'm," three times, and reported: "Mrs. Winslow wants a closed carriage at Oberheimer's store soon's you can get it there."

Darrell whistled through the tube ordering the carriage. When he returned to his seat, Standish perceived that his face was extremely thoughtful, not to say puzzled. He sat down again, but did not pick up the thread of his remarks.

Standish started a new topic. "I hear Winslow's bought the Patch."

"Good thing, too. He'll clean off the ground and make a decent place of it. They've needed cleaning for a long while. They're mostly squatters, but the ground belonged to an unsettled estate and couldn't be sold, and the heirs were in St. Louis and Europe, so nothing was done, though I guess they've got every known disease on tap there, and the place is a perfect fire-trap. Start a fire once down there in the west end near the lumber yards, and there's no guessing where it would stop. Fire's like the wrath of God, dreadful thorough, but not at all discriminating."

"You know Winslow, don't you?"

"I just do. Known him twenty year. Bought every horse, or its dam, he's got for him. He lent me money to go into business."

"He's a pretty decent fellow, isn't he?"

"You won't find much decenter when you git to Heaven, though he covers up his goodness as careful as most folks their sins."

Although Darrell was talking easily, he gnawed his lips and frowned in an absent way, at the first pause, and his eyes kept straying to the clock.

"That telephone bothers him," was the observer's conclusion; and he was right.

Darrell distrusted Mrs. Winslow with all his shrewd and prejudiced wits; he suspected that she was intent on some scheme to help Serge Vassilovitch escape. It is one thing, however, to suspect ladies of high standing, and perilously another to express one's suspicion.

Finally, smiling a dry sort of smile, he repaired to the stable, where he had a short colloquy with the man who was putting the horses into the carriage.

Returning, he went to the telephone. The two listeners heard him plainly.

"Hello! Give me Mr. Winslow's residence. Thirty-nine. This Winslow's? Mrs. Winslow in? Oh, well, Mr. Winslow'll do. Ain't he? Well, when he comes back, will you tell him to call up Darrell's livery stable? Much obliged. That's all."

Darrell whistled softly as he took his chair again. Standish thought that the men were a long while getting the horses into the carriage. His own buggy was waiting, and he had time to ask and receive all the details of the Winslow fire, and still the grooms were buckling straps and dusting cushions and finally rubbing the horses and joking with each other.

"That's how you hitch up in a hurry, is it?" said Standish.

Luke puckered his eyes over the leisurely stablemen, but without any rebuke. "I ain't quite sure of the direction," said he.

"Tom took the message—are you uncertain, Tom?"

The blacksmith looked stolidly at Darrell.

"I guess so," replied he ambiguously.

"So you're waiting for Mr. Winslow to enlighten you—or be enlightened?" said Standish. "I catch on."

"You young fellers are awful bright," said Darrell.

Standish laughed. "You might tell me the game."

"There ain't none," said Luke, "and where a lady's concerned there hadn't ought to be, either."

"You're right," agreed Standish heartily. "Good morning."

After he was gone Rand asked no questions and Darrell read the paper. There was no sound in the cool dark stable save the stamping of the horses' feet and the murmur of the voices of the two men still harnessing the horses for Mrs. Winslow.

Ten minutes passed. Fifteen. The telephone bell rang. Darrell answered it.

"Yes. That you, Mr. Winslow? Why, Mrs.

Winslow just 'phoned she wanted a carriage sent to
—Oberheimer's I think was the name, for *her*. Is it
Oberheimer's *house* or Oberheimer's *store* she wants
it? The house is off in the east end and the store's
west; I'd hate—yes, well, about thirty-five minutes
ago, it might have been longer. Wait a minute,
I'll ask the man who got the message. Was it two-
thirty when you got that 'phone, Tom?"

Tom Rand, with no sign either of curiosity or intelligence, replied it was two thirty-two exactly.

The monologue at the instrument continued.
"Two thirty-two, exactly. . . . No, but it is
ready. I tried to get you before. . . . Oh,
that's all right; don't want to make mistakes, that's
all. It'll be there in no time."

Luke smiled again as he issued his orders: "Go
in fifteen minutes."

Tom did not smile, but a glimmer of admiration
flickered in his eyes, and Luke passed him a cigar
out of the "good box."

All this while, at Oberheimer's little store opposite the Patch, Mrs. Winslow and Johnny-Ivan were
waiting. Johnny-Ivan didn't know why they were
in the store—a modest combination of grocery and
bakery with which Peggy and he were quite familiar, and many a nickel had they both spent upon
toothsome German dainties, the Berliner *Pfannkuchen* and coffee cakes, the sweet pretzels and
Marzipan; but munching a *Pfannkuchen*, his handkerchief spread on his knee for napkin, he was highly
content with the moment. His previous experience
was obliterated. He had followed his mother to the
house. Mamma had gone into her room (after she

had locked the doors) ; she had come out with the pretty leather bag with silver letters on it which he —helped, of course, by papa—had given her for Christmas, and she had told him to come with her. First, though, she had dressed him in clean clothes. Then she went out into the yard, leaving Johnny-Ivan with the bag on the piazza. She threw some cushions over the bag, and told Johnny-Ivan not to speak about it. He felt sure something was on foot to help Serge, but he asked no questions. After a while, mamma came out again, and they walked out of the yard together; they walked all the way to Oberheimer's.

"We'll rest here," mamma said.

They had a long rest, longer than mamma fancied, Johnny thought, for she kept going to the door and glancing down the street.

Finally she went out; she told Johnny she was going to telephone; when she came back she was looking less anxious; before her arrival, however, a carriage had drawn up to the door, a nice, shining, new livery carriage with two black horses. Into this his mother pushed Johnny and the bag, with an order to the driver which he didn't catch. They drove in the direction of Overlook. Johnny thought they were going to return home; but they halted outside the drive and there, strange to say, was Michael in the farm wagon, sitting on a trunk. And (which was funny) Michael had his white collar and tie under his blue blouse; they were sticking out.

Mamma said something to Michael in Russian; Johnny knew enough Russian to understand that it was something about a trunk. Then Michael hoisted the trunk on the back of the carriage. The trunk was all covered over with a rubber cloth, so he couldn't tell whether it was mamma's trunk, or what it was.

"Now it won't get dusty," said mamma.

Michael came and stood by mamma and looked at her and at Johnny. It was very strange indeed, but Michael looked as if he wanted to cry. Of course that was impossible, Michael being a big man and there being nothing to cry about. Mamma said more things in Russian, very low and very fast, and then Michael stepped back to his own horses, and their carriage turned around.

By this time Johnny-Ivan began to suspect that there was something very strange in the air.

"Mamma, what are we doing?" asked he.

"We are running away, Ivan, you and I," she answered.

"Where?" said he.

"Where papa can't find us and put you in a school far away from me, where you will be wretched and homesick and they may—oh, they may do anything cruel to you, my darling!" She caught him in her arms and held him tight to her. "Don't you know how angry papa will be for what you have done this morning?"

"I—I told him a lie," said Johnny in an awestruck voice, "but—it was like in war, wasn't it, mamma? I *had* to, to save Serge."

"You did right, darling. I'm proud of you. But papa will not understand. Ivan, I'm not going to call him papa to you any more; I can't, it's too dreadful—ah, it's all too dreadful!" She flung her head down on his little shoulders, but instantly she held it erect and dried her eyes.

The little boy kissed her. At this moment they were passing the Winter place, and all at once Johnny-Ivan realized that he was parting from his comrade.

"Mamma," he whispered, "would there be any objection stopping so I could tell Peggy good-by?"

Mamma understood: it was part of Olga Winslow's charm, this quick perception of distress however different from her own.

"I'm afraid not, Ivan,—anyhow, it would be only a few days—maybe you can write to Peggy."

Johnny-Ivan did not understand, he could not grasp the situation. He thought they were only to go for a few days to help Serge escape somehow; then papa would get over being angry and fetch them back. He nodded his head, quite reconciled. It would be rather grand to have an adventure to tell Peggy, if only mamma would let him tell the whole. Guess Peggy would reckon he was some good in a Blood Feud, after all!

In peace approaching complacency, therefore, he sat by his silent mother, while the fields and the little houses and the flowering trees and all the loveliness of spring drifted past them. Soon they were in the town, clattering through the streets.

They drew up before the tall red building with its big unsheltered platform, on the side of the many railway tracks. Mrs. Winslow got out of the carriage with Johnny. The driver hitched his horses and followed with the trunk.

"Don't seem in a hurry or frightened or anything," mamma had whispered; so Johnny-Ivan stuck his tiny fists in his pockets with a manly air, and sauntered into the station.

No one they knew was there, nor did any one come during the few minutes they had to wait.

But just as the long dingy line of cars pulled out, Johnny, who was at the window (having a wild hope, be the truth known, that Peggy might be passing on the street with her mamma or Aunt Winter), gave an exclamation: "Oh, mamma, there's our wagon and the grays, but there's a boy driving. Nor he don't know how to drive worth nothing!" he concluded scornfully.

His mother did not lift her head. "It's too late now," was her strange answer; "and he wouldn't be in the wagon; he'd have the buggy." As the speed of the cars slackened on the bridge Olga looked back a moment and studied the little city spread along the fair river which was barred with silver by the setting sun. Her eyes were dark with thought.

"For the last time," she said in Russian, "another leaf of failure." But before the words ended, Johnny touched her in some movement and she flung her arm about him, saying softly: "Golden one, you make up for the whole world!"

Johnny snuggled closer to her. But in a flash he sat up, exclaiming excitedly: "Why, mamma, *look!* there's Michael!"

Michael, truly enough, was coming down the aisle of the car in his American Sunday coat and white shirt. He looked deprecating and mild, and bent his head before mamma and spread out his hands—which wore his driving-gloves. "Me, too, your mercy," he said in his own tongue, his voice choking, "me, too. Ekk—r! Could not bear it!"

Then mamma and Michael talked a long while in Russian, and there were tears in mamma's eyes and they talked so fast Johnny-Ivan couldn't make out very much they said, only that Michael wanted to come. "Oh, let him!" begged Johnny-Ivan.

So finally mamma *did* let him stay. She wanted to buy him a ticket, but he smiled and showed the ticket to Chicago which he had bought already.

It was a good thing, too, Johnny considered, that they brought Michael, for the train being a "local" only went part way to Chicago, and they had to wait three or four hours for another train, at a queer little place where they couldn't get any supper. So it was dark night before they began to see villages on the prairie and then long rows of streets, winking stars at each other, and horse-cars and big factories with black windows or flaming chimneys. Johnny found it infinitely interesting to look into the back yards and the curtainless, lighted rooms where men in shirt-sleeves and tousled, black-haired women were eating and laughing and smoking. The wooden houses were painted a sooty gray with smoke. There were a great many rags and tin cans in the yards. The denizens of the quarter were unclean, often almost repulsive; but (which surprised Johnny) they all seemed to be cheerful.

"They're dreffle poor people, mamma, ain't they?" he whispered. She nodded. "But they're laffin', *mamasa*.* I guess they'll be rich pretty soon."

*Mamma.

But mamma paid no attention. She had risen to her feet and Michael had taken the bags. The train had left the houses; they were passing high, dark walls, and now it was darker. And overhead were iron rafters and a glass ceiling, and there was a noise of shouting which no one seemed to heed.

"We're there, dear," said mamma. With her words Johnny felt himself pushing in a crowd which seemed to tower bulkily far above his small stature. He was propelled forward and then down the car steps and along a path between two shining, coughing engines up to a little gate.

On the other side of the gate stood—papa!

CHAPTER IX

THE END OF THE GOLDEN AGE

It was most surprising, but papa did not seem in the least surprised.

"Ah, Johnny!" he said. "Michael, take my bag, too. Where are your checks, Olga?"

"Why, papa!" cried Johnny-Ivan, "I didn't know you were coming."

Papa made no answer; he had given Michael his bag and taken Johnny's hand. His arm was offered to mamma.

She accepted it without a word. Her veil was down over her face.

"The Grand Pacific, Michael, if you get lost; but you won't; keep close to us—only a step—yes, there are the hacks. Make a dreadful racket, don't they? It oughtn't to be allowed. Here, you! take us to the Grand Pacific."

In a daze between pleasure at the new sights and sounds and a sense of calamity and fright which he could not understand, but which none the less rested heavy on his young heart, the boy was lifted into the cab. He leaned his cheek against the window; he was on the back seat with papa, and mamma sat on the front seat. They had put Michael outside on the box with the driver.

"What are you going to do?" said mamma. Johnny was afraid she was still "mad" at papa, her voice sounded so queer.

"Oh, I think we'd better stop a day in Chicago, long enough for you to do some shopping, and then go back."

Mamma said nothing.

"I found out you had gone to the depot," said papa, "and I calculated you would take this train. I took the next one, the fast express, you waited for. I was behind you all the time in a Pullman. I took a state-room; that's how Mike didn't see me when he went through the train."

Mamma never answered. Papa didn't seem angry, however; he helped mamma out and showed her their rooms in the hotel. They were very large, with flowery velvet carpets and great windows draped in lace and velvet. The splendor was prodigious, almost like the royal palace in Saint Petersburg. More magnificent, however, was a vast banqueting hall to which his father took him at once, and where he bestowed on him a lavish dinner, with ice-cream and nuts and raisins. Mamma did not come down.

After the meal the two stepped into a very little room, and it moved right up through the floors in a most amazing way. Johnny's hand found a fold of his father's trousers and gripped it tightly, but his stoical little face showed none of his terrors. He did venture, however, to ask if Michael had something to eat; he had seen mamma's tray at the door before they went down the great marble staircase. His father reassured him as to Michael's case.

Therefore, it was without any deep misgiving,—on the whole rather with relief that papa had come and cut their journey short, since he seemed to have forgotten all about Serge,—that Johnny obediently let his father undress him and put him to bed.

"Mamma has a headache, but she will come kiss you good night," Mr. Winslow told him, and suspecting nothing, Johnny kept himself awake until his mother appeared. She sat down on the bed and he laid his head on her knee and sleepily kissed her hand, which was very cold.

"You better come right to bed, mamma," he advised; "won't you sleep with me?"

"No, Vanya, your father will sleep with you," she said.

Johnny reared up in bed like a colt. "Why, mamma, papa never slept with me in my life! why— maybe—maybe I'd *kick* him! I do kick when I'm 'sleep."

"He is going to sleep with you to-night," his mother replied.

"But—mamma, I'd rather have *you!* I do want to have you. I kep' thinking, now I'll sleep with mamma! and I was *so* glad."

Mamma—was it possible mamma was crying? He raised himself on his elbow. Not a word of all the words in his heart did he say, for at this moment Winslow walked into the room. He cast a single swift glance at his wife and child before he turned up the gas. He walked to the windows and to the doors. He examined the windows as carefully as the fastenings of the doors, and he looked into the closet. Then, he shot the bolt on the out-side door.

"Josiah," said Johnny's mother, "may I stay with Ivan to-night? But only to-night?"

"Come into the other room a few minutes, Olga," said his father, "I want to have a little talk with you."

But it was not a little talk. The murmur of their voices came through the heavy closed door so long that Johnny-Ivan's weariness conquered his desire to be sure his mother would come back to him, and he slept. Morning was breaking grayly through the city smoke when his heavy eyelids lifted, and his mother, completely dressed, was sitting on his bed, while his father, also dressed, his hat in his hands, stood by her side. And his father's face was darkened by the blackest frown that Johnny had ever seen on any living face. He tried to smooth it away when the child shrank; but Johnny had seen it.

His mother was crying, crying so that her tears wet his cheeks and her beautiful white throat trem-bled. She caught him when he would have risen and held him so close that he felt a pain in his ribs, but he was so startled and wonder-stricken that it was only afterward he remembered that he was hurt. She said things in Russian, loving things which he understood, because she had said them before, and dreadful things which he only caught in snatches, about some one who was ice and iron and cruel—crueler than death.

"Cut it short, Olga," said his father coldly.

His mother dropped her arms. She drew a long

breath; she looked into his eyes; it was the Princess Galitsuin, whose ancestors had been princes and brave soldiers for centuries, who began to speak very slowly, using the language which her son was surest to understand. Her eyes glowed through their tears.

"Ivan, my dear little son," she began, "I have to tell you something hard, and you must bear it bravely."

"Yes, mamma," said Johnny-Ivan; his heart was drumming in his ears.

"Listen," she went on, "can you hear me when I whisper—so?"

"Yes, mamma." But he felt cold.

"I have to save Serge,—or else he would be hanged. I thought I could take you with me; but I —I can't. Papa will take you home—Vanya, if you look that way" (for in spite of him his lips were quivering) "I can't bear it, I shall break down, I shall give up and then poor Serge will be hanged, and all my life, Ivan, I shall be a wicked, miserable woman—"

He made his stiff lips smile, saying: "I won't look any bad way, mamma."

"I *must* go, Ivan."

"But—but you'll come back, mamma?"

"I'll see you again, Ivan, be *sure* I'll see you again. I can't tell when; but I will. I surely will. And you —ah, thank you, my brave little son!"

It was only that Johnny-Ivan had made his chin stay quiet and set his teeth.

"Now, my darling, you must promise to be good, to remember what I have taught you, never to be

cruel to those who are weaker or poorer or more unhappy than you, and to try to help *all* who suffer.
Will you remember, my Ivan?"

He nodded, because he could not speak.

"And you will remember *me?*"—she was not the
Princess Galitsuin, she was Johnny-Ivan's own
mamma now, and he was kissing her wildly and telling her he would, he would, for ever and for ever.

"You will make the child sick,"—the voice
dropped into the tumult of the two excited creatures'
passion of love and despair as an icicle drops into a
whirlpool.

Johnny-Ivan felt himself gently laid back on the
pillows. "It won't be long. Be brave! I'll come
back," mamma had whispered, and she was gone.
Winslow followed, scowling as darkly as the stern-
est Puritan of his mother's stern race.

But although Johnny-Ivan lay awake a weary
long while, until the sun was shining brilliantly on
his white pillow, mamma did not come again.

At last he rose himself and went to the other
room, calling to her and to his father, asking if he
might get up. Neither of them answered; there
came in their stead a comely and cheerful Irish-
woman, who said she was the assistant housekeeper
and his mamma and papa were gone out a bit, but
she would dress him, which she did, showing a really
marvelous knowledge of boys' waists and buttons,
and being, besides, a very polite person who arranged one's bath and respected one's feelings by
keeping her place on the outside while one bathed,
merely calling directions about the rough towels.

She described a great many delightful and unusual things about to happen to him, a cyclorama
of the Chicago fire (a cyclorama was ever so much
finer than a panorama), and a drive, and stores full
of beautiful things; but when Johnny-Ivan asked:
"Will mamma stay to see them, too?" she shook her
head compassionately. "Well, you know your
mamma will be going to your poor sick aunt, didn't
you know?" said she.

"But she'll come back—she'll come back to say
good-by to me?" urged Johnny in a suffocated voice.
The kind creature said afterward that she fairly
couldn't stand the eyes of him.

"I know she's going away, she *told* me," cried
Johnny, with a forlorn pride, "but—she isn't said
good-by. Oh, you'll see! she'll come back and say
good-by."

He would not ask questions about the "sick aunt,"
because Johnny was already become a miniature
conspirator; mamma was fooling them, somehow, so
he wouldn't give anything away; but surely, surely,
mamma would say good-by.

Yet when he lifted his wistful eyes at his father's
entrance, a little later, and no one else was in the
doorway, the look in them cut Josiah keenly like a
knife.

The man tried to speak lightly: "Mamma's gone,
son. Aunt Wanda—you know how sick Aunt
Wanda's been. She—she didn't come back to say
good-by—she'd have missed the train. Michael's
gone with her to take care of her, and Augustine,
Mrs. Winter's maid's gone, too. She's glad to go

back to France. She'll take very good care of mamma."

He hadn't the nerve to look at the child, whom he felt he was striking with every sentence; so he didn't see the sensitive little features grow white and the eyes scared. He swallowed a lump in his own throat, nevertheless, as he concluded: "And mamma sends her love and says 'Be brave!' and I'm going to write her how—"

But he was shocked by an exceeding bitter cry. "I can't! I can't be brave any more!" And the little boy dashed out of the room.

"Leave him to me, sir," said the housekeeper, with a woman's instinctive scorn of man's inadequacy in an emotional crisis. She followed too quickly for Johnny to shoot the door-bolt.

He broke from her and flung himself on the bed in a paroxysm of grief.

"Oh, your poor mamma!" said the wise woman; "how she'll feel when your papa writes the way you've cried!"

Johnny rolled over on one side.

"I ain't crying!" he sobbed; "I ain't going to cry at all—I—I—just got a stomach-ache. Please lemme 'lone!"

"You sweet little brave lamb!" cried the woman, "ain't there nobody you got to home to buy presents for?"

"There's Peggy," said Johnny. "Oh, I want to see Peggy!" He felt the sobs choking him again; but it was not only mamma urging him to be brave and this strange woman he couldn't cry before, there was Peggy who missed her papa but never cried. He sat up in the bed and wiped his eyes and submitted to having the woman wash his face, and after a while papa came in and talked about presents, and said he could buy presents for everybody in Fairport if he liked.

"There's a lady from Fairport here, you know," papa said. "She's here with her sister, who lives here; her sister's going to send her carriage for us, and Miss Emma Hopkins—that's the lady—is going to show us where we can get things."

Johnny-Ivan was a polite child and he tried to be good; but Emma Hopkins long could see, too vividly for her comfort, the wistful little face which would suddenly cloud in the midst of its childish distraction. He remembered all the maxims of behavior in which he had been trained; his cap was in his hand as soon as the lady's face appeared at the carriage window; he said, "yes, ma'am," and "no, ma'am," punctiliously (according to Hilma's and Maum Chloe's code); he always let the lady go first, when she wasn't holding his hand, and he didn't ask any questions; but all the while there was that dreadful, queer feeling inside him,—all the while he knew that mamma was gone.

Emma Hopkins was alone. It had not occurred to her cheerful Western mind to bring Mrs. Raimund with her, because she might be going shopping with Mr. Winslow. She showed them both over the big, crowded, gaily decked store, and she guided Johnny's choice of gifts. Johnny was perfectly docile; he bought the cravats for Tim and Fritz, the beauti-

ful embroidered silk fichus for Hilma, the waitress and the cook, and the richly flaming scarf for mammy, at Miss Hopkins' suggestion. And he agreed that the white gloves would be nice for Aunt Rebecca Winter; only when Miss Hopkins took a pretty ribbon from the counter, saying, "And would this do for Peggy Rutherford? You would like to bring her something, wouldn't you?" Johnny shook his head. "*I* picked out Peggy's present," said he, his little finger indicating an exquisitely painted black lace fan on the opposite counter. "Peggy loves lace fans, and she told me she was sure going to have one when she was growed up."

"But that fan is twenty-five dollars, dear—"

"Thirty-five," said the smiling saleswoman behind the fans; "it's all hand-painted and *lovely* work—"

"We'll take it," said Mr. Winslow. It was the single sentence he had uttered since they came into the store; and, for the first time, Johnny-Ivan smiled.

"Oh, thank you, papa," he cried; almost unconsciously he shifted his clasp from Miss Hopkins' hand to his father's, which closed over his gently.

Johnny-Ivan felt better after the presents were bought. He had not been able even to eat bread and milk for his breakfast at the hotel, but he plied a nimble fork at the luncheon at Kinsley's, and he went with Mrs. Raimund and Miss Hopkins and his papa to the cyclorama, storing every detail for Peggy's use. Now and again the old horror of loneliness would clutch him; but he insisted to him-

self, in a child's flight of hope, that if mamma didn't
come back pretty soon he and Peggy would go after
her; and, meanwhile, there was Peggy waiting, and
wouldn't she be glad to get the fan!

He whipped up his courage in this fashion, until
his father and he were alone in the cars going home,
when he had to remember who had been with him
before in the cars. It grew harder to keep from crying, harder every minute. His papa sat on the seat
beside him, looking very stern. By-and-by, maybe,
he would begin about Serge. Perhaps he would be
angry. No, he wasn't going to scold him, else he
would never have given him the fan. Papa was
kind, too. Why was mamma angry with papa? He
wanted mamma now, this minute; he wanted to go
to sleep close to her. Where *was* mamma?

All at once he spoke. "I'm glad mamma's got
Michael to take care of her," he cried.

"She'll be all right; don't you worry," said Winslow. His voice sounded careless. Somehow, Johnny
felt a little chilled, and more lonesome than ever,
for papa was smiling. The poor man had forced a
smile to reassure the boy. When Johnny was un-
dressed at night (by the united skill of the porter
and his father and at the expense of at least three
vitally important buttons) he crawled into the little
berth, so heavy-hearted that even his presents, which
he had taken to bed with him for consolation,
couldn't help him. He cried himself to sleep, while
the unconscious father smoked in the next car, and
the porter, appointed guardian *pro tempore*, dozed
happily.

He was crying as his father came into the state-room, but he simulated slumber so successfully that Winslow suspected nothing.

Equally ignorant of his father's feelings, Johnny did not know with what a sorrowful and tender face Josiah Winslow stood, long regarding the little form only indicated by the heavy blankets, nor how he extended his hand twice as if to touch the silky curls on the pillow, only to draw it back lest his caress disturb the sleeper.

Nor did Johnny-Ivan, whose pretense of sleep had drifted into real dreams, know how long the man opposite looked wide-eyed at the darkness and the bolted door and his sleeping boy, while his thoughts were rummaging the years; and the son never heard the father mutter, at last: "Well, there's Johnny. I'll save Johnny out of the wreck."

Johnny's first conscious feeling, in the morning, was that he was lost; his next was his father's face. The curtains were up and it was broad daylight, and papa and the porter were bending over him. The porter was holding up his waist and talking.

"I done look ev'ywhar, boss, and I kain't fin' dem buttons, nowhar. Reckon we-all got to pin 'em."

"But won't the pins—ur—stick into him?" This was Johnny's father.

"Dey mought," admitted the porter, musing deeply; "but look-a-here!"—he brightened—"say, dar's a young married lady in number six, wid a baby. I'll borry some pins fr'm her, baby pins; dey'll sho' stick an' *kain't* hu't."

Thus, not nearly so neatly or so quickly as usual,

but very firmly, Johnny was attired, and only one really superfluous waist, which buttoned to nothing and naturally was not missed, escaped the rites of the toilet.

At Fairport the Winslow carriage was waiting, driven by Tim in Michael's beautiful Russian hat and caftan, but with his own honest overalls below. Mr. Winslow's mouth widened grimly, though he made no comment.

"All right at the house?" said he.

"Yes, sor. Splindid."

"Did they get Serge Vassy locked up all right?" Mr. Winslow went on.

"They did, sor. But the copper, God be good to him—he's dead."

"I'm sorry."

"They was talkin' how they'd be takin' Serge Vassy out an' hang 'im. 'Twas a big crowd at the jail, yesterday night, I'm hearin'—"

"Oh! Weren't you there to see for yourself?"

Tim grinned feebly, and found something wrong with the horses, which were very smoothly trotting out of the town.

"Well, sor, 'tis best not to be to sech onlawful gatherin's. But annyway they was makin' a power of noise outside; some dhrunk and all howlin'. Most loike ut scarit the cratur—they're poor timoreous craturs, thim nihilists, at bottom, I'm thinkin'. Annyway, afore they cu'd git to him, he'd taken some stuff he'd wid him consaled, and 'twas dead's nails he was leanin' forninst the door."

Mr. Winslow whistled. "Just's well, maybe," he

said finally; "that lets me out. He'll need no help now. Tim, how is the new colt?"

"Couldn't be better, sor." The talk strayed into Tim's province, the stable.

But Johnny stared at his father. This cold strength affected the warm-hearted, impulsive child like an incubus of terror; how could he escape it? And mamma would feel so bad about Serge! Was mamma going to Russia to beg the czar to save Serge? or was it true she was going to Aunt Wanda, who had been ill?

Johnny's childish wits sank bewildered in this maze; only one solid hope remained amid a quaking bog of fear. There was Peggy; pretty soon he'd see Peggy! They were passing the Patch. The smoke curled up from humble chimneys; the children were playing under the blossoming trees; at some of the windows were gray heads. And his father would turn all these poor people out on the world. But—there was Peggy!

"Any other news?" said Mr. Winslow.

"Jest the Rootherfords, sor. You was hearin' 'fore you wint away 'bout the woord come how the poor doctor was tuk bad?"

"Yes, the telegram came in the morning. Mrs. Winslow told me; they were hoping for better news before Mrs. Rutherford started. She's gone, I suppose?"

"They've all gone, sor, Mrs. Rootherford and the nagur woman and the little girl—an' Mrs. Winter, she wint to St. Louis wid 'em. They wint Wednesday night, sor."

"That's too bad!" said Mr. Winslow in real concern; "why, Johnny was fetching presents home to them. I'm sorry, son."

But Johnny hardly heard him; he had sunk back in the carriage. He was not crying; he didn't want to cry, not exactly; but his wistful eyes looked out on a wide and lonesome world, where no comfort was.

Book II

IVAN

CHAPTER I

STRANGERS YET

The noon train from Chicago to the Pacific on the "Great Rock Island Route" was an accommodation train. Limited trains whirled over the prairies before the day broke; their iron chargers rode

> "The late moon out of the skies
> And their hoofs drummed up the dawn;"

but the eleven-o'clock local linked no glittering Pullmans by dusty vestibules; it was only a vertebrated line of day coaches in which the plain people, with their babies and their luncheons and their antique hand-luggage, could swell the revenues of the railway the most for the least accommodation.

Few long-distance travelers took the local, so few that the ticket-seller was moved to look a second time at the handsome and very well dressed young man who requested a ticket for Fairport.

"The four P. M. is an hour and a half quicker and has a diner on," said he.

"Thank you," said the young man, "but it is a case of sickness; I can't wait."

There was something so winning in the young man's voice and his ready gratitude for a slight courtesy that the busy official spared time for a civil

145

"That's too bad!" and a glance after a fine straight back as it disappeared swiftly in the crowd.

"Say," said the chief ticket-seller, coming over from a customer, who was buying a ticket to California and trying to obtain unlimited information about the Pacific from a world-weary man who knew nothing beyond Omaha,—"say, I'll bet *that* was young Winslow; his father's taken awfully bad, and we were to stop him if he came here and tell him there's a special waiting for him; they must have missed him, somehow; Alan G. Raimund was down here, himself, about it. You wait; I'm going to catch him!"

But the hand of the clock touched the hour and the accommodation was slowly swinging out of the great murky station as the official reached the gate, while on a platform, smiling at a man who had caught his arm and righted him from his leap, stood the tall, slender, dark young man whom the agent sought. All the men about the gate were swayed by a ripple of gaiety.

" 'Is that the Fairport train?' he says"—a railway attaché seemed to be telling the story—" 'you can't get it, gate's shut,' says I; he never said nothing, just run and cleared the pickets like a race hoss, and hopped on to the train as easy!"

"Bag and all," another man chimed in; "he ain't feazed, that feller."

Meanwhile, unconscious of the trail of admiration sputtering after him like sparks after a rocket, young John Winslow, who had beaten the college record for hurdling at Harvard, was selecting the cleanest of the spotted red plush settees. He brushed off the peanut shells from his choice and, sitting down, instantly became absorbed in thought. The seat in front was occupied by the young fellow who had helped him on the platform, a short, wiry, round-headed and deeply freckled young man. He leaned his head on his hand, shading his face.

But he roused himself to greet a cheerful brakeman, who showed exceeding joy at the meeting and wrung the young man's hand. "I ain't seen you since the Federation election," cried he; "well, didn't us boys make good? Ain't you in, all O K?"

"Sure," responded the other; "I don't mean to forget who did the trick, either, you bet."

"Where are you going?"

"Fairport."

"Anything wrong there?"

"I'm going to see my mother; she's had another stroke."

"Pshaw!" exclaimed the brakeman softly, "I didn't know. Say, is it pretty bad, Billy?"

"Couldn't well be worse. And this train is slower'n the wrath of God." He ground his teeth in the irritation of his anxiety.

"That's so," agreed the brakeman, "but it'll git in before number four. But it *is* awful, traveling slow at such a time; you know when Tim got his leg mashed—Lord! I thought I'd never git to him— it was on this same old caterpillar, too. Well, I'll see nobody bothers you."

Johnny Winslow looked at the man whose dismal errand was so like his own. The brakeman had called him Billy. Billy must be a Fairport boy, or, at least, might have been one, since his mother lived in the town; and anything connected with the little city was of interest to Johnny now. Billy looked prosperous; his light gray suit was new; his linen was very clean; it was also gay, being striped with red and blue; and his silk cravat was of a rich, shot scarlet. On the seat beside him rested a soft felt hat of silver gray. He wore no gloves; his hands were freckled, but they were well-kept, and there was a diamond ring on one little finger, companion to another diamond flashing from his cravat.

"Too fine for a workingman, yet he's got the little ways of one," thought Johnny; "brushes his face with the back of his hand, and his walk's like one. Hands too white for machinist; may be a molder or steel man."

Probably Billy would have wondered at Johnny's confident opinions about mechanics. The truth is, during his last vacation Johnny had tried a job in a foundry. Here he had perspired happily all summer, having a river for his bath-tub at night, and a hot, dusty factory for his days, instead of taking the North Shore of Massachusetts with his people, and playing polo with the Myopia Club.

Therefore, Johnny knew a little of labor and felt the responsibility of knowing a great deal, because his knowledge was so new that it loomed up in the forefront of his imagination.

Only for a second, however, did his thoughts touch his companion; there was too much of grim and anxious importance at hand for consideration. As he sat, his dark eyes, which had not quite lost either the innocence or the wistfulness of their childish regard, were fixed mechanically on the drifting

landscape; but they saw neither houses nor smiling
harvest fields. His thoughts did not concentrate
themselves enough to distil into words; rather they
were a dim and irrelevant procession of scenes, rising like smoke wraiths out of the past. He saw a little, lonely boy playing about a great lonely house,
and always, all day long, watching, watching. No
one, at first, knew for what he watched, nor why
he would steal down to a corner of the hillside
whenever he surprised an unguarded moment; no
one knew of the letters with the foreign stamp which
came to another address and were brought to this
unsuspected mail-box. Dreary years of a child's un-
guessed sorrowing and remembrance—how bleak
they drifted before him! Years in which Johnny
learned to hide his deepest affections and his keenest
hopes; years in which he learned to meet his father
with a cheerful countenance of an evening, and
never to ask to stay up later than the legal hour of
bedtime, and to ride his pony at the sober paternal
pace; and to sit, a tiny, unconsciously pathetic figure, beside Josiah's broad frame in the buggy, when
the latter drove on Sunday afternoons. Josiah never
guessed that his son was studying him, bewildered
by him, yet judging him—this little docile son.

After Mrs. Burney, who was an unobtrusive
comfort, was obliged to go back to her husband
and children, there came a far-away cousin. She
was a prim but kindly New England gentlewoman,
who looked well after the ways of her household,
and Johnny learned to love her in a genuine if tepid
fashion. With her came her son to study for the
ministry in the infant theological seminary, just

founded in Fairport. The cousin was a widow; she was greatly respected in Fairport, and she was strict in the return of visits and the payment of "obligations" in feasting. She was a cousin on Josiah Winslow's mother's side, and came from Salem. It was she who had the front door remodeled, with a fan-shaped glass light above and green blinds on either side the brass knocker. She told Johnny-Ivan that it made her homesick for Salem, yet she loved it.

"Yes, ma'am," the child surprised her by saying, "I know; I've felt that way."

"What about, Johnny?"

"Oh, about the summer-house," said Johnny, whom nobody ever called Ivan in these days. The cousin understood. She remembered what she had been told of the Princess Olga's favorite haunt. She was too reticent a woman to express the sympathy really in her heart; but she patted the curly head under her hand, saying: "Well, Johnny, we know; but no matter how much we miss things we have to try to be cheerful and not make other people trouble."

Johnny-Ivan swallowed and winked his eyes before he answered, properly, "Yes, ma'am."

"And—I'm going to tell you a secret. You're going to Switzerland with papa next spring."

"To see mamma?" Johnny-Ivan had turned suddenly white with emotion. The cousin nodded. "But you had better not say anything about it."

"No, ma'am," breathed Johnny-Ivan very low. Suddenly he lifted the cousin's thin, blue-veined hand and kissed it in the foreign manner which he had disused of late. "I love you!" said the little boy, and ran swiftly away. When he reappeared his eyelids were red; but his eyes were shining and he was tugging a great basket of shavings. He had whittled them with his knife, he explained; Hilma let him. "You said you wished you had some shavings for your fire," said Johnny; "you used to have shavings in Salem."

He dated his affection for the New Englander from that day, while as for Mrs. Parker, the cousin, she pronounced him "a real Winslow, every inch of him"; nor did she ever swerve from her belief.

Then came, in scattered scenes, the visit to Switzerland. The young man drew his breath sharply over the child's remembered ecstasy of meeting. How lovely his mother was! How exquisite! What a beautiful life she led among the exiles, whom she helped and comforted! The fortune that Aunt Wanda had left her,—was it squandered because it went to a most noble if hopeless dream of liberty and human brotherhood? Yet—Johnny scowled, because he found in his own mind a far-away echo of his father's petulance. He recalled, almost with sympathy, a single speech of Winslow's.

"Good Heavens, Olga! let *me* take care of your money; it's better to have me take it and double it, while you can fool away the income on these maniacs, than it is for you to be dumping it all into their insatiable maw! Quite apart from the object, it's sickening to see money wasted so!"

Not wasted, perhaps, since so large a sum was needed at once; but he dimly appreciated his father's position. Even as a youth of fourteen he had begun to see the futility of his mother's dreams. During

the years between his first visit and that time, every
year (according to some never-mentioned but sa-
credly-observed pact between his parents) Johnny-
Ivan had spent two months with his mother. Most
of the time—not all of it—his father was an inmate
of the household, an unexacting and silent spectator,
observing every form of distant courtesy toward his
wife, and never seeking his son's company. To-day,
he could see the grave unresponding face beside
them in theater boxes or fiacres or sitting amid other
guests at the table. His mother was always the
Princess Olga now,—she was never addressed more
as Madam Winslow,—and while the visit lasted
Johnny was with her all the time; he breakfasted
and had luncheon with her, and he always came in
with the dessert at dinner, where he made acquaintance with bearded, feverish-eyed dreamers who had
less harm than noise in them, and several mild and
well-behaved plotters, to whom murder was merely
a distasteful accessory. They found him the same
gentle, polite and interested child, and how kind
they all were to him! His fingers touched the knife
in his pocket; it was a gift from the man who had
carried the bomb to and from the cheese shop that
blood-stained March morning when Alexander was
slain. One of his rings was the treasure of a nihilist
who slew a whole family in the effort to quench one
hated life. He still owned a book which came from
one conspirator, and a paper-weight from another;
and the most ruthless assassin in all the Russias had
spent hours whittling the little boy a ship. Toward
Mr. Winslow their attitude was different.

"They are a precious lot of egotistical cut-throats," he said to his wife; "I hope they know I think so."

"Do not fear," she replied calmly, "they are not ignorant of your good opinion, which really does not require writing to be read!"

Swiftly came other scenes to the sad young eyes at the window-pane, his mother's agony when they must part, her happiness when they met, only two months out of the year; but Johnny-Ivan lived in those two months all the months between, and there were always the letters; not the weekly letter which came to his father and was read with due respect and ceremony to him; the reading always prefaced with, "Here is a letter from mamma," as if a mother who never came to her husband's home and saw her child only two months in the year were the normal parent. Once a week—when the letter was read— Josiah Winslow would mention his wife; his lips never touched her name at any other time.

The year Johnny-Ivan was fourteen his mother seemed changed; she no longer lived in the beautiful villa which had been hers, but in a small house with only Michael and a maid; and the things to eat at dinner were not so good; but the same faces, lacking but a few to whom conspiracy had not been kind, were over the samovar, every afternoon. Michael and his father had frequent conversations apart. It seemed to the boy that gradually Michael had been growing more friendly to his father. His mother was sadder, but no less beautiful, and she wore the same charming costumes. Even then he guessed the reason.

"Does papa give you your clothes, mamma?" he

asked one day. Her lip curled. *"Ai da!* I should have very plain clothes if he didn't; he pays for everything now, *galubchik;* I have lost a great deal of my money."

"Well, *mamasa,"* said Johnny-Ivan with the shrewd little frown that she called his Winslow look, "I wouldn't give any more money to the patriots."

"Why not, Vanya?"

"Because, mamma, they only get sent to Siberia; they don't hurt the government a bit! They talk so loud and they twirl their mustaches and drink so many glasses of champagne, and they don't do *anything*, really!"

"But, Ivan," his mother returned, "shall we let all this wickedness go on and the people be more and more miserable?"

"No, *maman,* give them money to come to America."

"Are they, then, so happy in America?" she replied.

"They can't be sent to Siberia, in America, *maman!"*

"But there is the penitentiary in America; and don't you remember how Serge killed himself rather than go there? I went to Chicago to get our friends, there, to help him. Papa had promised he would help, too. Yet Serge killed himself rather than risk it. Not all the oppressors are in Russia."

"Well, anyhow, it's easier to reform things in America," the lad persisted; "that's where *I'm* going to try."

Sitting by the car window, the young man could

see the Swiss mountains, which caught his eye whenever it strayed from the beautiful pale face before
him; their opal peaks were strangely gilded by the
glow in a little grate. He could see his mother's slim
hands—which wore no rings—clasped over her knee
as she talked. That last year his mother was
changed—she was sadder, gentler. He wished that
his father (who spent barely a week with them)
had stayed longer. When they came to part it was
harder. Her last miserable smile haunted him and
he felt an indefinable yet deepening gloom. The
letters were fewer, and they did not, as usual, re-
gain the note of hope, for her temperament had as
much gift for joy as for pain. She reproached herself with failure. She wrote to the boy of fourteen
as if he were a man:

"What is the Secret of Life? Do we need happiness? Here is a strange poem by one of your Americans, a woman. That is right. Women have the
cruelest burden always, for they can never forget
pain in action. This poor woman, this Emily Dickin-
son, I know, has suffered. Hear her:

> "'The soul asks pleasure, first,
>   And then excuse from pain,
>   And then the little anodynes
> That deaden suffering.
>
> And then—a chance to sleep,
>   And then, if so may lie
> The will of its inquisitor,
>   The liberty to die!'

"Do you not find that dreary, my Ivan? And that
last image! 'The will of its inquisitor'—is it not

terrible? As if *le bon Dieu* were turning the rack handle. You are so young you do not consider the pervasiveness of misery. Is it we, ourselves, that make the world so horrible or—this is where I am affrighted—is it our nature, in the constitution of the world, that we should suffer? Do our very struggles of frenzy to relieve the weight that is crushing the soul out of a race—do they but press it the heavier? Once I saw a horse in a quicksand— *Ai,* if I could forget it! Every struggle made him sink deeper. A sight like that makes an infidel of one. Yet that is only a particle in the vast total of horror. How can any one, with a heart, be happy after twenty-five! But there have come moments better than happiness to me. One was when I bought the release of a true woman, born a peasant but with the soul of a princess, who has done more for Russian womanhood than any of us; and I never think that because of my help all she did after her escape was made possible, without an exquisite exaltation of the heart. I have longed inexpressibly for happiness; I have felt only its wing brush my hot cheek as it passed; but when I renounced hope for self and sought only to gain release from pain for others, then only did I find a deep and strange peace. Happiness is for the child, whatever his years, for some are always children; to the end, I think, your father, who has many, many noble qualities, will yet be a determined and blinded boy. But for men and women who have lived, peace is our best.

"You will not understand me, my poor angel. I forget your years; it is because in some ways you are older than I. But keep this poor vague letter; it is the last cry of my soul. Read it when you are older. I have failed, but you will succeed. You *must* succeed. Begin where I surrendered; do not seek the happiness of the senses or of the heart. But from the beginning take the vows of a priest of humanity. There is so great a multitude of downtrodden, helpless, hopeless, and, therefore, wicked people; there is so great a multitude of strong, careless, joyous souls who will pass to their own images of happiness over the bodies of their fellows if need be, just as boys will in games; but the pitiful, the unselfish, are so few. Alas! they often are so blind. And this is the most terrible of mysteries; we not only harm through cruelty and carelessness and ignorance; we harm most out of the blind folly of our best intents.

"Would it not seem that God might keep watch above his own that they should not destroy where they agonize to save! But He does not—always! I suppose we blunder, and to blunder is the only unpardonable sin! My life has been full of good intentions and blunders. I saw too straight—I did not look to either side. But thou wilt be different. I no longer ask thee to help in Russia. Thou art more an American than a Russian. But help those who need in America, my dear son, whom I have loved with the one absorbing, passionate love of my life. Do not grow hard with success. There is something nobler than piling up gold. There is something finer than your vulgar American power in politics. Lead the working people, my darling. They need a leader. Give your life to them. Be it in America or Russia the end will be the same, for it is true what the American poet says:

" 'For humanity's vast frame
Through its ocean-sundered fibres feels the gush of joy or
  shame—
  In the gain or loss of one race all the rest have equal
    claim.'

"There is one thing I wish to say to you. Be a good son. I have not been all a wife should be to your father. Pay my debts, my darling; give the consideration, the patience, the forbearance, which I did not give. There has been some talk in America, in Fairport, of your father's obtaining a divorce. His longer absence this year, his staying in the hotel, not in my house,—these things would indicate that he wishes to break even the shadow of a tie that has held us these many years. And I feel that, should he break it (a thing very easy, I understand, according to your laws), he will wish to marry again. I even surmise who is the lady. You will think it strange that for these many years I, who never willingly sought your father's presence, should still be horribly jealous of this other. I am, I confess it to you. She is what the world admires as a good woman. Nothing would induce her to do anything which the law and the church do not sanction. Yet I believe she loves your father and will marry him, so soon as he is free. I know that she is often at the house. I have asked you about her, and the pain it gave me to hear your artless confession of liking her shames me. For I know that she will be kind to you; I know she will give your father all the comfort which he needs and a companionship which *l'aimable* Madam Parker can not. Still this excruciating jealousy rends my poor heart. Little son, it is not so much for thy father, it is for thee. When she becomes his wife—and my health is not strong; she may not need the courts to help free him—then see to it she is not thy mother. Only I am that. Ah, God, how I have loved thee! And it were such a comfort when I go into the dark, to know I shall not be all dead; I shall still live in thy heart. And there is no one besides you. These are such foolish wild words and I began to write them, meaning them to be calm and forgiving and patient—*Nu!* these qualities are too foreign to me even to be feigned. Yet I know there is much in this woman to which I don't do justice. *Soit.* I can not help it. Be good to her, but do not love her. I will send this, now, that it may catch the steamer, and to-morrow, again, I will write."

But there was never another letter, and this John-ny-Ivan read only after he came back to America, having seen his mother laid in a foreign grave. It must have been the day after its writing that Michael's cable was received. The princess was ill, dying,—would not his mercy, the barin, send Ivan-Josiahvitch?

Johnny-Ivan did not see the message; but it is questionable if he would have suffered more if he had known what he guessed. His father was very gentle to him. Johnny's eyes filled with tears, re-membering how gentle and how silent.

It was a ghastly journey and too late. The prin-cess may not have realized the seriousness of her condition—she was a skeptic about doctors; and it is likely that an unknown affection of the heart com-plicated the mortal disease which she had suspected.

It saved her months of pain, but it took her away from her son without a parting message. A few hours of unconsciousness slipped into the everlasting release.

The train groaned and panted over open trestle-work; the sky had darkened. Johnny-Ivan was wondering how he lived through the year after his mother's death. There are some losses which are more than wounds; they are mutilations. The soul is never the same afterward. He put his hand unconsciously against his breast. That last letter was there,—he had worn it all these years. For a long time he read it almost daily. One day he read it with a convulsed face and streaming eyes, for on that day his father had told him that he was to marry Miss Emma Hopkins. Not a word did Johnny say; he simply turned pale and walked away. For the first time, now on his way to his father's death-bed, he was reproaching himself, not for the discourtesy of his behavior—for that he had apologized stiffly the same morning—but for its cruelty.

But during a long time he was too occupied with his own torture to think of anything else. He was in a frenzy of resentment and grief. He despised himself because of his former weak liking for the cheerful, ingenious, sympathetic "Aunt Emma," who used to tell stories of the Winslows and Endicotts and play Indian massacres in his childhood when he was so lonesome, and who was grand about algebra in later days. The half-obliterated memory of his mother's words to Aunty Winter at the Art Museum was burnished into scorching brightness by his knowledge, as brass is burnished by an acid. All the jealous suspicion of the letter, which he had glossed over as impossible, was justified. With the hot unreason of youth he accused Emma Hopkins (never more Aunt Emma, he swore) of being a heartless and calculating ˙schemer. All along, yes, all along, she had meant to marry his father and live at Overlook; she might, he could not help it; but she should never rule over him! His head was throbbing with plans to escape, to run away, to reach his mother's friends, plans which he was quite reckless enough to have tried to put into some sort of action had he not found a wise counselor in Mrs. Winter. She was become a great comfort to him since his mother's death. He knew that she loved his mother. Three times she had made a special pilgrimage to Switzerland to visit the princess. Johnny always had a little moving of the heart when he looked at the picture of his mother hanging above the solitaire table in Mrs. Winter's own little sitting-room. She had mourned the Princess Olga's death with a depth of grief which astonished herself. She said as much to Emma Hopkins.

"I thought," she said, "when my husband died, I used up my capacity of misery. It was some compensation that if I could never feel any keen happiness again, neither should I ever suffer so I should hate the sunshine. But I have been cruelly lonesome since Olga died. And she had really learned to love me; I had hopes I could help her." To Johnny she said: "Your mother had a beautiful nature; I shall miss her as long as I live."

So it was to Mrs. Winter that Johnny, grown a

tall lad of fifteen, brought his news. Again, he could see her narrowing her handsome eyes and nodding her handsome gray head over it.

"Yes, I suppose so. Well, Johnny, you know Mrs. Parker has to go to Keokuk, where Endicott has a call; your father would be very lonely. He was talking of your going to school."

"I *want* to go to school," said Johnny. "I want you to ask father, will you?"

Mrs. Winter eyed him a moment, thoughtfully.

"I shan't ever like Miss Hopkins," said Johnny; "if I stay I'll get so unhappy I'll run away. I mean it, Aunty Winter."

"I see you mean it; and of course you're unhappy, Johnny—"

"Won't you go on calling me Jo'nivan? I want to have you."

"And I dare say you are cooking up wild schemes of running away."

"I don't want to run away,—not if I can help it."

"Your father is uncommonly fond of you, Jo'nivan."

"I am fond of him, but I shall never obey that lady."

Mrs. Winter considered before she spoke: "I'll make a bargain with you, Jo'nivan. Be kind and respectful to your father and polite to Miss Hopkins. She is a clever woman. She won't ask anything more of you—now. And keep your bad feelings to yourself. That's your part. On my part, I agree to advise your father to let you go to school."

The young man at the window was sighing. He felt a queer distant pity for the lonely lad fighting his way through the hazing and fagging at a military school. Then he smiled faintly. The mild, slim young Westerner had organized the new scholars. By means of a secret society, at first covertly, finally openly, he had defied the hazers. There had been a bloody battle wherein clothes were torn and heads were broken and the new society held its own until the bugle for drill stopped the fray. The subsequent assault with intent to "bed-slat" the chief offender against school traditions ended Johnny's career, for he repelled boarders with giant firecrackers, smuggled to him by Michael, and set the building afire. Johnny's father was summoned. He came, said very little to Johnny, took long walks with the Head of the school; finally he announced to Johnny that he could come home with him.

"I'd rather stay," murmured Johnny. He felt a silly, childish longing to sit close to his father, to cry and confess how lonely and miserable he had been; but he choked it down, as unworthy of the chief of the K. T. F.

"You can't," said his father, "don't you know you could be arrested for setting the house afire? Besides, Kane,—isn't that the captain's name?—he might arrest you for that big burn he has where the cracker burned right through his shirt. It is almost assault with intent to commit murder!"

"He came at me with a baseball bat; there were six of them—"

"Yes, I know. It was a dirty business. But you shouldn't try any anarchist tricks with dynamite. That's un-American—"

"I tried to get a knucks or a pistol, sir, but I

couldn't buy one in town, and they were coming, and if they'd finished me, they'd gone on and chased every one of the society—"

"I see," groaned Winslow, "other folks' messes, as usual! Well, never mind; the upshot is, Johnny, I've agreed to 'take you out of school. You're not expelled; there's no record against you. Kane graduates this year, anyhow; he'll be allowed to graduate, but he'll lose his bars. The other fellows will lose their rank, too, and the sixth and fifth forms have agreed, if things are dropped and your society is disbanded, they will see that hazing and fagging are stopped. On the whole, it is a pretty fair deal."

"Then I've stopped the hazing?" cried Johnny; "they said there wasn't a boy or a teacher could do it!"

"Yes, young crowing cock, you've stopped it; but I advise you to let reform alone in your next school. I think you'd better make aunty a visit—for a few weeks. Then you can come home. No need of talking of a thing of this sort, and next September we'll try Phillips Exeter. You need a little Eastern conservatism."

"Papa," said Johnny, unconsciously reverting to his childish address—he had called his father father, ever since the announcement of his intent to marry, —"papa, I'd like to stay at aunty's all summer."

To-day, with its background of waving corn, Johnny-Ivan could see his father's face; why hadn't he understood, *then,* that he was hurting him? Why couldn't he have been touched then by his smothered sigh and the undertone in his words: "Well, son, if

you wish it so much; but I had been thinking a good
deal of what we'd do this summer. Your mother
was planning a good many things."

Johnny-Ivan remembered: he knew why he had
not been touched: it was that last sentence; well, he
was glad he had had the grace to keep from flashing
out: "*My* mother's dead, I don't want anything
from Mrs. Winslow." He shut his teeth tight—
sulky little dog that he was—and after a considerable pause his father had begun about the details of
the journey.

He regretted his coldness now it was too late.
He was in a mood to regret. All his past was colored with his doubt of self. Even his conduct to his
stepmother did not seem to him so unassailable as
usual. He had been scrupulously courteous to her.
He could not reproach himself with rebuffing ad-
vances; his attitude had been one to prevent any ad-
vances being made. Every week when he wrote to
his father he added as the last sentence, "I hope
Mrs. Winslow is well." She began as Mrs. Winslow and she never came to be anything else.

His ingenuity (and Johnny was of an extreme and versatile ingeniousness) spent itself
during term-time at school in building water-
proof excuses for absence from home through vacation. Once he went to a room-mate's; once he
joined a bicycle party, for the bicycle was then
in the height of its first fascination. He was most
duteous to all his eastern kindred as well as to
his aunt, whose husband had come to the command of an eastern arsenal. He needed a tutor for
his Harvard "finals," although his "prelims" had

been passed without any such aid. By such con-
trivances he had shortened marvelously his periods
of home-coming. Now he wondered with a pricking
pain whether his father had not missed him. But
then, he was accustomed to consider his father as
wrapped up in his colossal business, to the exclusion
of everything, save possibly his wife. He supposed
his father had been sorry when the baby girl born
to him died within the year. Johnny had seen the
little thing only during a single vacation, but a
strange feeling tugged at his heart when it first held
out its tiny arms to him.

"Why, she likes you, Johnny!" cried Mrs. Winslow, "take her, won't you?" For once he did not
secretly resent her words. He accepted the funny
little bundle with a secret tenderness.

"Hullo, little sister!" he whispered. No one (he
was sure) knew how many times during his brief
visit he had stolen to the nursery to chaff and romp
with the "Bunch," as he called her. She used to
jump with joy at his approach. Once, when she had
a passing illness, she went to him from the nurse.
He was queerly moved, and when no one was looking (he thought) he bent his black head over the
pale golden curls and kissed the round little cheek.
It quite startled him that Mrs. Winslow should come
in, directly afterward. Before Mrs. Winslow, he
maintained the proper nonchalance pertaining to an
Exeter Senior who was the head of the track team.
He called Baby Nelly "Miss Winslow," and whistled school songs at her, nor ever by any chance laid
a finger on her soft little cheek, before witnesses.
Yet when the telegram came that the baby was dead,

he took the first train home, and cried softly behind his curtains, in the night, because he should never feel those clinging little arms again.

But he was too young to master the embarrassment of sympathy, and the never-healed wound in his heart for his mother was reopened by the atmosphere of loss and death. He wandered desolately amid the scenes which they had known together, and his tears flowed anew in a lonely sorrow, hardening instead of softening the heart over which they flowed. No one missed her but himself; but he should miss her for ever. Dimly he understood that their common grief would draw husband and wife closer together. Even in the darkened room with the strains of the hymn on the air and the wee white coffin so near, he was passionately pleading his mother's cause, passionately resenting her wrongs. Poor lad! he did not comprehend that his resentment was the effort of an obstinately faithful nature to repel its own compassion, because compassion seemed to him disloyalty.

The morning of his departure for school he rode out to the cemetery, to the baby's grave. He looked down on the flower-heaped mound for a few seconds, then laid a cluster of violets and milk-white iron-weed amid the hot-house lilies and smilax. He had gathered them on the knoll by the summer-house. They were the flowers his mother used to love.

"My mother sends them to you, little sister," he said. He who had lost his childish faith and who wondered drearily whether he could ever behold his mother again, unconsciously used the loving fictions

which comfort the sore-hearted. And then the tall
lad rested his head against the shaft above his unknown grandmother's grave, while his tears flowed
out of a loneliness more bitter than grief. That
evening, as he was saying good-by, he felt a movement of pity toward the baby's mother. She kissed
him—for the first time in years—saying: "Johnny,
I shall never forget how good it was of you to come.
You were always good to her and she always
loved—" But even her self-control, which had been
marvelous all along, could not finish the sentence;
she turned away.

"Where's Johnny's dress-suit-case? Is it on the
carriage?" called Winslow.

"Yes, it's there," said Johnny. So he did not need
to use any reply—save a "Thank you!" which the
habit of politeness forced out of him.

Perhaps she was not feigning, perhaps she was sincere; good heavens! it would be too ghastly to suspect feigning at that moment. And to do her justice, she was as straight as a string; with lots of
sand, too, and a sense of humor which not all
women have. He could have been good friends with
his stepmother if he only were free to be. But he
wasn't free, and he shut the door of his heart, which
had been ajar for a second, with a resolute bang.
Yet she was assuredly a devoted wife to his father.
With that, his thoughts shifted again as thoughts
will shift. They left his stepmother to go to his
father. He wished he hadn't been—well, so argu-
mentative with his father.

"I'm afraid I came awfully near being bumptious," he repented, with a kind of discouraged dis-

gust. "I'll never learn to hold my opinions and my tongue at the same time, I guess."

He went back to those long Sundays at Manchester last year, and blended with the church-bells and the moan of the surf were his father's testy criticisms of "socialist gas-bags" and flings at Tolstoi's "inflammatory non-resistance."

At this time Johnny was studying political economy, and waving the Tolstoi torch with ardor. He was on fire with a passion of pity for suffering, and his young brain boiled with visions. The insatiable logic of his mother's race had begun to offer its word. Argument was fuel to flame. Consideration of impossibility, the magnitude of obstacles to his Utopia only stirred up the courage of youth. How many nights filled with wrangling could he remember in that loveliest of spots, where one ought to have sighed Symons' delicate verses and dreamed:

"I have grown tired of sorrow and human tears;
  Life is a dream in the night, a fear among fears;
  A naked runner lost in a storm of spears.

I would wash the dust of the world in a soft green flood;
Here, between sea and sea, in the fairy wood,
I have found a delicate, wave-green solitude.

Here, in the fairy wood, between sea and sea,
I have heard the song of a fairy bird in a tree,
And the peace that is not in the world has flown to me."

But the fairy bird which sang to Johnny Winslow sang of conflict, not of peace. His soul was not weary—whatever he deemed it—it was throbbing tumultuously; he was awakening to the glory of ambition; his imagination and his soul were kindling, at once. Had you known him, as a few, a very few Harvard men knew him, he might have shown you a portfolio most daintily carved with Russian devices, and reverently lifted from it two letters.

"One was to my mother from Tolstoi; one is to me," he might say. Ah! which of us has not had our day of hero worship, that golden time when the young soul prostrates itself in the purest of passions! Johnny had fixed his heart high. Some day he would do something worthy of repetition to his mother's noble friend; then he would write to him. A hundred times he composed the exordium to that letter which held all his dreams. The recital itself would take little time because Johnny expected his deeds to be in all the papers. Many a night had he smiled and stared at the moonlit ceiling, while his hopes and schemes chased sleep out of the window. And many a morning the pale arrows of the sun had pierced the artificial radiance of his lighted room, to find two or three eager faces still burning with the zeal of their themes while the overflowing *Aschenbecher* revealed the length of their vigil.

Unfortunately, Josiah Winslow had missed many things in not going to the paternal university besides a knowledge of dead languages; he had never known the dear delight of hero worship and literature combined. He had his own heroes; but they did not adapt themselves to fervid eulogy over steins and tobacco; he had never known the exercises of soul which eat up the evening hours as an ocean steamer eats coal. Indeed, it is doubtful if he ever sat up—unless to work—beyond ten o'clock, until after he had made a fortune. He was ignorant, to a degree, of the need of safety valves for the thunderous steam of youth. Any steam in him—and there was plenty—had gone to keep the kitchen stove burning with all the holes filled. He had crowded his laboring days so full that sleep took him whenever he sat down to breathe. When he stopped to think it was how to get a new carpet, so his mother would not have to patch the old one with her own delicate hands, or how he should pay for his sister's books, or buy flour cheaply by the barrel, instead of easily and extravagantly by the pail; or how the great sum suddenly owing the doctor should be paid by instalments. His youth had walked heavily under a sordid burden of care. His early manhood had been absorbed in effort like that of the swimmer in a storm who gains a boat and must steer it to the shore. Then he was winning the mastery of riches and the consciousness of power and command. There was not such a gulf—could either of them have come to the measuring of it—between Johnny, exulting over his leadership of a handful of school-boys, and Josiah, walking through the foundry of the plow factory the day he was made foreman, and was nineteen years old. But Johnny was too young to see any likeness, and Josiah did not come near enough to his son to perceive any reflection of his own traits. He was always dreading to bump against some stubborn heritage from Olga.

Furthermore, at this time, the rugged captain of industry was in stern straits of his own. He had begun to suspect that the hand of death was upon him and the days of his mastership were numbered. His first sensation was a kind of dull anger. He found himself struggling with a besetment of irritability which, oftener than not, would blaze out at his son: "Johnny, does Harvard turn out many such hotheaded and well-meaning idiots as you?" he would growl. "I tell you all your schemes come to, is devices to compel the thrifty and saving and industrious to pack the lazy scalawags on their shoulders! You'll never make the poor prosperous by curtailing production. We can't all get rich by stealing from each other! Don't you think it! . . . We may be obliged to take care of the weak and the damn fools; but we aren't obliged to take care of them *their* way! . . . The best government is the one that puts the smart men at the top and makes the fools work their passage! . . . Maybe I'm not to blame I was born blind; but I needn't brag about it or expect to boss."

Thus would Josiah wave—or rather kick—Johnny's arguments aside.

"Maybe I'm *not* logical," he would snort. "I never knew logic useful anywhere that horse sense couldn't do the job a heap quicker! I've had enough wits to leave you a rich man—*if I dare!*" His voice changed over the last word. He sighed heavily. "The influence of the mother to the third and fourth generation!" he muttered. "A man doesn't know the extent of his folly when he marries against his judgment." Johnny, pale with resentment, had held his tongue by sheer will and been glad to see Mrs. Winslow's substantial figure in the doorway. It was not his first relief of the kind. She often interrupted hot disputes; she often held both sides away from dangerous subjects. Perhaps he owed her gratitude as well as respect, Johnny admitted to himself now; certainly all through the summer she had been anxious. He could pity her to-day, and it was with a weary sigh that he turned away from the window, as if he could push his memories from him with the action.

CHAPTER II

FATHER AND SON

The brakeman was back again. Johnny found himself idly looking up at his good-natured young face.

"Say, are you Mr. John G. C. Winslow?" said the brakeman, putting a slip of paper into Johnny's hand. "Special waiting at Joliet."

The despatch was signed "Alan G. Raimund," and it simply announced that a special would be in readiness; but it struck cold on Johnny's heart, for he argued, instantly, that had there been any change for the better in his father's condition, it would have been mentioned by his stepmother's brother-in-law; nor would there be this ominous speeding of his journey. He was settling back into his seat and his dreary reverie, when his eye lighted on the man in front. With sudden thought of his kindred errand, Johnny touched his shoulder. The face turned on him struck some obscure nerve of memory.

"Aren't you going to Fairport to a sick mother?" said Johnny.

"Yes."

"I have a special waiting for me at Joliet; will you come with me? It may be only an engine, but I dare say you can get on, too."

So it happened that, at Joliet, the freckled young man took a seat diagonally opposite Johnny, in the car attached to the engine which was in waiting.

"Ain't you young Winslow?" said he; and on Johnny's assent: "I expect you're going on to see your father?" Johnny nodded.

"I was awful sorry to hear he was so sick. But you can't tell; often things will take a turn, even when the doctors have given a man up. And they would send for you as soon as there was any danger."

"That's what I have been telling myself," said Johnny. His eyes went gratefully toward the sensible young man who recognized facts under the surface.

"You look some like you looked when you were a boy," continued his new acquaintance. "I suppose you don't remember the last time we talked together —up back of your house? I came for milk, and you gave me a five-dollar gold piece. My name is William Bates."

"I do remember,"—Johnny felt a flicker of interest. *"Did* you run away?"

"Sure—my mother and I. Went to Chicago where I've got on fairly well, and I am glad of this chance to pay you back that V—"

"I dare say you have paid it more than once already, by giving it to some one that needed it."

"That doesn't count. Here it is." He tendered Johnny the money.

"No," said Johnny; "I gave it, I didn't lend it. Don't owe me money, owe me a kindness." The young man replaced the bank-note rather reluc-

tantly, more as if he did not know how to insist
courteously than as if he were convinced.

"I've always felt that way," he explained, "but
I'd sorter like to do something more direct. I did
smooth the boys over when the molders were getting
giddy and wanting to go on a strike at the Old Colony Plow Works. I guess your father's told you of
that. It was a year ago last spring. Your father is
all right. I wish there was more like him; though
some folks would say I might be out of a job if there
was."

"What is your job?" asked Johnny politely.

"Business Agent of Chicago Local 25 of the
Molders' Union. I was a molder—started there, but
I found out pretty soon that it would take a devil of
a time to make a fortune on two-sixty a day; so I
went in as an organizer. The boys rather liked my
style, and I found I could work with my head as
well as my fists; so I'm what you folks call one of
those damned walking delegates."

Johnny did not show the expected shock. "Tell
me," said he, "is this union movement going on in-
creasing, or will the men fall out?"

"It's going on all right," said Billy, "going to
grow like a prairie fire. And there's something
else will grow—the men that run 'em. There's jest
as much politics and jest as much need of smartness
in unions as anywhere."

"Just as much," agreed Johnny, "and *more* need
for honesty. It seems to me about the meanest man
going is a labor leader who sells out his union."

The walking delegate looked at him keenly as if
suspicious of masked sarcasm, but he nodded. "Oh,

I'm straight all right. There's a general impression we fellers cook up most of the trouble; well, we don't. More times than you'd guess, we're as moderate as we can be and hold our jobs."

"Who does make the trouble, then?"

"The radicals and the kids. The radicals always want the earth and the kids are always ready for a row just for the fun of it! They've no wives or homes or responsibilities and a strike's just a bully vacation."

"What do you mean by kids?"

"Oh, young larks between eighteen and twenty. 'Twasn't for them we could hold the others down; but they're just meat for the devil."

"You're not so very much older than twenty yourself, are you?" said Johnny dryly.

"Well, I'm not superannuated, that's a fact; but I've always had responsibilities, and I've thought the whole business out. I've never swiped a dollar I had trusted to me, and I've never given my word that I haven't kept it. Say, a reputation for always delivering the goods without writing is worth money, ain't it? Another thing, I made up my mind not to be a fool. I don't drink. I let the women alone. I never bet a nickel. And I mean to get on. I mean to have a nice house with a piazza and a bath-room with a white china bath-tub, and a horse and buggy and keep a hired girl for—" He stopped short with a sudden quiver of his face. "Say, how does a feller forget for a minute? I don't care much whether I have a house or anything, now *she* can't get the good of it!"

Johnny nodded a quick comprehension, and of-

fered a cigar in mute sympathy which the other
acknowledged with a nod. The conversation flagged
after this, while the two men made pretense to read
their papers. But a kind of comradeship had grown
up between them. They talked at intervals. Billy
told of his boyish struggles and his privations; his
mother's joyous pride over his least little advance-
ment; her nursing him through a fever; her happiness to go back to Fairport.

"I believe what she's always hoped for was that
I'd make enough to git back to Fairport and be an
alderman and hire a buggy to go riding, at Luke
Darrell's, every Sunday."

"Ah, Darrell! is he still keeping his stable?"

"Bigger and better than ever. Say, he's a dry
one, ain't he? His last cheerful greeting to me was:
'Well, Billy, I hear you're getting on fine; you'll die
a rich man if you don't get into the penitentiary!'"

"Not very complimentary."

"Oh, he's got to have his little joke; but he let
me have a hack on credit when my mother was sick,
once. He's *white.*"

Within the last hour of the journey both men became restless. Johnny felt the same gnawing impatience that he read in Bates' abrupt movements. As
the familiar landmarks swung into sight, the hills
and the river and the low sky-lines of the three
towns, Johnny suddenly found himself trembling;
he looked over at Bates; the paper before the delegate's eyes was rustling.

"It's hell, ain't it?" said Billy.

"Yes," said Johnny.

"I believe there ain't a mean trick I served her

or a sassy word I gave her that I ain't been going over this damn ride. Looks like if she'd jest say she'd forgive—though I know she has—I'd feel better!"

"Yes," said Johnny.

"We're on the bridge," said Billy. "You've done me another awful good turn and I ain't likely to forgit it."

"We're nearly there," said Johnny. In an agitation beyond his disguising he flung himself out of his seat. He strode to the platform. He looked on the mighty river, silver-gray and almost waveless in the calm of summer noon, and a depression, heavy and subtile like the mist from its waters, penetrated his being. He could not see Overlook. It was hidden amid the foliage shrouding the far-away hills. All the lonely grief of his childhood, all the conflict and disillusion of his youth, surged over his head as the waves surge over a defeated and sinking swimmer. His mother was dead, his father was lost and estranged, and now the grimmest of separations would make the estrangement final. The prosperous, trim little cities gave him the weary feeling one receives from the beauty of a cemetery; sun-dappled fields and waving woodlands were verily the tomb of all his boyish hopes and loves. Then Johnny smiled faintly; no, not all,—little Peggy remained! He had seen her a few times since that dismal day when he ran away with his mother, on their futile flight into the world. More than once she had visited Mrs. Winter; she was grown into a handsome girl with a train of admirers. Only a few months ago he had heard of her mother's death. Why should he be reminded of Peggy now, and with such a curious glow of comfort? The image of her helped to steady him through the difficult moment when he felt the jarring stop of the train, and he was back again in the old town.

His first sweeping glance about from the platform showed him his father's carriage. His eye brought back a blurred vision of clean-limbed, fiery horses tossing their proud heads, a high, light wagon, and a smart coachman in whipcord. He wished that Michael had come to meet him; but at that instant he heard his name. Looking down, he saw a slim girl in black, with shining hair.

"Peggy!" he cried.

"I came," she said. "Michael sprained his knee, and Aunt Emma couldn't bear that some one shouldn't come."

Johnny's throat failed him; but his eyes interrogated her.

"There is a little change for the better. The doctors hope he will live through the night."

"Thank you." Johnny said no more, but his eyes went after his companion, who was searching the street for a cab, of which there seemed no sign at that unusual hour. "He has come on a like errand," Johnny explained in an undertone, and afterward he smiled bitterly to remember how a faint quality of apology was in it, the self-same quality that had been so often in his tone to Peggy as a child, when he excused his undue softness of heart. "I wonder, could I take him with us?"

Peggy glanced sidewise at the young man's silver-gray hat which rested on the back of his head, and her features almost imperceptibly stiffened; but the eyes which turned upon Johnny were kind as well as beautiful.

"*I* will drive him wherever he wishes to go," said she. "I can go more quickly, and you don't want to lose a minute—"

"*You* drive?"

"Yes, I came in the runabout." She waved her hand at a big bay pirouetting and jerking away from a porter holding him gingerly at arm's length.

"Then perhaps you will drive *me,* and let the man take Mr. Bates," said Johnny.

She hesitated almost imperceptibly; but he perceived it and divined the cause: it was kind and like Peggy to meet him thus, to break that first desolate moment of a home-coming so unlike his others, and then to mean to slip away, leaving him unrestrained by any demands of courtesy. She couldn't know how she, of all the world, was the one he wanted.

"I don't in the least mind," she said.

"But I do," said he, approaching Bates.

"There's another favor," cried Bates in answer to his offer; "depend on it, Mr. Winslow, I ain't going to forget."

"I hope she'll be better than you fear," said Johnny. Their eyes met; there was not time for their hands, and with a run Johnny sprang into the runabout, calling his message to the coachman as Peggy drove him away. The big mare's great flanks went out like the bolt from a bow.

"Is that horse of yours safe, Miss Rutherford?" said Johnny.

"Oh, I can drive anything on four feet," she replied carelessly; "but Kentucky Babe's gentle enough. That man fretted her."

They were going like the wind. A policeman lifted his arm, but recognized the driver, glanced at Johnny and let it fall.

"Don't be afraid, I shan't run over any children," said Peggy. "I'm keeping a sharp lookout."

"You're a dandy whip; still, on account of the children, we might ease up a little here."

Peggy made no answer except to slacken their pace. She let him know somehow without telling that she did not expect talk from him. His few questions about his father's state she answered with concise intelligence more bracing than sympathy. He felt grateful to her, afresh.

To steady his mind he forced himself to look at the streets. They were changed and grown metropolitan since that other dreary day of arrival when his father had borne the little fugitive back from Chicago, although the line of shops and houses still seemed quaintly low. There were many little variations, many signs of the march of wealth. The courthouse lifted gray stone walls and towers amid a velvet lawn and formal beds of geraniums and particolored bavadias and lavender and pink hydrangeas in shining green tubs. In place of the old grove there was a careful rank of elms, giving ample arm room. A park looked down on him from the terrace below his home, and the hills which had embowered modest cottages were cleared to reveal glimpses of new colonial mansions or gaily stained villas. By some obscure law of association the change depressed him; he had not expected to find the old town; indeed, most of these very changes he had seen before; yet he was disappointed that the old landmarks were gone.

The Patch was covered with little houses so fresh with paint that they seemed of yesterday. He remembered how the lonely child used to dread the scenes of spoliation and dispossession which he imagined; how he had stolen down to the Patch, to find empty houses and busy carpenters, and could get no easing of his pain, since loyalty to his father (which he never violated save for his mother) forbade him to inquire into the former's crimes. For years he had brooded over possible tragedies. He wondered where the outcasts had hidden their heads and who would give them a crust; nor did he ever discover how readily they had taken the peace offering given them and scattered into the country, where most of them were thriving, or into other streets, where the plague of their presence, being scattered, was felt less. Now, recalling the squalor of the past and contrasting it with the present scene, he excused his father. Perhaps his father had always meant well; surely he ought to have believed in him, he, his only son.

One by one he numbered over the times of their better acquaintance, the gifts which had been showered on him, the lavish generosity shown his college days. How often had the two seemed only a hand's breadth, a hair's breadth from each other! yet, always, fate or the ineffaceable antagonism of temperament had intervened. Had his mother lived there might have been moments when he would have sided with his father against her; dimly, in this solemn hour, he realized that she was not always just, not always merciful; alive, the battle between the two was more equal than appeared; but dead, every tender and loyal impulse of the boy who had adored her rallied to her side. His imagination helped her, with none of her living frailties to interfere, as the frailties of our dearest will interfere with our ideals of them. Dead she won, where living she might have lost; when she was borne from the field her husband found her memory stronger than her living presence; he was worsted by a shade. The fancy flitted for a second through Johnny's brain: Would his father, too, be the victor when he seemed to have lost the fight?

The horse's head had turned. Johnny came out of a fantastic and somber reverie to feel the thicker beating of his heart and the chill of the Overlook trees. No sign of tension showed on the grounds; the lawn-mower buzzed along the terraces, and a man with a hand-mower supplemented it in corners and near trees, pausing at intervals to wipe his brows with a red and yellow handkerchief. Johnny felt the unreasonable resentment of sorrow at the unmoved world, at the inevitable progress of the routine of life. The smoke was drifting from the kitchen chimneys; a grocer's cart rattled down the hill. But as he passed the mowers, there was a simple sign that the observers of the tragedy were not unmoved. The men took off their hats to them, gravely; even the grocer's boy gave a motion toward his head.

Johnny lifted his own hat. With the quick response of his nature, he felt the tacit sympathy. He glanced at Peggy.

"You always were brave, Johnny," said she; her own lips were held tightly.

"All right, Peggy," said he.

As they reached the house the atmosphere changed. There was no one in the garden or on the lawns. And the strange maid, who opened the door, stepped with elaborate softness and gloom. A man took Johnny's luggage silently, with a respectful bow, before he went to the horse; but behind him hobbled painfully a homespun figure that he knew, and the rugged face with the tears streaming down its cheeks he had loved all his life. Michael caught him in his arms, with a sob.

"He *would* come; I told him not to," explained the maid in the lowest tones that escape a whisper; they vibrated with the righteous indignation of a person who knew the proprieties and observed them; "but he promised he'd be quiet—I hope you *will*, Michael."

All the while she was steering both of them into the room which had been Josiah Winslow's den. "Mrs. Winslow will be down directly," she concluded, having shut the door and bestowed one more eloquent glance of contempt on Michael, weeping aloud in mingled Russian and English. Johnny looked about the room. He recalled his father's pleasure in it; now he would never see it again. But Johnny did not weep, and he wondered why Michael must be so moved, when he was calm. When a dress rustled he turned composed and melancholy eyes to the doorway. He had been troubled by vague visions of Mrs. Winslow in some strange new attitude of distempered excitement; yet he knew that this quiet, almost stolid face, which his eyes found for one glance and left precipitately and feared to find again, was the face of his assured expectation. The controlled, emotionless voice was the voice he had known that he should hear. But he had been afraid that he should have to kiss her, at least to shake her hand; it was inhuman how much he had been afraid of this. And, really, she did not expect him to touch her. She said: "Can you come up stairs now?" Nothing else. He felt grateful to her as he had felt grateful to Peggy.

A young woman in a white cap and apron and a blue and white striped cotton gown opened the door for them, while she herself passed into the hall. Johnny caught a murmur that she would be outside. Then he stopped on the threshold to get his breath, which was coming very quick, as if he had been running.

"Here's Johnny, dear," said Mrs. Winslow.

"Hullo, Johnny; you made good time!"

There was something in his eyes, and it was harder than ever to breathe. His father's face wore a strange waxen pallor, and the eyes had grown bigger; but it was his father's old face, and it was his father's old voice that hailed him.

He got his own voice and he said something—about the special; he was glad to find it.

"Ought to have told you before—she wanted me to; but the blamed thing has been going on so long I got off my guard, and then it came all of a sudden. Johnny, I've a lot to say to you; but I'll wait—have you had something to eat? I feel pretty bad, Emmie."

When Mrs. Winslow hastily put a glass to his lips, she motioned to Johnny, and he lifted his father's head.

"You've a nice touch, Johnny," murmured the sick man. "You must take care of her; and—she'll explain. I've a lot to say to you, when you're rested."

"Never mind, father dear;" Johnny stumbled over the lump that was choking him. He was aware that the nurse had come back, that Mrs. Winslow had beckoned to her, and that she was doing something with a syringe and a spoon.

His father lay back on the pillows, smiling strangely, when Mrs. Winslow bared his arm. "There's little Peggy," said Winslow, "dear little Peggy." His eyes opened brightly; he took Johnny's hand and laid it on his wife's. "Help each other, you two," he whispered.

"She's been an awful good wife to me, Johnny. You won't quarrel with her, Johnny?"

"Never, father; never!"

"That's good. I've a great deal to say to you, son; but I want to get a little sleep first. He's going to come out all right, Emmie; our boy'll understand."

He closed his eyes in content; and the two, who loved him best and yet were so far apart, sat hand in hand until he was quite asleep.

Before the sun set Josiah Winslow was safe from all human perplexities. He never awoke again to more than a fleeting recognition of Johnny's presence or his wife's, over which he would always smile; and a little space before he died he looked in Johnny's white and care-worn features with a grave yet not unhappy look, saying: "It was because I loved you, son; if I get well, it won't need—"

The sentence drifted into silence, only broken by faint mutterings of a wandering mind, back again in the past. After a while he lay very quiet, the sunset on his face; but of a sudden he lifted his hand and his face was irradiated with a smile, as he cried in a clear, pleasant voice: "Here, *here,* little Johnny! let papa help you climb!"

Still smiling, he laid his head on his wife's arm.

It seemed a long time before the doctor gently raised the head; yet the sun of the same day was dazzling on the river which the dead man had loved, when Johnny led a silent woman from the room, and saw Peggy Rutherford come swiftly out of the brightness, to twine her arms about the other's waist and walk with her into the shadow beyond.

CHAPTER III

BY THE TERMS OF THE WILL

Every one who has been in Chicago recalls the dressmaking department at Marshall Field's. In 1894 this important feature was on the fourth floor. There was restfulness in the high ceilings, which looked the higher for the red, low partitions; in the shining floors and wide spaces; in the ample wicker arm-chairs wherein reposed tired-looking women, usually of comfortable presence, gray hair and rich clothing. The quietude was soothing after the noisy bustle below; nor was it disturbed by the occasional apparition of a handsome woman in black, who would emerge from one of the doors in the red cherry wall which inclosed the court, followed by a youthful attendant bearing great bundles swathed in white cambric,—evidently a high priestess of beauty with her acolyte.

Two years after Josiah Winslow's death, on a pleasant July morning, two gentlewomen entered this temple of art. One was slim, graceful, languid. Her exquisite toilet was the most perfect accompaniment of a warm summer morning, and a carriage,—for the crisp freshness of an embroidered lawn and a filmy hat would wilt into dingy limpness in the hot and grimy streets. Wearily, she

189

drew a white silk glove from a white hand which had no ornament save two priceless pearl rings. The beautiful hand adjusted her hat on her brown, wavy hair. Not a silver thread showed in the hair, nor in that soft light did the minutest of wrinkles disfigure the charming pink and white skin. About her bearing and her motions, her gracious recognition of the shop people's salute, her careless smile for the cordial, almost florid, greetings of her acquaintance, there was the serene although gentle pride of an amiable woman who has become so accustomed to her social power and her personal beauty that they are no longer a luxury to her—only a necessity.

The other lady was a contrast to her in almost every way, unless possibly in her repose, being frankly gray-haired, of large although well-proportioned figure, clad in widow's weeds, her sober bonnet draped in the lighter veil which succeeds the suffocating fall of crape. As the two ladies sat, it so happened that each had extended a foot a little beyond the shelter of her skirts. Nothing could symbolize the difference between them better than these feet,—one clad in open-work stockings of black silk and wearing the least substantial of high-heeled slippers; the other, shapely, not small, shod in a substantial low shoe with a heel made for comfort alone.

The woman with the shoe was Mrs. Winslow, formerly Emma Hopkins, and her companion was her sister, Mrs. Raimund.

Helen Raimund and Emma Winslow were the two daughters and only children of a very able man who rose from the estate of a common day laborer to that of superintendent and partner in the Old Colony Plow Works. He was now the president. They were born in the same little village on the Housatonic River, but with this difference: Emma was born eight years earlier than Helen and of another mother. The first Mrs. Hopkins was a farmer's daughter who had thought it no disgrace to work at her husband's side in the mill, and who saved him many a dollar by her mechanical readiness when he was perfecting the inventions that were to make his fortune. She was one of the best women in the world,—a patient, sweet-natured, sound-headed creature, but no one ever called her a lady, and no one ever called the second Mrs. Hopkins anything else. For the second Mrs. Hopkins was an army officer's daughter; and it goes without saying that when she married Benjamin Hopkins he was a prosperous man.

Nelly grew up into an extremely pretty girl, who was barely out of her teens and her expensive "finishing school" and back in Fairport, where the family had removed, when she met Alan Raimund, whom she married after a short engagement. Raimund was a Chicago railway man, very wealthy even then and since described in the newspapers as "a magnate." They had one child, a handsome boy of sixteen. The marriage entirely satisfied Mrs. Hopkins, but she often said that she was not surprised by it; she had always felt that Nelly, with her beauty and her charm, would make a great match. Emma's "great match," however, frankly abashed her. Not so did it Nelly, who "didn't see any won-

derful workings of Providence or inscrutable wan-
derings of a man's fancy about the affair," saying
frankly that Winslow had sense and he wasn't a
particle too good for Emmie, who made him happy,
and very lucky he was to get her! Nelly was fond
of her sister, and probably respected her more than
any one else in the world.

"Emma never nags you," she used to say, "and
she never bores you. Before you've had enough of
her, she always goes away. I wish she'd give lessons in the Art of Leaving in Time, in Chicago!
I'd treat a whole crowd of people to them at twenty-
five dollars a course, the proceeds to go to some
indigent charity."

To-day she had just met her sister, who had
come to Chicago to see her, before she went to the
sea. Emma was to spend the summer in Fairport.

"And a hotter place," Mrs. Raimund affirmed,
"there isn't outside the tropics!"

"Not always," objected Mrs. Winslow placidly;
"and we always have a breeze at Overlook—"

"From electric fans. Oh, yes, I know. And the
temperature stands at ninety when it's over a hundred outside. Still *I* consider ninety tolerably hot.
Why, it *has* to be hot! Fairport's in a corn state
where they brag they never have a crop failure, and
weather that's good for corn is awful for human
beings. Corn's insatiable; it's not enough to swelter
all day for it; you must have nights like an oven,
too. Emmie, why don't you just take Peggy Rutherford and come visit me and be cool, not *cooled off*,
which is the best electric fans can do!"

Mrs. Winslow shook her head.

"Perhaps you think I don't guess why you're roasting yourself and Peggy—it's all for that silly boy—oh, don't worry, nobody is anywhere near! You are planning something awfully deep, and sending Peggy to be my secretary through Miss Starr's vacation is part of the scheme."

"By the way,"—Mrs. Winslow did not trouble herself to deny the accusation—"by the way, isn't Peggy nice? Doesn't she keep your correspondence and your accounts all straightened out?"

"Oh, she's nice, really very nice, but she's pestiferously proud. I can't give her a thing—I can't even lend her a thing. And she's just the figure one wants to dress up. But she's so stiff about it, she's nasty. I'm positively ashamed of her, she's worn that one black net dinner-gown of hers so often. If she didn't have so much ingenuity about changing it, and hadn't such a stylish figure, she would actually look shabby."

"I think she always looks neat and trig and sweet and—distinguished." Mrs. Winslow's face softened as she spoke.

"Yes, she does, that's the maddening part of it; it shows she'd be positively *ravissante* if she would only let *me* dress her! But she won't, proud little Southern fire-eater! Such a joke! your fastidious socialist has fallen in love with her!"

"Johnny!" Emma Winslow's calm cheek was mottled with spots of red which slowly widened until they blended in one flush.

Mrs. Raimund opened her beautiful eyes. She laughed suddenly. "Emma, you absurd matchmaker! I believe *that* is why you sent her to me."

"Certainly," nodded Emma; "but respect my confidence. Is anything settled?"

"No, nor ever will be, I fancy. He's over head and ears in the Pullman strike, which she hates."

"But—she doesn't hate him?"

"I don't believe she's in love with him, if that's what you want. She's as easy as another boy with him; she is a sort of tomboy; well, all girls are now. It's very tiresome. If I had a daughter I should want to slap her. But to go back to those youngsters. Is that truly your scheme—to marry them?"

"Yes. I wish Johnny would marry Peggy; marriage would straighten him out quicker than anything else. And"—Nelly marveled over the change in her voice—"I promised my husband to try to save Johnny."

"Oh, of course," Mrs. Raimund agreed vaguely. "I suppose," she continued, "it was hard on him, having Johnny abroad so much with—with the princess. Why did he let him go?" She had never ventured to discuss Josiah's first wife with her sister; it was forbidden ground which Emma could guard in her own way; but now she was made aware, subtly, that the gates were down.

"He was conscientious about it," Emma answered with a little tightening of the lips; she might be willing to discuss the subject, for reasons; but it was none the less painful to her. "He knew how she loved Johnny and how he loved her; he couldn't bear to hurt them both so much."

"Why didn't they send her to Siberia? She was a nihilist, wasn't she?"

"Hardly that. She was a socialist and worshiped Tolstoi, and wanted to give every cent she had away. I fancy she did. But I don't know that she wanted to kill the czar or burn up property or any such violent things. Besides, she lived in Switzerland. They couldn't get her. After she died and we were married, I hoped that Johnny would forget what she must have taught him, and"—Mrs. Winslow smiled a little sadly—"I suppose I had all kinds of nonsensical fancies that he would learn to care for *me*. Well, he hasn't changed. And I haven't succeeded in making him care for me." In spite of her self-control, she sighed.

"Then he ought to be ashamed of himself!" cried Mrs. Raimund, "good as you were to him! But he was a most obstinate boy, with a horrid will of his own. Don't you remember that horse of his that he had when I visited you? and say what I would, he wouldn't have a bearing rein for it or have its tail docked! How it *looked!*"

"But he has a good heart," said Mrs. Winslow, "even if I couldn't win it. Well, now you understand why Mr. Winslow made such a will. It would be no kindness to give Johnny such a great property to squander in social propaganda. And it would be a mischief to society itself. As a good citizen, Mr. Winslow couldn't do it; he felt he had no right to do it."

"Certainly not," agreed Mrs. Raimund cheerfully; "a great deal better for you to have it, Emmie."

Mrs. Winslow did not seem to hear her,—she was looking absently out of the window. "Mr. Winslow knew I would do my best," she said.

Mrs. Raimund deemed it a good opportunity to satisfy some queries that had been in her mind for a long while.

"Didn't the will give him a hundred thousand outright and two-thirds of the property if he keeps that sum intact until he is thirty?"

Mrs. Winslow nodded.

"And if he has lost it, or any part of it?" her sister continued.

"It all goes to me."

"Well, I think you will get it, Emmie."

Mrs. Winslow smiled faintly; she changed the subject.

"Perhaps not," she replied,—"if he has really fallen in love with Peggy Rutherford. When is your fitting?"

"She's ready now, I think."

"I'll meet you here, then."

After Mrs. Raimund's dainty skirts had flitted behind the red wall the older sister sat in frowning abstraction. She was roused by a man's voice, speaking her name.

She looked up at a young man bowing before her, —a short young man with big blue eyes and long fair lashes and freckles on the bridge of his nose.

"I guess you don't know me, Mrs. Winslow," said the young man, "but I used to live in Fairport, and you used to know my mother. My name is Bates, William Bates, Business Agent Molders' Union No. 25. I called at Mr. Alan G. Raimund's to see you; but the young man who waits on the door told me you were both gone here to get some dresses tried on; so I took the liberty, as I thought my busi-

ness would interest you, to come right here. I hope
I don't interrupt."

"Carstairs isn't usually so communicative,"
thought Mrs. Winslow, "but I imagine this young
man has his own ways of getting information."
Meanwhile she was inclining her head in a courteous
but not responsive manner; she was trying to place
Mr. William Bates in her memory.

"My business," said the young man, "is about
Mr. Ivan Winslow; I know him well."

"Ivan?" said Mrs. Winslow. "Do you mean Mr.
John Winslow?"

"Yes, ma'am, but he signs his name Ivan now.
I wanted a word with you about him, if you please."

"Yes, I *do* remember you," said Mrs. Winslow;
"you had a very good mother."

"She did washing for you,"—his voice was carefully subdued,—"I can tell you, though, she had a
girl to do *her* washing before she died."

"I know she did; she had a good son."

"Not so good's she deserved; she deserved the
best there was; and I know it better all the time.
'Twas her told me about you. I know you are a good
woman. Good! If I didn't I wouldn't be coming
with this story. I've heard all about the Winslow
will. It might seem as if you would be the last person in the world to stop that boy from making a
fool of himself and squandering his money; but
I'm betting certain that you'd do a lot to keep him
steady till he's thirty. You've got a whole lot of
money, anyhow. And you haven't chick nor child
but him, and any woman would get soft on *him*.
He'll keep himself straight once he has that big for-

tune to handle and gets into business. All this is only to show why I'm speaking to you, madam. I expect you know that I've seen a good deal of Ivan, —I may say I know him well."

"So I understand," said Mrs. Winslow composedly; she did not show any emotion either of surprise or incredulity; she had fixed her calm, keen eyes on the young man's face and listened attentively, but if in assent or in disbelief was beyond Billy Bates' guessing. He drove on doggedly to his object.

"He has got in with the socialists pretty deep. And I'm going to talk confidentially with you, Mrs. Winslow, if you'll let me and keep what I say, my opinions, I mean, to yourself. You know I have got my position in labor circles to maintain. When I think our folks are making a mistake I can't always say so in the newspapers, can I?" He looked up at her in a manner she found very winning.

"I understand. This is a confidential interview so far as your opinions are concerned," said she.

"That's right. Thank you. I always heard you were a perfect lady. You see I have got a lady friend in Fairport—well, no, ma'am, she ain't quite that; I don't know her quite well enough to call her that; I wish I did,"—he smiled in a kind of shamefaced way first, but then openly, as if he tasted the humor of his own embarrassment—"well, she tells me considerable of the things which everybody knows, and I always drop in at Darrell's when I'm in town, so I get more. Maybe I'm wrong, but I've sized it up in my own mind that Mr. Winslow and you tried to save Ivan, and this leaving the money conditional was *your* way to hold him in. I know I seem to be taking a liberty, an awful big one, talking this way—"

"I suppose you have a reason," said Mrs. Winslow quietly.

"A good one, I think. I want that boy to have a show for his white alley! It ain't only the money; he's going to get most terribly disappointed; and he'll take it hard. He's the sort that takes things hard. I think he is beginning to find out we've got a slick lot of skates in labor circles here in Chicago, and he squirms a good deal sometimes at the meetings; but so long as he has any dough left to give, the insiders are going to be easy on him and not let him git on to any dirty work—I mean what he'd call dirty—these college folks are particular, you know." William Bates gave her a smile of significance, so confiding and humorous that Emma Winslow, whose sense of humor never caught cold, returned it slightly. "Well, maybe you and I would, too," he went on, warmed by the smile, "still, the sum total of it all is: Ivan is getting just a little bit disgruntled. You see, the lot here is pretty rabid, left over from the Internationals and the anarchist outfit of 1887. Ivan, himself, started in out east with a nice mild lot called Fabians. So he's rather sick of these bloody bums. But that's the very time he's likely to do something desperate, just because he begins to doubt everything he's believed in. He's pretty obstinate, you know—"

"Obstinate as a pig," said Mrs. Winslow calmly.

"And he'll be doing something to convince *himself*, see?"

Mrs. Winslow looked intently at the young man beside her, sitting in Mrs. Raimund's chair,—and such a contrast to Mrs. Raimund! She had called him, in her own mind, "ordinary looking"; but there was something in the set of his firm jaw and the outline of his head which was not ordinary.

"Yes," she assented thoughtfully, "I see. Well, what is he going to do?"

"That's what I came about. I suppose, what with one fool thing and another, he has dumped about sixty thousand dollars in the dust-heap already—"

"I dare say. He's had two years."

"But if he'd take what he's got left, and put it into a good business, these cheap times when things are going for a song, he could get enough more to make good by the time he's thirty. Besides, he's the right to git a good position in the Old Colony, ain't he? By the will?"

"Yes,—if he will take it. And no one would be gladder to welcome him than my father and I."

"I was *sure* you would. But you see,"—Billy Bates was confused all at once, and fidgeted with the arms of his chair—"he ain't opened his mouth to me, you understand; and yet I—you'll excuse me; I take it you want me to be frank and free, madam?"

"I know what you mean, I dare say," said Mrs. Winslow quietly; "he imagines that my father and I want the Old Colony for ourselves. He is quite mistaken."

"I *knew* he was. I knew it all along," exclaimed Billy, with an enthusiastic blow on his knees, "but —I admit to *you,* ma'am, I don't venture to introduce the subject to him, except on the side. He is so high-strung I don't know what crazy act he won't do if I was to mad him. But as I was saying, *if* we could save that forty thousand and convince him, at the same time, that you was his friend, why —we could begin to *talk!* See?"

"But how are we to save it?"—Emma Winslow had unconsciously accepted the tacit partnership offered. "He has some scheme on foot to make ducks and drakes of it, hasn't he?"

"Oh, sure," agreed Billy, grinning; "he's spent a lot, already, on the Pullman strike, which" (his voice sank almost to a whisper) "is on its last legs now, and *bound* to lose; and he has been persuaded that if he'll give a *big* lot more they can win (but they *can't;* they couldn't if he had a hundred thousand to squander!); and so he has sold out all his stocks, and he has got the money."

"Has he given it to the Railway Union?"

"Not yet. I'm coming to that. A fellow named Walter Tyler has done most of the work with him. He's on the executive committee and (this is in confidence) he's the man who has attended to most of the riot business. He's hand in glove with some of the old Spiess-Engel-Parsons gang; and he is a pretty thoroughgoing rascal, to my mind. Maybe I'm prejudiced; but if it hadn't been for him and his influence, we might have got them to call off the strike. There was Miss Addams, of Hull House, and a newspaper man with a mighty level head and a few of us who weren't fools, and we came almighty near getting the fat out of the fire before it blazed. Wally Tyler's more to blame than the pigheaded fools on the Pullman side. But that's not the point.

I only mentioned it to show you what Tyler's like.
Mr. Winslow thinks he's a high-minded patriot,
extreme in his views, perhaps, but awful unselfish
and self-sacrificing; while I give you my word,
madam, only two years ago he was treasurer of
a lodge and lost four hundred dollars,—pretended he was held up and robbed! And he went out to
Pullman, only *one* year ago, and sold fake titles to
some Kensington lots. That's his kind—"

"But why does the Union employ such a man?"

"He's got a tongue, and it's amazing how much
more a man's tongue counts than his head 'mong
workingmen. He's a mighty slick one. And then,
too, he's awful clever with his hands. He can break
your head if he can't beat you talking, you know.
He'd great luck; he killed a man in an election row
in ninety. Got off, of course. He was bound to get
off for that. So that gives him a reputation of a bad
man to tackle. And there's no doubt he's got a big
pull. But I guess he's overreached himself this
whack. That's why I've come here. He knows
about the money. He knows it is in Ivan's room—
somewhere. And he could git into the room even if
it was locked, for Ivan's boarding at a hotel."

"What hotel?"

"You wouldn't know it by name, ma'am; it's just
a cheap place, Chris Wulf's, off Clark Street. But
Tyler's well known there, and he could get in, on
some excuse. This evening Ivan was intending to
give over the money, and jolly up the boys. But,
meanwhile, I happen to know Wally has made preparations to light out—I mean to escape, abscond.
He's bought clothes and a mustache—"

"But he may mean nothing worse than amateur theatricals—"

"This ain't no time for amachure theatricals! He means to skip—I mean abscond. Now, if we was to catch him and get the stuff and show him up, wouldn't that kinder sicken Ivan of the whole bunch?"

"Perhaps," said Mrs. Winslow meditatively, "but what is your plan to catch him, presuming, for it is only presumption, that he really is running away with the money?"

"Of course he is; he wouldn't let such a chance slip; I only knew this morning that *he* knew about this money, and then I caught on to his buying those things. I sent word right straight to Ivan, but he was out; when he gits back, or the man I sent hunts him up, they'll 'phone me if the money's gone. But I know it is, all right. Next we'll swear out a warrant; I've a man in plain clothes shadowing Tyler, now. We'll give him rope, and the minute he tries to run we'll be on to him."

"But I don't quite take it in yet, Mr. Bates, what you want of me," said Mrs. Winslow, with an ironic smile which yet was not unfriendly.

Billy Bates' own smile met it, gaily. "I rather guess you do, Mrs. Winslow; I've tried to explain Ivan needs to have it proved you're his friend as well as me; and *this* ought to do it."

Emma held out her hands. "I trust you, Mr. Bates; do you want me to go with you now?"

"Well, ma'am, I've a cab below, waiting," said Billy, as he deferentially surrendered his own fingers to her firm, calm grasp.

CHAPTER IV

THE THOUGHTS OF YOUTH ARE LONG, LONG THOUGHTS

"Jo'nivan, you're a plumb *idiot!*"

Peggy was speaking,—Peggy very flushed, with her hazel eyes burning and her little firm chin in the air.

She looked—and the likeness flashed over her beholder—exactly as she had looked in their childish squabbles; excited, petulant, desperately in earnest, although now the white hand, which whisked in the air, flashed jewels from its slim fingers; but it was the gesture of the child Peggy, just the same.

The young man on the same bench in Lincoln Park with her viewed her actions with an unaccountable gloom; for, certainly, the girl showed affection even in her anger, and she was adorably handsome. She had a charming, supple figure, that loveliest and freshest of skins which goes with the hair which painters worship; and these same locks, which Johnny had once likened to copper, now were a warm bronze, with glorious lights; and little tendrils of them curled on her milk-white neck. She had the carriage of the head, recalling a mettled horse, which belonged to the child Peggy, the same unconscious dilation of her nostrils when she

SHE CAUGHT HIM WHEN HE WOULD HAVE RISEN AND HELD HIM CLOSE

Page 131

grew excited, and the same trick of opening her eyes and bending her brows at once. A fair picture she made amid the velvet grass with the gray-blue lake before her, fading into a luminous blue-gray sky.

Nevertheless Johnny Winslow sighed and frowned. "*Is* it so foolish, then, to sacrifice a fortune to help other people?" said he.

"Yes, when your sacrifice won't help them," retorted Peggy sternly. "Oh, I know what I'm talking about. At first, when you began on me with your grand schemes for making the world over, I felt sure they were all hot air; but I couldn't prove it, so I kept quiet."

He smiled.

"When was that? I don't remember that quiet time; I think you have been slating me ever since we met, again—"

"I may have thrown in a word, now and then," interjected Peggy with hauteur, "but I didn't really *argue* with you. I didn't know enough about the subject. No, it's more than a year,"—she sighed— "think of it! I went straight to Mr. Raimund and asked him to tell me all about the labor question; I was under the impression that I could gobble it up in the hour after dinner. Well, I soon found out my mistake; I've been at it ever since. I was bound to convince you you were wrong, Jo'nivan—"

"And *that* is why you took a class at Hull House?"

"Of course. I taught the violin—they were much too grand for the fiddle. Nice little Italian mites, who loved candy and music; I suppose they'll grow up anarchists, but they are very nice now. I expected it would be awfully stupid; but it wasn't, that part; it was the grown-ups' jabber tired me. There's one special socialist I met there I reckon I could slay with my own hands, she's so tedious in her violence; but I listened politely, for I was determined to hear both sides. You said I was so partizan; *that* isn't partizan, is it? I met your social labor leaders and your socialist leaders and every other kind of a leader who scorns a nailbrush; and I listened all around the subject; for, after these, I would go straight back to the capitalists and hear *their* side. And I tell you, Jo'nivan, the sensible men on both sides came to mighty near the same conclusions. And they weren't *your* conclusions a little bit!"

"I dare say not."

"I tell you, you are not going to pull people out of the mire by jumping in and getting mired up beside them; you'd better keep on firm ground and throw them a plank!"

"Won't it do to carry them the plank and get close enough to pull?"

"Not nearly so well. You are simply going to ruin yourself, without helping other people. I know right well what you're fixing to do *now;* you have got the notion that this strike will succeed if *you* can dump a great heap of money in, just at this moment when it is going to pieces."

"Who says it is going to pieces?" Johnny-Ivan spoke softly, as he had spoken all the time; but a flicker kindled in his dark eyes, a spot of red burned on his olive cheek.

"I shan't tell you; but I *will* tell you that all my information doesn't come from the Pullman crowd, as you call them. Some of it comes from men who hate Mr. Pullman, but don't shut their eyes to facts, like you!"

Johnny-Ivan laughed. "Dear old Billy, he's the frankest labor free-lance going! Do you know what an opportunist is, Peggy? I don't, I never could make out when I was taking Economics, but I think Billy's *it*."

"No, I don't, and I don't want to know. It's bad enough to have to find out about American politics without having to dabble in French nicknames. Bates has sense. And it's true about the strike."

"But it comes too late, anyhow, your wisdom," said Johnny-Ivan. "I have given my money almost all away."

Peggy jumped as if he had hit her; she towered above him in a flash of terror which had the showing of anger; her voice sharpened in pain. "You don't mean it! You—Jo'nivan, *don't!* You scare me!"

"I thought nothing would scare you," said he, with the unmirthful smile that was beginning to carve its fine wrinkles about his mouth, so often did it flit there nowadays. "But I'm in dead earnest, Peggy. You see, dear, it had come to this, I *had* to help them. The strike, as you very shrewdly guess, is lost—unless they get a lot of money immediately. Well, I've supplied the money."

"Jo'nivan!"—but Peggy clenched her tiny fists, pressed her lips close and achieved an agonized silence.

"Oh, turn it all on, Peggy!"

"Jo'nivan!"—Peggy's voice was fine and small and of an ominous mildness—"when did you give it?"

"Yesterday."

"How much was it?"

"Altogether it was thirty-nine thousand five hundred and twenty dollars and fifty cents, to be accurate. You see I couldn't get par for my stock these hard times or it would have been more."

There was a thud; it was the bump of two slender, clenched hands falling on the wooden seat of the bench.

"And to whom?" It was marvelous Peggy could keep her composure so well.

"To the proper men. The committee I want to have it; you don't know any of them, even by name, unless it is Walter Tyler—"

"Johnny, he's an unscrupulous villain. I *do* know him."

"How? At Hull House? Peggy, you ought to be a little careful making acquaintances—"

"Oh, ought I? How about you? But I never spoke to your precious friend. Yet I know just what he is, because, sitting in another room, I heard him bragging about such a dastardly thing. Bragging!"

Johnny said nothing. All at once, as her proud young head tossed, his mind fell away from the moment; it was seized by a sudden idiotic anguish, because he would never now be able to give Peggy a rope of pearls for that lovely neck! There was a tiny pearl brooch at her throat,—the simplest old-fashioned trinket, which he had seen Mrs. Rutherford wear. Her rings, also, had been her mother's, relics of the old days when Peggy Rutherford had not dreamed she would need to earn her own bread, he thought bitterly. Perhaps some other man who was not vowed to a hopeless quest—it was here Peggy saw Johnny set his teeth hard. She misunderstood and took fire in a flash.

"You needn't get so angry," she cried, "it *was* dastardly, *vile!* And I heard him bragging! He was a picket on a strike and he 'did up' a lame man; jumped on him from behind and pounded him so his wife had hard work to know him. That's how he expressed it—and laughed. Do you approve of *that?*"

"A strike's war, and war's infernal," evaded Johnny, "but don't you see if they *didn't* terrorize the scabs, they would run in and steal all the jobs? The union would fight and starve, and the scabs would get the benefit of the rise in wages."

"And you think anything's fair in war, do you? You don't believe in fighting fair?"

"Yes, I do. And I think it was atrocious, if you ask me," said Johnny doggedly; "but I should like you to see that there is some excuse for men when their passions get red-hot with injustice and suffering—"

"His weren't. I heard he sold out that very strike."

"You hear all sorts of tommy-rot. But never mind Tyler, he won't get it. I promised all but fourteen thousand of it yesterday and wanted to give them checks then; but for some reason they wanted the *money,* notes and gold; so I got the whole sum in money yesterday, carried it home in the street-cars, and this morning I hunted up the committee and handed them their twenty-five thousand. I didn't mean to give any more, at least, not now; but they are in straits, so I promised to give the rest at the meeting this evening, to jolly up the boys. I had a rather theatrical notion I'd like to give it myself; being the last of my stake—"

She caught the words off his lips: "Oh, Jo'nivan, it isn't too late, then; you haven't really, truly given it all, you've a *little* left. Even a little will help. Oh, Jo'nivan, please, *please* listen to me and consider before you throw away such a fortune, for you never in this world can make a hundred thousand out of nothing before you are thirty—"

"I know it, Peggy; I realize what I am doing, and, of course, I know the terms of my father's will. Mrs. Winslow will get it all. Frankly, I don't enjoy that part of it a bit. She will have all she has been scheming for."

"She isn't scheming. She's so good, and it is a shame, a *shame* the way you have been so prejudiced against her all your life. Jo'nivan, you think yourself so awfully fine and high, and you are, too; but you have been mean as dirt to Cousin Emma! you have been unjust and cruel ever since your father married her. He had a *right* to marry her; she made him happy—"

"I deny none of that. Peggy, can you talk this over quite calmly, just as if it were a thousand instead of forty that I'm giving?"

Peggy flashed her great eyes at him; he caught his breath with her beauty and scintillating power.

Like a sword-thrust the consciousness came to him
that she was more precious to him than all the world
besides. And it was too late.

"Of course I *can't*, Jo'nivan," she said with spirit,
"I should be a—a—*stick* if I could; but I can be
reasonable. Jo'nivan, have you considered that if
you fling away your money you won't have anything
like as much to give to these people you want to help,
by and by?"

"Yes, Peggy, you crafty little temptress, I have
thought that all over. I see the bait my father holds
out. He counted on my being anxious to do big
things and be a leader in a new social state, and so
waiting until I could have several millions instead
of a bare hundred thousand, and meanwhile, I
would be tempted by the luxury I should live in
and by the chance of making money as well as
handling it, and by dealing with big things in a big
way; you see by his will I was to have a position
in the works at Fairport; if I kept that position
and kept the money, when I was thirty I was to have
two-thirds of the whole fortune. Well, of course he
counted on my getting to like my job. He knew
part of me awfully well. There is a fascination in
handling large affairs. It's tremendous. He reck-
oned I'd feel it, and I'd be tempted. I'd get conservative. When a fellow gets hardened to the poor
devils' sufferings outside, and determined to hang
on to all that he has, *that's* getting conservative. To
be conservative is to despair altogether of improve-
ment—"

"No, it isn't; it is only finding out you can't mend
the world in a minute. Johnny, you've got common

sense; I do wish you wouldn't let your heart sit down on it and squash it!"

"And, maybe, I wish you wouldn't let your common sense, as you call it, which is only the conventional name for a mix-up of cowardice and selfishness which one generation hands down to another as the secret of getting on in the world, getting on over other people's necks—I wish you wouldn't let *that* sit down on your heart. It's such a good heart!"

"Never mind my heart," returned Peggy coldly, "or rather assume I have a regular geyser of a heart and can't see suffering without its spouting. My heart isn't the question; it is, *What* is the best way to help people? It has puzzled the wisest men in the world. Do *you* find it so easy to decide? Why not go a little slow?"

The minute puckers of his under lip, so like his father's, used to mean a quick shift of perception with Johnny; she guessed that shooting at random she had sent a bolt home; like a woman, she pressed her advantage.

"Wait, Johnny," she pleaded, "wait a year, *six months,*—try the life your father, who loved you so dearly and who was such a good honorable man himself, wanted you to try; only *try* it!"

"I admit I meant to try, Peggy," he said—his head was on his breast, his eyes fell before hers—"I thought I would give the life of a man with a fortune who tried to make other people's lives a little less miserable, a fair trial; what my father said to me last summer didn't impress me so much as—as—when I came home and he died. Peggy, all at once I realized that he had really loved me; it wasn't his pride and his effort to keep a great fortune in his name—"

"I know, Jo'nivan," murmured Peggy gently, "he did love you mighty well. I always knew that. He used to talk to me about you; he was so proud of you—oh, Jo'nivan,"—she lifted eyes swimming in tears, and both hands went out to him in an unconscious gesture of appeal—"this would be awful to him—*don't* do it!"

Something was choking her just when she needed to be calmest; she bit her lips in a spasm of self-disgust; but he hadn't lifted his eyes from the blue sky-line; his lips twisted in the same way that little Johnny-Ivan's lips used to twist when he was carrying a heart-ache off, boastfully.

"But I didn't *dare* to wait, Peggy; I was getting such a lazy, luxurious dog and valuing the properties of—well, a gentleman's chances, so highly, that if I'd waited I might be a selfish sneak myself and break all my promises to my mother; no telling. Besides, this hundred thousand my father gave me with his eyes open; he knew exactly what I might do with it; but to save it and scoop in the big fortune, only to use it in a way he would have detested —oh, you see I couldn't do that, Peggy, dear!"

"You're a nice boy, Jo'nivan," sighed Peggy, "but you never did see things all round them. You *have* thrown away your chance of getting your father's fortune; you don't need to worry about that. But why must you throw away your chance of making a fortune of your own? Why must you strip yourself to the bone as well as bare? Bless you, honey, there will be plenty of distressed socialists waiting for your money next year! Save a little for *them*. Why not wait a year—wait six months?"

"The strike would be lost then. I'll admit I hesitated, I wanted to be sure my little stake, which was all the stake I had, wouldn't simply be swallowed up; but it's now or never with the boys; so it's now with me. I've burned my bridges. There's another thing: I never could quite win my mates' confidence! They always have felt I was outside; I had this money to fall back on. I was only a kind of curiosity workman; I'm the real stuff now."

He spoke lightly; but Peggy detected the sadness she was too irritated to regard.

"I reckon it is no use talking with you, Jo'nivan, —you were always the very obstinatest boy on earth!" She burst forth hotly: "Oh, of course I know you are doing all this terrible foolishness from the *best* motives. You think it's your Russian sympathy with suffering; but it isn't, it's your nasty New England conscience twisted round. You're getting over your Russian crazy sympathy, but your hateful New England doggedness won't let you let go! And the worse it hurts the more you'll be sure it's your duty to hang on! I almost wish Tyler would run away with all your money,—then you'd see for yourself what an infatuated—*mule* you are!"

Instead of answering, Johnny, who was facing the stream of carriages while her face was averted, sprang to his feet and raised his hat, with a bow and a perfunctory smile, and Peggy was aware of the blended flash of silver harness trappings and the sleek satin skins of pawing horses, and of the soft billowing of a lady's gown over a victoria.

"Why, Peggy!" exclaimed the lady. She smiled mischievously.

"I happened on Miss Rutherford, here, by a lucky chance, Mrs. Raimund,"—Johnny offered his explanation with a nonchalance that Peggy admired.

"Then you've happened on me by an unlucky one," said Mrs. Raimund, "for I must take her away. There is barely time to get back to luncheon and see me off—unless she wants to desert me, like my sister, who mysteriously disappeared at Field's."

"On the contrary, it was a most lucky chance," said Johnny, with the smile his friends liked, "for I wanted to bid you good-by and thank you for being so good to me, and it is impossible for me to get down to the train."

"I got your note and the flowers. I didn't know Tolstoi permitted flowers."

Johnny laughed. "I'm afraid he doesn't. But, you see, this is my last day as a gilded trifler. I've got a job, and I'm going to be a mechanic for keeps to-morrow. So I'm taking the privileges of farewell."

"Take more and come to luncheon and explain yourself. Oh, that's too bad!"—at Johnny's murmur of excuse—"well, if you can't, why not come up in the evening and dine with Mrs. Winslow and Peggy and Mr. Raimund? Emma and Peggy go to Fairport to-morrow—no, don't think up another engagement. Come."

"I will, if—if I may, Peggy?"

"Of course, do come, Jo'nivan," said Peggy in a carefully matter-of-fact way. But why, she demanded angrily of herself, in the victoria, why need she have blushed?

CHAPTER V

THE SOUTHERN WAY

Mrs. Alan Raimund was passing through the gate which guarded the Michigan Southern and Lake Shore railway tracks, at the Old Rock Island depot. The procession was impressive. First came two porters bearing (under the eye of Mrs. Raimund's maid) dress-suit-cases, lizard-skin bags and a bundle of rugs, for Mrs. Raimund abominated "the boards the Pullman Company calls blankets;" next the maid laden with Johnny's flowers; then the lady of quality herself, dutifully escorted by her husband; and last, her son, Cecil, with Peggy Rutherford.

Cecil, for reasons of his own, had insisted on carrying his hand-bag. He was chatting very busily with Peggy, who was a great chum of his. Peggy had forced her chagrin and actual misery out of sight. She found it the easier assuming the mood of her friends since Mrs. Winslow had not yet returned—to Mrs. Raimund's vast annoyance, peppered with alarm, which expressed itself in so many ways that every one had a chance of failing to assuage it, and a slight dejection in the hearers seemed no more than polite.

"What did she say in her note which was handed

you at Field's?" asked Raimund, taking his turn at ineffectual comfort.

"Said that she was unexpectedly called away by important business and would see me, she hoped, at luncheon; anyhow, at the train. Now we have *had* luncheon, and she isn't here. I shan't wait for her. I don't think it nice of her at all. You *don't* suppose she could have been enticed away to be robbed?"

"Hardly," observed her husband dryly; "sister Emma wouldn't be a healthy subject for kidnappers!"

"Of course the train couldn't be late! Alan, won't they wait the train if you say so? What if it isn't your road, they might be a little obliging, I think. I don't see what Emma was *thinking* of! Why did she come to Chicago to see me if she is going to act this weird way?"

"There's eight minutes yet," said Raimund, "come in and get settled. I'll watch for her outside."

It was really an unworthy device to escape from his marital duties, and his wife detected it instantly. He needn't do anything of the kind, she told him; Peggy would wait.

"And I'll wait with Miss Peggy," volunteered Cecil.

"And have some one kidnapping *you!*" interrupted Mrs. Raimund. "No, come in and let Peggy keep watch. She won't come—just as likely as not it's some foolish old woman run over by the cars, and she saw it and rushed down to help her. Emma is too ridiculous sometimes, you know she is, Alan! I do think that she might have waited until I went; there were several things I really wanted to talk to her about, now I'll have to write, and that is a nuisance—"

In such bewailings and complaints her voice faded plaintively and was lost within the car. Cecil was giving his own last messages to Peggy, regarding Aunt Emma, and Best, the coachman, who must not allow Tom, the groom, to drive Arkansas Traveler (Cecil's own horse) *ever;* Best must exercise him himself, and he was awfully sorry not to see Aunt Emma and—

"You really *must* go, Cis, honey, your mother will be worried!"

"Oh, there's five minutes. Tell—where are you going?"

Peggy had darted from his side; he lost her in the crowd at the gate and stared until a man pushed him to one side with a curt: "Excuse me, but I'm going on this train."

"First Aunt Emma and now Miss Peggy!" cried Cecil; "what in *thunder's* up! Mysterious disappearances are getting a lot too common here!"

He swung round to perceive Peggy at his elbow, breathless, with curious burning spots on each cheek, and their reflection sparkling in her hazel eyes.

"Cis, please go on, I'm going with you."

"But how about Aunt Emma?"

"I'll explain later; now get on, Cis, *quick!* I have to see your father."

Cecil was so propelled by the impetus of a certain suppressed but intense excitement in her manner, that he obeyed without question.

In the car vestibule they brushed past the man who had jostled Cecil. He was a tall man, very well dressed, and he was carrying a dark red, russia-leather bag with a silver monogram on the outside. This man turned, giving Cis the sweep of a heavy black mustache and the gleam of a full black eye, before Peggy went by.

She saw Mr. Raimund at the state-room door; he read the scarlet mounting to her cheek and the fire dancing in her eye with a better trained perception than his son's, and quietly drew her apart.

"Anything doing?" he began.

"I haven't seen Mrs. Winslow. But"—her voice sank—"don't show any interest in what I'm saying! Do you see that man behind us, the tall man in the light-brown suit, with a black mustache? He is holding a russia-leather bag with a silver monogram on it. That bag belongs to Johnny Winslow and there are fourteen thousand dollars in bank-notes and gold in it; I am almost certain the man means to steal it. He has bought a ticket to Buffalo—"

"Sorry to hurry you, Mr. Raimund,"—the porter was bowing at one elbow.

"No hurry; I'm going on to Englewood," replied Raimund, who had a business man's habit of hitting a decision on the wing.

Peggy gave him a grateful glance.

"And I reckon a lady's trying to catch you-all's attention," said the porter.

Peggy was at the window before Raimund; she saw Mrs. Winslow hurrying toward the gate, too late. Perceiving that it was, she gave over the effort and smiled and waved farewell. Doubtless she was not surprised at Peggy's presence with the party, as Englewood is only twenty minutes from the central station, and Nelly might have taken a notion to have company so far. She did not look disturbed in any way. Mrs. Raimund was calling out of the drawing-room window something about sending a telegram. The great wheels were grinding faster; the words were drowned amid the heavy din of motion; in a second Mrs. Winslow's face was gone, lost in a blur of faces, replaced by the barren spaces of steel arches and sheds and gleaming rails.

"And now, Miss Peggy," said Raimund, seating himself, "get on with the tale."

Peggy glanced with apparent carelessness over her shoulder before she sat down.

"He's safe in the seat," she breathed, "now tell me, can you arrest him?"

"What are the facts?"

Peggy gave them succinctly.

Raimund shook his handsome gray head and smiled a little under his mustache. "I'm afraid, Miss Peggy, that you are relying more on your prejudices than your facts. Tyler knows about the money. Tyler is a villain. Tyler is carrying Winslow's bag. There is the case. Suspicious, maybe, but nothing proved. Winslow may have *given* him the bag. We'd be in a pretty box if we arrested him and found it full of clean collars and cigars."

"I noticed the way he carried it. Cigars and collars are light; that bag pulled his arm down."

"That may mean something. But there are other heavy things besides gold, say revolvers and bottles. These fellows are traveling all over, making mischief for us, but they generally go deadhead because we've been afraid to refuse them passes. But *he* bought a ticket. *That's* suspicious, I grant you. I think, Miss Peggy, we've grounds to watch him but not to arrest him until I can hunt up Winslow and find out if the money has been stolen. If it has, then I'll swear out a warrant and have him arrested at the next stop the train makes. I'll speak to the con ductor and the porter to watch him, and if he gets off before you get my wire, why, wire me at once *where* he got off—"

"Can't we stop him?"

"We could if we were sure he had the money. The conductor could arrest him all right. But we have to be sure the money has been stolen. You are sure this man's Tyler? I know all about him, of course, and a pestiferous rascal he is; but I've never seen him."

"I'm quite sure," answered Peggy steadily, "though his hair's a different color and he has a mustache, and he *was* clean-shaven; but he can't change his eyes—they are rather full, you notice— you can see him?"

"Distinctly. He is reading the *Chicago Times.*"

"Don't you see his eyes are—not what people call pop-eyes, but prominent; you aren't near enough to see another thing; in one of them is a large brown speck—in the iris. I noticed that, and the way he wrinkles his eyes when he smiles, the first time I saw the man."

"You should be a detective, my dear Miss Peggy!"

"Don't you notice little things about people? But Mr. Raimund, don't you think his disguising him-self that way is suspicious, too?"

"Yes, rather. Although he may be on some other scoundrelly business. But really, I'm coming round to your theory. You're sure of the bag as well as the man?"

"Absolutely; it used to belong to the Princess Olga; I've seen it a heap of times; it has her coronet on it, and initials. Part of the coronet has been wrenched off, but I know the bag; there's a black stain just under the coronet—Johnny got it on, trying to black my shoes when we were little and I put my foot on the bag. I remember I fairly loved the princess ever after, because she didn't scold us that day."

"Risky to take the bag; that's against the theory. But criminals are always taking fool risks, being amazing subtile in nine out of ten ways, and then idiotically rash in the tenth. But now about ways and means? you'll want a section—"

"A lower berth—"

"A section, my dear young lady. You couldn't keep awake in a lower; you would have to go to sleep in self-defense to forget your misery. And you ought to stay awake and watch every movement until the policeman gets him. I'll attend to that; they are running light now, so there ought to be no trouble in getting into the same car with him. Does he know you? Has he seen you at Hull House?"

"He may have; but I have never spoken to him."

"The chances are he knows you, as you know him. But he won't know you have recognized him, unless a guilty conscience is particularly far-sighted, and he can't very well know that Winslow has confided in you. I hope we'll trap our gentleman; it may sicken young Winslow of his crowd a bit. He is too good stuff to waste on this socialistic rot. Miss Peggy, if you have any influence, get him out of Chicago as soon as you can!"

"I'm afraid I haven't," said Peggy, "or he would have gone long ago."

"A great city is always bad for men whose minds are in any kind of ferment. There is the nervous strain of the life, for one thing, and in a case like his, the sight every day of a mass of misery and howling discontent plays the mischief with a young fellow who is sensitive and kind-hearted and has his notions all upheaved, anyhow; why, he is ready for *any* scheme that promises the moon! Yes, Cis, tell your mother I'll be there in a minute. Well, Miss Peggy, what shall I say about your presence?"

"Tell Mrs. Raimund the truth, please, she will understand."

Raimund nodded approval. "And you'll get the boy off to Fairport and green fields and general prosperity as soon as you can, won't you? He has seen enough to give him bad dreams the rest of his life, already. Well, I'll attend to your ticket and your section; but you will want money for your return trip and to give the train-boys something, maybe. Fortunately, I brought a wad with me to the station lest Nelly shouldn't have fetched enough; no, best take a hundred; one needs plenty, and you can have Winslow return it; it's his affair, really."

"Thank you," said Peggy. The thought flitted through her brain that if they failed and the money was lost, Winslow would have as little as she to return; there was, strange to say, an obscure pleasure in lavishing dollars which came so hard to her for her old playmate. She seemed to be back in the old protecting elder-sisterly attitude. At Englewood, Raimund left them, and Peggy had a lonesome slump of the heart, as she watched his handsome iron-gray head dwindle down the platform.

But Mrs. Raimund was in delightful spirits. She was immensely relieved by the glimpse of her sister, and she hailed the prospect of rescuing Johnny Winslow's thousands from the Pullman strikers, with a keener species of the same interest with which she would have welcomed an exciting novel to read on her journey.

"Of course," she explained, "I didn't really think anything had happened to aunty, Cis, but those grip-men are so irresponsible, and I had a friend once—a very sensible woman, too, and a member of the Fort-nightly and one of the Colonial Dames—she had her foot *chopped* off by a cable-car and never knew it—"

"How could she *help* knowing it?" Peggy shuddered.

"I don't know how, but she did. She never knew there was anything wrong until her husband cried out, 'Look at your foot!' She was lame ever after. I always think of her when Emmie will go off without the carriage. Where do you suppose she went? She is the most unexpected creature. Why didn't she come on and go to Englewood with us?"

"One reason was she *couldn't,* mamma," said Cecil, "the train was moving when Aunt Emma came up."

"That *was* a good reason," admitted Nelly, who

had a sense of humor, "and I'm awfully relieved, anyhow, to know she was all right; but I do wonder where she has been."

The porter's head was insinuated through the open door: "One of you ladies Miss Rutherford?" he purred in his soft negro accent.

Peggy nodded.

The porter smiled a smile in which abode a respectful and confidential intelligence. "Mr. Raimund engaged number seven for you in the next cyar. Gen'lman with the bag we're keepin' an eye on, he's in number eight opposite. If you'd like you' berth made up ruther early, you could go any time you liked, and maybe not 'tract his 'tention, if he was in the smoking-cyar. Make it up in one, I suppose, and all the pillows haid to the engine?"

"Yes. And you can tell me when to go in," said Peggy, "and be sure to bring me any telegram quietly, you understand."

"Yes, ma'am, I do, ma'am," said the porter, as he permitted himself a flash of eyes and teeth together; they flashed again at the touch of a large round silver coin on his palm. Peggy smiled back; she felt the mounting excitement of combat, the wild stir of the blood which had sent the men of her race into a hundred reckless adventures.

"He wouldn't in the least mind shooting me to escape with that loot," she thought.

"Some of us ought to watch him *all* the time," said Mrs. Raimund, while Peggy was considering deeply. "When he goes into the smoking-room you might go too, Cis; but mind! you are not to smoke. Listen and pretend you're one of those preposterous boys who like to hear men's yarns. When he goes back to his berth, Valerie can have her seat in that car. Peggy would better not show *any* interest. She and I can look out when the train stops."

Valerie, Mrs. Raimund's maid, was so new to the country that she accepted amateur detective work as a normal part of a highly paid lady's maid's duties, and instantly went on guard, while Mrs. Raimund tried to piece her own recollections of *The Sign of the Four* and *A Study in Scarlet* with Peggy's memories of the same and of Gaboriau.

"The main thing is not to rouse his suspicions," said Nelly. "I hope they won't come roaring your telegram through the car when it comes, the way they have."

But the telegram did not come. The time slipped by. Mrs. Raimund and Cecil took dinner at a table behind Tyler. "And, *mon enfant,* he had that bag with him at dinner," said Mrs. Raimund; "he had it in the smoker, too. There isn't a *doubt* in my mind about him. He's a hardened villain; I have no sympathy with him; he actually seemed to *like* the awful things they served us and *ate* the orange-colored butter! He also drank a Martini cocktail and a pint of champagne, and gave the waiter a quarter. His table manners are only *rather* bad. What do you think of me as a sleuth?"

"You're *great,* Mrs. Raimund," laughed Peggy.

"No telegram, yet?"

"None yet."

"Have you seen the conductor?"

"I've had a heart-to-heart talk with him,—he's a most intelligent man."

"Has anything happened since I saw you?"

"No; we are on time, and shan't stop again until we reach South Bend."

Peggy was a particularly truthful person. Nothing really had happened, she would have said, yet she felt much better equipped for adventure than an hour ago. Then she had contemplated Tyler's possibilities with misgiving.

"If he gets wind of anything, he'll jump off at the next stop," she decided dolefully, "and where'll we be if we let him? I don't even know whether that conductor has a gun. I reckon that fat porter has a razor, but the chances are he'd be too scared to use it. *I* ought to have something." "Something" to the Southern girl meant any kind of lethal weapon. It is almost impossible for a Northerner, especially a native of the older and more densely settled sections, to understand the naïve feeling of the Southerner about private bloodshed. He expects to defend his own as naturally as a Northerner expects to be defended by the strong arm of the law. Peggy's father had taught her to shoot a pistol the first year they lived on a plantation. Her prowess with small arms was not only a jest to him; it gave him a continual sense of security in their lonely and isolated life. It was not from parental pride alone, by any means, that he would call his negro tenants and workmen to "watch Miss Peggy shoot the eyes out of the scarecrow."

As for Peggy, she shot wild turkeys, but she would not shoot quail; she said they were too tame, it was like shooting chickens in the hen-house; and once she shot a panther in the sheepfold, thereby lengthening the days of several hound dogs that had been under suspicion of a dog's worst crime. It was characteristic of Peggy that she took the suspects under her protection ever after.

Stories of valor and carnage Peggy had heard at her nurse's knee. One of the vivid memories of her childhood, not all unpleasant, either, in its strong thrill, was of mammy's lifting her over a gutter in Memphis, in the days when they had gutters, before the yellow fever forced sewers upon them; mammy lifted her, and as she felt her little bronze slippers dangling in space, she threw a glance downward.

"Mymy! mymy!" she squeaked, "the gutter's all red!"

"Nev' you min' de red gutter, my lamb, an' doan you look roun'," warned mammy. Of course, Peggy immediately "looked round," to behold two men lying in a queer attitude, all crumpled up on the sidewalk, and then she knew what was the matter with the gutter. "Oh, poor men!" the child cried; "run quick, let's make haste and get papa to make them well!"

But mammy answered sternly:

"No, you leave dem men 'lone; dey ain't no frien' you-alls; dey is evil-doers, an' you' paw'll live de longer kase dey is a layin' dar; you hark to me!"

So Peggy pleaded no more; if the bad men would have hurt papa it were well they should be "killed up"; children are not squeamish.

During her youth, she heard more or less of the violent happenings which are the inevitable result when a high-spirited race has its feudal state rent from it by war and is forced into a new order of

things for which it is not ready. Therefore, in the
present stress, although Peggy was a gentle and
merry creature, her mind flew instinctively to fire-
arms. She owned a beautiful pistol; but it was lying in a perfumed drawer of a dressing-table in her
chamber, at Mrs. Raimund's. She gazed wistfully
around the stuffy luxury of Drawing-room A; but
directly she chuckled. Her eye had fallen upon
Cecil's hat. It went from the hat outside the room,
to Cecil's section and a smart new bag on the seat.
Cecil wouldn't be a normal boy of sixteen, to Southern thinking, if there weren't a revolver inside that
brown alligator skin. But hard on the thought came
the amendment that perhaps Northern boys were
not so fond of fire-arms as those in Tennessee.
"Never mind, he's a *boy,* and he spent a winter in
Arkansas," she comforted herself, and she recalled
how he had insisted on carrying his bag himself.
No sooner did Cecil come back than she made an
excuse to get him into his section, and very sweetly,
as his own chosen chum, she asked for the loan of
the pistol.

"How do you know I have one?" said Cecil.

Peggy laughed.

"Anyhow,"—with a man-of-the-world gravity—
"I couldn't think of lending it to a lady, especially
if she *might* use it."

"Your mother would make an *awful* time, Cis,
if she knew you were carrying a revolver."

"But you wouldn't tell tales. There's nothing
mean about *you.*"

"You see, if your mother *knew,*"—quite disre-
garding this artful speech—"she'd confiscate it, and

give it to me. I'd hate to get it that way. But we *must* have a pistol."

Cecil wriggled. Peggy pathetically set forth the defenseless plight of the conductor. She promised to give the latter the pistol if he needed it. In the end, the lad capitulated and she obtained the pistol.

After this her mind was at rest and she despatched Cecil to take his mother out to dinner.

She took the opportunity, so soon as she had the drawing-room to herself, to examine the cylinders, making sure it was loaded. "Mighty trifling little pistol," sighed Peggy sadly, weighing it on the palm of her hand. "Not even thirty-two caliber, I'm afraid, and short cartridges, too! But what can you expect of a boy! Well, it's better than nothing."

At South Bend, Valerie appeared breathless in her zeal to report: *"Il est parti, madame!"*

But Mrs. Raimund, already at the window, merely said *"Regarde!"* and pointed to the group outside,—Cis and Peggy looking at the car-wheels and the conductor affably conversing with Tyler. "All aboard!" shouted the conductor. Tyler swung himself on to the platform, Peggy and Cis after him; last of all the conductor grasped the shining rail.

"The conductor is all right, mamma," reported Cis, a moment later.

"Then do let us sit down together and be comfortable," said Mrs. Raimund, "and let poor Valerie finish her dinner in peace; she can sit in the car afterward. What is it, porter?"

The porter was chewing an apologetic smile in the door, a yellow envelope between his black fingers.

"Miss Margaret C. Rutherford? Telegram fo' you, miss."

Peggy had the envelope open and the telegram under her eyes before the words left his lips:

"Money gone. Will have man arrested at Toledo. Tell conductor to arrest him if he tries to leave train.

"A. G. RAIMUND."

"I'm sorry, Miss Rutherford," said the porter, "but the despatch jest being addressed to Lake Shore Limited, the other cyar porter got it, and he was going through the cyar hollering 'Telegram fo' Miss Margaret C. Rutherford'; but I stopped him mighty briefly, I asshoo you. The gentleman didn't seem to be payin' no manner of attention."

"Well, he'll be arrested next stop; and he can't get off the train before."

The porter grinned: "He sure can't, miss, that's a fac'!"

"Are we on time?" she asked.

"Well, no, ma'am," he admitted. "We'd a hot box at South Bend; that's why we stayed so long. Los' thirty minutes, and we los' 'bout forty with the engine bein' slow befo'; altogether we are ovah an hour behind; but we'll make it up by the time we git to Cleveland."

"Is there any trouble with the strikers any more on this road?" asked Mrs. Raimund.

"No, ma'am. We been running smooth for 'most a week now."

"I thought so," Mrs. Raimund replied, "but I wanted to be sure. You may shut the windows and leave the ventilators open."

After the porter was gone Peggy summoned the

conductor and showed him the despatch. He somehow inspired her with trust because he was bald-headed and talked about his wife and his little girl. The conductor promised to notify her at Toledo, when the officers came aboard, in order that she might identify the bag.

"But we must keep watching that man," said Mrs. Raimund firmly, when the three were alone. "I've told Valerie on *no account* to go to sleep. The engine might stop to get water or something, you know; they are always stopping when it's not on the folder!"

She continued in this mood of vigilance until she tired of dummy whist, about ten, when she became convinced that the engine had plenty of water and Tyler would not run away, and she advised Peggy to go to her berth. Valerie, also, was relieved from guard duty.

"Only be sure you wake me at Toledo," said Nelly. "It is no use depending on Valerie; she sleeps like the dead; always has to have an alarm clock, and she wouldn't hear one on the train if she had it—which she hasn't!"

Gladly Peggy departed. The porter notified her that Tyler was in the smoker, so that she retreated behind her curtains without being observed, the porter further shifting suspicion by hanging a well-worn derby hat of his own from the large bracket of number seven.

"Only two hours more," sighed Peggy; "that's not long!"

But the time dragged heavily, watching and waiting. Peggy never forgot those hours; in their aloofness from all natural usual experience, they were like the woeful night-hours by sick beds which had been hers. Always her watches were sorrowful, for always in her conflict with death she had been worsted. Pale dramas of past struggle and sorrow enacted themselves again, until she fled from them to the landscape outside her window. It was a moonlight night, and she could see the shadowy stacks of hay in the Michigan fields and the cascades where the reaper had left a shining path. The train shuddered and flinched and seemed to pull on the engine as it slowed. They must be stopping! But coughing and panting, without halting, the engine pulled out from the cavernous spaces amid the blue flashes of electric light, swept past the black hulk of the flaming chimneys of great factories and the scattered lights of sleeping streets, then, screaming as if in sheer rapture of flight, tore out again into the long, dark sweep of the prairies.

To keep her memories at bay Peggy took to song, humming, under the whir of the wheels, all the old-time songs which her mother had loved to hear her sing. She wished, how she wished, that her mother had lived to use the old piano after it had been tuned! Peggy had to save so long before they could hire a man to come from Memphis to tune it, but Mrs. Rutherford never came back to rock gently on the creaking floor of the wide old veranda, where the Japanese honeysuckle swayed its dim silhouettes over the cypress boards; and the cotton-fields stretched, green in the moonlight, far away, up to the wall of gum-trees and the black mysteries of the bayou.

> " 'Those dear old days are past and gone,
>   I sigh for them in vain;
>   I want to see the cotton-fields
>   And the dear old home again!' "

sang the Southern girl with the tears on her cheeks, and checked herself in a sob.

"That's worse than studying," cried Peggy; she burst into a popular jingle, heard, those days, on every street-organ:

> " 'Comrades, comrades, ever since we were boys,
>   Sharing each other's sorrows, sharing each other's joys.' "

"That's like Johnny and me," giggled Peggy; "he was a boy and I was a tomboy."

For a little she was silent, then she found herself fitting an air to a poem not so well-known ten years ago as now. She sang it, softly, while the moon rode high in a wonderful cloudland of sky:

> " 'Love blows as the wind blows—
>   In the crowded mart
>   As the quiet close.
>   By ways that no man knows,
>   Love blows into the heart!' "

The night wore on. Still she sang; and still the train beat its even, tremendous rhythm of speed. And still the moonlight flooded the earth, which was no longer the work-stained scene of sorrow and struggle and greed which the sun found every morning, but a new world, such as love alone can create,—mystic, wonderful.

Lost in reveries of music, deep as sleep, Peggy

awoke with a start and a jar through all her nerves. The car trembled under the vast purr of the engine; they had stopped. Yet outside was nothing but a few cottages crouching on the ground like black ants, and the moonlight flooding a wide, level landscape. She went on sentry duty, instantly. Tyler's curtains never moved, but a brakeman bustled through the shrouded aisle, swinging his red lantern. Him the porter encountered, and their colloquy was audible: "Why we stopping? To water?"

"That's right."

"How long behind are we?"

"Oh, hour'n half, mebbe hour and three quarters."

A hand, only a hand, came out of the curtains which Peggy watched. The fingers unbuttoned a flap. Next the curtains bulged. Finally they parted, letting Tyler step forth. He was completely dressed, his hat on his head, and he was carrying his heavy bag.

For the merest second he hesitated, peering to right and left, before he briskly walked after the brakeman.

Peggy slipped out of her section. She reached the vestibule just as Tyler jumped off the steps. Almost at the same moment the conductor appeared out of the other car. He sprang after the man with the bag.

"We've only stopped to water," he called; "look out for the engine!"

True enough, another engine was drawn up to the huge dripping red tank on the parallel rails and its headlight shed a luminous stream around its black nozzle. In the disk of light, Tyler's figure showed plainly. He did not turn his head; but he began to walk faster. His evident intention was to get behind the engine of the freight train, where were some sheds.

"Arrest him!" cried Peggy.

The conductor ran; he called on Tyler in the name of the law to halt. He caught one flap of his coat, but Tyler wrenched it away and broke loose, running at right angles. Instantly Peggy fired. She aimed at his leg. He fell, dropping the bag, but was up almost instantly. He snatched at the bag, but could not reach it, for the conductor was on him again; but all the railway man got was a blinding blow between the eyes from his quarry, who had whirled in a flash, struck, and darted across the track. The conductor righted himself on his feet; but he did not pursue, for the freight engine was moving. He saw Peggy standing by the bag. She had leaped from the car steps and run to it. She lifted it with an effort, and came toward him, stumbling a little as she walked.

"Did he hurt you?" cried Peggy; "he was right in line with you, and I didn't dare shoot again. When you got out of range I couldn't see him. I reckon he'll tumble down, anyhow; I know I hit him in the leg. *Did* he hurt you?"

"Not worth mentioning. Just as well you didn't fire again," responded the conductor philosophically, "so long's you got the loot. Is it all right?"

"It *feels* all right," said Peggy, extending the russia-leather bag.

"Thunder!" exclaimed the worthy man, surprised

out of his manners; "why, it weighs a ton! It's locked all right."

"No, only a spring catch. I know it. This way." She suited the action to the word, and opened the bag a narrow chink, wide enough for the conductor to give a single glance ere he shut it with a snap, muttering: "Best not let anybody see that again, Miss Rutherford. I'll carry it in for you. You folks best take charge of it; you know where it belongs. I'll have to report this at the end of my run, and I guess Mr. Raimund will explain to the police." He bent his head and lowered his voice. "Chuck full!" muttered he; *"gold!* No, nothing's the matter, Dan,"—to the engineer, who had clambered down and was running up to him—"just a thief tried to sneak off with this lady's bag. Had to fire a pistol to make him drop it. No, nothing wrong; no strike,"—this to two dark heads protruding like anaglyphs from the side of the car—"just a thief. Good Lord! here's a fresh batch of 'em!"—as two porters and a passenger panted into earshot—"yes, you did hear a pistol; but it wasn't of any consequence. A thief; fired to scare him; he'd stolen a lady's bag. No, Peter, I don't need your pop or your razor, and it is against the rules for you to carry a pop,"—he was now addressing Peggy's friendly porter, who straggled up, last of all, armed to the teeth, but less sanguinary of aspect than of equipment; for he was wearing a demoralized grin. "Hullo, Mr. Raimund; you're too late for the excitement; but you can take the victor back to the car. I'll carry the spoils."

Cecil looked deeply aggrieved; he explained that

he had kept awake for hours, and then merely dropped off for a minute, and nobody waked him.

"Never mind, honey," laughed Peggy, "you are the one that really did it and saved the bag, for it was your pistol hit him. Come on in!"

Her eyes were like stars, her face glowed even in the moonlight. Every man in the group had a sudden sense of her beauty, and at the same time of her own unconsciousness of it; the bald-headed conductor smiled upon her with a kind of fatherly pride, while Cis caught his breath and whispered: "Peggy, you've got sand to burn!"

But Peggy noticed nothing; she had saved Johnny's money; she would win Johnny away from his ruinous dreams; on the whole, she was glad that she had not hurt Tyler much; she did not want to hurt anybody in the world. Away, far down the horizon, she saw the western train, a wavering, jointed worm of fire, crawl through the darkling fields: she had never been so happy in her life!

CHAPTER VI

THE PRINCESS OLGA'S DAY

A tall young workingman stood in the Raimund vestibule. His sack-coat was buttoned over his blue flannel shirt and his heavy boots were varnished. Carstairs, the second man, opened the door. "Other door,"—he began in languidly haughty tones, viewing the smiling artisan under his eyelids; but at the second glance he started palpably, a thing which he had not been known to do during his five years of office at Mrs. Raimund's. "Mr. Winslow! I beg pardon, sir," he gasped.

Johnny smiled the grim sort of smile which recognizes rather than relishes the humor of a situation.

"I've got a job, Carstairs," said he.

"And I'm no glad to hear it, sir, if you'll pardon me saying so, sir," said Carstairs.

Johnny laughed. "Jobs are good things, Carstairs. I hope I'll do mine as well as you do yours. Are the ladies in?"

"Mrs. Winslow is out, sir; but Miss Rutherford is in, sir."

"Tell her I am here, please."

Johnny's hand stole to his pocket, fell on the monition of his conscience, then defiantly went back, and he slipped a coin into the Scotchman's hand.

As Carstairs departed he wagged his head. "I doubt he's no blate," commented Carstairs in his own tongue, "but he's an awfu' gran' lad!"

Johnny sat down in the reception-room and looked about him. The familiar splendor of the noble hall, the vista of beautiful and stately rooms came to him as if to a stranger, as if he were the mechanic to whom his boots belonged. His eyes strayed from the soft tracery of the lace curtains to the rich hues of stained glass in the great stair-window, and the duller but equally rich dyes of the marvelous rugs woven centuries ago by a patient skill that triumphed over time. In the mood of a stranger he felt their taste, but more their luxury. The shifting sea-green of the heavy silk, with which the walls of the little salon were hung, was broken by exquisite old French etchings in frames that looked like carved ivory, etchings of the same date as the curiously inlaid table and cabinet and formal chairs, or the faintly tinted tapestries half hiding the doorway. The whole room exhaled the atmosphere of an alien pomp, the delicate arrogance of a vanished generation of aristocrats who had died for their pride, and died smiling. Beyond was a court, with palms and hydrangeas and luxuriant vines framing the white serene beauty of the fountain, a charming court in perfect harmony of detail, but as alien as the charming room.

Johnny smiled. "Yes, I'm outside," he said, "clean outside. And I'm afraid I don't like it."

"Miss Rutherford says, would you kindly walk up stairs to Mrs. Raimund's parlor?" announced Carstairs.

Meanwhile Peggy, in Mrs. Raimund's parlor, had risen from the davenport and was standing. Thus she awaited Johnny. She was beautiful in her simple white gown, which, nevertheless, had been adjusted in every fold, and immaculately fresh ribbons added to its pleasantness. The faint shadows under the oval of her cheek rounded her rose-white throat, and her cheek flushed and faded with her thoughts.

Johnny's eyes grew darker; he wished he were free to kneel at her feet.

But she was thinking that there never was a knightlier young man than he. And with an indescribable glow of pride she, who was older two years by the sun and ten by her knowledge of the world, compared his stainless life with that of most of the gilded youth that she had known. Her heart overflowed with a half-maternal affection, dating back so many years. She felt for him the love of his mother or his sister, so she told herself. He smiled up at her. The wind had ruffled the shallow waves of hair on his shapely black head; his olive cheek was as smooth as a woman's—had he not spent an hour shaving himself! Indeed, never in his days of luxury had he taken such thought and pains with a toilet.

"Well, Peggy," said he, "accept my congratulations and a tremendous scolding for being so reckless! You'll shorten my life, scaring me so! And so you actually shot Tyler, you little fire-eater! Oh, Peggy, it was horribly reckless; he might have shot you, dear!"

"He was too busy running," laughed Peggy. "*I* did the shooting; but it was just a toy pistol, you understand, and he only stumbled and got up again. Boys don't know anything about pistols."

"I know the kind. They say out West, 'If you ever shoot me with that popgun—*and I find it out,* you'll get hurt!'"

"Yes, just that kind. But do sit down, Jo'nivan!"

She seated herself on the davenport and let Johnny get on one knee and kiss her hand, with a jest. Johnny looked very nice in that attitude. But when he rose he sat an unnecessary distance away, and of a sudden he had grown very pale.

"Who told you?" said Peggy, returning to the important subject. It was extremely entertaining to have Johnny in such a proper frame of mind.

"Billy Bates. He got the story from Mrs. Winslow. Billy is pretty sore," said Johnny dryly; "I can't help enjoying it a bit, for Billy always pulls things off, you know, and he had Tyler's passing so beautifully planned out: Rescue of the Lamb by William Bates and Mrs. Winslow. Tyler sent to the pen, and me weeping tears of gratitude on both their noble shoulders! Then Tyler was too slick for him. But Billy's a real sport and he's wild over *you!*"

"How was Tyler too slick? You tell me your story, and I'll tell you mine. This is cozy and comfy, —like old times, isn't it?"

Now, why should a kind of shadow fall over Jo'nivan's face? Perhaps it was her fancy, for immediately he chuckled.

"Why, it was this way," said he; "Billy found out that Tyler knew I had the money in my room, early in the morning. He had seen Tyler buying a money-belt at a pawnshop the day before, and also a mustache at a costumer's, or barber's, or somewhere, and Billy suspected him at once, for he has locked horns with Wally before; I am afraid he was right about his not being square, now; I'll own up and tell you that I didn't exactly like some things about him, myself; yet he stood by me so stanchly in some rackets I had that I wouldn't believe the stories; and, to show my confidence in a friend, I was a fool and told him about that money. Well, he was the main one, I see now, who induced me to get cash. It was a plot from the first, and he didn't expect I would give away that twenty-five thousand, not he; he meant to nab the whole.

"But to get back to Billy. He was confident Tyler had stolen the money or would steal it that day. So he set a man to shadow him. But Tyler got on to the shadow game. I figure that he got it out of the room that morning while I was with you. It was easy enough for him to get into my room, pretending I had given him the wrong key and he was to fetch me something. He had a horse and buggy waiting; and he had an appointment with me to go to half a dozen places, about the strike, all over the city. I say, Peggy, he had his nerve with him, all right. He drove around all day with that bag in the buggy under the seat! I got on the wrong side once and hit something with my feet—must have been *it!* And Billy's poor sleuth was roasting and frying, running after us. Why, once, we met Billy himself (in a cab), and I told him Tyler and I were just going out to Pullman. That was almost five o'clock.

Billy naturally concluded Wally had put off swiping the money until night. He made beautiful preparations for passing the night at Wulf's, in the room next to mine. Then, about ten minutes after, Tyler stopped at a saloon to telephone to his sister, who was ill. He wanted me to get out and take a schooner with him; but I didn't feel a thirst, so I stayed and held the horse and guarded that bag without knowing, while he stepped inside. Hadn't he his nerve with him! He did send out the barkeep, though, to ask me some questions."

"Why did he go in?" said Peggy.

"To get his excuse. Don't you see? Sister was worse; he'd have to go straight over to the West Side. He got me on the street-cars like a little lamb, and then *he* sprinted over to the Rock Island depot, picked up somebody to drive his buggy back to the stable and just had time himself to change his hair and his mustache in the depot, and hop on the limited."

"Then *that* was how he risked taking that bag?" said Peggy thoughtfully; "it puzzled us a little."

"He *had* to take it. He hadn't time to make a change. I suppose he meant to change his clothes, too, but there wasn't time."

"How did the money happen to be in gold? That hampered him, too."

"Why, that was—well, it was what you call my theatrical streak, I suppose. There is a lot of rot talked nowadays among workingmen about the demonetization of silver, and I'm an out-and-out gold man; so I'd a fancy to give the boys gold. Pure nonsense, you know, but it turned out to be lucky nonsense, for Tyler might have got off if he could have wadded his money-belt with paper—"

"Oh, Johnny, I meant to tell you—there's an awful oversight—"

"That I'm a thousand or two shy? Yes, I couldn't get it all gold. I dare say he stowed away the long green the first thing. But there were a couple of thousand he missed; I didn't put them in the bag. I hope, Peggy, you remembered the train boys."

"Yes, Mrs. Raimund said she would if you wouldn't. I hope you won't think we were too lavish. We gave the conductor a hundred; he got such a lump on his forehead where Tyler hit him, and he was such a nice man with a large family, and he wants to send his daughter to Smith College—"

"That's all right. Thank you so much, Peggy. And the porter?"

"Oh, we gave him twenty; he wasn't very efficient, but he was watching—then you don't really mind so much, Jo'nivan? I was afraid he might have taken more. And there is a 'very tidy stake left'; Mr. Raimund says. You can make a lot more out of it—"

Johnny shook his head. "I shan't be in a very money-making business," said he; "but no, I don't mind, perhaps, as much as I ought, for the poor fellows needed every cent of the—"

"Johnny!" Peggy almost screamed; "do you mean—oh, you *can't* mean that you have had this warning and then this escape, and *now* you will go on, the same—Jo'nivan, it isn't fair to me! Do you reckon I would have risked my life for the Railway Union and those murdering lunatics that stoned women and little babies? I'd rather Tyler got every last cent of it! I would *so!* You've no *right* to give the money that I've fought and bled for,"—her voice broke in a hysterical little laugh—"you've no right to give it away!"

"I've no right to keep it," said Johnny.

"You never did give it over to that horrid lot—"

"I promised it; it truly isn't mine."

"And do you mean that after you have found out how cruel and selfish these demagogues can be, after you've seen for yourself that they are just as hard and grasping as the capitalists, and dishonest to boot—do you mean that you are not willing to please the friends who have helped you in your trouble and who care for you more than anybody else, you are not willing to wait and think things over and see for yourself whether these dangerous experiments are going to help? Jo'nivan, I never did ask you anything on earth; but I ask you, now, one thing, only *one* thing—wait six months, only six months; then, if you feel that your honor and your conscience demand you should throw away such great opportunities and break all our hearts, I promise you, on my honor, I will not say a word to dissuade you. Won't you, *dear* Jo'nivan?"

"The strike would be lost in six months, Peggy; and—don't you see, dear, I have promised the money? I have to give it. Besides, I ought to give it. Tyler's being a rogue isn't the fault of the Railway Union. He was stealing their money, not mine, really."

"Do you still cling to those anarchists?"—Peggy caught his words away, with a stamp of her foot—

"and is that why you are wearing those ridiculous clothes? You have carried out the threats you made me, have you? You have thrown in your lot with the proletariat; you want to level us all; and your money will go to help cut our throats and burn our houses——"

"Peggy, if you would just be calm, be reasonable——"

"I *am* calm," declared Peggy, whose eyes were flashing and cheeks burning, while Johnny looked paler every moment, "and I say to you, now, Jo'nivan, that if you refuse the first and only favor I ever did ask of you,—I will never speak to you again, to —*save—your—life!*"

"Is Miss Rutherford in Mrs. Raimund's parlor?" The two excited young creatures heard Mrs. Winslow's voice; the tones were particularly clear; it was almost as if the speaker gave warning of her approach. Johnny sprang to his feet.

"I have to go," he cried. His voice was unsteady; he had lost his temper a little, too. "I was wrong to expect you to understand. But I will do the only thing I can to show my gratitude. I will never trouble you again."

"We're in here, Aunt Emma," called Peggy sweetly, but she curled her lip for Johnny's benefit.

Johnny shut his teeth and darted out of the room; the red russia-leather bag lay on the sofa; he would have left it in his haste had not his foot caught on a rug which slid on the slippery floor under the impetus of his plunge, and in his effort to save himself he touched the sofa, and thus perceived the bag.

He picked it up as his stepmother entered. He greeted her with an effort at composure and the gratitude which he had determined to have.

"I must go," he said, "although I have not half thanked Peggy for what she has done for me. Thank you, too, for your efforts. I feel glad that my father's estate will be in such honorable and careful hands. It is as he would have wished. Good-by."

"I understand," said Mrs. Winslow; *"please* stay, Johnny!"

But Johnny went. He held his head very stiffly and did not turn back once, nor hesitate a second, until he was in the hall below. There he paused; he cast a defiant glance at the mocking beauty of the *Louis Seize* room and the court. "This suits her better, I dare say," said he, and his heart was hot and bitter within him; but as his eye ran over his own image in a mirror, from his rough clothing to the bag in his hand with its faded and battered elegance, something rose in his throat. He kissed the broken initials.

"Oh, *mamasa, mamasa!*" he murmured, unconsciously reverting to the speech of his childhood and his first passionate love, "I've done my best to keep my promise. If you only could come back a *little* while!"

Book III

JOHN

CHAPTER I

PEAU DE CHAGRIN

In the late autumn of the year 1895 John Winslow stood in the grim little Kensington street which fronted a winter-stung prairie, looking across its dreary acres, at the spirals of smoke curdling in the sky above the factories of Pullman. The street was in its winter disarray, the more unkempt for the many windows gaping like blind eyes before empty shops, and the litter of rubbish on the sidewalks. The low wooden or brick buildings looked dwarfish beside the broad roadway. There was the dinginess of soft coal smoke about the paint, about the glass, about the whole town. Bare trees and skeleton shrubs could mask sordidness no longer, with the transient gaiety of growing foliage. The place had the battered and slinking mien of a drunkard on the morning after.

From one of the vacant shops a footpath stretched a line of yellow-brown through a hatching of withered herbage. How many dragging feet had traced, by infinite, weary pounding, that clear line! Johnny, sadly and bitterly following its oblique course, beheld again the procession of ill-clad, tired men with their flour sacks, which had moved over it a year ago. The load in the sack dwindled every day; but the heavy-hearted men trod the path steadily, through the pitiless heat of that rainless summer, until the empty counter met their empty hands and the curt scrawl in the window warned them away.

Remembering the summer, Johnny's face darkened. It was a thinner and more haggard face than when Peggy flung her parting flash of petulance at it. He was dressed in a dark suit which was a little shabby, although tidily brushed and pressed. (Johnny had pressed it himself.) At his elbow stood Billy Bates, cheerful of countenance, but much chastened in toilet since he had become Johnny's friend. With more or less writhings of soul he had relinquished divers snowdrift grays and vigorous effects in plaids, as well as a diamond scarf-pin and the general morning wear of a tall silk hat. He did not yet know that he might wear his tile on Sundays at any hour; wherefore his freckles were shielded with a plain black derby, and a crimson neck-scarf flaunted the only bit of gay color about him.

Billy continued the subject that had occupied them.

"Well, I don't believe we are going to be able to flag Bloker this bright, beautiful Sunday morning, as the story-books say."

"How was he off when you heard last?"

"Bad enough. He stuck it out at Pullman to the last ditch, run errands and was cat's-paw for the slicker fellows, who saved something out of the wreck. You know his wife died?"

"I don't know anything but the fact; how was it?"

"Pneumonia. And the daughter killed herself—"

"What?" cried Johnny. "I knew she was dead, but not—not—"

"Well, she fell into melancholy, and one night when he was off she turned on the gas. She meant to kill the children, too, but they pulled through. They offered to take 'em to an asylum, but he skipped out with them. I wanted to dig up a fiver for him, myself; but I couldn't find him. Some men are so damned unlucky. Now, you wouldn't believe it, but that fellow opposed the strike—"

"I know he wanted to give in, at one time. That's why I'm after him now." Johnny rammed his hands in his pockets and took a turn to warm himself.

"Why didn't you wear your overcoat?" grumbled Billy.

Johnny laughed, while a faint red crept up under the pale olive of his cheek.

"Say! you ain't—?"

"No, I haven't sent it to Poco. This weather isn't cold enough for coats!"

"Did you give it away?" demanded Billy, in the stern tones of a physician dragging out a patient's misdemeanors in diet.

Johnny laughed peevishly. "Let my clothes alone, Billy! When was it—"

"You tell me about that good overcoat, first. Have you got it now? No? I can see you ain't. All right. I tell you one thing straight from the shoulder; Ivan, you ain't fit to live in a city!"

"Well, if you will have it,"—Johnny's inextinguishable sweetness of disposition had asserted itself and he smiled as he laid a hand on Billy's shoulder; thereat Billy grunted—"it was this way.

You remember when the boys got so discouraged just before I plunked all my little pile into the hole?"

"You made more than you intended happy by that virtuous but driveling act," observed Billy, pulling out his cigar-case. "Have one? Now,"—as Johnny shook his head—"now, there you are again, carrying economy to a vicious extent; *you* ain't paying for those cigars!"

"I know, but I'd be pampering an extravagant taste, and maybe should want them when I couldn't have them, smoking them; a pipe'll do me. But I was going to tell you; when I made that speech at the meeting out there—"

"I remember. Hell! that was a jimdandy! I knew it was playing against a cold deck and the boys would have to take their medicine, and the quicker the better; but when I heard you talking I felt like a quitter; I was mad at myself for having good judgment. Ivan, I've heard a damned sight of slick talkers, but I never heard a feller that pulled you up by the roots like you did that night! It wasn't the money you were giving, either,—that only proved you meant what you said. It was *you*. Why, the men next me were crying out loud! And next minute they were laughing! They'd have followed you straight to hell that night if you'd asked them!"

"They did!" answered Johnny gloomily. "Poor Bloker for one, anyhow. He came to me after the meeting, his face quivering and his hair standing up different ways all over his head—"

"Red hair," explained Billy; "maybe that made him so emotional. He was awfully easy worked, too. Anybody down on his luck could get Bloker's last quarter. You've *got* to be a little hard-hearted in this world!"

"He said that he had about made up his mind to give in and advise the others to give in. It was no use; the odds were too big, but now, said he, you've put the sand in me, I'm game to fight to a finish! He did, too; and now I know what it cost him. Billy, it's an awful shame; but there were so many fellows clapping me on the back and hugging me that night; and I had been feeling like a limp rag, wondering whether I hadn't made a blooming idiot of myself letting myself go the way I did, and when I found out they didn't think so, I suppose it went to my head, and I didn't notice things. Bloker was just one of the crowd to me, and he slipped out of my mind. Yet he was giving up more than I, for he was sacrificing his wife and children—"

"Which he hadn't no manner of right to do," Billy amended through a puff of smoke; "there's reason in all things."

"I led him on to do it. But for me he would have given in and gone to work; he'd never have lost his wife, or she'd have died in comfort; and the girl would never have worried herself crazy. Billy, I saw their house once. It was such a pitifully neat, comfortable little parlor, and that poor girl was singing at the little melodeon; they hadn't begun to sell the things off bit by bit—oh, damn *me!* And I didn't even keep him in my mind; I missed him and forgot all about him until I almost ran into him on the street last Thursday. He gave me one look and ran as if I were a policeman. He was thin, he was ragged, his eyes made me sick—"

"You didn't catch him?" asked Billy.

"No; if I'd had more'n my nickel for the cars and hadn't got to get to my job too quick to run it, I'd have chased him; but I hadn't had him in mind, and it was so sudden, he was off before I really got on to the situation. But I asked some of the boys, and they told me what they had heard; and—well, I was low in cash and that's where the coat went. I sold it to an opulent rooster, who only gets one-fifty, but has got it all summer and a cinch on it all winter."

"And you are hunting up Bloker to squander it on? Well, we'll come to that later. Just now I want to find out why you're damning yourself."

"I've ruined him; I've broken up his home; I've killed his wife, driven his daughter crazy—"

"Don't get excited! Say, what sort of nights do you expect big generals and kings would have if they got to thinking what happens to the soldiers? You gave up everything you had; you know you did; you're a gentleman, and you left your crowd and your relations and—and everybody. If he gave up his wife, you gave up *having* a wife; you say, yourself, you hold a man with your opinions ain't got the right to ask a girl to marry him. You worked like a dog. Damn it, you're no more'n skin and bone yourself! You were perfectly honest, and you didn't ask no more'n you were willing to give! I'm sorry for Bloker. I'm sorry for all the Pullman chaps, but I say he hasn't got the right to reproach you, nor you haven't got any reasonable reason to reproach yourself."

Johnny kicked a tin can off the sidewalk, scowling. "I've gone over all that, Billy. In the first place, while I went in, I thought unselfishly to help the fellows who didn't have a chance; it wasn't *all* to help them; it was a good deal because long ago I promised. Then, I wasn't going to be coerced by my father's will. I resented it, and I resented having my stepmother have the control of things, and I wanted to be a leader and show the people who were sneering at me what I could do—oh, my motives were mixed—"

"Lord, ain't they always! It's healthier and more natural they should be. Don't you know you can't work pure gold? it's too soft!"

"In the second place, no man has a right to urge other men into a fight that may ruin them without having a reasonable assurance he is going to win. A strike is a devilish thing. It was my business to be sure it was a righteous strike in the first place, and that there was a good chance of its winning in the second. I didn't do either. I jumped in over my head without knowing how I'd get out. In short, I've been a damn fool and a damn scoundrel."

He kicked another tin, this time a sardine box. "Don't you think we'd better be heading for the city? There'll be a lot of our fellows hanging around the committee meeting, and though they've taken mighty good care not to put me on the committee, I may get at the men all the same and head off Tyler. Maybe I'll get a chance at Bloker at the factory. I was told at his house that the shops were doing a little repair work to-day, and he was at it. So I think I'll try there—after the meeting."

"I don't *think*," mused Billy,—they had turned

and were walking toward the station,—"you'll git them to call off the strike at Wethers'."

"What's going to be the trouble,—Tyler?"

"Tyler," pronounced Billy, puffing at his cigar.

"And what's his little game?"

"After the dough, of course. *As* usual. I have it pretty straight that he's dickering with the old man, to settle. But they haven't come to his figure. Till they do, he'll be hot for holding on, at least a while longer. Besides, it makes him safer if there's any talk. No, you won't get the strike called off before the last of the week."

"That will mean bloodshed; the boys are getting desperate about the new men. Billy, what are *you* here for?"

"Me? Oh, they want a sympathetic strike of the molders in Fairport at the Old Colony; that's in my district now. They've a contract to make Wethers' patterns, and they are naturally doing it. Some of your crowd want them called out."

"Shall you let them go?"

"I shan't. I am down on monkeying with contracts. I'm not altogether particular about keeping the commandments; but I'll keep my word if it busts me. It's kind of maddening, though, to be playing Tyler's game, for he'll lay the strike failing on to me, see if he won't, while he'll work to call it off the minute he gets his price. Oh, he's a slick assassin! Wouldn't it kill you dead, though, to see that infernal plundering thief toddling back and bossing the very fellers he stole from!"

"He knows our mouths are shut," said Johnny between his teeth.

"They are that," said Billy. "I didn't understand at first, but"—he flushed over his high cheekbones—"I guess you've made me enough of a gentleman now, Ivan, to understand that we can't drag a lady's name into our fights. Oh, he got a good bargain. Fifteen hundred for a game leg for a month!"

Johnny laid his arm affectionately on the other's shoulder. "You *are* a gentleman, Billy. And I can't claim any credit. If I could it would only be a fair deal, for if I have made a gentleman of you, I hope you'll succeed in making a man of me."

"You're one already. Take away the taffy! But I tell you, Ivan, if I am not a gentleman, now, before God, I will be some day. We've had them in the family; I've heard mother tell of them. But I'll tell you, Ivan, you've done a thundering lot to help me. I used to think the whole business was a skin game; rich folks on one side, poor folks on the other. The rich trying to skin the poor, and the poor getting the knife in deep whenever *they* got a show. Any slick trick was good enough so long's it was real slick! If you were a mighty decent feller (as I meant to be), you played fair with your own gang, but the more you could fool the other side the better! But since I have known you I have come to see that there are things you can't talk about that count more than tin. You *can't* cheat the other side. You've got to keep your word if you give it to a Chink! It's *your* word just the same, no matter who gets it, or what they do with it."

"That's being a gentleman, Billy," said Johnny.

"Well, besides,"—Billy was so full of his theme he did not notice Johnny's growing abstraction—"besides, it has been beaten into my head that there are lots of things the biggest union or the biggest king, either, can't do! Like this: if you've got a little corn crop, as we had last year, nobody can make it into a big one. All the strongest union could do would be to get a fair share. But the biggest share of a small crop mightn't be as big as a small share of a big crop. So I say this question of bullying folks into giving big wages has got its limits. The size of your share don't cut any figure if you've only got an empty basket to divide! The unions are a good deal like a lawyer. If you've got anything coming to you, he'll see you ain't beat out of it. But he didn't make it for you. All the same, lawyers are necessary; and so are unions. Your boss, Wethers, for instance, always cuts wages a *little* in winter after the men get settled, always snooping about to see how much the fastest men can do in a day; and then cuts the piece rate on that basis. And he's making a fortune while decent men have hard sledding to keep from failing. Well, I guess he's lost money by this strike. I hope so. Pretty mussy world, ain't it, Johnny—I mean Ivan."

"Yes," said Johnny, knitting his brows; "but I guess Wethers and all of us have to pay for our diversions. Billy, do you know what I was thinking about just now? Not in relation to Wethers, though he will have to pay his lawing, too, in one way or another. But about myself."

"Ask me something easier," said Billy.

"Well, I found myself thinking of one of Balzac's

novels that I had read in my French course in Harvard—"

"Never heard of him,"—Billy was puffing hard on a nearly extinguished cigar—"you never told me of any of the French duffers, except Hugo and Corneille and Molly something and—what's his name? sounds like troches-for-a-cold."

"De la Rochefoucauld? Balzac was different; he wrote novels. This one my professor called his 'most splendid' novel. I didn't think so much of it —then. It is the story of a tremendously ambitious young man who is on the point of suicide when he falls into possession of a piece of wild ass's skin, a magical charm, which is—well, you remember Aladdin's lamp?"

"Yes, saw a play of it once. Play wasn't much, but the ballet was out of sight. I expect the Skin gave the Frenchman whatever he wanted, didn't it?"

"Yes, but with a difference. Raphael—that was the sweep's name, and a full-blooded sweep he was, too, with no sand in him—Raphael can get anything he wishes from the Skin; but with every granted wish the Skin shrinks. When it is all gone—that's the end of him. So he gets fame and wealth and love—and dies horribly, in a little while."

"Why didn't he stop wishing?"

"He did try; but he couldn't stop. None of us can. He was a selfish cur, and I didn't in the least sympathize with him. Neither did I especially take in the allegory. But I do now. You see, the greater the wish, the more the Skin shrank. And it is the same with us all. The bigger the thing we try to do, and the more intense our own feeling, the more we have to pay. I tried to help turn the world upside down. It was too big for me; but I am paying now, and it's a big price!"

"Look here, Ivan, you are getting daffy."

"If one could undo anything! But one never can—"

"Well, you and I, together, can do considerable to help Bloker. One thing, let's get a good square meal inside him before to-night." Johnny brightened. He began to discuss ways and means of help with Billy. It was a pity the poor chap hadn't waited. But Billy would persuade him to give up scabbing for Wethers. They would get him a job. All the way into the city Johnny was making plans; he did not look up once at the white towers and golden dome of the West's dream of beauty as the train passed them. They were growing a bit discolored and shabby now, and there were piteous charred gaps where graceless tramps had destroyed their shelter, either through carelessness or wanton brutality. But still unconquered, that stately and lavish architecture held its wonderful sky-line against the pale November sky. Billy felt a thrill and drew a long breath of approbation over his own delight.

"I'm coming on," sighed Billy. "Great Scott! I can remember when I thought a mansard roof was stylish. I'm a long way from those days."

He wanted to talk about the trips Johnny and he had taken to the Exposition together, but after a single eye-blink at his friend's moody profile he shook his head. "He'll have to have it out with

himself," said Billy.   "Well, he's got to, and I can't
help him.   Damn it!"

He looked at Johnny with that admixture of worship and familiar, protecting affection which is
about as unstained an emotion as our weak and
complex human nature allows.   Johnny, to him,
was not only the most beautiful and noble gentleman in the world and a leader by divine right; he
was the creature who needed him, Billy Bates, the
most, as well as the one who helped him the most.
His own elation of mood vanished in a compassion
so keen that it irritated him.

"Suffering!   Suffering like hell, all the time," he
raged inwardly, "and he's *got* to.   He's got to find
out we ain't a bit more saints than his own sort.
We're all cut out of the same piece, pants and coat.
The under-dog would chaw the top one's throat if
he could; 'tain't a sweet disposition's got him
under!"

So, unmolested, Johnny sat, his head on his
breast; nor did he speak once until the magic of art
was displaced, first by the commonplace comfort of
the better-class residence section, and then by the
grimy ugliness of the work-a-day part of the down-
town streets.

He followed Billy passively out of the train and
down the stairs of the station platform, but turned
sharply on the last step, with a low-spoken but
staccato query: "You don't suppose Tyler would
get the meeting put ahead half an hour so's to down
me before I got there?"

"What's that?" said Billy sharply.

"He told me it would be at eleven-thirty at

Einert's place," Johnny explained. "Did you get
any word?"

"I only came this morning, unexpected and un-
welcome, I guess. I go anywhere, you know. I
took your word for the time. But Tyler is up to all
sorts of dirty dodges."

They discovered that their suspicions did Tyler
no injustice when they reached the room above the
saloon where the meeting of the committee was to
take place. A crowd of men waited outside in the
undetermined hope of some news which always ani-
mates strikers.

Johnny fancied that in spite of their truculent talk
they were secretly hoping for a recommendation of
peace. With a throb of admiration, Billy noted the
instant change in Johnny's own bearing. He was
smiling, cheerful, friendly.

"Do you get on to one thing, Ivan?" Billy whispered, as they neared the door of a closed room on
the third story; "the fellers here are the peaceful
crowd, mostly married men. The tough guys have
got their tip and are off raising hell somewhere. I
wish I knew where."

By this they were in the hall amid a crowd, staring at a closed door which opened immediately.
There came out a stout man with bright blue eyes
and a head cropped so closely that it was a soft
mouse-color and wrinkled in the back.

"Hullo, Bates, you come to help us out?" cried
the man, a business agent for the molders' local to
which Wethers' men belonged, a good-natured,
shrewd fellow, who did his best to steer his own
craft in troublous waters. His name was Conrad;

he was of American birth but German parentage. He looked rather suspiciously from Billy to Johnny.

Billy greeted Conrad cordially, but the next man who came out he addressed formally as "Mr. Tyler." "Well, what have you decided, Mr. Tyler?" said he.

"Oh, the strike's on, all right," replied Tyler, striking a match on the sole of his shoe in order to light his cigar. The shoes were varnished, his clothes were new, his linen shone; he looked sleek and prosperous; Johnny thought of Bloker, shabby and disheartened, risking his bones that moment in some striker's place, that he might earn a few dollars.

"The boys will be disappointed, won't they?" said Billy mildly.

"I think they will," said Conrad.

"They've got the remedy in their own hands if they want to surrender," Tyler observed carelessly; "I'm not a quitter myself,"—and Billy, close to Johnny, gave him an imperceptible nudge to call his attention to this preparation for the future on the labor diplomat's part.

"Unless it's worth your while," sneered Johnny—which Billy justly assured him afterward was rank folly; but he was angry past weighing his words, just then.

Tyler seemed as if he had not heard the words; his features were behind a cloud of smoke; he only puffed a degree harder on his cigar.

"You didn't even make them a proposition?" asked Johnny of Conrad, who merely shook his head.

"Course not; they'd know we was weakening"—this came from a big, black-browed admirer of Tyler's. His name was Reilly; he was the president of the blacksmiths' local; he was personally honest, but of a sensitive and pugnacious vanity. Before Johnny found his measure, he had made fun of a pet scheme of Reilly's, thereby earning his ill-will. "We've found out they've got a new contract, and they *want* to run."

"Not enough to keep wages fifteen per cent. higher than they need," said Johnny; "besides, they've got some men now."

"Scabs," sneered Reilly, "and some of the old bunks and the apprentices."

"They'll have protection, whatever they are; and the public will stand by the cops," retorted Johnny. "The company will win this strike, and our only chance of getting our men their jobs is to let them come back now. I believe if you propose to call the strike off and let the boys go back Monday, they'll take about all of them back." Johnny was very much in earnest.

"Will *you* carry the proposition for the molders?" asked Tyler with a grin.

"I'm not eager for the job," said Johnny, the red creeping up his cheek, "but rather than have the strike go on another day, I'll take it now."

"They kicked you out of the shop when you went to talk to them, didn't they?" said the chairman of the committee. It was composed of representatives of the various striking trades employed in the factory. He was secretary of the machinists, a ready, shrewd man, not too scrupulous, and very close to

Tyler. He shot a keen glance at Johnny as he spoke. Tyler laughed unpleasantly.

"They tried to," returned Johnny, who seemed amused rather than abashed; but Billy's mellow, rotund voice struck in for the first time, although his eyes and ears had been busy.

"Yes; the old man had three regular toughs who call themselves plain clothes men. He got himself in a wax, and told Galitsuin he couldn't go through the shops. Galitsuin was simply bearing the answer after fighting against it; *he* was against striking, all the while; but the old fellow for some reason was mad's a hatter. He may have heard some lies about Ivan,"—without malice or apparent intention, Billy looked at Tyler—"so they had a scrap; but Ivan carromed one of the guys against the other, and gave the other guy a job for his dentist before *he* jumped out of the window. Take it all together, I guess they hadn't anything to brag of."

Conrad and another man laughed; not so Tyler or his two allies; and the chairman judged Galitsuin to have been insulted.

"It makes no difference. I'm not in this business for my health, and a few biffs don't cut any ice," said Johnny. "It isn't the question whether I was insulted—"

"The union was insulted," Reilly burst in, "organized labor was insulted. We had ought to resent that—"

"We can't hunt up insults when our men's families are down to dry bread and a potato apiece for the day!" retorted Johnny. "I haven't a word to say for the Wethers'; they are anything you like.

And I hope I get a chance to hold them up some time. But they've got the drop on us now. Our men have been out three weeks; we haven't a cent in the treasury; we haven't had for—not since Wednesday, anyhow. What's the use?"

Conrad looked uncomfortable; the others exchanged glances. The hall was filling up with men. They did not say much, but their murmurs were not of approval of the committee.

"Well, we've another meeting to-morrow," said the chairman. "Wethers may see a great light before then."

"I'm convinced they're with Tyler, too," Johnny muttered in Billy's ear; "maybe not Conrad; but the others are greased, too, damn them!"

"Maybe not, maybe not," soothed Billy. "I'm getting on to their curves, though. The strike will be called off by Wednesday, anyhow, if not to-morrow. Wally is putting up some sort of a bluff to bring Wethers to his terms. You best get a day off, to-morrow, from your loading grocery wagons, and watch 'em. You can out-talk 'em and out-fight 'em, but you can't hold a candle to 'em playing politics, and don't you forget it!"

"And till Monday—"

"Well, being Sunday, Wethers won't be running and there won't be any mischief—"

"But they *are* running to-day," exclaimed Johnny. "Billy, those fellows—"

"Down there? Sure!" cried Billy. "Why didn't you tell me before! Let's get a move on!"

Johnny was hurrying after him when he was arrested by a decent, elderly man who caught at his sleeve. "I jest want to ask you in confidence, is there any show for them calling the strike off?" he whispered. "My woman's real sick and she needs things; if I knowed for *sure* it was to be called off, I'd raise a bit of money and git a bunch of grapes and a bit of bacon."

"I'm so sure it'll be called off to-morrow or next day I'll lend you a dollar," said Johnny.

His face wore a tiny smile as he joined Billy.

"I'd have given him more, but I think it belongs to Bloker."

Billy merely wrinkled his nose. The two friends stood out on the car platform, and as they approached their destination the conductor illuminated the situation.

"Lively time at Wethers' this morning, I guess," he began.

"What they doing?" said Billy, between puffs of his cigar.

"Pulling out the scabs, I guess. Heard they 'most killed a feller last night. Well, I ain't sorry. If folks won't stop scabbing from decency and regard for other men's rights, they got to be scared out of it. Stop here? Listen to the racket!"

The car landed them on the corner opposite Wethers' shops. It was an unsavory neighborhood, filled with mean shops and lean rookeries, grimy with soft coal, and fluttering the ragged laundry of the occupants over the rickety platforms and staircases which made fire-traps in the rear. The signs of the shops were in strange languages and grotesque lettering, and a polyglot din rolled out of any open shop-door. The uneven pavement was diversified by a few raw piles of brick, which showed, by their presence, an intention of the corporation to repair, but, by their battered condition and the veil of mud and litter over them, the remoteness of their coming and the uncertainty of their final end.

Over everything lay the shadow of the great, dingy bulk of factories. The foundry chimney rose out of the pile, volleying black smoke, such as a raw fireman always spouts from his furnace. Sooty clouds hung low over the stained thoroughfare, roaring, now, with a crowd of boys and disheveled women. The women were bareheaded in the sharp air; bare-armed, occasionally, as they rushed out from their household toil; all feminine softness, as well as feminine vanity, ground off them in the fierce attrition of the daily conflict for life. The boys were mostly half-grown lads who had learned English and deviltry at the public schools; but the women shrieked out their fury in their native tongue; wherefore an undistinguishable Babel swelled above the roofs, pierced continually by one English word, "Scab! scab!"

"They're at it," said Billy, shrugging his shoulders; "they've smashed the stockade."

Johnny had seen more than one such scene of mob passions breaking their leash; he looked for the center of the storm and discovered it: one man with glaring eyes and white face fleeing before a crowd down the middle of the street, darting under horses' feet and worming himself between wagons. His hat was gone, his clothes were torn, there was blood on his face, but he ran with the swiftness of fear.

"Here!" yelled Johnny, *"here!* We'll protect

you!" All the while he was forging his way through the crowd, Billy at his elbow.

The fugitive turned. His eyes, staring like bits of glass, went to Johnny's. Whether he had heard or not, he suddenly swerved in his course, dove like a rabbit under a wagon and made straight for the two friends. But the pursuers were hot on his heels, and the leader, a lad of eighteen who worked at Wethers', in Johnny's own shop, sent out a shout: *"The bricks! Give him it with the bricks!"* Instantly a dozen hands were at the convenient pile and a shower hurtled over the wagons. More than one of the missiles went astray, but one hit the mark. The fugitive toppled over at Johnny's feet.

A horse was plunging, a woman was screaming, and Billy Bates' robust tones penetrated the confusion, calling a halt to the fusillade. Johnny was on his knees beside the fallen man. He lifted the head, which sagged on his arm. A tiny thread of blood trickled down the matted hair from one temple. The hair was red and stiff, and on the features was fixed a ghastly caricature of that twitching, eager smile Johnny had seen before.

Billy threw a glance behind him, and turned a grim and white face to the nearest of the crowd. "Keep back!" said he. "He's *dead;* you've killed him, all right!" Then as he, too, knelt beside the limp figure, he uttered an exclamation: "Hell! If it ain't Bloker!"

Johnny, with pale lips that stiffened, was fumbling about the man's ragged shirt.

"Only one shirt," muttered Billy; "ain't he dressed poor for this weather? Oh, damn them!"

"Haven't you got any whisky?" said Johnny, in an even, little voice. "Don't you worry, Bloker! *You're* all right. *We* won't let them touch you."

"They're skipping fast enough," muttered Billy, "leaving us to be pinched. Don't rub him, Ivan; all the whisky in the world won't help him. Look at his eyes!"

Johnny shifted the head to an easier position. He did not speak. Billy looked helplessly about him; half the crowd had vanished, but shops and windows were full of them, gesticulating and chattering; and a black-haired, white-toothed fruit-vender was volubly and politely convoying two policemen to the scene.

"Three lives," said Johnny in the same small, dry voice, "three lives,—thrown away because I made a fine speech! It's a good deal for a man, who tries to be decent, to carry on his conscience all the rest of his life."

PEGGY

CHAPTER II

A "SCRAP"

Mueller, the shipping clerk of Moulton and Company, looked up and squinted his eyes dubiously; a very critical man was the shipping clerk in those days of abundant supply of "rooster" talent; but he liked the quick-witted, athletic, cheerful-tempered new recruit whom he suspected both of another name and far different previous surroundings. "This morning off, Gleason?" said he. "Why?"

When he engaged the young man, he had wondered to himself: "Is it a newspaper lark, a quarrel with his friends, or has he got to this, spreeing?" Before the new roustabout had been with him a week he decided against the last theory. "Reporter studying us at first hand to write us up in the *Record* or the *Herald*," he mused; "but he never takes out any pad, and he doesn't ask questions." The shipping clerk crossed off number two from his mind. "I guess it's a row with the old man, and young mister is on his uppers and going to show his stuff," he decided finally; and he was confirmed in his opinion when Johnny answered, "I don't mind telling you, but I'd rather not tell the whole crowd. If you would be so very good as to step this way a minute.

"It is only this," Johnny explained. "I worked at Wethers' works until the strike; I opposed the strike, but I didn't count. I went out with the boys; but I couldn't afford to stay idle, so I got a job here. Now, they are going to discuss ending the strike to-day. I was out late last night getting the boys together and having them come—"

"I thought the thing was left with the Executive Committee."

"It was. But they would have to submit anything to the whole of us. And if I've enough backing outside, they won't oppose me. I've got it, too. But they've a meeting at nine-thirty, and I need to be there."

"They had some pretty nasty rioting, didn't they, yesterday?"

"Yes," said Johnny.

"I suppose they'll take you back; so really it don't matter whether I give you the day or not, hey?"

"It matters to me; I'll have to take the day, but I don't want to lose this job, for they won't take me back."

"Why? Did you stir up the trouble?" The shipping clerk looked puzzled.

"No. I didn't think they ought to strike; but—" the smile that won every one who met Johnny flickered over his face—"do you mind my confiding a bit in you? The fact is, early in the business I got into a scrap with the firm. I came to try to get some agreement, but instead of getting even the least little concession, which I could have used to persuade the men to end the whole racket, they wouldn't give a thing—convinced me, in fact, that they wanted the strike as an excuse to get out of a losing contract. I said something they didn't like. They had some Pinkertons handy—we had a scrap."

"Who licked?"

"Both of us, I fancy. I jumped out of the window, but I knocked some teeth out for one of the Pinkertons."

"I see. You're *persona non grata* at Wethers'. But will they take the other men back?"

"I think so. I'm told they have made a new deal with their contracts, and some fresh ones have come in. They want to run, and they've only a third of a force."

"But look here, if you don't get on there, and you come here, will you be kicking up a row here? It wouldn't be very bright of me to be hiring that sort now, when I can get my pick. Our roosters ain't organized, but you might be organizing them."

"Ah, but," suggested Johnny, "I'm trying to make peace. *I* didn't stir up the strike; I got into hot water myself opposing it. All I want here is a steady job until I can get something better, in steel or as a molder, which is my trade. You needn't be afraid of me as a mischief-maker."

The shipping clerk took a turn. "Ain't he the slickest chap!" he was thinking, with a sort of admiration. "What *is* his little game?" He wheeled on the young fellow suddenly and surprised, not a smile, but a look of settled melancholy which gave an unexpected twist to his calloused sympathies.

"I can't quite make you out," he cried sharply— the more sharply that he was touched; the American sympathy is likely to be irritable when it is not humorous. "You can't git back yourself, you say; yet you want to pull things up by the roots to get the rest of the push back. Say, if I won't let you have this morning off, what'll you do? Throw up your job?"

This time Johnny smiled: "No, I'll take the morning, but try to hang on to the job till you fire me."

"What you so keen about freezing on to your job for? You ain't married nor widowed?"

"I'm not. But"—he hesitated as he looked with a kind of appeal at the clerk's shrewd, city-hardened visage, "I do have some kids that look to me; the poor fellow who was killed yesterday left three little children, and some of us boys are looking out for them."

"You best not go into the dry-nuss business in *this* town—you'll git too much on your hands! Say, tell me one thing. Ain't you a gentleman?"

"I hope so," said Johnny.

"Didn't you have a pile of money, once?"

"I did," said Johnny, "but this talk is in confidence."

"I guess I know *who* you are," said the clerk, nodding his head. "Allow me to tell you you've been a damn fool!"

"I suspect as much myself," said Johnny.

"If you wanted to help other fellows you'd best have hung on to your rope to pull 'em up. But I guess you'll come out, some way. Mind putting it there?" He held out his hand, and Johnny, with a little flush, clasped it.

"You can have the day if you like; but say, we're

pretty rushed.   Load that truck first, will you?   Get busy there, everybody!"

He did not know how gratefully Johnny's eyes followed him, but he marked with a grin the mighty heaves of the young man's muscles.   And although Johnny did not know it, he had made a good friend.

The truck was not long in loading under the impetus of such energy, and Johnny found he had time to run to the meeting, saving his car-fare.   The exercise of minute economies had lost its savor of novelty and become habit, but this morning it pricked with a fresh zest.   How well and how easily once he could have helped the poor little Blokers!   But that was the least of the remorse which had robbed him of sleep the night before, and which he doggedly put out of his mind until his work should be done.   It was beyond him to-day, however, to assume the blithe mask of yesterday, when he walked into the swaying mass of men at Einert's.

He returned, gravely, salutations from men almost as grave and stern-looking as he.   To this there were exceptions: Tyler's party made a clatter of jokes and laughter; and Tyler himself moved about the hall, his handsome, florid features dealing smiles and his big fist hammering arguments, jocose or belligerent, into his changing audience.   Already Johnny was grown quick to gather straws from men's reticence as well as their talk; he marked how Tyler's hot confidence fell upon cold gloom; how his hearers edged out of his way or slipped out of the circle, or, unable to escape, returned vague and non-committal murmurs instead of applause.   These were men who would have cringed to him, alone; but nothing is so bracing to courage as company. Each man's known defiance emboldened the others. Tyler's gang couldn't lick them all. Besides, they were sick of the strike. They had begun to suspect Tyler. And they had found a leader. Once or twice Tyler shot lowering glances in Johnny's direction, but he made no move to approach him. On the contrary, he imperceptibly changed his own position lest they collide. This, too, Johnny marked. It puzzled him. But, had he known, the explanation was simply the presence of Mr. William Bates.

Billy was leaning against the bar, drinking the sweet white soda-pop which had become the standard subject for jokes about him in the daily journals. He made no pretense to total abstinence, but no one ever saw him drink anything stronger than soda water.

Billy's garb was studiously chosen in black and grays; his clean-shaven, amiable, entirely unfathomable countenance was serious. Even his cronies got no more than the flicker of a smile.

"This is bad business, gentlemen," said Billy between sips. "It's no affair of mine, only I can't let my men get mixed up in it."

This neutrality and the neutral's known conservatism acted as a magnet to the older and colder men. The group about Billy's innocuous glass swelled by natural attraction. Forth from it, in thread-like undertones, fluttered sinister reflections on Tyler. Not Billy's reflections; Billy, the discreet, simply listened, shook his head and settled himself, morally, more firmly on his fence. But he denied as little as he affirmed; he admitted that he had heard things, how true he could not vouch.

"Who's paying out all this here stuff 'bout Tyler?" finally demanded Reilly, wedging his big shoulders between two of Billy's listeners.

"I don't know who began it," returned Billy, cutting the tip of a cigar with much nicety, "but you can hear it all round. They say he's greased or he wants to be, and he's holding out till they come to his figure."

"I guess we ought to know by this time that Tyler's all right; he's done more to git us recognized and git decent wages than any man in the union," snapped the blacksmith. "I'll say that to anybody."

"I don't know what he's done, so I can't deny it," answered the pacific viceroy of the molders. "I've no light on him at all. Gimme five cards!"

"I guess there ain't anybody in Chicago but knows what Tyler's done and how he's worked and sacrificed for organized labor."

"*What's* he done?" came from the crowd in several sullen voices. One elderly man said that one sure thing was Tyler hadn't raised wages—" 'cause look at 'em!"

"But he's kep' 'em from fallin' lower," urged Tyler's supporter.

"Lord! So've I," said Billy, "but I ain't sending out a brass band about it. You make me think of a kid's composition: 'Pins have saved the lives of many people, by their not eating 'em!' But I'm glad to hear you say these stories are all hot air. Still, I guess we'd best not send Tyler by himself to dicker with the Wethers Company. You'd be a

good one, and Ivan Galitsuin; there's no question-
ing your squareness."

The friend was not beyond the shaft tipped with
honey; he vociferated his belief in Tyler's impecca-
bility, but he admitted that there might be wisdom in
the cautious course.

Billy's further persuasion was interrupted by a
telephone call. The barkeeper, with much defer-
ence, said that somebody from Fairport wanted to
talk with Mr. Bates. And Billy, for once off his
guard, betook himself to a long and baffling wrestle
with a man whose name he couldn't gather, and who
purported to come from Fairport ("not *in* Fairport,
no, in Chicago—came from Fairport") and wished
to relate a wondrous tale of a projected strike.
Three minutes sufficed to rouse Billy's suspicions,
two more to confirm them and to ring off with a
curt excuse; but in those five minutes and the addi-
tional two which may be allowed for transit, something had happened in the saloon.

Tyler had not avoided a clash with Johnny
through any disinclination to fight. Hitherto he
had beaten his way with the mailed hand (or, to
use the locution of the street, with "brass knucks"),
and he was not minded to abandon his tactics. He
could see his hold on his followers parting like a cut
rope; "Gleetzin" was openly and carelessly defying
him; he knew only one way to quiet criticism; that
was to send the critic to the hospital. If he could
pummel Johnny insensible, he could pass his measures and keep his men in line, even with Bates
against him. He needed only a day longer, a show
of antagonism, and Wethers, who was wavering,

would come to his terms. It was only to keep Gleet-zin quiet. Nor did he have much doubt of his success, for he was of Homeric prowess, and had stood up two rounds with the mighty John in his prime. Therefore, the instant Billy's soft gray hat swung round the door-lintel Tyler made straight for his man.

"I've something to say to you, Gleetzin," said he threateningly.

The bystanders hushed, as if by an incantation, and stood on one another's toes to get nearer.

When Johnny perceived Tyler before him, with the lust of battle in his eye, his own eyes lightened and the corners of his mouth curved slightly, but he inclined his head in all courtesy.

"I'd like to understand what you mean"—Tyler's tones grew rougher—"by sneaking around insinuating that I'm a thief and a liar and trying to sell out my best friends to these bloodsuckers?"

"I suppose I mean that you *are*," said Johnny in his gentlest tone.

Tyler's blow was like a flash, but it found Johnny's guard, not his head. It must have been given with too furious an impetus, and thus unbalanced the striker—how else no one could explain—for the next second there was a swift rush of fists, a ducking of heads, Johnny's left, in scientific parlance, jabbed Tyler over the heart, and, as he countered, Johnny's right found the great fighter's neck just under the jaw. There was a frightful crash, a big man, a table and three beer glasses tumbled on the floor together. The table and the glasses were in pieces; the man lay as inert as the wood, covered with beer and blood, while slowly his florid face whitened.

"You've done for him, by hell!" gurgled a bricklayer, who had seen the fight. "He can't put up his hands for one while!"

"He—he ain't killed?" hesitated the barkeeper, running around his counter, with first aid to the injured in the shape of a whisky bottle.

"No, worse luck!" said Johnny; "he'll live to do plenty more mischief."

"You all are witness he struck Galitsuin first," called Billy Bates, from the door. To be truthful, Billy had not seen either the first blow or the second; he spoke on those sound general principles of the conduct of life which the natural leaders of men follow by instinct, and which serve as a very good proxy for experience. He had not seen the fight, but he knew Tyler's trick of getting in the first blow, and he knew that Johnny fought fair. "Call you all to witness," bawled the astute Billy, "this is a clean case of self-defense."

"So 'tis!" cried many voices. The spectators stole admiring glances at Johnny.

He looked indifferent; he was indifferent. To the mood which had held the lad since he lifted poor Bloker's head off its cruel pillow, Tyler's slaying was a duty rather than a crime. His heart, full to bursting, was eased a little when he saw the fomenter of all the tragical strike lying dumb at his feet. His color did not turn nor did his expression change. An electric tingle of fear of the soft-spoken, gentle fellow stirred the beholders. They liked him for his generosity and his courage; but they admired him to the verge of awe for his callousness to bloodshed.

"He don't give a damn whether he's killed him or not," one man whispered to another. "Wally's met his match at last," sniggered the bricklayer. Whatever the resentment of the Tyler men, it did not lead them to reprisals, legal or otherwise; and any sympathy was blunted by Tyler's showing plain signs of life under the barkeeper's skilful ministrations with cold water and whisky. Billy looked on.

"I guess he got what was coming to him, all right," observed the sagacious neutral, "and if I was you, Carl,"—to the barkeeper—"I'd get him off before the police get on to the scrimmage."

"Gentlemen," said Johnny, "I think it is time for your meeting."

"I'll bet you a dollar to a nickel the strike's called off," was the sentence Billy heard before he left the room. But there were no takers, and the result justified the wisdom of the better. Within the hour the committee waited on Wethers; within another hour the general meeting had accepted the manufacturers' terms. As Johnny halted on the sidewalk for his street-car, a hack drove away from Einert's private rooms, and there flashed past him Tyler's pale and sullen face.

"In some ways, Ivan," said Billy, linking arms, "it's kinder a pity you didn't *kill* that skunk; he's going to give us the devil of a time yet!"

CHAPTER III

The misery of the months which followed the Wethers' strike neither time nor happiness ever effaced for Johnny. Remorse stamps the soul deep with its sinister hall-mark. Never again, although his perfect health and his natural elasticity of hope restored him to daily cheerfulness, was life the same light-hearted thing to him. He was caught in that awful mesh of the evil consequences of the action of good intent, which has bewildered conscience and made the unhappy "follower of the gleam" doubt God Himself.

Could a mistake, an honest mistake, be accounted to a man for worse than sin? Rash he might have been, he was; impatient, not strong enough to wait; all sorts of idiotic dreamer; but not selfish or cruel or base; yet did the men whom he knew,—the careless sinners of his college days, who sought the desire of the eye and the delights of the flesh at any cost to their people at home, who were toiling and stinting for them,—did they suffer as he did? They couldn't. And Tyler, who lied and stole and dipped his hands in blood, did he suffer? Not a pang.

"It is not just!" groaned the wretched boy in

those terrible nights which would come, unless he was so exhausted that he could not help sleeping.

One circumstance added incalculably to his torture. He was never free from a view of the consequences of his folly. The first impulsive movement of his remorse was to assume the charge of Bloker's children. He was not earning enough to support them, away. By boarding himself with Mrs. Delaney, who had befriended the children, he could see to them far more efficiently and at less cost. He did not consider the consequences to himself, nor could Billy, who was more far-sighted, dissuade him.

"You'll be jest like those pilgrim guys,"—Billy's journey to the higher education was now leading him through the Crusades, in his leisure hours—"who used to wear sackcloth and put peas in their boots; didn't do a mite of good, but made them bloody uncomfortable every minute. You'll be hearing about Bloker all the time, and you won't make them stop talking, because you'll think they mustn't forget their father. I tell you, Ivan, it won't work; it would be safer to take to drink."

"It's all I can do for him," said Johnny, "and don't row me, else I'll get so I can't talk to you about it. And you're the only one." The little muffling of his voice which was not a quiver, because he held it, in time, quite routed Billy.

Johnny moved his trunk and bath-tub to Mrs. Delaney's that night. Billy's only grain of consolation was that Johnny had agreed to let him contribute to the children's maintenance. Had he known it he might have claimed another; he was more help

than he or Johnny himself realized at the time, because he insisted on Johnny's talking out his black
thoughts. "They won't hurt me," he urged, "I
haven't been to church since my poor mother died.
I'm tough and you can't shock me."

He used to spend a deal of thought, himself, on
the situation, trying to work it out logically enough
to appease what he once called Johnny's "terrible
Russian imagination."

"They're so damn logical, but haven't got good
sense," he would grumble; "now look here, Ivan,
this is how I look at it. I see plain enough you
can't run away from this. You've got to face it and
count every rib in the skeleton, and then you've got
to down it, once for all; smash it and bury it away.
Now, here's how it puts itself to me. Punishment is
what comes from breaking every law. Maybe the
feller who breaks the law don't get it, but *somebody*
does. If the world is a big machine, anything that
smashes a cog will make trouble, whether a man,
who means to make mischief, smashes it, or an innocent little kid. As for knowing, we *can't* know;
we've got to find out to the best of our ability, and
then let her slide. 'Do better the next time, and not
worry,' is my motto, sonny. Why, hang it! the only
use of repenting is to fix your good resolutions in
your mind. There ain't a bit of virtue in the bare
crying over things. When I lived in Fairport, there
was a family I used to work for,—weed their garden
and carry coal for their base-burner. It was an
awful nice family and there were two little girls in
it, younger than me, Sadie and Lily; Lily, when she
did anything bad, would weep and howl and go

without her dinner, she felt so awful bad; the whole house would have to turn in and chirk her up a little. Then she'd subside; but after she subsided, she wasn't especially good,—just same's usual, that's all. Sadie was kinder offish, a proud little piece; she pretended she didn't care so very much and had a good appetite, and didn't need anybody to go up stairs with her nights, but I noticed afterward she'd be a good, minding child, and think up things to do for her mother for a *long* while. I've often thought of those girls. No, Ivan, don't use up your energies feeling bad; you'll need 'em all in your business."

"I do work as hard as I can, Billy," said Johnny quite meekly, "and I don't whine."

"Sure!" cried Billy heartily, throwing an arm around his neck but restraining a desire to be sympathetic. "For what he needs is *brace*," was Billy's faith. "*Sure,* you're sandy! I saw you playing blocks with the baby and I heard your funny stories. That's the sort! It's only skin deep, I know; but if you persevere, you'll find it'll work in!"

Billy's homely consolation did help; but Billy was away much of the time; he had been elected a vice-president of the molders, and the district head of a labor union leads as peripatetic a life as a bishop. When Billy was gone there was no one, so Johnny worked the harder. Long afterward he told some one who loved him, that neither love nor religion was the salvation of a man in despair, like work.

"Every case of melancholia needs to work until he perspires freely," he said; "perspiration is a great moral agent. Billy thinks so, too; he expresses it succinctly, but rather bluntly; he says, 'You can sweat a lot of meanness out of you!' And work is a wonder. I used to work so hard I couldn't help sleeping. And Sundays I would take the kids to Lincoln Park. I didn't dare go to church. I used to mend my clothes; sometimes I helped Mrs. Delaney wash."

Yet there were days when the heavy and weary weight of all this unintelligible world crushed everything save dogged endurance out of him. Once, during such a mood, he read over his mother's last letter; it seemed to him that he had never understood it before.

"I have failed as she failed," he thought dully. He was no longer angry with himself; he felt numb with despair. Yet in that self-same hour, a new purpose began to stir in him, for he felt a disgust at his own apathy. "My father would want to kick me,"—thus he scorned himself—"well, in effect he has kicked me already, good and hard!" There had been a long time during which he had resented his father's lack of confidence and resented his stepmother's assuming to guide him. When he left Peggy he vowed to sink out of his old world, beneath the wave entirely. Therefore, he had taken his mother's name, the better to throw in his fortunes with her. His father had disowned him, disinherited him. Very well, he would accept the dictum and live his life according to his own conscience, not another man's.

But now, having let the idealist in him go its length, the reaction came; he revolted at his own impetuosity, and the silent, stubborn resentment against the tyranny of a dead hand began to flake

away like a lump of coal in a furnace. After a while
he turned to the study of his father's motives. Perhaps it was to save him from mischance, huge and
woeful as this which had befallen him, that Josiah
Winslow had plotted. Little by little there came
changes in his image of that grim, undemonstrative,
strong man, whose awkward and reticent tenderness
he began to suspect. He went back, groping through
his childish memories. They showed him more than
he expected. How many times his father had been
gentle to him! Once, on that tragic journey, after
his mother's death, he had fallen asleep on deck, and
he wakened, wrapped in his father's rug, his head
on his father's shoulder. He lay there, embarrassed,
yet finding a certain consciousness of rest and shelter. The tears which he had shed were still on his
cheek. He thought it the wind on his hair, the touch
of his father's lips was so light; but, now, he did
not think it was the wind.

"Pretty bad to be a disappointment to him, too,"
said Johnny wearily; "not a thing I've done but
would sicken him—unless—I wonder if he wouldn't
chuckle over my downing Tyler!" By a swift transi-
tion, his thought went to another phase of Winslow's conception of life and duty; he wondered if
his father would not detect some alleviation in his
tragic blunderings. Might he not take some such
view as Billy's; if so, would he not find his son's
nightmare of gloom intemperate as his former
hopes? Johnny's first gleam of comfort came with
these fancies. He found an obscure satisfaction in
rating himself after his father's manner, giving his
father the rôle of judge, and repenting to him. "Oh,

if he only *could* come and whack at me as he used to!" longed Johnny. Often he thought: "Peggy's the only real person in the world who would understand why it dulls the pain for me to let my fancy run away with me so! Oh, Peggy, Peggy!"

Sometimes the homesick yearning he had for the mere sight of Peggy so goaded him that, but for the Blokers who took his every dollar, he would have gone to Fairport only to steal a look at her by night. He believed himself disguised enough by his dress and his mode of life, which he fancied had battered him out of all his former comeliness (Johnny still went to extremes while vowing warfare on them), and his mother's noble name had been corrupted variously into Gleetzin and Gleason, while Ivan was docked into Van; Van Gleason most of his mates called him; surely there was nothing to call the attention of the curious in Van Gleason.

Probably it was at this time that the plan of removing to Fairport began to shape itself in Johnny's mind—a mere adumbration of a plan, now, which had not even the shadow of detail, but which never left him.

Meanwhile, Billy puzzled over his friend's case more than was good for business. He used to seek counsel of the wisest of his acquaintances. Here is the way he would put his puzzle. "Say, suppose you know a man who has been as good a friend to you as one man can be to another; suppose he is straight as a string, never did a mean trick in his life; but terribly conscientious and sensitive, and suppose out of sheer good-will—and ignorance—he gave some bad advice to another man, who took it and came to smash in consequence; in fact he got killed, poor fellow, and the first man is about distracted over it —say, what would you propose to pull him out of the hole?"

The wise men—generally magnates of the labor unions—differed. One advised going to a new town and getting a change. Another, of a drastic temperament, opined that getting religion or getting married would be enough of a change to divert from despair. He admitted that it was a kill-or-cure prescription. Most of the counselors believed in work! "And whatever you do, Billy," said the youngest man, "don't let him try to drown the grief."

"No danger," snapped Billy, "he's not that kind."

"Many mighty good fellows are," returned the other quietly, and Billy remembered that the speaker had won a hard fight against that enemy, himself.

"I know it," he amended in penitence; "but he— why, he went to college, to Harvard College; I guess he had wine or beer to drink every day; he's used to it and yet he doesn't care for it. He ain't that sort."

"Sentimental lot?"

"No, *sir;* he's the best company you ever saw, and —you ought to see him put up his fists! It's simply lovely!"

"Where'd he learn?"

"College."

"I didn't know they taught anything so useful in college," observed Billy's friend thoughtfully; "can he make speeches, too?"

"He made a speech that would get you to jumping!"

"He must be a kind of a wonder."

"He just *is*."

"Nothing of a organizer, I expect?"

"He euchred Wally Tyler out of a deal he was trying to make in the Wethers' strike."

"So?" said the other. "I guess I'm on to the man you mean. He doesn't belong with our crowd, Billy; try to steer him back to his own side; he'll help us more there."

"I think so, too, Hindman; but you see he's broken with his folks and lost his money, and now he thinks he's the cause of that unlucky Bloker's getting killed."

"Sensitive sort of man?"

"Very."

"Look here," the labor leader took out his pocketbook with a half-embarrassed smile, and found in it a printed slip. He tendered it to Billy.

"Funny sort of thing to carry round like a rabbit's foot, isn't it?" he said. "But ever since I fell on it in a newspaper, I've kept it. I'm not much on poetry; I don't know anything about the fellow that wrote it; but, say, it hits you in the neck, don't it?"

Billy read the poem; it was Henley's immortal defiance of despair. For a moment both men were silent. Billy drew a long breath.

"That's big!" said he in an undertone as if he were in church. "That man knew how it feels to be down. And yet—he won." He repeated softly:

> "'It matters not how strait the gate,
>   How charged with punishments the scroll,
>   I am the master of my fate:
>   I am the captain of my soul.'"

"Will you let me write it down, Hindman? That's my friend, exactly."

"Take it," said Hindman, "I know it by heart."

Billy carried it to Johnny, explaining: "I guess Hindman knows what trouble is mighty well. He'd a brother he was saving his money to educate and make a priest of, and one day when they were shooting he accidently shot him—killed him. Hindman nearly went crazy; took to drink and nearly lost his hold. But somehow he's pulled out. Everybody respects him now. I guess he knows about that first verse though:

> "'Out of the night that covers me,
>   Black as the Pit from pole to pole!'"

Johnny finished the stanza:

> "'I thank whatever gods may be
>   For my unconquerable soul.'"

"That's the stuff!" cried Billy, "and that next verse, too:

> "'In the fell clutch of circumstance
>   I have not winced nor cried aloud.
> Under the bludgeonings of chance
>   My head is bloody but unbowed.'

"That's you, Ivan!" He stopped and his voice changed a little: "Here's the summing up:

> "'It matters not how strait the gate,
>   How charged with punishments the scroll,
> I am the master of my fate:
>   I am the captain of my soul.'

"Ain't you, Ivan?" he said affectionately. "Say, you've got to be,—for me. 'Cause you've been all the religion I've got."

"All right, old chap," said Johnny, smiling. "I will; just to oblige."

Yet under his affected lightness he felt a thrill. A man does not serve honor or duty or his country for reward; the constraint is upon him; he follows the gleam, and if it lead to exceeding narrow ways and the final plunge into night, that is the concern of the Powers that were before him, not his at all; he acts a man's part because he is a man.

"After all, I've something left to lose," said Johnny; "I've been a fool, but not a coward; my father would tell me not to begin being pusillanimous, now!" He took the little worn newspaper slip thankfully, and placed it in his pocket, wearing it over a heart only less sore than that of the man who had sent it to him. "His luck was worse than mine," thought Johnny, "I ought to consider I'm not the only one."

Meanwhile, a quarter, whence Billy had anticipated excitement, showed none; Tyler was very quiet. Half-hopefully, Johnny had expected reprisals. None came, although it was now a month past the time of the fight. No one molested Johnny by so much as a word.

For this, however, there was a good explanation. It was no fault of Tyler's. His anger burned more fiercely than ever. He caught a heavy cold when he went out, the very day after his felling. Johnny had nothing to do with the cold; but very naturally Tyler laid it at his door, as he caught it tramping through the rain for a consultation with two doughty followers, who were to help him "do up Van Gleetzin." The cold turned into bronchitis, so Tyler had plenty of time to stoke his wrath. Considering his purposes for Johnny, it was rather unreasonable that he should make it a cause of grievance that the latter did not pay him a visit; but he argued: "If he wasn't meaning to fight it out, he'd have sent round to see if I was going to pull through or have the pneumonia. But he'd rather I'd die. Then he'd crow! But I'll show him who's boss in Chicago!"

Harder to bear than the blow was the damage to his prestige that it had wrought. He fancied that associates, who had been close, neglected him during his illness, while the commonalty were lukewarm. And the election of officers in his local was coming on. He wanted to be president. Some stroke was necessary to hearten the faithful and intimidate the backsliders. He watched his chance and was not long in finding it. It came in the first week of December, after a meeting of the Federation of Labor. Conrad and Tyler had clashed over one of the innumerable efforts of the socialists to drag the labor unions into politics. Tyler was working with the socialist wing at this time. Johnny had drifted further and further from them during the year, and he gave his best to Conrad. There sprang up one of those unexpected squalls of discussion, to which unwieldy assemblages are prone, and which may disconcert the craftiest skippers. Thus it happened that Johnny captured the floor from an inexperienced parliamentarian of the social labor party, and succeeded in making a speech. His old friends, the socialists, interrupted him continually; but he kept his temper and the rough and ready badinage learned in college debates stood him in good stead.

"He's no workingman," yelled a socialist Johnny knew and respected, for he was a very honest man who nearly starved himself to help his household of faith; "he graduated at Harvard College!"

There was a laugh; but Johnny brought another when he retorted, "Yes, that's true, I have been exposed to education; but I only took a very mild type. I don't know half as much as the gentleman who interrupted me. But he is a doctrinaire and expects the earth; I'm only a practical man and *as* a practical man—" He plunged into his argument.

"I see your finish, Wally," whispered one of Tyler's friends, as applause and catcalls contended when Johnny sat down.

"And I see his," said Tyler grimly; "you wait!"

His nearest friends exchanged glances and they looked at each other again curiously, when the ballots were announced and Tyler's man proved himself a true prophet of evil. Tyler simply ground his teeth, rammed his hands into his pockets and left the hall.

His departure was unnoticed by Johnny. The light had faded out of his eyes, and he sat pale and unmoved amid his friends' joyous tumult. Presently he slipped away while they were celebrating their victory, and walked, alone, to the cross-street which he must traverse to reach his car.

Billy had cautioned him never to walk alone at night. He was docile under the warning and tried to obey it; but to-night he had been roused out of his apathy, and the excitement drowned Billy's warnings no less than his own resolution.

He plunged out of Clark Street, blazing with electric lights and gaudy signs, reeking with stale beer steaming through the iron gratings of its sidewalks from basement restaurants, and roaring with the unnamable din of street-cars, horses and humanity, into a shambling, low-roofed, ill-lighted dwelling-street where the shadows of the houses devoured the feeble space illumined by a single gas-lamp. The street was so lonely that he was the only wayfarer. It was so quiet that he could hear his own footfall. As he walked, the brief elation of conflict and oratory fell from him; the deep abiding melancholy of his common mood asserted its rights.

"How little I can help them!" he was thinking. "I barely hold them; I've given them my fortune, my future, my chances of happiness, my peace of mind, even; yet I'm an alien still. They'd like me better, they'd believe in me more if I'd stayed where I belonged!"

Just in front of him a shadow fell athwart his path. His wits acted as alertly as a rabbit's; he sprang with a mighty leap to one side and a man staggered and stumbled on a thwarted blow.

"Put up your hands; we'll have it out now," called a deep barytone which he knew. He saw the two other men skulking in the shadow. When he would have jumped back, one of these ran between him and the street, the other kept his place.

"No running now; stand up and take it," cried Tyler.

Johnny's coat was over his arm and his knife was

in the pocket. He struck the guardian of the road between his eyes, ducked the blow which Tyler aimed at long range, and put enough space between his assailants and himself to slip his closed knife between his clenched fingers! Tyler was able to land two blows, while the smaller man danced between Johnny and the light. Johnny struck Tyler only once; but he reeled and Johnny gained a few steps more in his retreat to the lighted highway. When the second man would have stopped him Johnny's armored fist struck straight, first at his arm, then at his jaw, and as he fell a little space more was gained. Tyler rushed forward again, followed by the third man. He tried to clinch, but went down before his follower's eyes. The third man darted at Johnny as he whirled. Johnny felt a sharp prick in his side, but he landed a swinging blow on his assailant's eye, which stopped the onset for a second.

Then Johnny ran, ran for his life. Tyler was on his feet again and they would use their knives if not their pistols; it was either to get to the lights and the crowd, or be stabbed to death under the shadow of the rotten wooden porches. He ran as he never ran on the track. Something whizzed by him,— what, he never knew, for he made the street and hailed a car. No sooner was he seated than he realized what had befallen him, but he knew enough not to ask for aid. Tyler had too many friends on the police force. He sat in the car, holding his arm tightly against his side, where he had jammed his handkerchief. He sat until the car reached the corner next a celebrated hospital; nor did the conductor suspect anything wrong until, a moment after, the pale young man had stepped with careful steadiness off the front platform and walked up the street.

"Say, Mike," cried the motorman, "look at the platform; that feller's been stabbed!"

The conductor threw an experienced eye over the boards in question.

"That's right," he answered carelessly; "well, he's got his nerve with him; he's minding his own business and not troubling the police, and he's toddled into the hospital."

Nor did Johnny come out for a month.

CHAPTER IV

IN HOSPITAL

A hospital is a quiet place. Suppose one to go to a public ward, say the surgical ward, and there be the only patient during a large part of a four weeks' stay; he were like to have his fill of lonely gazing on the white-coated walls, and white-spread cots, and white-shaded windows; of the fugitive persistence of iodoform; of straining the ear for a vanishing footfall on the rubber-deadened passage without, a nurse's smothered, girlish voice, a young house-surgeon's important tones, the soft swish of unstarched skirts, or any of the hushed hospital sounds which awaken out of the silence, at first muffling everything.

Moreover, in such a case, too weak to read, too poor to buy privacy with its consequent allowance of company, seeing no visitors except on the bi-weekly visiting day, one might have a surfeit of leisure to think.

After Johnny passed the danger point, when his mind crawled out of the mists of delirium and deathly weakness, when the pain was gone and the day nurse smiled every time she went to the window with her thermometer, he thought a great deal. He lay through the day and watched the morning sunlight flicker a diffused prism on the corner of the white ceiling, and the afternoon sunlight paint gray and violet shadows such as are made delicately by a water-color brush. He used to puzzle out the objects in the ward which they represented. He lay through the night, and when he wakened he watched the grotesque shadows of the night-light, smudged on the white walls, as if by a crayon stub. If he closed his eyes on the shadows, he drifted back into the scenes of his life. In his delirium he had been tormented by a vast longing for home,—he who had no home. He brought tears to the eyes of the nurse by his appeals to take him home.

"Please let me go to my own room; I could always sleep in my own room!" he would say; or: "This is a very pleasant place and you are all kind; but isn't it nearly time for me to go home?" or: "After the doctor goes is there any reason why I can't put on my clothes and go home? I am very anxious to go home."

Sometimes his sick fancy feigned his mother in waiting; she would bend over him and kiss him; he would see her eyelids half closing, in the way they had when she smiled; he would feel the cool satin of her cheek. For the most part, however, he did not lose his consciousness that she was dead. But often his father walked out of the great hall to the portico of Overlook to welcome him. Once he woke out of a feverish dream and smiled and cried: "Why, father dear, I thought you were dead, isn't this *corking!* Oh, but I made a mess of things, just as you said I would." Sometimes his stepmother would give him his medicine or his milk, instead of the

nurse. This did not in the least surprise him, because nothing surprises us in delirium or in dreams;
but he said once: "You are very kind; I didn't know
you were so kind,"—and then was vaguely worried
by the suspicion that he had been rude.

"I wouldn't say anything harsh to her," he explained to the night nurse; "you know I wouldn't—
why, I promised my father."

Usually the night nurse was Peggy; not the
beautiful, haughty, grown-up Peggy, but little
Peggy with her red curls and her temper, his childish comrade. He never was a child again, himself;
nor did he ever lose the consciousness of the weight
on his heart, although he could not make its cause
distinct, and several times said: "It's very queer,
Peggy, very queer, why I am so unhappy; but there
is a good reason if I could only remember."

With returning strength the visions faded, leaving him the lonelier for their loss. In their place he
had his relentless questions. There was no narcotic
of work to stupefy him.

"I'm up against it," he told himself. "I must find
some way to brace me up, or I shall die, and I have
no right to die—a man with a family like me!"
Therefore Johnny lay and let the Anglo-Saxon in
him have its word, at last.

At first, no one but the shipping clerk at the grocery and Mrs. Delaney came to see him. He had not
sent word to Billy. Billy was in Indianapolis trying to avert a sweeping cut of wages without a
strike, and Johnny would not "bother him." There
was no one else who cared enough about him to require a notification—so he thought. Conrad was an

ally, rather than a friend. The other molders were friendly acquaintances and comrades to whom he was glad to render a kindness, but of whom he never dreamed of asking one. Johnny had more pride than he imagined. He loved to give and hated to receive, which is a trait of the young. Either they receive quite unconsciously, as their right, since it is the business of the elders to make them comfortable; or they resent the oppression of a debt. One college boy will borrow so long as his friends' good nature or ability holds out; another will live on "hot dog" and oat-meal and pawn his overcoat, or, worse, his dress-suit, rather than ask an acquaintance for a loan.

It is only living that teaches us the right of our friends to help us. Mutual obligation is like rotation of crops and saves friendship from sterility. But Johnny was too young for such philosophy. He deemed his misfortunes of no importance save to himself; indeed, he sent word to Mueller only lest the latter should find his absence inconvenient. But the next day (being Sunday) he was surprised by a visit from the clerk. Johnny's fever had not yet appeared in serious form, and he was allowed a short interview. The clerk heard the particulars of the fray. With difficulty he compressed his feelings into language befitting the presence of the nurse.

"And you don't know who knifed you?" he asked at the end.

"I can guess; but I couldn't swear to any one's face," said Johnny.

"Then you can't have him arrested. What are you going to do?"

"Get well and thrash the man who put up the job. Make him stand up to me with his two fists; drive him out of his union."

"You'll do," Mueller approved, grinning; "say, how are you fixed? This will take a week, most likely," (the doctor had told him three). "Can you send an understudy for your job?"

"Yes, I know a pretty good fellow, Mark Delaney; he's young, but he's tough. I board with his mother and she'll be glad to have him have the job."

"All right; he'll keep it for you. I'll take him on that understanding."

"You had better let him have it for keeps, Mr. Mueller; he needs it."

"And I need *you*," grunted Mueller; "say, another thing; how are you fixed for money?"

"Oh, I can manage that all right," said Johnny, smiling. He thought of his ridiculous dress-suits, his cravats, his frock-coat, his books and pictures— only they were in Fairport, and he could hardly, yet, ask for them to be forwarded him. His watch his father had given him, and his studs were gifts also, as was most of his jewelry. The few trinkets which he had bought himself had gone long ago; but there was enough left. "Oh, I can manage!" said Johnny cheerfully.

"Better sell 'em to *me!*" growled the clerk; at which divination Johnny grinned and felt the better for it.

Mueller's kindness took shape in more ways than one. He sent the *Fliegende Blätter* and the best grapes in the market, and (though Johnny was soon beyond knowing it) he called daily.

Another visitor was Mrs. Delaney, to whom Johnny intrusted the mission of turning his past pomp of raiment into cash.

"I will if I have to; you rest aisy," she replied, soothing him with a pat on his hair. "I'll git a whole lot, I know that. Now, don't yous be talking, for you do be raising your temperschure, the nuss says, and then I won't be let to see you."

The next visiting day she returned, and he questioned her. What had she sold? With placid mendacity she described his tuxedo suit, and reported that she had obtained thirty dollars for it. "Dirt chape it was, but the bloody ould Shylock wouldn't give a cint more. Will I kape it or bring it to yous?" she asked with calmness to be admired, in view of the fact that she had but two dollars on earth, the same being given her the day before by Mueller. But Johnny made no demands. He sighed in content and told her to keep it and see that the children had all they needed.

"Sure, I will do that!" said Mrs. Delaney. She wondered how she would do it. Johnny, however, slept quietly for the first time since his entrance.

After this, for weeks, no one was allowed speech of him; then, through Mueller, the news reached Conrad, and he appeared laden with sympathy, oranges and fresh eggs.

"Got 'em in the country myself," he explained; "they're reasonably fresh, I guess." He told Johnny that Tyler was in high spirits of late, and that he had just got a tough friend a place on the force. "Tyler's got a big pull in the City Hall, some way. The boys do say it's the same man knifed you. He's a dog named Gweesip Something." For years, it may be added, Giuseppe was a terror to all penniless or contumacious evil-doers. Finally he was killed by one of his own countrymen; why, there are doubtless men who know; but the newspapers have never explained.

"Does Wally Tyler boast of doing me up?" Johnny asked.

"Not exactly. He jest laughs and says you were too fresh and got what was coming to you."

Johnny set his lips firmly; he didn't speak. Conrad changed the subject. That night he wrote a letter to Billy. It was a long letter. The next train brought Billy to Chicago, although he stayed only half a day.

After Billy's return from Indianapolis, the hours did not drag so heavily. True, Johnny would not let him hire a private room; but Billy's influence relaxed the hospital rules, the more readily that the nurses and the hospital orderlies had become interested in their patient.

"He's sandy. That's why I like him," said the ward orderly to Billy. "Ought to have seen him when the doctor was dressing his wound and probing for the bit of knife in it—broke off sharp in the ribs, you know—pyrexia threatened."

"He ain't dangerous?" cried Billy. "Conrad said he was convalescing; you don't mean—"

"Oh, it's out all right; but it was a close call. You look rattled."

"He's the best friend I got in the world," returned Billy ironically, "that's all. And probably not having had the advantage of a medical education like you, I'm easy rattled by your damn technicalities. But you were talking,—I know how he took it. Did everything he was told, never so much as said 'cuss' and thanked the doctors for hurting him. *I* know."

"Well he did. He's mighty nice to everybody. You ask him how he is, and he always says the same: 'Pretty well, thank you.' Did all the while he was sick. I don't care what kind of a ward he's in, I know a gentleman when I see him. And he's one. Mrs. Rand, the day nurse, says the same thing. She's from Kentucky and she'd ought to know."

Obscurely, Johnny was affected by the kindliness about him. It comforted him, in a small measure, and awakened his gratitude in a large one. Before he left the hospital, he made Billy fetch some of his belongings. He gave the pearl cravat-pin to one nurse, and some sleeve-links to the other. They had been his mother's and his heart contracted a little as he handled them; but he was sure that she would not ask him to keep them.

"Nor would my father, either," he thought. He had prepared a little bundle of his two best neck-scarfs to give to the orderlies; but Billy espied it on the bed, and confiscated it imperiously.

"What's the matter?" asked Johnny, the color rising to his pale cheek. "Do you think they look second-hand?"

"No, I don't; they're splendid," snapped Billy; "much too splendid. They belong to you and you've got to keep 'em—and wear 'em Sundays. You'll give these guys this box of cigars."

"But what shall I give you for the cigars?"

"You'll give me a civil 'Thank you,'—something you don't seem willing to give your friends a chance to earn from you. Now, shut up and don't argue. I've got a carriage and I'm going to take you to ride."

The carriage had been carefully picked out by Billy, in person, at the stable of his choice. "Coachman in livery with cloth buttons, and no number on the lamps. Plain and handsome like a private rig," dictated Billy.

Johnny was properly enthusiastic; he said he felt as an imported duke would feel going to be married.

"Oh, it'll do," observed Billy carelessly; "not half as good as you'll take *me* to ride in, if you follow my advice."

"What is your advice?"

"Gimme back my word not to peach to your folks. They'll do the rest."

Johnny's lip curled. "I dare say. But don't do that. I know I'm a blooming ass. I know you've got to be just before you're generous, or you won't be able to be generous very long. I'm learning, all right. But don't call in my stepmother to be kind to me and my old friends to tell me they knew just how it would be, and they're glad I've come to my senses. I nearly drowned once, Billy; the drowning wasn't hard, but coming back to my senses was the very devil; I fancy it is always. I don't care for an audience; I like to be off by myself, so I can kick and swear all I want!"

"Mrs. Winslow isn't that kind," said Billy.

"I know she isn't," Johnny agreed after a difficult

pause; "but there are all the family friends. No doubt they'd improve the occasion. No, Billy, you can roll me in a barrel and stand me on my head and thump me black and blue all you like; but nobody else, please, old man!"

Billy wagged his head in dismal reproof; but he had not really expected success. Most likely he was only after a bargaining basis. The man who refuses the large demand is the more willing to grant the small one. So, at the tail of a few picturesque remarks about fools, he came to his real purpose,—the loan of some money to Johnny.

"I don't need it," said Johnny airily. "I've sold some truck."

Then, in a flash, doubt smote him. "Has Mrs. Delaney been fooling me?" he cried; he was so weak that his voice trembled.

"N—no, she hasn't, she's sold a lot of things!" Billy stuttered in his eagerness.

"She's sold 'em to you, then," said Johnny. He turned his head lest Billy should see the tears gathering under his eyelids.

"S'posen she has?" said Billy sternly—he winked his own eyes and frowned out of the other window. "Why not?"

"Because they don't *fit*," retorted Johnny, with a queer squeak between a sob and a giggle.

"The tailor'll make them all right."

"He can't. You won't ask him. You are only pretending. How much money have you spent on me already?"

Billy folded his arms, casting a haughty eye upward at the satin tufting of the brougham.

"I don't know and I don't care," said Billy; "if I was down on my luck you wouldn't know how much you put up, nor give a damn. You haven't got the right to refuse to let me do for you what you'd do for me in the same case! You haven't!" Billy repeated almost with ferocity. "You insult me! What kind of a damn lop-sided thing do you take friendship to be? Are you so damn much above me that you've done everything on earth for me, made a gentleman out of a mucker, and you won't let me do a thing back! *Damn you!*" gurgled Billy, sniffling.

As South Park is lonely in winter, no one was on the drive to see an athletic looking but very pale young man lay both hands on the slight shoulders of the noted labor leader and try feebly to shake him.

"Tommy-rot!" cried Johnny. "Billy, you're a lovely liar! When you die you'll wheedle St. Peter out of passes for all your friends! I surrender; you shall lend me the money. It'll save you storage on those suits. Only don't try that injured racket when you *know* I love you better than any man in the world, and you've saved my soul alive."

"Oh, rats!" snorted Billy. "You don't be moving about or you'll do yourself a mischief; you know you're all sort er wobbly inside yet. Lean back and play you're the duke. Got your feet on the hot-air box? Let me tuck you up."

He covered Johnny as tenderly as a woman, and his heart leaped when Johnny gave him something like his old merry smile. "You *are* chirking up!" he exulted.

"I am," said Johnny seriously; "I'm *obliged* to,

as a Southern friend of mine would say. Billy, I've
done a sickening lot of genuine thinking, not moon-
ing or dreaming or slanging myself, but straight
thinking things out. And it comes to about this: if
I'm ever going to be able to look Bloker in the face,
in another world—I believe there is another world,
Billy, some sort—or look myself in the face in this,
I've got to do better by Bloker's children than he
ever could have done. Then he ought to forgive
me. To do that I have to make some money. I
have to make it, even if I abandon plans of another
sort. I shall have to quit reforming, except as an
ordinary good citizen, and go to hunting up cash,
just as my father did. He started with nothing, you
know. I don't expect to be as much of a man as he
was, but I'll try to be decent. I'm going to learn
the implement business in all the branches; and then,
when I'm worth their taking, I'm going to ask
Hopkins to give me the job my father would. But
not until I am worth it. And so I've got to keep
my eyes open and be cheerful—or at least be as
cheerful as I can."

"Good *work!*" cried Billy joyously; he had absorbed Johnny's Harvard slang like a sponge. "I
knew you'd come out all right."

"You remember that poem of Browning's you
read to me yesterday, Billy?"

"Sure."

"And those lines,

> " 'That I aspired to be
> And was not, comforts me.'

"Well, that's my case, I guess. They made me

think of a remark of my father's.   Some busybody had come to him with a story about one of the men's just coming out of the penitentiary. *'We've* got to judge a man by what he does,' my father said, 'but I guess the Lord will judge *us* more than our doings.' "

"He kept the man?"

"Oh, yes.   He worked for the Old Colony until he died.   He was a very decent fellow."

"Your father was always a good man to the poor," said Billy, unconsciously dropping into the simple phrase which he had heard his mother use.

"Yes," said Johnny, "he was." There fell a silence; the young dark eyes swept the desolate, wide spaces and formless shrubbery of the Park; but they were seeing Overlook, with its white terraces, and his father's rugged, ungraceful figure was in the doorway, one hand shading his eyes, as he peered down the road, watching for his only son.

"And, really, I never came," thought Johnny heavily. "I'm the Prodigal Son; I've wasted my substance in riotous giving, and I've no father now to meet me afar off." With a pang he recognized that it was his father, not his mother, to whom he would have turned, in this darkest passage of his life. At last the hard-headed, faithful old Anglo-Saxon ruler of men was claiming his own.

CHAPTER V

"ROGER MACK"

There was a little room in Overlook which Peggy Rutherford loved, yet it had witnessed some of the saddest hours of her life. Nevertheless, she had loved it when she was a little child, when it was the Princess Olga's sitting-room, where Johnny and she used to play with innumerable paper dolls, for which they feigned wonderful romances; and she never lost her childish sense of happiness in it, even after the happiness, like the childhood, had dwindled to a pensive memory.

The room was on the second story, with a Palladian window filling most of one wall and giving on the river and the dim Illinois hills. Wainscoting and mantel-piece, lintels and jamb, massive, tall doors and crenulated molding on the ceiling and under the mantel-shelf,—all were as Peggy's childhood knew them; painted, to-day, the same smooth, glossy, but not glittering white which always had assembled in her mind the mingled sensations of the white of lilies and of a certain delectable candy that Johnny and she named "cream pull."

The house had been built before the days of grill-work, and the interior construction was supervised by an old German, a craftsman of no mean skill who

313

died ignorant that he was an artist, hence had never muddled his vision with ambition; and, being an honest man, used only well-seasoned lumber and plenty of nails, and never trusted his rabbets or mortises to any eye save his own. Stanch and true Winslow found the old mansion, inside, whatever havoc the weather had played without; and stanch and true it was to-day. There was the same vista past the door, which Peggy's childish eyes had admired; the ample hall with the well in the center, up which wound the great spiral staircase with its white balustrade and mahogany hand-rail. A long-deserved paddling did she, Peggy, once receive from dear old dead mammy for sliding down those balusters from the third story, closely followed by Johnny, with Hilma pursuing by the stairs, a bad third. Through another door could be seen the mahogany four-poster of the princess' time, and the same low-boy and high-boy that she had used, with their glass knobs and brass escutcheons. The curtains of chintz and swiss muslin on the windows and the bed, and the chintz on the chairs, as well as the wall-paper, had been renewed often; but so pious was the copy of the past that Peggy seemed to see the same sheer whiteness of the valance that she used to covet for a frock, and the same sprawling roses on chintz and walls.

In the room where she sat, the walls were tinted grayly-green as of old, and the white curtains of the window might have been the very curtains she had watched the princess push aside, so many times, to look down at the humble roof-trees of the Patch. Almost with the vividness of reality Peggy could

see that exquisite light shape in the trailing dove-
gray gown which made delicate shadows as it fell;
she could see the long arm in the elbow sleeve of the
period, the white, lovely forearm emerging from a
filmy fall of lace, and the beautiful hand with its
flashing rings; she could see the shining dark head,
so like Johnny's, in that proud and graceful poise
which her son had inherited. The image in the
girl's mind was so strongly colored that it made the
portrait which hung in the bedchamber seem less
real than its spectral beauty.

The portrait was new. It had been painted since
Mr. Winslow's death, since Johnny's vanishing.
Mrs. Winslow had an enlargement made of the
miniature which was done of the princess during
her visit to Russia, after her marriage. Her husband never spoke of it; whether he ever looked at
it or not his closest friends, even the closest friend
of all, his wife, did not know; but two years after
his death Emma came across it in a secret drawer of
his writing-desk. She planned to give it to Johnny
on his next birthday, and she had the water-color
copy made to give at the same time. She hung it
in Johnny's chamber, which had been his mother's,
placing it on the wall to the right of the bed, at such
an angle that the beautiful face would meet his eyes
as the sun met them, when he woke in the morning.
She took infinite pains with the gift, and perhaps
spent on it some hopes that his pleasure would in-
cline his heart more kindly toward the giver. But
it was never given. Before his birthday Johnny
had disappeared. So the picture hung beside the
bed which was always kept daintily ready for the

son of the house, who never came. Always the room was swept and garnished, but only the maids entered it, unless Emma Winslow went there, alone and unobserved, to think her own thoughts.

There were other pictures in the room where Peggy sat, that Johnny and she did not see, as well as some that they knew. Over them all dominated the portrait of Josiah Winslow, painted by a great artist, during the last year of his life; a rugged and yet indomitable face, wherein the marks of care showed, but power showed, also, and a softer look not always visible, but which his friends knew. On another wall was a group of photographs, large and small, all different images of Johnny; Johnny as a laughing, dimpled baby; Johnny as a solemn little boy; Johnny in his cadet's uniform; Johnny at Harvard, smiling above his track sweater with its hard-won H, or languid and elegant in his class picture; and, larger than the others, Johnny holding the little sister that died, on Varonók, his own horse.

But the new pictures in the room and Peggy's typewriter were almost the only changes. Peggy's desk was the same George Washington which Mrs. Burney had once given her brother, and the desk which Mrs. Winslow used was the old "secretary" purchased by Josiah's agent in Salem, in the eighties, not only because of the beauty of its leaded panes of glass above and its curiously inlaid drawers, but because tradition gave it to a luckless Tory Winslow of Josiah's own line. On the mantel-shelf, now as always, stood small copies of Marc Autocolski's Ivan the Terrible, and his tremendous Mephistopheles. Between the two, above them both, on the wall, was a bas-relief of Joraslav the Wise. The princess had bought the Ivan, saying: "Ah! there, there is the true spirit of despotism!" Josiah merely grunted, but when the statuette was unpacked in Overlook he took out another carefully shapeless bundle and unwrapped the Mephistopheles, with the remark: "You are right about Ivan; he is the symbol of despotism; now here is his pretty twin, Nihilism." Then, as the princess gazed in silence: "Your countryman is great, Olga, great! Look at this creature; he's not Goethe's gentleman devil, not a bit; he's a brute, with a head on him. Look at his clever, sneering head and then at the horrible hands and feet of him, an animal and a fiend—oh, I'll chance with his ugly stick, rather than him."

Their positions had never been altered. The Mephistopheles and the Joraslav were Josiah's only work in the room. Otherwise it was all Olga's. And it had not been changed. There were the same ikons on the wall, the same Russian bronzes of troikas and wild horses, the same figurine of a Tsigane, the same Venetian glass vases filled with violets, as she used to keep them, although their iridescent fragility had been the despair of a dozen housemaids. And in the window-box, with the earliest spring, bloomed hot-house azaleas and hyacinths like those which had brought the Russian a perfume of home. The waxed floors were polished to the same perilous gloss that had been the small Peggy's undoing more than once, as she skipped recklessly across them, and on the floor were the same Persian and Daghestan rugs from the Nijnii Novgorod fair. The two strong souls that had clashed and suffered, each in its own fashion, violently or dumbly, had been defeated by the stronger years and driven forth from the shining of the sun; but these insensate objects were scarcely marked by time. Below, and in the other rooms, Emma Winslow had given her own taste or temperament some indulgence; but here the least detail was respected.

"Johnny will come back," she said once to Peggy. "I want him not to feel strange in his own house, especially in his mother's room."

In the Princess Olga's room, then, Peggy was sitting before her desk, a week after Johnny took his convalescent's drive, the time lacking two days till Christmas. She had dropped her pen, and her eyes were exploring, idly, the snow-enchanted slopes, slanting down to the chill, white roofs of the flat fields below and a wide, frozen, opal-tinted plain that had been the flowing river. The bend of her head disclosed how fine was the texture and how snowy the skin of her pretty neck, and what graceful tendrils of silky bronze hair had escaped from its coil, to curl below. Her long lashes fell on a paler cheek than Mistress Peggy had used to show; there was a sharper oval to the face, and the mouth was set more firmly.

Mrs. Winslow, who was writing at the secretary, watched her for a few moments, while she seemed to be looking at the paper under her hand.

"Peggy!" she called; but she did not look up.

"Yes, dear?" said Peggy. As she turned it was as if she had slipped her features into a mask of attentive interest.

"Peggy, I suppose you had nothing in *your* mail

about Johnny?" Had Mrs. Winslow been looking she might have seen a flicker of color, like the shifting, luminous cloud of a cat's-eye, waver over the nape of the girl's neck; but Peggy's tones were clear and cool: "No, Aunt Emma."

"There is nothing but the two letters from Billy Bates, since he left Chicago," Mrs. Winslow went on, "and he says he can't tell anything, except that Johnny was well and he thought on the right road to come to his senses, and the last of those was five weeks ago, from Indianapolis. He hasn't answered my last letter yet."

"You wrote to all the list that Harvard man sent you, didn't you?"

"To every one, begging him, if he could, without betraying any confidence, to tell me how I could reach Johnny. I have written to his tailor, and his haberdasher. I have hunted up his shoemaker. They have never heard from him since last summer. He closed up his account at the bank; paid all his small bills—if he had any, and—simply slipped under the wave. His aunt hasn't heard a word—nobody has heard a word. You see, Johnny's most intimate Harvard chum died."

"But Billy Bates?"

Mrs. Winslow thought a moment before she answered, rather slowly: "Yes, we've Billy Bates. Do you know what he has done? He came round to me and asked me how he could get some of the Old Colony common stock; he had a few thousands he wished to invest. I gave him a chance to buy at a reasonable figure—"

"That is, you sold him some of your own, cheap?"

"Why not? He was good to Johnny. I made him promise that if Johnny should be ill or in trouble, he would give us a chance to help him."

Peggy only nodded; but in a moment she made an excuse for getting stamps for her letters, which brought her near enough to drop a light kiss on Emma Winslow's hair. The older woman put her arm about the supple waist and held her tenderly close. "I suppose you know, Peggy, you are a great comfort to me?" she said.

"It's my business to be," laughed Peggy. "I get a large salary for being; and then—oh, I do love you, Aunt Emma!"—while she caught the hand and held it to her cheek and her lips.

"Don't you suppose that's a comfort to me, too?" said the elder woman. "Plenty of people like me; I trust a great many respect me; but who loves me besides my good old dad and you? Well, maybe Elly and Cis a little, and Claudia Loraine and a few friends. You see, it's not a long list."

"It's a heap longer than you know," said Peggy.

"Do you remember,"—Emma Winslow's tone had changed—"it was in this very room Johnny came—that day my husband died; and you stood, there, in the other doorway? For months I hated the shine of the setting sun on the river, just because it was shining, shining in that blinding way, then. And, do you know, the first thing that roused me was that I must comfort Johnny, his father's only son. But—he wouldn't let me. He was perfectly gentle, gentle as snow, but I couldn't reach him. And yet he has so kind a heart,—too kind, too easily touched!" She turned away and stood with

her back to Peggy, looking out on the snow.
"Christmas is a hard season," she said; "I don't
know how I am going to bear it without—and
Johnny gone, too."

"Oh, Johnny!" Peggy broke in loftily; but her
heart ached for the uncomplaining pain that she
knew was in the other woman's face. "Johnny'll
come back all right. I'll answer for *Johnny.*"

Emma Winslow tried to laugh, but the laugh
broke; she laid her head against the window-pane.
"Peggy," said she, "do you mind if I cry? I think
it's the season and the holly and the sleigh-bells;
they get on my nerves."

Now, never before had Peggy seen any intimation
of nerves about her friend and protector. Mrs.
Winslow's self-control seemed a fastness which none
of the afflictions or perils of humanity could storm.

Such conquering of her own spirit was beyond
Margaret Rutherford. It held her at arm's length,
as those qualities in our friends, which we admire
but have no hopes of imitating, generally hold us.

And now Peggy saw a tear splash on the clenched
hand at the window-pane; and she was abashed. It
had not been philosophy or indifference, then, which
had kept Aunt Emma so tolerant, so uncomplaining
about Johnny. Johnny had hurt her all along, just
as he had hurt Peggy, and Peggy felt a sudden pain
in her throat sweep in a curve to the roof of her
mouth.

But even as Peggy thought this, Emma turned
her quiet face, wiping her eyes, with a kind of apology in her smile, and sat down calmly in an easy
chair.

The chair was just under the large portrait of Winslow. While his wife talked, she looked into his face. On hers was almost the expression it might have worn, had the painted man been a sentient listener to her words. "I'd like to have you understand," she said, "how I feel about Johnny. I took him to my heart from the first, when he was a little, lonely creature mourning for his mother, but never making any fuss about it. There never was such a sweet little chap in the world!"

"No," said Peggy, "I reckon there never was."

"I think at first he did like me a little. He seemed to."

"I know he did," said Peggy.

"But after I married his father it was different. He never forgave me for usurping his mother's place. I suppose that was how he put it. I tried to understand his point of view. I think I do, in a way. He wouldn't *let* himself grow attached to me. But —he loved baby, Peggy."

"I'm *sure,*" said Peggy.

"The day after we buried her he went out to the cemetery. He gathered some wild flowers, and I found them there on the little grave. That night, when he went back, I thought there was something different in his face. But when I saw him again it was gone, or else I only imagined it. I don't deny his coldness hurt me, but I tried to be reasonable and never let his father suspect that it did hurt. I felt all the time that if Si could only find his son and Johnny find his father, and they could understand each other, I would have no right to grumble, whether he ever cared for me or not. But while I feel convinced that Johnny really loved his father, very deeply —"

"He fairly *adored* him!" asserted Peggy stoutly; "he somehow got all wrong about him; but he was awfully fond of him and admired him, just the same."

"Yet they seemed to drift apart. And I could do nothing to bring them nearer because he mistrusted me—"

"Shame on him!" exploded Peggy. "He was always the pig-headedest little boy, even! Oh, the things I am going to say to him when I once get hold of him again!"

"It's his conscience, of course. I often told Si he shouldn't blame Johnny for inheriting the Puritan conscience. The trouble was, he had a Puritan conscience and a Russian imagination—"

"And his *own* obstinacy."

"I don't agree with you; I think he is open to conviction, if it is only rubbed in hard enough. But, Peggy, don't you see that with his convictions there was danger that he would wreck not only his fortune but himself, if he were trusted with it? The times we have talked about it, Mr. Winslow and I, thinking one plan and another! The weight it was on his father's heart—I don't suppose anybody can know. At one time Si made a will giving me everything for my life. 'I can trust Johnny with you,' he said; but I tore the will up, and he made another before he went to bed very similar to the one last made.

"Our idea was to let Johnny see for himself. We knew he would lose the hundred thousand. But we expected then that I should show him his father's letter to him and his father's letter of trust to me. See, I will show my letter to you, dear. I can't have any secrets about Johnny with you."

She took the letter out of a locked box, in which she replaced it after Peggy had read it. Peggy, with a moving of the heart, perceived in the box a pile of the small diaries which Mr. Winslow used, his watch and chain, and such personal trifles.

"Well?" said Mrs. Winslow.

"It's very generous," said Peggy, "but I knew you would be. I suppose meantime you meant to help Johnny."

"I meant to lend him money, and let him show the stuff he is made of. But—we can't find him."

Peggy was standing by the window. "You said we should have no secrets," she said slowly. "I think so, too. There is a little thing. It didn't seem worth while—until I found out more—but—I'm going to tell you everything just as it happens. There's Mishka*; *he* must hear from Johnny."

"Yes, through Billy; no more than *we* know."

Peggy raised and dropped her eyes; she blushed faintly, finally laughed. "I was trying to get round to it. To-day—well, to-day, Michael showed me a letter from Johnny. I'll go get it."

And she hurriedly left the room. Emma smiled and thought: "I dare say if I could follow her I should find she was wearing it on her heart. Oh, how ridiculous are girls!"

Then she looked from the baby girl on the wall

*Russian diminutive of Michael.

to Johnny's last picture. Where was he now, this Christmas-tide? With no money, no friends—but her dismal reverie halted on the word and she smiled. Wherever he was, she knew right well that Johnny would not be without friends.

Peggy returned with an open letter. "The paper is off a block," announced she; "the envelope is a stamped one and postmarked Chicago. That tells nothing except that Billy Bates must have been in Chicago last week."

"As I am hunting Billy, that's something," said Mrs. Winslow. She unfolded the paper and dropped it. "In Russian!" she cried.

"Of course. He always writes Russian to Mishka, but I made him translate it. He says kind things to Mishka and sends him a Russian picture-card and tells him that he would send him more, but he has been in hospital, ill for six weeks, and, while he gets good wages, he has to spend a good deal, for he is helping take care of three little children."

"Three children!" repeated Mrs. Winslow; "whose children?"

"You wouldn't suppose Johnny could have carried his nonsense so far as—as—to marry somebody?" Peggy made the speech with elaborate carelessness.

"No, I *wouldn't*," retorted Mrs. Winslow.

"A widow," suggested Peggy, who had never harbored the suspicion until this moment, but instantly began to color it with the hues of life. "One of those right helpless, silly, deplorable sort of creatures that look pathetic and always have their shirt waists parting from their skirts. Husband probably

killed by machinery and the children are all about
the same age, one born about every six months—"

"That, Peggy," Mrs. Winslow interrupted, "is
impossible."

"Not to that sort of woman. They are bound by
no natural laws. No doubt she's pretty in a driveling
fashion—"

"But, Peggy," Mrs. Winslow objected, "he says
he was in a hospital. If he were married his wife
would take care of him."

"Not *that* kind," said Peggy firmly; "she's too
trifling."

"But he says he takes part of the care of the children."

"She takes the other part; she's so trifling she
can't even take care of her own children; it's awful
to think what Johnny probably has to eat."

"Peggy," asked Mrs. Winslow, "do you believe
that rubbish, yourself?"

Peggy's white teeth flashed; she owned up with a
laugh: "No, Aunt Emma, I only like to pretend,
just as Johnny and I used to, as children; there is a
sort of joy flinging oneself thoroughly into a dramatic situation. Don't you ever want to get into
some one's else skin? But Johnny?—I'm pretty sure
Johnny is taking care of some mate's kit of humanity, and the man's dead. I reckon Billy's the other
partner in the kindergarten."

"That would be likely," mused Mrs. Winslow,
"and like Johnny. Peggy, do you suppose he was
very ill? Why didn't Billy Bates tell us?"

Peggy supposed because Johnny would not allow
him, and Billy was straitened in resources by

some promise. But why couldn't there be a letter sent—through Michael?

"You write a letter, you mean?" queried Emma Winslow.

"Of course not,"—Peggy's tone and pose were full of dignity—"*you* write him a letter."

Emma smiled wearily. "But, you see, I have written, with no result. I only got profuse and humble apologies from Bates because he had promised that he would not forward any letters. Ivan considered it was the same as if he had died—"

"Oh, can't Johnny be mawkish, sometimes!" cried Peggy, tossing her head. "I'm *glad* I called him a plumb idiot."

"I don't think Johnny even thought of opening the envelope. He didn't."

"He'd have to open this, for it would be inside Michael's."

"He would know the handwriting; that would stop him at the first sentence."

"I'd typewrite it."

"And if he read it, read it to the close, he would steel his heart against every word I say. If you wrote it, he would read it in the first place, and it would move him in the second."

Peggy took a turn up and down the room. "I don't see how I can, Aunt Emma; I told him I wouldn't ever speak to him again, *to save his life!* It was so silly and cruel and horrid of me; but I did. And I don't see how I *can* break my word."

"It was only a foolish expression. You didn't believe you would keep your word; he didn't believe you would."

"Oh, yes, ma'am, he did. And Johnny never breaks his word. Oh, I shan't break mine."

"But this isn't speaking,—since you are so absurd."

"Besides—I *have* written him," said Peggy in a very little, soft voice.

"Peggy!"

"Oh, not as myself; dear no; that would break my word. I wrote him (through Michael) as a—a boy —a Fairport boy, who used to steal rides on the cars and who was once chased by the constable and rescued with two or three others by Johnny. That rescue really happened. I said I was one of that crowd. I was, in fact, hanging on to the caboose, and the brakeman didn't know it until they slowed down, and he spied us and signaled a policeman. I don't know what we should have done; the prison doors yawned for us, as they used to say in the stories; but in the very instant of doom Johnny and Mishka appeared. Mishka was driving the big landau and Johnny's nice little face was at the window. The policeman was pounding down the street after us. We dived and doubled, shot into one shop and out the back yard and came out behind him, and made straight for Johnny, who had the door open. He sheltered us; and Michael drove away while the policeman hollered to stop. There were three boys and I. I never saw any of the boys before or after; but I pretended to be one of those boys. I called myself Roger Mack; Mack, after my horse down in Tennessee, and Roger I chose for pretty, as old mammy used to say. I told him I lived in Fairport and worked for my living and had half-way educated myself. It would be a great help to me if he would write me and tell me of any job he might hear of in Chicago, if he was there. I was giving the letter to Michael to post for me. What's more, I got Michael to say 'Roger Mack is a good boy.'"

"But the handwriting; you couldn't disguise that?"

"I didn't try. I consider that right clever of me. You know the Martins? The older sister sews for Cousin Rebecca Winter. Well, Sadie Martin is a typewriter, and she taught me a little stenography; she's giving me lessons, right along. She is really a fine girl, and she's as trustworthy—as trustworthy as your William Bates, who admires her very much, by the way. Sadie is my fellow conspirator; that is, she is one of them. She has heard so much about Johnny from the *fidus Achates* that she is very interested. But the best is, she can hold her tongue."

"And she wrote the letter?"

"She did. She admired it very much."

"And whom else have you in the plot?"

"Why, Michael, of course; and only Luke Darrell, else."

Mrs. Winslow laughed a little. "We never can seem to get along without Luke Darrell in Fairport. But what is *he* for?"

"Address place to send letters *to*. Care L. Darrell, Livery and Feed Stables, Fairport."

"I see, dear. What did Luke say when you told him?"

"He was right nice. He screwed his eyes up— after he had put himself, his office, and his office stationery at my service—and he said: 'Well, Miss

Rutherford, if you'll excuse me saying so, you're showing good judgment. You can't drive a high-stepping colt in harness, first jump; it's better to start with a halter.' Well, I don't know how much we'll get out of it, but there is my secret, Aunt Emma; I won't have any more."

Thus did Roger Mack begin his career,—a longer one than his sponsors foreboded.

CHAPTER VI

TYLER PASSES

Tyler was a cheerful man these days. It is doubtful whether he really meant murder by Johnny, although his comrades in the assault would not have stopped short of it after their tempers were roused. He was well content when the affair ended with Johnny's losing five weeks and his job (as he thought), besides having a bad time in the hospital. He didn't hesitate to say to his intimates that he had taught the young cub a lesson, maybe he'd behave himself now.

But it was with some misgivings that, one evening, peacefully playing poker in his favorite saloon, and holding at that moment a full house of high character, he perceived Johnny's dark head in the doorway.

Johnny was accompanied by two molders, generally leaders among the radical element. He was still pale from his illness; but he walked with a light, springy step. He wore his working-clothes.

"I'm out," said Tyler's neighbor, dropping his cards.

Secretly Tyler wished that he were out, too. But he studied his hand and then carelessly shoved a pile of blue chips into the heap on the table.

"Fifteen better," said he.

Two more men dropped out.

The fifth put out his hand with his cards in it, as if to throw them on the table, but in the act hesitated, because he saw Johnny at his elbow.

"Hullo, Gleason!" he called; "glad to see you're out."

"Don't let me interrupt your game," said Johnny, "I only want to speak a word with Mr. Tyler when the hand's out."

"That decides it," laughed the man. "I call; Wally, take my pile." He pushed the last of his blue chips into the center.

"Full house, queens up," said Tyler.

"Not good; kings over here." Then, as he raked in the swollen aggregation of rising and falling jackpots he gleefully confessed: "I'd made up my mind Wally had fours and was going to pull out, when I saw Van here, and my mind sort of shifted."

Tyler kept his easy smile (he prided himself on being a good loser), but his thoughts were as ravening wolves. He greeted Johnny perfunctorily.

"I have only one word to say," said Johnny in a low voice, with extreme gentleness. "I'm not going to ask you who was the man who stabbed me last month,—I don't care who he was. He was only a tool—" Tyler's strident tones overrode the other's quiet tenor:

"Look here, young gentleman, Gleetzin, or whatever you call yourself, I fought you with my hands, nothing else; and you fought me with knucks!"

"And I'll fight again with knucks, any time," returned Johnny in the same gentle accents, "when three men jump out of the dark at me. At any time you wish I am willing to fight you, fairly and squarely, with bare knuckles or with gloves; and may the best man win! But if you set on me again with knives or crowbars or pistols, I go ready to protect myself, and I shall *kill* you. That's all. Good evening." Johnny wheeled half around as if to go.

"Aw, cool off," sneered Tyler; "I ain't fighting with a typewriter and can't keep up with your lingo; but I'll fight you, all right—*and this minute!*"

He had been measuring Johnny; it came to him that the young fellow was enfeebled by illness and should prove an easy mark; he was sure of it when Johnny seemed about to depart so tamely. But he found his mistake before the end of the first round, —suspected it the minute Johnny peeled off his coat and showed his undershirt and the belt about his waist. "He meant to pick a fight, by hell!" darted through his brain, and his heart beat more quickly. The next second a body blow sent him reeling. He recovered himself and made a rush.

Tyler's terrible rushes, wherein by sheer force and weight he broke down his opponent's guard, were known wherever he was known. He hurled himself on Johnny with the force of a battering-ram, but what avails a battering-ram against a tiger which leaps out of its way? Before he could rush again, Johnny feinted with his right, and easily parrying Tyler's half-hearted jab at his eyes, sent a crushing left-handed blow straight at the big man's heart.

The fight was ended again. Tyler, who had toppled over, got on to his knees; but the barkeeper, the recognized representative of the Red Cross on such occasions, hauled him behind the bar and held him with arguments and arms, while he (secretly thankful for his bonds) made futile struggles to escape and get at Johnny, and swore ungratefully at his guardian angel. This latter simply winked at the crowd in the door, whence emerged a tall and burly policeman.

"Do yous make complaint, Mr. Tyler?" asked the tall policeman, with much civility.

"No, I don't make complaint," Tyler replied sullenly. "I can settle my troubles outside the City Hall."

He hadn't lost all his shrewdness, and he knew the popular view; moreover, to do him justice, he had plenty of confidence in his own powers.

"Aw, go get the drinks on me," he added with a forced grin. On the whole, he slipped out of the humiliation of the occasion with considerable deftness. But never had Tyler hated a man as he hated Johnny from that day henceforward. The hatred was not violent, as it had been before, but it was virulent. And when he lost his election as district president he gave the credit where it belonged and hated Johnny a little more. All the same, Johnny won. Before six months had passed he had forced Tyler out of the molders' union.

They had only one interview. They were alone together, with a newspaper man at the keyhole of one door and Giuseppe, in Tyler's interests, at the other.

Tyler came straight to the point: "What do you want to let up on me?" said he.

"You to leave the molders' and leave Chicago," said Johnny.

"I'm going into the machinists', anyhow," said Tyler carelessly, "but why should I leave Chicago?"

Johnny's reply was given close to Tyler's face, so low that the newspaper man could not catch it, which was a sore chagrin to him.

"Because I know you made Evers and Hastings pay you three hundred dollars to keep on hiring non-union men. And I can prove it. Because I know you sold out to Wethers; and I've got one of your letters."

"Maybe you'll show it to me," jeered Tyler, but his color turned.

"I'll show you a copy," said Johnny, and took out a slip from his pocketbook, which (always keeping his eye on the man), he handed to him.

Tyler read it. His face was undecipherable. He pushed it back to Johnny.

"It's good," said he, in poker parlance, "but I was going, anyhow. I'm not stuck on Chicago. But you're not through with me *yet*, Mr. John Winslow."

But Johnny was not disturbed. He was interested in politics, for the most exciting presidential election since the war was drawing near, and the entire American people were studying political economy. He was also interested in his work, which now was in a steel mill; and he frequently told Billy, with a touch of his old enthusiasm, that steel was the most wonderful and interesting thing in the world. He got good wages. The little Blokers were no longer a continual goad to his remorse; they were not only

Bloker's children, they were their own often puzzling but interesting selves. In short, he was recovering his spirits. He was desperately unhappy often, and lonely beyond expression; but his life began to creep out of the pit.

CHAPTER VII

JOHNNY MEETS AN OLD FRIEND

Not long after Tyler's flitting, Johnny ran against an old Fairport friend. Several times he had seen familiar faces on the street, had dodged them unobserved and, finally, fled from them when he feared their notice; this time there was no fleeing. The friend was Mrs. Winter, and he met her in the last place which he would have feared as holding any danger of that sort, a street-car, since all Fairport knew Mrs. Winter's detestation of street-cars.

"So long as I have fifty cents left in my pocket," she was accustomed to remark, "I will never ride in those disobliging pest-houses!"

But there are two things, besides the good will, necessary to take a cab instead of the cars: one is money, with which Mrs. Winter was amply supplied, the other (quite as necessary) is a cab to take. This day she found that, by some mistake, the cab on which she counted was not at hand; rather than be late for an appointment she stooped her proud spirit to the plebeian transport.

The car was full. A young man gave her his seat. He was a handsome, tall, clean-shaven, dark, young fellow, who wore a blue flannel shirt and

337

trousers that had seen trouble with grocery barrels; but his battered soft hat came off with the grace of a courtier, as he said: "Will you take this seat, madam?"

"Thank you," she began with perfunctory courtesy; then she looked him full in the face. "Isn't it Johnny Winslow?" she inquired calmly. Johnny hesitated, he flushed.

"Don't bother to deny it," said she; "this isn't the place for a talk, but won't you come to the Annex— after you've got on some other clothes—and take dinner with me? Better. If you wish, I'll never mention seeing you."

Johnny's wits were stampeded by the surprise; moreover, he felt a traitorous weakness of the heart at the sight of those kind, familiar features; he was disgusted with himself, but he was glad; he was so glad, he couldn't keep his lips from curling as he stammered: "I can't come to dinner; but I will come in the evening, if you are not engaged." He did come. He appeared in his workman's Sunday clothes, and sat in front of Mrs. Winter, clasping his hands over his knee and lifting his boyish smile to her keen eyes.

"Well, Johnny-Ivan," she said, "have you been knocked down in the crush yet?"

"Knocked down and trampled on," he answered, "whichever way you mean."

"Mind telling me, or haven't you got there yet?"

"I'm not quite there yet, I think, Mrs. Winter; I'm too sore."

"Very well. Only you used to call me Aunty Winter."

"You are such a very great lady—"

"Provincial, only, Johnny-Ivan; but what if I were? You haven't, I take it, done anything unworthy of a gentleman or of Governor Josiah?"

"No, I hope not. Tell me, Aunty Winter, does the portrait of the old governor still hang in the library?"

"Just the same; Emma Winslow has good taste, I will say, though she *has* stolen Peggy from me."

"Is Miss Rutherford with Mrs. Winslow?" He looked at his boots.

"Peggy is with your stepmother, yes. Good thing, too, although I wanted her myself, and she's *my* kin. She makes Emma mighty comfortable; and I think Emma means to do the right thing by her."

"She's well, I hope," said Johnny constrainedly.

"Who? Mrs. Winslow, or Peggy?"

"Both."

Mrs. Winter smiled, and rumpled his hair. "It's good to see your curly head again, Johnny-Ivan. What are you up to?"

"I'm a rougher in a steel mill."

"It *sounds* rather discreditable; but I suppose it isn't."

"It isn't, at all. It's rather high up."

"What do you do, by chance?"

"I pull out red-hot billets from the furnace and—"

"Gracious! Don't you get burned?"

"Oh, I have some tongs."

"Jo'nivan, will you give me your word you don't get burned?"

"Not now. And, cheer up, the worst is yet to come! I'm going to be a heater's helper, next week."

"That sounds dangerous, too."

"It's not. It's a big promotion. I shall earn four and five dollars a day."

"Is that good wages?"

"Very."

"Where do you live? Write it on a card, will you?" And as Johnny obeyed: "Take one of my cards and tack it on to your clothes; how many suits do you have? Take a number and tack one on each coat, so if you meet with any accident I'll know it. I don't think much of your trade for safety. Talking of accidents, I wonder were you ever in the Presbyterian Hospital?"

Johnny admitted that he had been in the Presbyterian Hospital.

Mrs. Winter nodded. "I heard of you; the nurses and the superintendent were very taken with your polite manners."

"I'm glad I didn't discredit my class. Workingmen are fine fellows."

"You still think that, and still know more than your father?"

"I still think that; but so did my father, and he knew a *lot* more than I."

"About labor?"

"About everything."

Mrs. Winter leaned back; a strikingly handsome, elderly woman—past seventy, Johnny knew, did he stop to think, but no one ever stopped to think about Mrs. Winter's years. She did not defy the approach of age for a good reason,—age did not approach

"KEEP BACK!" SAID HE. "HE'S DEAD; YOU'VE KILLED HIM, ALL RIGHT!"

her. The supple and erect form on the red brocaded sofa, which had waltzed with the blue and gold uniforms of the Civil War, two years after this speaking was agile enough to tread a measure with the clay-colored khaki of the Spanish volunteers; her lustrous eyes were undimmed and her delicate skin singularly free from wrinkles; if her black hair had turned gray, it was still, to all appearances, abundant, with a burnished gloss, not a dead or faded grayness; and when she smiled she showed her own white teeth. She was not smiling now, but viewing the young man with much gravity.

"Do you prefer your new class to your old class?" were her first words.

"No," said Johnny.

"Do you prefer your new mode of life to your old?"

"No," said Johnny.

"Well, why don't you give it all up and come back?"

"Ah, that's too complicated. I can't get back, for one thing."

"But you can. Have you ever thought, Johnny, that the loss of your fortune isn't irretrievable? You have until you are thirty. If you can make one hundred thousand dollars before you are thirty, you will have all your share of your father's fortune."

Johnny studied the toes of his best shoes, and his mouth puckered rather ruefully. "I have, since I left college, up to date, been able to save just forty-eight dollars and fifty cents," said he; "that doesn't look as if I'd be a bloated capitalist in a hurry, does it? But I'll tell you my plan. I wanted to learn the plow business—go through all the branches; but the union requirements for apprentices are pretty stiff; so, as I had a chance to get into steel in an open shop, I went in. I mean to learn the business, all the branches, be able to be rougher, finisher, roller, heater, melter, mechanic—know the *business*. Then with customary assurance I shall try to convince some company that I'm just the man they want to put in charge of a rolling-mill or an open hearth plant. I shall jump to three or four thousand a year and have my dress-suit pressed, if the moths haven't eaten it up. And then—well, then, I shall have my foot on the ladder. But it will take longer than five years to make good so I could claim what I might have had."

Mrs. Winter drew a deep breath. "Johnny, your father would be mighty happy if he could hear you talk that way. I believe, for all your charm, you have a heap of sense."

"I'm afraid you think I am expecting to get on too fast. Very likely I am; but that is what I am trying for. Then I have another chance. I can be organizer, business agent, what you would call a walking delegate, and try to make the unions stand for something better than striking,—be the kind of labor leader Billy Bates is. That is what I set out to be."

"Well, but—"

"That's it. *But*. Maybe my 'but' isn't the same as yours, but it comes to the same conclusion. I am not free to try. Maybe, anyhow, I can help them better as an employer than directly on their side. But some one, I hope Billy Bates, is going to show the unions that they haven't begun to do half what they can do for their men. Why, just take this one point of protection; the union only protects the workingman from his immediate employer, who, in nine out of ten cases, is the mildest of his oppressors; the poor fellow has no shield against the instalment Shylock, who takes three or four prices out of him, and then the goods, themselves, if the last ounce of the pound of flesh isn't forthcoming! Or against the rascally landlord who charges extortionate rent for pestilential fire-traps! Or the charlatans who fatten on the poor fellow's trustfulness in those who profess to be his friends! Or the sham doctors who fleece him and poison him and kill him, and charge his widow for the murder! The destruction of the poor is their poverty; there's nothing truer in the Bible. But only in a few cases does a man's union lift a hand for him, outside of his shop. They ought. And, in the shops, the root of the whole matter, as Billy says, is that the unions haven't yet learned, though they have *begun* to learn, that the real way to better the condition of workingmen is to make them better workers! The unions have taken about all they can from the share of the employer. The only way for the men to get more, permanently, is to *produce* more. It used to make me tired when the boys kicked at my doing so much. Putting up wages and prices all round helps no one —instead, it is apt to bring on a collapse—but I beg your pardon, Aunty Winter, I am going on like a house-afire, not giving you a chance to escape!"

"Never mind me, Johnny; I like to hear you."

"But I may be tiring you; as for me, I never go

to bed so long as I can get anybody to listen to my artless prattle."

"But, Johnny-Ivan, tell me; how do you expect to convert your unions?"

"Well, I told you; I don't; there are Billy Bates, and Arthur and Sargent, and there's a young fellow named Mitchell coming on,—that's the crowd I expect to do the John-the-Baptist stunt. As I'm situated, I can only be the man behind the gun."

"It will amount, virtually;" said Mrs. Winter musingly, "it will amount to converting the unions; and, for that matter, the manufacturers are about as stupid; and sometimes I think they are not so willing to learn. The trouble is, it is only a question of interest, and they haven't either of them the sense to see where their interest lies."

But Johnny, who had jumped up and was pacing the floor, spouting jets of oratory, like a perambulating volcano, broke in: "There is where I disagree with you, Aunty Winter; on all hands you hear the same story; how materialistic we Americans are. We are *not!* We are sentimental idealists! I know the workingmen are—"

"The socialists may be."

"All of us. There's a notion nowadays that most of them are forced into the union. Undoubtedly some are; but a good many more pretend to be, to stand in with the employers and carry water on both shoulders. Do you think that it is the material benefits of a union that attract the men most? My dear Aunty Winter, a skilled workman doesn't need the union; he can get his price, even a bad year like this, without paying dues and risking having to

stop work to help somebody else. Yet he joins.
Why? Because he is an idealist. Because he is willing to sacrifice himself to help the others. He is the
fellow who goes into a strike last—and gives it up
last! Well, there is another reason why he believes
in the unions; it isn't such a high reason, but it is
purely sentimental, too. You don't know how lonely
a poor man is. He is so unfriended and so bewildered. He is always being shoved aside. Sometimes he is crushed by his loneliness; sometimes he
turns sullen. In either case, put him into a union.
He feels he is part of a great organization of
brothers. Send him on a committee to anybody, no
matter how unimportant; he is no longer insignifi-
cant; he has a power behind him, and he can give
back talk freely. He does, too, if he is fresh, in a
new union. But you see that is all sentiment."

"Well, don't you think there is a heap of sentiment in this envy and hatred of the poor for the
rich, which seems the fashion? Johnny, the manufacturers don't continually grind the faces of their
men nowadays, whatever they used to do."

"Poor people have a hard time, you see; and
they don't always hit the right quarter guessing
where their misfortunes come from. Oh, yes, there is
a lot of sentiment about that, of course. Part of the
bitterness comes from the fact that the men and their
employers have so little personal intercourse. You
can't feel so bitter toward a man that calls you by
your name, and perhaps has advised you in difficulty,
or lent you a little money in trouble, as you can to
an unknown corporation. Why, even boys, who are
less accessible to compassion than any known ani-

mal, I do believe, even boys show that. After they get acquainted, they let up on their hazing. It never lasts the year through.

"Another reason is not sentimental at first sight, yet it has its ideal side. Unhappily, the old notion that any saving, self-denying, industrious working-man might rise to be something better and employ men on his own account, is about gone. Most wage-earners expect to live and die wage-earners, and it makes an awful difference. Their whole effort, now, is not to get on, which involves making their em-ployers' interest their own; not at all; they don't *expect* to get on; what they strain every nerve for is to get as much money for as little work as possi-ble, so they will be able to work as long as possible and lay up as much."

"That's short-sighted."

"Of course, but natural,—almost inevitable. And it is hard making them understand. I think I could show the advantages of a good job as well to an employer as a workingman."

"I do, too, Johnny. And now let's come to the point. I believe in you. Why don't you let me lend you some money—"

Johnny stirred as if to speak, but she stopped him, autocratically. "You'll refuse, of course, but let me make the proposition. It will always be open. Let me lend you ten thousand at six per cent. for ten years. I'll lend it to you in Old Colony Plow stock at par—"

"It's worth more," interrupted Johnny.

"Not in the open market. You'll be a stock-holder; you can go to the meetings; you can look at the books, and you can have a position with us. Oh, we'll get the worth of our money, Johnny."

"Thank you, Mrs. Winter, but it's impossible."

"You needn't be cross and stiff, Johnny—that's better." Johnny was on one knee before her.

"You know I'm grateful," he cried; "I can't tell you how awfully good I think you are! I'll never forget it and it will cheer me up always to think of your having such confidence in me. But let me make myself worth helping first."

Mrs. Winter rumpled his thick hair with her delicate hand, which did not look like an old hand; she smiled on him pensively, but he could not see the smile, and her voice was light: "Very well. It will all come right, Johnny. But tell me more about the unions. They seem about as biggitty now as they can be."

"That's your beautiful, feminine ignorance, Aunty Winter," said Johnny, rising and sitting beside her on the sofa. "Wait until we organize the waiters and shut up the dining-rooms of the Annex and the Metropole; wait until we organize the teamsters and make you burn coal in summer instead of natural gas, so we can have the job of hauling it; wait until the retail clerks and the servant girls are organized, and the organized laundry-workers shut off clean linen from Chicago; wait until the cabmen and the undertakers' men strike, and you have to be buried in an express wagon or a street-car—you would dislike that—"

"I certainly should; but I don't think you will go quite to such lengths; if you do, the long-suffering public will organize, too, and put a stop to your foolishness, if not to your unions. I don't think you take a very cheerful view of your case, after all."

"Well," Johnny corrected, "the cheerfulness isn't on the surface, but it's there, all right. Whatever their faults, the unions have done a great big lot apart, quite apart, from any question of raising wages; they have educated the men to work together. The leaders can organize."

"Yes, they have organized plunder."

"You will admit it is organized," bantered Johnny, "and if they have learned to work together in a bad cause (mind, *I* don't admit that), why shouldn't they work together for something better?"

"Well, what else?" The situation pleased Mrs. Winter. In the first place, she was genuinely delighted to capture Johnny. Her vanity was tickled, and a certain softness, which she always felt for the lad, grew with every glimpse of his handsome face. On the whole, she liked the face better for the changes in it, although the lines about the eyes irritated her. "The boy has been most absurdly miserable," she grumbled within herself. Mrs. Winter felt repelled by suffering as by snow in spring. But it was distinctly exciting to have found him, to have succeeded, when Emma Winslow, who was so clever, had failed.

"Well, we've learned to respect our word, that's a lot. We've learned to obey,—a lot more. We are getting acquainted with our employers—fighting them. But it is better to get acquainted fighting than not to get acquainted at all! We're not dumb, driven cattle any more, even if we're not heroes in the strife. Our discontent has ceased to be inarticulate despair. Now all these things will not be lost even though the high tide of unionism recedes. The wrecking party will find them."

"Then, you have really got over your socialism, Jo'nivan?"

"I wouldn't say *quite* that, Aunty Winter," Johnny corrected, his eyes narrowing as they always narrowed when he was trying to think with exactness. "But laws have to be made for men as they are, not as they ought to be. I have discovered, too, that underneath a lot of this raging against great fortunes is not so much pity and patriotism as hatred, envy and malice. Some of this comes out of real misery; that's dangerous. But that will disappear in a great measure with better times. But the feeling against these swollen fortunes isn't, by any means, *all* selfish. It has ground. But it is blind; it can't see that it isn't the size of a man's fortune that is dangerous to the public; it is how he made it."

"For instance?"

"Well, to increase the production of the world, whether that production shall make for beauty or happiness or material comfort or moral elevation, we need *brains!* And, as a rule, brains will not work without reward! Without big rewards. Now, speaking only of the industrial world, I don't grudge millions to the men who can get hard wheat planted instead of soft, or run the corn-yield up from thirty to fifty bushels an acre, or irrigate the desert, or increase a man's capacity by machinery a hundred-fold, or devise ways of economy in manufacturing or using up the by-products. Men who use other mens' muscles and brains to increase the working capital of the world are worth more millions than the luckiest of them get—I see that now. There's one big division. Men who see clearly have no kick coming against the real captains of industry; but it is the men who make their money, not out of the earth, but Wall Street, who get more than is coming to them. If the wreckers can make more money than the ship-owners, it's bad! And if manipulating is a lot more profitable than producing, that is very bad."

"You mean—well, apply the case to the Old Colony!"

"That's easy. If you can make rakes and cultivators cheaper and better than your competitors, it's for the public interest that you should have the most business,—all you can get. But if you get rebates on the railways, so that you strangle your competitors who make just as good stuff as you—that's distinctly against the public weal. You get your market not by production, but by manipulation."

"And you think the Government ought to interfere?"

"Yes. But here comes up another point. There are public and private businesses. I am socialist enough to think that if you mix these up you will come to trouble. For instance, a railway is distinctly a public business; as a public business it should play fair to all. Every one ought to have as much right to the highway as every one else; and the railway is the highway to-day."

"Then you believe in Government ownership of railways?"

"No. See how far I have traveled. I believe the Government has a right to run the railways, but I am sure it would be a stupendous folly for them to use it. We want to encourage initiative, not repress it; and our civil service has a long way to travel before it can be trusted with any such job. Besides, no more shaking of values. No more panics for me! I've seen one, and it will do me. Wherever it starts, it's the poor man always gets the ball at the heaviest! No; if railway stocks are watered, better evaporate than squeeze. Let the Government regulate the railways, not own them! Give them a show for their white alley! Go slow!"

Thus Johnny unbosomed himself, and Mrs. Winter led him on. By degrees he confided some of his experiences to her. Her cynical enjoyment of the humor of them and her gliding over the deeper emotions was better for him than sympathy, for it made talk easy. Johnny came again, and more than once. Some obscure fiber of pride in him would not let him dine with her or go out with her to amusements; but he would present himself later in the evening, and the hospitable Southerner, who could not conceive of friendly intercourse quite bare of eatables or potables, was likely to have large cups of coffee with cream, and liqueurs or cocktails or wines on the table with the cigarettes.

By degrees Johnny slipped into confidences of the lighter order. And one of his first subjects was "his kidlets."

"What kind of clothes ought little girls to wear?" he asked one Sunday afternoon.

"Oh, any simple things," returned Mrs. Winter,

who was innocent of much beyond the rudiments, not having interfered with any child's toilet since Johnny's childhood.

"Well, they ought to be fastened by buttons, not by safety-pins and shoe-strings, oughtn't they? Amelia Ann's got the greatest layout of shoe-strings I ever discovered on one person; she picked them up in the street, I guess; she mends her clothes with them—that isn't quite good form, is it? Mrs. Delaney told her it was naughty, and Amelia Ann, who has considerable spirit, felt wounded and ran away— Amelia Ann's protest against the conventionalities always takes the form of running away. Or rather, she doesn't run away, she hides; and poor little Franzy goes without his own piece to feed her. It doesn't strike me as quite right—child's going without her bath and skulking about out of school that way, but—I can't make up my mind to let Mrs. Delaney beat her, as she hankers to do."

"How many children are there?"

"Three. Franzy and Thyrza are all right, but Amelia Ann is a handful. Thyrza takes to housework—why, she's a wonder!"

"Does *she* mend with shoe-strings?"

"Well, no; that's Amelia Ann's patent; but she doesn't look just right in her clothes. Mrs. Delaney is so afraid they'll outgrow their clothes that she buys a size or two ahead; and she generally buys the bargains that are left over and marked down and have been shopworn or stained or saved from a fire or whatever; so poor little Thyrza, who has hair inclining to red, usually trips about in a Harvard sweater, or a blue and green Highland costume.

And once Mrs. Delaney purchased some off numbers of union suits that had gone through fire and water and been scorched in the legs. She cut off the legs and took tucks in the arms, and Thyrza wore the shirt as an outside rig. Exclusively for the house, you know. I got her a little blue jacket to go to school."

Mrs. Winter held an interview with her own particular salesman at Field's, in Johnny's behalf. She invested the money which he had given her. The sight of the money, neatly inclosed in a pay envelope, gave Mrs. Winter's seasoned old heart an unexpected twinge; it was so small a sum, yet it represented so much self-denial.

"Johnny, Johnny," she exploded, "will you never learn to look after your own troubles and let other people's alone!"

"Ah, but, you see, these are my own troubles; and, bless you! you needn't think I tote this load all by myself; there's Billy, who joshes me worse than you, but has bought Mrs. Delaney a cook-stove and given the kids their shoes—I do wish Mrs. Delaney wouldn't buy needle-toes because they're cheap— and he got the biggest boy on the city pay-roll and the youngest apprenticed to a plumber, and helped get Delaney into the pen."

"The pen?"

"Penitentiary; he's got fifteen years; so *he's* off our minds for a while. Billy is the best ever! You must see Billy."

"I've seen his picture. You know he's a sweetheart in Fairport?"

"Has he?" parried Johnny.

"At least he comes to see her often. She has a sister who does dressmaking, and does all my simple things. She has told me. He sends her candy and flowers and books and I suspect valentines."

"Well, that looks serious,"—Johnny, having written the valentines, would have liked to question further.

"I think it is serious, because she has never shown the valentines."

"They were probably original and awful," suggested Johnny placidly.

"Maybe. Then, it's *more* serious, for she seemed impressed with them. She's a nice, quiet girl,— pretty, too. And Peggy Rutherford says both the girls have been very good to their mother. Peggy and Emma Winslow both seem to take the most amazing interest in your Billy Bates."

Johnny felt his heart grow warmer. "Billy's a good one," said he, "and he is going to be a great man. A labor leader like Arthur or Sargent is a big force."

"I have noticed,"—Mrs. Winter looked, languidly, full at Johnny as she spoke—"I have noticed, Johnny, you seem to know a heap about Fairport doings. Does Billy Bates keep you so well informed?"

Johnny laughed frankly. "Oh, Billy isn't my only link with the good old town—Roger sends me the *Fairport Citizen*."

"Roger?"

"Roger Mack is his name. He's the link. Did you ever hear of him? I think he is employed in Luke Darrell's livery stable."

Mrs. Winter shook her head. "Never saw him."

"It's rather interesting. I never saw him, either— to remember. Last Christmas I got a letter from Michael, and there was a letter from Roger Mack in it. He's a Fairport boy who used to live near us and steal rides on the railway. Once he got into our carriage when the coppers were after him, and Mishka, of course, was in sympathy with any victim of the law; so he whipped up and saved the crowd. There were two or three of them. I don't know whether Peggy was among them or not."

"Ah, I see!" murmured Mrs. Winter softly.

"He recalled the incident and wanted to tell me— oh, a lot of tommy-rot about my giving that money. He was pretty nutty, there, and I told him so. Then —well, I thought it a good chance to hear a little about Fairport, and I asked him a question or two, which he answered. I've had a number of letters from him. I heard about your building from him, and about Varonók having the fistula—he calls it 'tishulow'—and the big new horse you have."

"I see," said Mrs. Winter again. "Then you know your stepmother has given up her plan of going to Europe, much to Mrs. Raimund's disgust."

Johnny nodded, flushing a little. Then he began to describe Roger Mack, who, it seemed, now wrote him every other Sunday night regularly. Roger appeared to be a bright boy. Johnny didn't know his age, but he should judge he was about twenty. He was an orphan who had been obliged to hustle for himself ever since he was a little boy. It was rather a pity, Johnny thought, that he should be in a stable. Still, Luke Darrell was an exception—

and Roger Mack was a clean, decent, honorable little horseman, to all appearances. He was trying to educate himself, too; wrote a very fair hand, and could use the typewriter; trying to get into the office. Yes, he had a letter of Roger's—he kept the letters. He would bring it round.

He brought the letter. Mrs. Winter was going home on the following morning, and she had declined several rather tempting invitations for that evening, not because Johnny had promised to come, for he had not, but because she felt sure of seeing him, since she had written him that she was going. But it was nine and she was in a very testy humor before the bell-boy brought her maid the card.

She did not see her path shining clear before her. She had promised Johnny not to write or to speak to any one about their meeting, if he would come to see her. The reticence was easy enough in Chicago, but to-morrow she would be returning to Fairport. She had a well-defined suspicion in regard to Roger Mack; her suspicions seldom played her false. Yet there was a possibility that a real Roger might shamble into Luke Darrell's office, to her confounding, or some other than Peggy might have stolen his rôle. She guessed that both of her neighbors were unhappy, however cheerful. She wanted to comfort them; she also wanted to display her own success with the prodigal. All of which increased her irritation when Johnny did not appear early for the appeal which she was plotting. Her good humor was so far in arrears that even his coming did not restore it, and she greeted him less cordially than usual.

"I had some very nice sandwiches and some coffee

ready for you at eight," she complained testily, "but I don't know what condition they're in now."

"We had a rush order, you see," deprecated Johnny. "I'm awfully sorry; I didn't know you expected me."

"Of course I expected you, when I was going away the next day."

Johnny sighed, looking around him. "How lovely it looks! How I am going to miss you!"

"Are you going to give me a chance to see you some more?"

"I don't know."

"You would better know. Johnny, I've been uncommonly patient for an impatient old woman, such as I am. You might promise me something; will you?"

"It seems most ungracious to bargain with a lady, you know; but won't you tell me what?"

Mrs. Winter laid her hand on his arm; she was not used to stoop to conquer, and she had never studied persuasion; but her tones were almost pleading.

"Let me tell your people, Mrs. Winslow—and Peggy—about seeing you."

"If you wish," said Johnny. But although he said it quietly, he was on his feet with the words, professing a hunger for coffee and sandwiches. It was evident that he did not want any discussion of his surrender. After the repast he took out Roger Mack's letter. By that time Mrs. Winter judged it wise not to give him any chance to hedge in his consent by conditions or reservations; hence she avoided the subject as warily as he. However,

Roger Mack's letter did something to enlighten her. It ran as follows:

Fairport, October 15, 1896.

Friend Johnny:

Yours of the 10th is at hand and contents duly noted. I have learned the poetry by heart. I guess I know how that man felt. I'm a pretty lonesome chap myself, with no near kin in these parts, though I oughtn't to say that, for I have good friends. Well, old Fairport is about the same, only dirtier since the rain. It certainly did make a mess of the country road, and I pity the washers these days. I drove Mrs. Winslow and Miss Rutherford out yesterday. They were down town and their carriage broke down, and I drove them home, while their man stayed and had the carriage mended; it was the whiffletree broke. They don't build carriages like they did, Mr. Rand says.

I will remember what you say about betting on horses. Right you are, too. I don't smoke much; and I don't care for whisky, it makes me sick. Once in a while I take a glass of beer or such, but I never got drunk in my life. There's no money in it. I don't go with any girls, and I don't mean to. Mr. Darrell has had his stable painted, and he has got the loveliest new landau for pall-bearers. Mrs. Winslow gave me a dollar yesterday. I wish I could get to drive for them. They are such nice folks. Say, maybe I hadn't ought to tell it, but I think they are awful cut up about your leaving them. Miss Rutherford she said, as we were down below on the Hill Road and looked up, "Don't the place look sweet,

Cousin Emma?" And I felt sorry for Mrs. Winslow, her voice sounded so sad when she answered, "Johnny ought to see it. Do you think he will ever come back, Peggy?" says she. But Miss Rutherford spoke up as chipper, "Of course he'll come back, honey; Jo'nivan will come back soon's he finds how sorely we need him." Then they spoke so low I couldn't hear them. I guess they didn't know I heard so much. Excuse the presumption of me giving you advice, but I wish you'd write to them or something. It looked lonesome to me, that big house and the gardens. The gardens look beautiful now. Please write to me sometimes; I value your letters very high and try to live according.

Your friend,   ROGER MACK.

"Well, what do you think of Roger Mack?" said Johnny, when the hand holding the letter dropped in the lady's silken lap.

"He seems a niceish sort of boy," said Mrs. Winter. "I hope you'll keep track of him. Another thing, Johnny: I hope you'll keep track of *me!*"

Not until she was gone, not, indeed, until she was speeding through the whitish-yellow cornfields of Illinois, the next morning, did she recall that, in all his pleasant gratitude and his affection Johnny had made no promises. But she was jubilant over her right to tell about her triumph. It was evening on her arrival in Fairport; nevertheless, she was driven directly to Overlook, and, finding Emma alone, gave her the news.

Emma listened with her exasperating stoicism to the recital, only interposing a question here and there. At the end she said: "Did you have any address?"

"None," said Mrs. Winter; "he wouldn't give me any, only promised if he had to go to the hospital again to let me know. And I couldn't spy on him while he was trusting me. I did suggest some clothes I bought for him should be sent to his address; but no, he *would* tote them from my hotel."

"Certainly, you couldn't," agreed Emma, "but we can. Only I'm afraid, Mrs. Winter, that he let you tell us because he meant to make another move, and that if we find his lodging house or who employed him, we shall find him gone."

Mrs. Winter's smile wilted. "The deceitful boy!" she exclaimed, "and I had his superintendent's address all ready for you."

"He will be gone," said Mrs. Winslow sadly.

And she was right. They wrote to the superintendent, receiving a civilly curt reply to the effect that Van Galitsuin had left the employ of the company on the twenty-third. They had never had his address. He was an industrious and skilful workman. They were sorry to lose him, but understood he was changing to better himself.

So the clue which promised so much broke off short in their hands.

CHAPTER VIII

AN DIE FERNE GELIEBTE

The golden woods of Overlook had crisped into russet and drabs; once more the Christmas snow was chalking the tree-boughs. Snow was everywhere, on the fir-trees and the maples, shrouding the forests, glorifying the hill-slopes, freshly fallen, shadowed with the subtlest violet tints, or powdered with diamonds in the sun, so beautiful, so mystical, that the sense of its chill was melted by a poignant thrill of delight.

On the twenty-third of December, with Christmas two days away, Peggy and Mrs. Winslow sat together in the Princess Olga's writing-room much as they had sat, a year before, when Roger Mack first stepped upon the stage. And both of them were remembering that day.

"How much longer is he going to keep it up?" sighed Mrs. Winslow. They had not spoken Johnny's name, but there needed no speaking.

"He was always the most obstinate thing in the world," declared Peggy; "he owns to Roger Mack that he misses his people and his friends and his old life, but he would despise himself, he says, and they would have reason to despise him, if he returned before he had shown that he had stuff instead of stuffing in him."

361

"Did you get a letter to-day?"

"Yes. I was just bringing it to you to read."

When the initial letter from Johnny came (that first intelligence direct from him, which was greeted so hopefully and yet brought them so little), Peggy would have handed it to Mrs. Winslow, but the latter shook her head, saying: "No, dear, I've thought it all out. You must be able to speak freely to Johnny, and he wouldn't speak so freely to you if he knew I had the reading of his letters. I shouldn't like to take that advantage of his ignorance. You will make Roger Mack a nice boy, and Johnny will get fond of him, and I hope you'll be very good friends. Read me anything important, but keep the letters."

She noticed how the color flickered on Peggy's cheek, and she smiled within. "The child wants her letters to herself," thought she; "there is no partnership in love! Thank God, I do believe Peggy is in love! If she only doesn't coquette with him."

But Peggy scorned the guile of the weak. If Jo'nivan came back he should come of his own free will, not prodded by jealousy; and, indeed, since they had seen Billy, during the summer, and he had told them of Johnny's dreary hospital experience, there had grown up in the girl an intensification of the semi-maternal tenderness of her childhood; not even to win him could she hurt him. It is not to be inferred, however, because Peggy despised the help of jealousy, that she was above setting feminine snares.

Once Johnny had written to Roger: "You must tell me all the gossip. I know there is mighty little goes on in Fairport which they don't hear about at Darrell's. Who die and who are married and who give parties? You can't find anything too trivial to interest me. Why, I'd like to hear what they have at the Opera House, and what kind of clothes Mrs. Winter or Mrs. Winslow or Miss Rutherford are wearing, when you see them pass on the street. Who goes to Overlook now? Have they any parties? You don't know how an exile loves all the details." (Peggy giggled; "doesn't he think he's mighty coony, the way he brings that in!") She wrote in response: "I guess I know just how you feel. There's a town I'd like to hear the same sort of thing about. And I'll tell you all I can. They are pretty quiet at Overlook now. Folks drop in considerable and they have some little dinners, but no big parties. Several young men go there to see the ladies, but nobody seems to be Miss Rutherford's steady. Just friendly. Miss Rutherford has got a new sealskin jacket. It's a bute. When I make some money and get married, I mean to give my wife a sealskin jacket; they make a girl look so stylish."

Peggy had, indeed, entered into her drama, and the growth of the character of Roger Mack was remarkable. He read the books Johnny advised, he reformed his grammar; his morals and political views reflected his mentor's counsels to a degree that was flattering, if it were not suspicious. And as Emma had predicted, Johnny grew fond of the lad, sending him quantities of carefully studied advice and occasional magazines, and once he inclosed a note to Mrs. Winslow (very civil but a little cool and curt; poor Johnny was having a bad attack of nostalgia, and not daring to be anything else), requesting her to give Roger Mack, the bearer, for whose responsibility Mr. Luke Darrell could vouch, certain books of his which had been left in Fairport. There was no place of writing on the note, only a date.

Some of Johnny's advice, over which he had plainly taken vast thought and pains, Peggy did not read to Mrs. Winslow, but as she read it, herself, the tears rose to her eyes. "Jo'nivan," she whispered, "you are just the *decentest* boy since Galahad, and I'm afraid, Jo'nivan, he's the only gentleman I know who can run in your class!"

She told Mrs. Winslow a little, although she could not bring herself to repeat Johnny's words, in which a man showed very simply his heart and his aspirations.

"His father would be proud of him!" was all Mrs. Winslow's comment; but she began so irrelevantly to talk about sending Johnny his winter flannels, that Peggy was sure she was touched.

"Has he any flannels here?" Peggy asked innocently.

"Not exactly," returned Mrs. Winslow; "there were some worn things which I gave away. But I shall get him some in place of them and send them by Roger Mack."

"Roger has to send everything to Billy Bates. But he'll get them in time. He always gets the letters sharp on time."

"I think," said Mrs. Winslow after a little pause, her eyes on Josiah's portrait, "if I could only know where he was, so that I could be *sure* he was having proper food, and getting his stockings mended and putting on his warm underclothes when it first began to be cold, I think I could be reconciled, and let him take his own time about coming to us."

"Oh, I've no doubt somebody is pampering him," said Peggy.

Johnny consented to receive some of his own books and pictures and any clothes which might be in Overlook.

Roger Mack covered his large sheets of office paper mainly with apologies for the box. "It's kinder a whale," he wrote, "but the ladies kept thinking of things, and I couldn't seem to stop them. They really got excited, and Mrs. Winslow would keep saying to Miss Rutherford, 'Don't you think we might venture to send some preserves for the children?' You see Mrs. Winter told them a lot about you and 'Melia Ann and Thyrza (I'm glad Thyrza liked the cook-book I sent) and Franzy. Then Miss Rutherford wanted cans of soup put in and hard water-crackers and some smoking tobacco. I told her you smoked Cowboys' Delight and *I* got it for you, but she said you used to smoke Hymans' and she would put it in. They put in a doll, too, that Miss Rutherford said used to be hers and you and she played with it, and once you were going to cut its head off or something, but your father stepped in and saved it. There's some hair-ribbons, too, for Thyrza and 'Melia Ann and a shawl for Mrs. Delaney and a pair of skates for Franzy—used to be yours when you were little. I had to stop them finally and ask them if they wanted me to hire a car. But I hope you won't feel you can't take them, for it

would hurt them awful. Please don't hurt them so
bad as that."

Johnny did not hurt them. His letter in return
was the one which Peggy brought to Mrs. Winslow the snowy day which was so like the day of a
year before.

"That's not all," explained Peggy, whose glowing
eyes showed her suppressed excitement, "there's a
box! Johnny is sending Christmas gifts!"

The two women bent over the box with flushed
cheeks, in an excitement that was almost joyous. It
was a starch-box, packed with great care and at the
expenditure of a large amount of tissue paper. There
was a white silk muffler marked "Roger," a Russian
ikon ("I suppose he got it at Field's," muttered
Peggy) for Michael, and three envelopes of ample
size addressed respectively to Mrs. Winslow, Mrs.
Winter and Miss Rutherford.

Peggy lifted up the muffler; she unwrapped it
with delicate, almost caressing touches; she looked
at the shop-mark and giggled,—a half-choked,
tremulous giggle which was close to a sob. "I feel
like a thief, but I'm going to keep it, just the same,"
said she.

"Johnny ought not to spend his money on that
Roger Mack!" Mrs. Winslow reproved. But Peggy
laid her finger on the little gilt circle on the white
satin lining. "Noyes Brothers," she announced.
"Do you think he would send to Noyes Brothers for
Roger? I reckon not! It is a relic of his past
splendor. Jo'nivan used to be mighty gorgeous, you
remember. He maybe has worn it once or twice, and
he had Mrs. Delaney press it; I reckon I can see

some shiny marks where the iron went—on the wrong side. Very nice and sensible of Jo'nivan!"

Mrs. Winslow smiled from her own gift, which was not a Christmas card, but a calendar. It was an ingeniously contrived bit of work. The gray mat was cut into a frame and a photograph, evidently taken by a kodak, but with considerable skill in posing and lighting, made the oval above the little pad of the months to come. Three smiling, childish faces met Emma Winslow's half-wistful eyes, and she read, on the obverse of the card, the words which Johnny had written: "Three little children, whom you have made happy, wish you a Merry Christmas."

"It is better than nothing," said she.

Peggy was reading her own card; she was determined not to be disappointed if Johnny made the small Blokers his interpreters in her own case.

"But I do think it is not exactly polite; he ought to say 'Thank you,' himself," thought she. He had said it. Peggy's was a Christmas card, very simple; a single passage of Scripture, illuminated in the medieval manner: "Glory to God in the Highest; on earth Peace and Good-will to men!" And when she turned the card over she read, between smiles and tears: "Dear Peggy, you were right and I was wrong; but I have begun over again; won't you wish me well? When I feel I have the right I am going to thank Mrs. Winslow and you for your kindness. But that takes time. Peggy, I stole the doll from little Thyrza; she never could appreciate a doll with associations; I got her a perfect horror she adores, and I'm keeping yours for a mascot."

"That," said Peggy, "requires an answer, per Roger Mack."

"He certainly is softening," said Mrs. Winslow. "If we only could wire him to come to Christmas dinner."

"He would wire back that he hadn't the proper clothes, most probably," said Peggy; but they made their jests out of lighter hearts.

Yet for months Peggy did not hear from Johnny —nor write to him.

Billy Bates came to Fairport, and his heart swelled within him, for he was asked to dine at Overlook. Billy had been less flattered by an invitation from the rulers of the earth. He telephoned to Chicago for his new dress-suit, and he waited after hours to walk home with Miss Sadie and seek counsel of her as to the weightier matters of etiquette. Thanks to that noble invention, the telephone, he put himself into communication with Johnny, exciting, be it said, a lively though transient apprehension when the superintendent of Johnny's shop understood the quality of the invisible visitor who would not be denied.

In the event, Billy displayed a tempered magnificence of toilet, a radiant neatness, and an anxious and vigilant politeness. He contrived to seat both ladies before the butler; after dinner, if either of them moved in her chair, he was on his feet; his manners were admirable. It was apparent to Peggy that he had not only been tutored for this special trial, but that he was well-grounded in the daily use of the spoon and the fork. He said little and he watched Wilton, the butler, narrowly; it was not that Billy's bold spirit was cowed by the functionary's imposing presence or his irresponsive attention; rather he was silently armoring any vulnerable points of decorum about himself against a possible sally of criticism.

"He'll see I can behave as pretty as any blamed dude of them all!" Billy was declaring within. There was another reason why one ought not to lose oneself in the pleasure of the moment, the exquisite sheen of the damask, the lights, the wine, the flowers and the silver, all so deftly blending that there was but one impression on the brain, a soft harmony of splendor. Billy felt that he enjoyed it and that with familiarity he should enjoy it more. "I always did like things clean!" was the way Billy expressed it to himself. But because of the butler, whose respect he coveted almost angrily, and of the other reason, Mr. Bates held his esthetic glow well in hand. The other reason was his dread lest the expansion of the hour would be used to find out something about Johnny's whereabouts.

Such inquisition, however, did not comport with his hostess' ideas of hospitality, and as little with Peggy's. Johnny, who was in all their thoughts, was not once mentioned during the meal. Afterward it was Billy, himself, who spoke the name, in a casual, accidental way. Then said Mrs. Winslow: "We don't want to ask you any questions, Mr. Bates, but you know we shall be glad to hear anything Johnny would be willing to have you tell."

After that, conversation flowed easily, and while Billy never forgot his guard over names and localities, he told innumerable anecdotes of Johnny and of the small Blokers, to an audience as eager to hear as he could be to tell.

"Amelia Ann's a handful," he declared frankly, being safe out of the bonds of Johnny's remorseful compassion; "she will either go on the stage or astonish the police court. Sometimes she takes to pursuing Thyrza with the carving-knife or any old thing, and, one time, she threw a can of hot lye at Mrs. Delaney. It was lucky Mrs. Delaney had the boiler cover in her hands—she was lifting it off the boiler—and she held it up for a shield, so it got the hot lye instead of her. That was the day Amelia Ann did get paddled, good and plenty. The wooden stick you stir clothes with, you know, was right at her hand, and Mrs. Delaney simply walloped Amelia Ann. I don't know that I blame her."

"Did it do Amelia Ann good?" Peggy asked.

"It ought to," said Billy, "but as Ivan—Mr. Winslow—says, Amelia Ann is not as all other women are, like the lady in the poem. She took the beating to heart so much that she borrowed a quarter Thyrza had accumulated in pennies, and went out and got some carbolic acid, which she tipped to her mouth after she got Mrs. Delaney in front of her and swallowed it—"

"My word!" cried Peggy; "did it kill her?"

"Why, no, ma'am. Mrs. Delaney knocked the bottle out of her hand, giving her a good box on the ear, and Johnny, who happened in, by good luck, at that time, tickled her throat with a feather and gave her white of egg and flour and mustard water until she nearly had convulsions. She was the limpest little rat you ever saw; but Johnny's the only creature she has any regard for, so she stood it. He was perfectly gentle and quiet. He always is, you know; but he didn't sleep all night, he was so worried. The next night, if he didn't take the kid and Mrs. Delaney to the theater and let them see *By Mistake of Law,* a fool play where the villain takes poison and half an hour to die in, and dies all over the stage. 'That's how *you'd* a been!' says Mrs. Delaney, who likes to rub it in hard. I suppose she gets that way washing. Amelia Ann only stuck out her tongue. Mr. Winslow didn't say a word. But the kid sidled up to him, going home, and said: 'You won't let me git killed, Johnny, will you?' He seems to know how to manage her. She used to wear the craziest things and look like a rag-bag. Mrs. Delaney couldn't get her to keep her clothes decent. But one day Ivan comes in with a dress that Mrs. Winter had helped him buy at Field's and she put it on and he said: 'What a pretty little girl! Isn't it a pity she'll go back to those ragged clothes!' 'I won't,' says she; 'I'm going to wear pretty clothes all the time!' What's more, she has. She makes Thyrza mend them. But she sings and dances for Thyrza. She can dance to beat the band, and twist herself into more shapes than a rubber jumping-jack, and mimic! she can imitate anything from the Mooney's dog fighting the Sigelfritz's cat to Mrs. Delaney's brogue, scolding. She's better than the 'Barnyard' on the graphophone."

"Is she fond of study?" said Mrs. Winslow.

"Hates it," said Billy; "hasn't got only to words of one syllable, and Thyrza can beat her figuring; but she can climb better than any boy on the street, and she can ride the goat that the Dago fruit-man keeps to draw his cart, and she can smoke a pipe and not be sick. As Ivan says, her stunts aren't exactly lady-like, but they're striking."

"Poor child!' said Mrs. Winslow.

"Well, I don't know, madam; you see, Ivan has taken her in hand, and he seems to have a way with people. She's improved. She chews gum instead of tobacco now, and she only makes faces at Mrs. Delaney instead of shying things at her. Mr. Winslow thinks she will come out all right."

"She needs to go out in the country," said Peggy; "the city is too stimulating for her."

"That's right. I mean you're quite correct, Miss Rutherford. But they have gone out in the country,"—he grinned over some recollection—"Amelia Ann tried to ride a cow; I don't think the cow let her! So Amelia Ann tried the calf because, she said, she wouldn't have so far to fall, and she'd learn on the calf. She hadn't learned at last accounts; but she was persevering."

In such anecdotes, the evening passed before Billy realized; he forgot the discomforts of his state collar and his new shoes; he forgot even Wilton's hauteur, and permitted him to slip on his coat at parting quite as if he were a waiter at his favorite restaurant. But he never forgot to keep Johnny's secrets. He spoke with feeling and sense about his friend. Although his argument was against them, his hearers felt some touch of conviction from it. Mrs. Winslow had said: "These privations which he must feel, this actual suffering he has, isn't it all unnecessary?"

"No, ma'am," Billy had answered, "I don't think it is. It's hard and God knows I have tried hard enough to send him back to his folks where he belongs, for he seemed to me like a lobster with his shell off, and the new one not grown, and everything could bite him. But these last months I have seen something. He's learning. He's learning fast. He's getting to be a large-minded, tolerant man. Yet he hasn't lost his gift of being sorry for people in trouble; he has only found out that the loudest squealers aren't always the ones the worst hurt. 'Twas a true word he once said: 'You have to be just before you're generous, or you won't be able to be generous long!' He has naturally got an open hand, and he's never had to tie it up until lately. He has learned a plenty of other things—to manage men, for one. He's maybe a bad politician, but anyhow he's a born leader."

"But isn't a good politician a born leader?" queried Peggy, whose eyes shone bright with amusement.

"No, ma'am," said Billy scornfully, "he's a born dickerer. He leads if he can, but he follows and dickers when he can't. When I was a kid, here in Fairport, and used to trundle my infant piety about among the Sunday-schools, as long as the Christmas-tree season lasted, there was a fat chump named Easterly; his mother or his aunty promised him a Rugby football, which he was keen for, if he'd get to the head of his class. Do you know that duffer paid us a cent apiece for *missing;* he learned just one question and for nine cents he got that ball. Well, *he* was a politician."

"Yet you are a good politician, Mr. Bates,—at least, so reputed."

"Oh, I'm a good dickerer,"—Billy waved the implied question aside. "I follow when I must. If I didn't I couldn't keep my job. There isn't a labor-leader going who doesn't have to swap some of his opinions for his place. He'd lose it if he didn't. Not only that, he'd have a successor who wouldn't restrain the men at all, while *he* can, a little. And if he waits and dickers, his time will come."

Then Billy added in a different tone: "But there is a limit. Mr. Winslow has taught me *that,* and no honorable man can either conceal or betray his convictions past that limit. Some things are expedient, and some things are right; you can give in on questions of prudence, but you can't on questions of honor. I can see why. I couldn't always; but he has taught me that among many things. I owe him a lot; a terrible lot it would be, if I didn't care so much for him."

"I think," said Mrs. Winslow, "he owes as much to you. We may be grateful he has so good a friend. I know *he* is."

Billy left Overlook that night with a sense of knowing Johnny better than before, and, curiously enough, he left the reflection of his own feeling behind him. Perhaps he left some tinge of resignation also. Peggy and Mrs. Winslow settled themselves into helping Johnny indirectly. Peggy wrote to him. It was the same kind of letter which she might have written to him had they never quarreled. He was her dear Jo'nivan on the first line; she forgave his being too good for this selfish world on the second, and told about Fairport and Overlook for three pages.

Johnny got the letter in the evening when he came home from his work. He didn't open it in the family circle where Amelia Ann, having just slapped Franzy, was doing penance (and making faces) in a corner, and Mrs. Delaney was frying bacon, while Franzy sniffled and Thyrza comforted him, between the placing of dishes on the table.

Johnny carried his letter into his own bare room. How many times he kissed the dear, familiar handwriting, how he opened the letter on his knees as if before his queen, any lover can fancy. But he sighed as he read. This Peggy, who wrote, was not quite the gentle creature of Roger Mack's picture, sending him the doll which was the sign of their old childish amity. In a moment, however, he smiled just as in his childish days he would smile when he was hurt, for some whim of consolation.

"Well, anyhow, she *has* spoken to me!" he said, "or doesn't she call this speaking? Oh, Peggy, Peggy, how sweet you are!"

Billy's visit was in the winter. On Valentine's Day a box of violets came to Peggy with a sealed envelope beneath their fragrant masses. The single sheet of paper, within, contained only Emerson's lyric, which once Peggy had sung for Johnny:

> "Thine eyes still shined for me, though far
>   I lonely roved the land or sea,
> As I behold yon evening star,
>   Which yet beholds not me."

There was no word, no signature; none was

needed. Peggy told Mrs. Winslow that she had had
some poetry with the flowers, and the wise woman
did not even smile.

The winter softened into a muddy slush of spring;
the spring opened like its own flowers into aureolin
sunshine and emerald hillsides and the homely
sweetness of newly turned earth; almost unawares,
the summer came with the breathless western heat.
But Peggy, herself, had not written to Johnny.
Perhaps she thought that Roger Mack did enough
writing for two. Roger had taken to the typewriter
of late. It was only in the beginning that Sadie
Martin copied the letters. Peggy had known Sadie
since she was a little girl. In the simple democracy
of Fairport, they often met. Sadie knew more than
Peggy about Johnny's life and conduct, for many
months, because Billy Bates used to talk to her. She
was more than willing, when Peggy proposed her
part in the scheme.

"I would do anything in the world for Mrs.
Winslow," Sadie said instantly, "she has been so
good to mother." And Peggy was rather glad to
have the onus of obligation thus shifted. The
Southern girl was far too wise to suggest any business basis; she accepted the proffered aid gratefully,
and took Mrs. Martin to drive and asked her fellow
conspirator to luncheon or to the play.

But a disinclination to have the kind Sadie read
Roger's letters to Johnny—naturally she had never
read Johnny's letters to Roger—had increased; the
solution of the matter was simple; Roger learned to
use a typewriter. That he had not used it in the beginning was due to Peggy's supersensitiveness; she

was always trying to imagine possible suspicions, and she fancied Johnny might suspect a typewriter; a written letter in a strange hand was much more plausible.

But Johnny's possible suspicions having been lulled by seeing the strange hand, there was not the slightest objection whatever to the typewriter, and Peggy kept advance sheets ready signed, always by her.

Was it her fancy, Peggy asked herself, that either Johnny was growing attached to this mythical Roger, this hard-working, poor wight, with his pathetic story of a neglected childhood, or—Peggy blushed and did not pursue the question. The change was intangible; but she felt it with every letter. In some ways he was more reserved; gone entirely were those austere moral reflections which frankly admitted some of the more elemental of man's temptations, even while they warned against them— Johnny's present letters could have been read to a girls' club—but gone also was the attitude of a teacher. Johnny never had a particle of condescension in him; he never put on pedagogic airs with Roger, but he had talked of the simpler matters of the intellect. If he spoke of an author, he was likely to fling in a bit of biography, and he was particular to keep his terms of logic very simple. Now he wrote as one educated person might write to another. But more important than all: hitherto Johnny had been reserved, in the midst of his sympathy. He never had spoken of himself, his own fortunes, his own daily round, or his own feelings. Now, he was equally silent about the material concerns of his life, but half-shyly he was unpacking his heart of its faiths and its problems.

He wrote every Sunday, that being his one leisure day. Roger wrote Fridays, in order to give Johnny a chance to answer his letters at once. The interest of the situation increased all the while. By degrees, Peggy dropped any talk about Roger Mack's personal experiences; a certain shamefaced doubt in her audience's credulity held her fingers; but she wrote out Roger Mack's heart, which was much the sort of heart Margaret Rutherford had had in a poor boy's place.

She also contrived to get in the daily life of Overlook and Fairport. And with a skill she did not realize, she sketched most delicately, in half-tones which could not offend, the character of the only woman to whom Johnny had been unkind. Grace was given her to do it with so light a hand, in so few if strong lines, that Johnny himself never suspected her purpose. Mrs. Winslow appeared in the letters, because there was no telling the incidents without her. As for her character, it revealed itself. Because his attention was not asked, Johnny gave it without reserve. He did not come to the reading critical, but interested, out of his armor and off his guard. "Could you have wronged her, dear?" he asked once, to the image of his mother that he summoned so often to his thoughts; "we made mistakes, you and I. And—let us be just—she had a right to marry my father if she loved him. She did, *mamasa*.* She made him happy; I fear we didn't."

*Darling.

These changes in the correspondence Peggy came eventually to date back to a certain day of July. It was the day she found a note from Luke Darrell in her mail, after reading which she telephoned Michael not to unharness her horse, but bring it around again, although she had just returned from town. Within half an hour she was in Luke Darrell's private office, and Luke was hastily shoving his white shirt-sleeves into his clerical-looking black alpaca coat.

"About Roger Mack?" said Peggy. Luke had been her faithful and willing confederate on almost the same terms as Sadie. He did not know whether Peggy or Mrs. Winslow was Roger Mack. He forwarded the letters to Overlook marked "For Mrs. Winslow or Miss Rutherford," and kept any surmises to himself. Now, he rubbed his clean-shaven jaws and looked solemn as usual, as he remarked:

"I'm afraid, Miss Rutherford, they are on to Roger Mack."

"Why?" said Peggy.

"Well, I was out this morning, and everybody else; we had two funerals, and only the new washer and Henderson were in. Henderson stepped out for his dinner, come to think, so he *wasn't* in. A young fellow strolled in and asked for Roger Mack. The washer said he didn't work here. Then the young fellow asked had he left? The washer had never heard of him; but he said he was new, himself. Then the young fellow left."

Peggy held herself impassive by an effort: "That was this morning?"

Luke said it was.

"And what was the young man like? A working-man?"

"That man who saw him—August his name is; he's got another but it's too long to be handled on work-days—he said he was a gentleman. I asked him how he looked and he said: 'Oh, like any gentleman.' I asked him how he talked: 'Oh, just like any gentleman.' I couldn't git a mortal thing out of the dumb tyke, he couldn't tell so much as the color of his eyes or whether his hair was curly. It was just as I wanted it. Were they brown? Yes, maybe. Or perhaps they were blue? He wasn't sure; they might be blue. He's as dumb as they make 'em, even Dutchmen—and they're next to a wooden Injun, if they want to be. But I thought I'd ought to tell you."

"Do you think the gentleman *could* have been Mr. Winslow?"

"I haven't got enough of a tip to give odds, it's even money *who* it was. That stick couldn't be sure whether he was tall. Might be little Billy Bates— only he'd be likely to stay and chin with me."

The unknown never returned to unravel their puzzle. But Roger Mack wrote that he had been in the interior of the state buying horses and was back that day. Johnny did not speak of coming to Fairport or Darrell's; but it was after that unexplained visit that his letters began to strike a more personal note, at first faintly, one may say tentatively, then with a firmer tone.

And this is why Peggy did not write to Johnny nor Johnny to Peggy.

CHAPTER IX

HAST THOU FOUND ME, O MINE ENEMY

The office-boy was not in the habit of eavesdropping; he was a decent little creature, as office-boys go, and his mother considered him the best boy in Fairport. Nevertheless, on a certain May morning, a year later, Axtel, the boy in question, made unnecessary excursions to the large office out of which opened Mr. Hopkins' private room; and whenever the typewriter was looking the other way he glued a very sharp ear to the keyhole under pretext of picking up something. The typewriter, the slender young men at the tall desks, the foremen and other workmen who came in with messages or questions, all wore the same air of suppressed emotion. And Axtel knew, as well as the others, that the excitement in the office was only a reflex of the excitement lurking in the two thousand eyes bent apparently on their work in the great shops outside; from the "daubers" who dipped machines in their first coat of paint to the foreman and superintendent, an electric agitation was spreading in tingling waves. Axtel was not the only one with ears and eyes open.

Within the office three men sat smoking. The tall, portly, white-haired man, whose noble dome of brow was nearly bald, was William Hopkins, president of the Old Colony; the shorter but more rugged figure, topped by a Roman head with a thatch of iron-gray hair above beetling brows and keen steel-gray eyes, belonged to Jabez Rivers, head of the Edgewater Steel Works, across the river; the third man's features showed (as the other men's faces did not show) the plain marks of care; he was vice-president and largest owner in a great Chicago corporation, manufacturing farm machinery. "Yes, I guess we are in for it, Dunham," Hopkins repeated.

A grunt was Mr. Jabez Rivers' only comment. Rivers' feelings never were much more than semi-articulate.

Dunham, the Chicago man, glanced from the plow manufacturer to the steel man.

"Then I understand you'll both stand with me?" he asked.

Hopkins laughed. "I guess we have to; we kept our foundry about running on your castings, all through the dull seasons ninety-six and seven, and you've got the contract from us for this year; what else is there for us to do but keep it, whether the molders like it or not?"

"Well, that's the way it strikes us, of course," the Chicago man said, nodding his head and waving his cigar; "but—how about you, Mr. Rivers?"

"The Edgewater has a contract to supply the Old Colony with steel," grunted Rivers; "none of our business how they use it."

"Well, I thought you'd feel that way,"—the Chicago man spoke more rapidly in his relief—"but of course I wanted to make sure. It's such an abom-

inable trickery—the whole business—that you don't
know what to expect next. *We,* ourselves, haven't
had a bit of trouble with our men, and have always
tried to treat them fairly. Why, last winter old
Wethers was chuckling to me about how he'd cut
his wages forty per cent. Just took it right out of
the men's skins and put it into his own pocket. We
hardly cut wages at all. And the trouble *began* at
Wethers'. *His* men struck for a rise and a recognition of their union; then the Colworthy men struck
and the thing spread till we have a peck of trouble;
it's 'way beyond the original cause. Been going on
a month, and now a vile anarchist they used to have
in Chicago, who used to be a molder, but now is a
light among the machinists and can make more
trouble than a candle in a powder factory, has taken
a hand, and *we're* roped in. No reason on earth
except that we sell to Colworthy and Wethers. I
am about certain that this Wally Tyler, who used
to be the most corrupt and mischievous labor-poli-
tician in Chicago—"

"That's a big contract," interjected Rivers.

"He'll fill it, never mind. He's the kind that
holds us up with his right hand and steals from his
union with his left. He's killed one man himself,
with his own good right arm, they say, and two or
three by proxy, and I'd hate to guess how many men
his gang has done up. Regular hospital feeder. It
was a mercy when he cleared out; now he's back.
He must needs take a hand for the machinists, and
demand that we stop selling to Wethers or Colworthy. We refused. We're not yet asking the labor unions to run our business for us. It's bad

enough to have them virtually hiring and discharging our men. We were perfectly civil about it, but we refused. Next day our machinists walked out. We don't mind a partial shut-down, though orders are coming in with a rush now. But we can manage. We've got considerable stuff on hand, and we're delivering it; and we've got a few fellows that will stick to us. If we can only get our stuff from you on time."

"You can," said Hopkins.

Rivers grunted something, presumably assent.

"But they've served notice on you, too?"

"Served notice and got their answer, and Mr. Walter Tyler is in town, raising all the hell he can. How much,"—Hopkins blinked at the clock on the wall—"we shall know in about ten minutes."

"Say they'll walk out then?"

Hopkins nodded.

"And how about Edgewater, Mr. Rivers?"

It was an open secret in business circles that the Edgewater had made a deal with the Old Colony, being virtually their silent partner.

"Well, we've no machinists to hurt, and what we have don't belong to the union," said Rivers; "but Tyler got at our strand boys, and the bumptious little beggars, who are always making trouble, went out last night—and came back this morning."

"Indeed? How was that?"

"We've a brand new superintendent at the Open Hearth—young feller who went through the mill. Used to be in Chicago. I have had my eye on him for two years. Didn't say much for fear of giving him the big head before he was old enough to stand the disease, but I watched him. He's been a strand boy, a rougher, a finisher, a roller, a heater; he knows the whole business; what's more, he knows the *men*. Those little cubs knew they could shut down the whole shop, and they were mighty cocky. He said he thought he could call them down. He did. I don't know how, but I've a notion he got at some of the older and more responsible men and they did the trick for him. I guess they promised the boys a good hiding. Lord, they need it! *Cubs!* Still, some of them are decent, Gleason says; he's teaching them to box."

"Has he a head on him?"

"He has. Good head,—but he's modest."

"Say, lend him to me for a while," laughed Hopkins. "I'm always on the lookout for young men that can work and haven't got the swelled head."

"Want him myself," rejoined Rivers.

"I guess *we* could use him somewhere, too," the Chicago man jested; his spirits were rising.

Rivers had lumbered to his feet and was looking at the clock. "Five minutes *of*," said he.

The three men left the office together so precipitately that Axtel barely had time to jump to the screw of the hot-water pipes for a lawful reason for his presence. They walked through the office and across the narrow street to the largest shop. The huge building, with its iron beams and cement floor, was penetrated by the staccato hum of machinery and luridly aglow with myriad flaming blasts, in front of which stood the dark figures of the artisans.

The three halted in the great doorway. Usually their presence would not have attracted a turn of the head. Absorbed in their work, the men would have hardly known that they were there. To-day more than one man cast a backward glance. The man next Hopkins smothered an oath, as he threw something into the scrap at his feet.

"Spoiled that bolt," argued Hopkins; "all of 'em rattled this morning. Who's that young feller just come in?"

"He's all right; he's *my* young man. I told him to come here." Jabez Rivers, with his hands in his pockets, was grimly unmoved. But the Chicago man's eyeballs glittered in the flare.

Mr. Hopkins gave the young man a long look. A handsome young man he was, over six feet tall, well-knit and erect, with a clean-shaven, young, oval face, and his head carried well in the air with the chin down. The head was covered with wavy black hair, which would have curled were it not cropped so short. He wore a negligée shirt and yellow belt, and there were straps on his trousers, as if he had just dismounted from a wheel. The president of the Old Colony Plow Works whistled softly.

"T-there's Tyler h-himself!" stammered the Chicago man, whose hands were clinching and opening, he was so nervous.

Tyler swung through a side door almost opposite the group, with his accustomed jovial swagger. His toilet had been made for the occasion, which he anticipated would be one for display rather than action. Therefore he had a red silk handkerchief peeping out of his coat pocket, a new tweed suit and tan-colored shoes to be seen across the shop. In-

stantly he took in the trio in the big doorway. He
knew Rivers, whom he respected as a good fighter,
and whose gruffness put him rather at his ease,
being quite comprehensible to him; he knew Hopkins, of whose quality he was yet in doubt; and he
knew the Chicago man. Their presence was an
unexpected tidbit for his vanity. He felt sure of
at least three-fourths of the busy hammers dropping
at his whistle. He hoped for more. All the men
leaving mightn't remain out; indeed, he had passed
the tip that there would not be a long strike, and if
the non-union men would but walk out they could
go back in a few days, should the strike not succeed, as he felt it must. He calculated that Hopkins, who had never had serious trouble with his
men, and who had rush orders of great magnitude,
would be frightened by the stampede. He counted
on the obscure yet enormous force of contagion and
the mightier force of clan prejudice. On the whole,
he was fairly sure of his stroke. His confidence
curled on his mouth as he turned—and saw the
young superintendent from the Edgewater.

The latter looked at him with grave, almost solemn eyes. Nothing passed between the two but
the single glance. Then Tyler lifted his whistle to
his sneering mouth and blew a blast that cut, knife-
like, through the vast buzz of toil. As if in answer
to a magician's call, every arm fell. The very
belts above slackened their mighty revolutions. The
noise of machinery dulled. One would say that the
heart of the great engine had been struck and was
staggering slowly into dumbness. Like statues, the
men stood, holding their breath, their eyes glued on

Tyler. Before Tyler could send a second blast the new superintendent (to whom Rivers had nodded, after a swift colloquy with Hopkins) strode in front of him and laid a hand of iron on his arm.

"Didn't you see that sign?" he demanded, but in the gentlest of voices. " 'No admittance.' We mean it. You've no business here. Kindly go away."

"If I say no?"

"I'll fling you out."

Tyler looked at his antagonist, and the pith went out of his courage. He knew himself to be the weaker man, and he had no mind to be discomfited before his following. He shrugged his shoulders. "We'll *all* go," he gibed. "Come on, boys!"

"The molders have refused to go. Don't be fooled, boys!" shouted a voice from the doorway. Tyler marched out, his shoulders back and chest expanded. About half the men followed him. The moment Tyler's back was over the sill the door swung, and the Edgewater young man, whose movements were of exceeding swiftness, turned the key and slipped it into his pocket. This stratagem obliged the striking employees to file down the aisles and pass out the large door under the very eyes of their employers. A clerk in his shirt-sleeves, with hair parted symmetrically in the middle and cut regularly around his girlish face, was taking down on his pad the names, which a perspiring young man in a flannel shirt, with an unintentional smudge on his nose, was repeating to him in a low voice. This procedure had a dampening effect on the finish of the drama, since a number of the malcontents flagged, a few even slipped back to their benches; only about

a third of the men held steady. These walked doggedly past Hopkins, staring straight ahead. But
one halted and turned his face, where toil and years
had whitened the bristle of a stubbly beard, up at
Hopkins, and the tears rose to his tired blue eyes.

"That man broke his leg and was laid up for three
months, and the company paid his doctor's bills and
full wages," the clerk recited. "Look at him now!"

"I'm sorry to see *you* quitting, Dennis," said
Hopkins.

The man drew his hand across his eyes.

"Thirty years," he muttered; "I never quit before,
never. You mind that. But I belong to the union,
and the word's gone out."

"Oh, damn your union!" snapped the Chicago
man; "much your union would do for you if you
were in trouble."

"The union's all right," called a cheerful voice;
"the thing to do is to get the union to send all you
boys back in a hurry." The young superintendent had crossed the room and was standing behind
the elders. The words drew from the Chicago man
a freezing look, but Rivers clapped him on the back.

"Right, sonny; you've sized up the situation," his
deep bass grumbled.

The young man sent back a bright smile and a
"Thank you, sir," as he took his own way outside.
He could hear Hopkins thanking the machinists and
the others who had remained, in the language of a
man who had not forgotten that once he had worked
with his own hands. The young fellow linked his
arm in that of one of the strikers, a man he knew,
who had recently been in trouble.

"I was sorry to hear about it, Ellison," he said. "I knew what a good wife she was and what a good woman." The man's chin quivered.

"That's right," he muttered. "Say, I ain't thanked you for the flowers. Say, they give me the day off and jest the same in the envelope, Wednesday."

"Too bad you had to go out," the young man continued; "get the boys out of this ridiculous notion as soon as you can."

"I didn't know but you'd be mad, me going out—"

"When a man belongs to a union he has to obey orders; but you can do your best to get them back—" He stopped, perceiving Tyler in front of him, a man on either side.

"You—damn—renegade!" he drawled with a kind of ferocious simper. "I'll be even with you *this* deal, Ivan Gleetzin!"

"I'm no renegade, and you know it,"—William Hopkins, in the doorway, heard the voice with its neat, clipped Eastern modulations strike every word clearly, although its pitch was not raised—"and don't call me Ivan; my name is John Winslow."

None of the men quite took in the significance of the speech except Rivers and Hopkins. Rivers wagged his great head without a sound, but Hopkins strode up to Johnny, extending his hand.

"Glad to see you back, Johnny," said he heartily; "will you come round this evening and dine with Mrs. Winslow and us—or ain't you quite ready for that?"

"Not yet," said Johnny; "but thank you. Thank you, awfully."

CHAPTER X

AMELIA ANN, HER HORSE

The manner of Johnny's coming to Fairport was this: Mueller, the shipping clerk, had a wife and family. The wife was accustomed to declare that the city was no place for growing children. After the cable-car ran over the baby under his mother's very eyes, Mueller was of his wife's opinion. Granted the baby was not hurt, being run over purely as a figure of speech, since the fender caught the chubby three-year-old body and rolled it into its beneficent lap, while Mrs. Mueller gazed in horror passing speech, still there was no gainsaying the awfulness of the risk!

To complete the chain of conversion in Mueller's mind, his brother-in-law, who was a bookkeeper at the Edgewater, wrote him of a shipping clerk's position vacant there, and, with the American facility of shift, Mueller turned from groceries to rounds and ovals and scrap-iron.

It was a natural sequence of events that he should write to Johnny and praise the Edgewater as the best place on earth for a young man to learn the steel business. "Open shop, and you won't have no trouble about apprenticeships; and you'll find the old man will push you as fast as you're worth it!"

Therefore Johnny came. From the first he got

on. He went through the customary steel workers' horse-play in trial of his fortitude and his good humor; these, to a man who had "run for the Dickey" in Harvard, were but artless fooling; he was soon matriculated as "not afraid of hot iron" and always good-natured. His strength and dexterity counted as such manly traits count wherever life comes down to its elemental basis. His sweet temper and his sense of humor won him friends from the first. In his new experiment he made no secret of his intention to become a master instead of a man. To his surprise, the frankness, which he had expected to alienate, seemed rather to attract confidence. As a social reformer, a little brother to the poor, who would strip himself and share their lot to the dregs, he had met an intangible barrier of suspicion, a nameless doubt whether there were not some ulterior motive of ambition behind this reckless philanthropy. Just before he left Chicago a socialist came to bid him farewell. He was a man whom Johnny regarded with loving respect because of his purity of soul, his absolute devotion to his cause and his unlimited self-sacrifice; and never did any change of faith or alienation of circumstances affect the feeling. Writing to Roger Mack of this man, Johnny said, "I feel like calling him St. Francis, for he comes nearer that gentle and broad-minded saint than any one I ever saw." St. Francis had suffered when Johnny fell away from his first ardor, but his soul clave to the boy, even after he became a castaway. Several times he had visited Johnny in the hospital, always bearing him some gift of flowers out of his poverty, for he was very poor—not that he did not earn a good sum, for this he did, being an expert and exquisitely careful silversmith, but he spent all but the barest subsistence on the needs of his party. St. Francis looked sadly at Johnny when he bade him farewell.

"You will never come back," he said. "You will go to your own class. You didn't know it, but you never really left it. You were never a socialist; you were only an adventurer in benevolence."

"And my adventure has failed," said Johnny, attempting no useless denial.

"It ought to fail," replied his friend, with a gesture of his thin hands, one passing swiftly over the other, as if flinging something away; "it ought to fail. The redemption of humanity is not an alms; it is a religion."

Perhaps an undefined resentment against the compassion under Johnny's impulsive generosity may have worked with the men whose friendship he coveted most, and the taint of it may have affected his fellow workmen, at least at first. Whatever the reason, he never quite lost his sense of their unexpressed, unconquerable distrust. But, now, as a workingman who meant to strain every nerve to rise out of his class, he met with the friendliest sympathy. His lovable qualities were loved without question. He found himself nearer his mates than ever before, and at the same time he felt a keener interest and more brotherly compassion for them than when interest and compassion were his imperious duty.

It was about this time he wrote to Roger Mack: "I believe Amiel was right: 'What is normal is, at once, most convenient, most honest and most wholesome. Cross-roads may tempt us for one reason or another, but it is very seldom we do not come to regret having taken them.' The whole socialistic scheme is abnormal. It would only be possible in the millennium when we were all saints—and then it would be unnecessary."

Peggy sighed from pure delight as she read the letter. "And he forgot to explain who Amiel was! Or else he was ashamed to take the airs of a teacher," she cried.

The very Saturday before the strike Johnny won his promotion. He was nearer at rest in his mind than he had been in years. To celebrate the occasion he took all the children to drive in the country. They enjoyed the occasion beyond words, particularly Amelia Ann, who was allowed to drive.

Amelia Ann, also, was less unhappy than she had been. When she first came to their neat new abode, where they had the whole of five rooms, a yard and a pump of their own, Amelia Ann was a rebel who loathed her lot. She did not take to the country. She was an urban child. For her the multitudinous din, surging all day and far into the night about their tenement, which reared its eight wooden stories against the brick walls of the great brewery, was soothing as the hum of the water-wheel to a miller. The sickly sweetness of stale beer which was wafted from the gutters, the ether-like odor of banana and the pungent savor of the restaurant onion stung her nostrils pleasantly in remembrance, and she sniffed contemptuously at the pastures smelling of new-mown hay.

"Ain't it nasty?" said Amelia Ann. She pined

for the incessant variety of the pavements, the motley crowd, the blare of the brass bands, the thrill of the plunging fire-engines which could run over people and the driver never be arrested, the occasional glorious pageant of a military procession, the breathless interest of a street fight.

She yearned for the vanished audiences before which she danced or sang or was the "India Rubber Gymnast." The stout policeman often flung her an orange or an apple—they cost him naught—unconscious of the times a gurgle of laughter had followed her mimicry of his pomp as she followed his stately passage down the street. The saloon-keeper, opposite, served her a dainty from his free lunch. Even Tony of the push-cart would sometimes part with a banana over her *Bella Napoli*. She didn't understand a word, but she gave an absolute copy of an Italian's rendering, homesick pathos and all. Yes, no doubt, unpleasant as Mrs. Delaney could be, Amelia Ann had enjoyed her city life. Here she had Mrs. Delaney still—a larger dose of Mrs. Delaney— for she only took in fine washing and kept the house, now—with none of the compensations of Chicago.

They lived out of the town, past the shops at least, if not past the houses, on a street-car line which ran twice an hour only, and the motorman would stop the car if you stood on the track! What kind of street-car was that! She asked one of the motormen how many people he had run over, and he said, "Not one," and that he never meant to. Secretly she despised this pusillanimous mercy.

The first week of her exile Amelia Ann was so wretched that she had serious thoughts of setting

fire to the house—a drastic measure which she finally abandoned as useless, since Johnny would only
rent another. Besides, it would worry him, and
Amelia Ann was fond of Johnny. He was, also, for
all his gentleness, the only being whom she feared.
He made her want to cry when she had been bad.
But with the second week came relief; she discovered
the cow, the calf and the horse of the Millers. The
Miller twins lived in the next house—the same
Miller twins whose priceless old delft Johnny remembered as the cause of some of his liveliest emotions when he was a child. They were grown older
and, thanks to a departed kinsman, richer, although
far from rich; and they had purchased a "place." A
venerable cousin lived with them. Their larger income also permitted a maid-of-all-work and a boy,
who tended the horse and cow and worked in the
garden out of school hours. The family consisted
of the three women, the maid, and the horse, which
was named Ally after one of the twins. Neither of
the sisters recognized Johnny, but he recognized
them, and his heart warmed to them. An occasion
of acquaintance soon presented itself.

One winter evening Miss Tina appeared at the
fence and hailed Mrs. Delaney. She was much per-
turbed. She explained that the boy hadn't come,
although it was now half-past six; the cow ought—
Miss Tina had her old habitude of deserting her sentences at the crucial phrase—really the cow *ought*,—
the young man who boarded at Mrs. Delaney's, did
he know how to milk? Johnny volunteered to try,
vaguely recalling milking under Michael.

"If you would attempt the manual part," stammered Miss Tina, "sister and I are acquainted with the *theory;* we could direct and hold the lamp. One of us could hold the lamp, and another have a pail of water in case—but our cow *never* kicks. Perhaps, together—"

Amelia Ann admired Johnny's careless ease. He said he could manage. He let her (Amelia Ann) hold the lantern. The sisters only flitted in and out, in shawls, their white hair blowing. Amelia Ann heard one of them whisper to the other that he (meaning Johnny) seemed a very respectable young man, how much—? And the other returned, "Oh, I don't know; he seems almost a gentleman; do you *think*—?" Johnny helped them out of their dilemma by cutting into Miss Tina's hesitating: "You have been so very good, we feel—we ought— may—" with a smiling: "Oh, don't mention it; we are your nearest neighbors, you know. Good evening."

Next day the sisters sent over a hot steamed apple dumpling, and Amelia Ann thought better of them. From this time there gradually grew a dependence on Johnny. When the horse was cast in her stall, he rescued her and got her on to her feet without a scratch. One night the Millers chased sleep from the cottage by an alarm of fire screamed by Miss Tina out of the window. On Johnny's appearance (clandestinely followed by Amelia Ann), Miss Tina and Miss Ally appeared, clutching each other, and clad mostly in quilts, and Miss Ally explained that the alarm of fire was a "subterfuge." "There were burglars breaking in, and we thought—" The burglars proved to be the calf, which had escaped from its pen and, with bovine stupidity, was trying to find its mother under the front porch, where she could not possibly squeeze; however, there was no less need of a manly arm, since the bewildered and desolate calf must be restored to its home.

But it was as an amateur veterinary that Johnny was most resplendent.

The day after the calf's unsuccessful attempt to "break and enter," Miss Tina appeared at the fence. It was a point of dignity with her never to go farther than her own fence, the gifts of small fruits and vegetables, which set in with the coming of summer, being always borne over by the Swedish maid-of-all-work, with Miss Miller's compliments. Mrs. Delaney cherished a bed of pansies near the Miller fence. When she weeded it, what more natural than for her neighbor to approach and forget the difference of station in an amiable effort to instruct? What more seemly than that the welfare of the different households should be approached politely; that, by degrees, Miss Tina should learn the sickening rapidity with which the young Blokers wore out their shoes, the housewifely virtues of Thyrza, the sweetness of Franzy and the heart-breaking "devilishness, no less," of Amelia Ann, or, on the other hand, that Mrs. Delaney should discover that the Millers' girl broke more dishes than any other the household had ever had ("and when my dear mother was alive we kept two," said Miss Tina), and that Cousin Matilda was such a terrible sufferer from nervous dyspepsia, that Miss Tina feared it might go to her heart!

Mrs. Delaney was full of sympathy; Miss Miller

with dignity responded kindly. Having never been married, naturally she had distinct theories regarding the management of children, which Mrs. Delancy received with respect. By temperament Miss Tina was of a plaintive cast, Miss Ally inclining to hope and even liking to joke at broken dishes. As Mrs. Delaney's Celtic politeness made her take the color of the other's mood, Miss Tina and she would often wade in sorrow up to their eyes. Consequently, this morning, perceiving the sad approach of Miss Tina, Mrs. Delaney's smile fell off and her brow puckered into decent gloom.

"And sure, what is it has happened, Miss Miller?" she hailed, so soon as it was decent to speak, for some sentiments it is not decorum to shout; "I can see plain yous have a new grief. Don't be tellin' me your poor cousin—"

"Oh, no, no," choked Miss Tina, with an inflection which almost hinted that the trouble was worse than Miss Matilda's demise; "no—oh, Mrs. Delaney, a most dreadful, dreadful calamity—"

"Whist, now!" deplored Mrs. Delaney. "I knowed it the minute I seen you come by. But what *is* it?"

Miss Tina's utterance was broken; she almost sobbed: "Our Ally—our Ally—"

Not for a second did honest Mrs. Delaney recall the Miller horse, which was like one of the family.

"Oh, what's come to her?" she gasped in real concern, for she had a true regard for the cheerful, hard-working, frivolous Miss Ally.

Miss Tina gurgled the words behind her handkerchief:

"She—*she plunges at sheets!*"

"Hivins!" groaned Mrs. Delaney. Exactly why poor Miss Ally should plunge at sheets the sympathizer could not imagine, but such behavior in an elderly gentlewoman could portend but one awesome fact. She glanced compassionately at Miss Tina dabbling at her eyes.

"And your poor cousin mabbe on her dying bed!" she bemoaned. "Have yous had the doctor?"

"Oh, yes, I had him twice. Poor cousin doesn't know, yet."

"Oh, 'tis most distressing! What doctor was it, plase?"

"Doctor Smith."

"*What* Doctor Smith?"

"The *good* Doctor Smith."

"What was he saying? Maybe 'tis a passing disorder that will yield to the good tratement?"

"He says," bewailed Miss Tina in a fresh access of grief, "he says she's going *blind,* and—and she'll *have to be killed!*"

Horror and amazement struck Mrs. Delaney dumb one second; then "The murtherin' villin!" she cried hotly; "you ain't manin'—oh, ma'am, try the asylums—" but in the very flood-tide of her protest her ear caught a squeak of ungovernable mirth proceeding from the wood-pile, and a rapid glance that way discerned the tip of an untidy shoe. It could belong to but one person—only the abominable little Amelia Ann could giggle over murder! Mrs. Delaney's outraged soul overflowed. Three strides brought her arm into focus, one masterly spring caught and clutched the skirts of the fleeing. The other arm rose for a box that should make Amelia Ann's head ring; but Amelia Ann ducked, grinning and squealing: "Asylums for *hosses!* It's Ally, the hoss, she means! Oh, my!"—and went into impish cachinnations.

Now, another than a Celt might have been abashed, and, in her embarrassment, have loosened her grip; but the Celt's wits are nimble. Mrs. Delaney took mental breath while she shook Amelia Ann.

"You're a wicked child and me heart's fair broke wid yous," she bawled, "laffin' over a kind lady's misforchunes wid a beautiful hoss that's like her own kin! Take shame, ye hard-hearted little viper!"

Then, still firmly holding the writhing little shoulders, she made her apology to Miss Tina, who had ceased to weep, in the shock of the spectacle. "You'll pardon me, plase, ma'am. But this wicked little cratur drives me out of me mind. Sure, don't be so desparit about the poor hoss. They'd orter be asylims or hospitils—'twas the word in me mind. I'm not eddicated like you, ma'am—hospitils for hosses, if they ain't. But, annyhow, don't give up till you've seen Mr. Gleason; he'll know. And I mind me, now, he cured a hoss of the blind staggers, no less, in Chicago; 'twas a hoss in the brewery near us, and he said at the time that he got the way of it from a man lives right here, keeps the big livery stable in Fairport, his name's Durrill, or some sech like—"

"I know *him,*" ejaculated Miss Tina; "this is wonderful, really providential! My poor sister Ally was saying this morning, she couldn't bear—we've been so fond of the horse, you know. I'll speak to Mr. Gleason this afternoon. He'll know what's best."

"He will that. And now, I'll bid you good day, ma'am, for me arrm is aching wid the pullin' and scratchin' of this little wild baste and I'll take her in and lick the stuffin' outer her, plase God. Don't be dishturbed when yous hear the screeches."

Amelia Ann cast a frantic glance townward, but it was too soon for Johnny's car, and the present angering of Mrs. Delaney was but the cap-sheaf of days' iniquities. Even her stubborn courage quailed at the glint in the matron's eye. But help came from an unexpected quarter; Miss Tina herself interceded for the little girl who didn't mean any harm to poor horsey, she was sure.

"You ain't seen her trying to ride your caff, then, I'm thinking?"

Miss Tina's compassion was proof. "I'm sure she wouldn't hurt it," said she. "I'm not so sure the calf mightn't hurt her," she added, for the dejected Miss Tina owned a saving streak of humor. Eventually she foiled justice, and Amelia Ann had the grace to feel a tepid shame, remembering how she had misused the cherished Miller calf with a limber switch.

Johnny, however, repaid all favors. He carried the day against the "good" veterinary; he persuaded Miss Miller to take Ally to Luke Darrell's and, later, he took charge of that gentle plunger himself. Thus it fell out that Amelia Ann became acquainted with a horse. Johnny knew too much to leave any unprotected beast in the path of Amelia Ann's reckless curiosity. He met the danger in his own way, by disarming the foe. He took the child out to the little pasture where the horse was; he told Amelia Ann what a faithful, kind horse Ally had been always; he described the sorrowful fate menacing her. "But I think," said Johnny very seriously, "if *you* will help me, I can cure her."

"Why don't you ask Thyrza? sneered Amelia Ann; "she's a good girl, I'm a devil."

Johnny smiled and patted the thin shoulders shrugging out of her frock.

"Thyrza *is* a good little girl, but she doesn't know so much about some things as you and I, and I have more confidence in your judgment about horses. Now listen." He detailed all the simple measures of care, the feeding and giving the horse drink, the flax-seed in the food, the bathing the eyes. Would she attend to them and not let anybody bother Ally?

"Yes, I will," said Amelia Ann carelessly, but with inward mounting pride; "you show me, once."

So Johnny took Amelia Ann by the hand and led her up to Ally. He patted Ally's neck while he spoke. "Ally, this is your own particular vet. She is going to take care of you and never let any of the boys ride you, or the flies vex you; she'll never let you be hungry or thirsty, and she will help me bathe your poor eyes every morning and evening. And when you get well, we will ask Miss Tina and Miss Ally to let her drive you."

This is the way Amelia Ann learned that she had a heart, and grew to love a horse, which, in her case, was the beginning of wisdom.

None suspected the part Ally and Amelia Ann were to play in the fortunes of Johnny and the Old Colony Plow Company.

CHAPTER XI

The morning after the strike, Johnny sat in the office of the president of the Old Colony Plow Company, which had been his father's, and looked about him with a strange moving of the heart. How familiar it all was! The oaken wainscoting, dull and substantial, the walls calcimined in serviceable brown, the ceiling of a lighter shade, the comfortable leather-covered arm-chairs built for men of generous mold; the map of the river, the island and the three towns hanging beside the pen-and-ink drawing of the Old Colony shops in their modest beginnings, between the windows, and the good old war governor of Iowa, wearing the famous "dickey" and shoe-string black tie, on which Johnny's childish eyes used to gaze.

The sole change he could find was a large photograph of the portrait of Josiah Winslow, the original of which hung in Mrs. Winslow's writing-room. Johnny looked from it to the red baize-covered table, by which Rivers and Hopkins sat; the same table where he had seen them both, aforetime, because the business relations between the Old Colony and the Edgewater had always been intimate; the same table, the same group—save one. But it was that one Johnny saw more clearly than the living, breath-

404

ing men before him. He sat as he used to sit, one
arm flung over the back of his chair, one elbow on
the table, untidily chewing the end of his cigar as he
smoked, his heavily molded, patient, tired face in
its undecipherable mask of attention, broken now
and then by a dry sort of smile.

The child Johnny used to be allowed to play with
the catalogues, even to cut out the dazzling two-
horse plows and cultivators with a pair of round-
pointed scissors which his father kept for him. The
young man was beginning to remember how his
father never seemed to weary of his company, but
rather, in a shy and awkward fashion, devised entertainments which should keep him content in the
shops. Many a tour had he made, holding on to his
father's big hand, through the roaring machine-
shops and the flaming, beautiful, terrible foundry to
the peace of the painting room, which proved most
dangerous of all, since after he had tipped a pail of
green paint on his white sailor trousers and got red
paint in his hair, the shop visits were forbidden.
Yet, usually, his disasters to clothing were treated
most leniently by the Princess Olga. There was a
closet in the wall—yes, it was there now; very likely
it held bottles of the same stout aspect, the same little tumblers, and in the cigar boxes with the ships
sailing over the cover, were big, brown, moist cigars
with bands of paper about them, such as a little boy
had admired; and there used to be a box of gum-
drops, which wouldn't stick his hands up or do very
much harm to his stomach, and which were always
fresh. Johnny used to wonder at a big man's being
so fond of gum-drops.

Rivers and Hopkins sat as they always sat; Rivers all over his chair, glooming at his big boots, Hopkins figuring and drawing on a pad, as he talked. In his youth he had had a taste for drawing, soon diverted to mechanical art; but a trick of sketching idly as he thought clung to him, and by the time a business meeting of the Old Colony directors was finished, the table would be littered with stray sheets covered with primitive landscapes, heads of men and beasts, or very capable machines.

Winslow had a habit of drawing these illustrations to him, when the meeting was over. On such occasions Hopkins' face wore a singularly mixed expression. It was a blend of amusement and admiration, with a dash of apprehension.

"Humph! that's what you were thinking, was it?" Winslow was apt to say, after his examination, laying one square-tipped finger on some particular object depicted. This object would meet the eye on most of the pages. It was a key to thought which Josiah alone knew how to turn.

The fancy wandered through Johnny's mind now, as he watched Hopkins' fingers busied with his red-ink pen and his pad, that he should like to see the pictures and try his luck at the cryptic iteration of the shrewd old plow-maker's thought. Just then Hopkins spoke:

"I sent for you, Johnny, because I guess you've got some stuff in you and want a chance to show it. Hey?"

"Thank you, sir," said Johnny.

"Your father would be glad to see you here to-day," said Hopkins.

Johnny's olive skin grew a thought paler; that and the darkening of his eyes were his only signs of emotion, yet he felt strangely shaken.

"I miss your father a good deal, a good deal," repeated Hopkins. "I'm a kind of ordnance officer trying to be general-in-chief. It's not my best hold, this bossing the whole show. It *was* his. A great organizer, Johnny, great, and nobody had better judgment about the markets. There was nothing small about him either; he saw things in a big way; he had a long look ahead. We're doing things, now, he planned before he left us." Hopkins sighed. "We'd never had a strike if *he'd* been here, think, Rivers?"

"Don't know," said Rivers; "he'd a lot of sense and he held the men well in hand; but this thing is getting too big for any of us to hold."

Johnny was silent, attentively listening, struggling underneath with a great rush of memories. He looked at the map of the river and the arsenal between the towns. His father had held a little boy up before it and pointed out the one building on the island, nucleus for the vast storehouses of destruction which were drawn up on their own streets now; he had traced the river's course and come to their own town and to some tiny rectangles. Johnny found that he was recalling his very words: "Here we are, sonny, *our* shops, mine and yours. I had hard work to get them, Johnny; be careful with them when they come to you."

All at once the unreasoning hopes of youth swelled his heart. "Some day," he swore to himself, "I'll have a stake in this again. *Here* is where I belong."

"Well, Johnny," said Hopkins, "I guess Rivers has explained the situation. We thought we had piled up a whole lot of cultivators and sulky rakes, but we underrated the shortage. Everybody cleaned up—clean. We have got a sickening lot of rush orders, and some of them are new customers in Australia and Japan. If we can't fill the orders we'll lose 'em. They'll go elsewhere. Of course, we are keeping a stiff upper-lip; but a strike just now hurts like the very devil. We are like to lose seventy thousand dollars if it lasts a week and no counting *how* much if it lasts longer. We've got to keep the shops running."

"Yes, sir," said Johnny.

"Well, what's your notion? You know the men better'n we do."

"I think you're right in what you were thinking of doing," said Johnny. As he spoke he drew a sheet of paper toward him and the tip of his index finger rested on a scrawl.

Rivers and Hopkins exchanged glances. They were smiling, but there was something solemn and moved in their elderly faces.

"His father, over again," Rivers muttered under his breath.

"Did you see his hand? He moves it just the same way," Hopkins whispered. He turned to Johnny with his question:

"*What* was I thinking?"

"Thinking of getting men in and lodging them in the new sheds."

"How do you figure that out?" Hopkins replied.

"BUT HE SAYS HE TAKES PART OF THE CARE OF THE CHILDREN"

Page 326

"That cot, sir. You've drawn a cot, half a dozen times."

"But the new sheds?"

"There's nowhere else for them to go," said Johnny.

Hopkins drew a deep breath. Rivers smoked hard.

"Got a good many of the old man's ways," said he.

"Well, how does it strike you?" Hopkins' voice had a queer little vibration; it was like the shiver that lingers in the metal, after a gong has been struck and the ring is over.

"I'm sorry," said Johnny. "I wish we might have a chance to influence the men; but you haven't got the time. I suppose you have some new men in mind. Negroes, I judge." His fingers touched a sheet of paper.

"Yes, there's a nigger's head in the pile," admitted Hopkins; "we can get a lot of 'em if we want them, down the railway. Don't know a washer from a bolt-head, regular forest primeval of blockheads; but the Association will send us a dozen strikebreakers who are A No. 1 workmen. We shall have to pay them big money, though. You know the manufacturers have a Protective Association, I suppose?"

"I was a union molder once," said Johnny laconically; "but these fellows, how soon can we get them? We ought to have them in time to blow the whistle Monday. They aren't expecting any such move, and the pickets will go home. We could have them come in on the three A. M. train, march them up to the shops and get them inside before they know anything about it."

Hopkins grinned.

"You are a hustler! I thought of waiting a week for the boys to come to their senses. And I expected you to approve. I thought you'd be for handling them with padded gloves and offering 'em ice-cream. You were so soft-spoken to those fellows yesterday."

"They're all right. We want those decent fellows back, don't we? And I believe they couldn't help themselves. In their places, I should do as they did. When I was a union molder at Wethers' I did my best to prevent a strike; but I went out with the others when the firebugs won. But I didn't rest until the conservatives got them to declare the strike off. The union men have to strike together, or give up their cards. We'll have to try to undermine Tyler and get the strike called off. That's our best hold now. The non-union men will come dribbling back as soon as we can protect them."

"There'll be trouble about that," Rivers remarked casually; "the mayor's going to run for Congress; he's laying his pipes now."

"Then the policemen won't work," groaned Hopkins; "they'll see the pickets pounding our men—"

"No, they won't; they won't see a thing if it's right across the street. They're blind," growled Rivers.

Johnny struck in: "Excuse me, only in one eye. You'll find if our men resist and seem likely to win, they'll see fast enough. But we can keep the new men inside, and take care of them pretty well, can't we? The main thing is to prevent the whole shop catching the fever and going out. They'll all go to the meeting to-night, of course, and Tyler's got some good news for them—"

"Not about Wethers?"

"Yes, sir. Wethers has signed the scale."

"The damn skunk!" was all Hopkins' comment.

"You got it from a sure source, Johnny?" said Rivers. He had begun to call his young friend Johnny, almost unconsciously.

"Sure, sir, though I can't give it."

"Probably. The surer the less likely you could give it. Well, I suppose now Wethers, who made the trouble by his damned greediness, has pulled out, they'll concentrate on Collamer—and us. Collamer called me up this morning, William, and told me Wethers was dickering; he'd get his pelt under cover and the whole pack would be yapping and yarring on Collamer's heels."

"Well, the Association is helping him and it will have to help *us*," said Hopkins.

"Do you mind explaining to me about the Association?" asked Johnny; "you see, I'm a tenderfoot."

Hopkins smiled soberly. His associates considered him to have a fad for clever young men; in fact, to push them too fast and make too much of them. "Gone daft over young Winslow," he knew they were whispering among the gray-beards. If they heard that speech they would consider him reckless to intrust great interests to a tenderfoot. "The Association," he explained, "is merely a protective combination among manufacturers in our lines to help out each other in case of strikes. We don't entirely lie down and let these gentlemen walk over us, though we are pretty meek. But to get back to business. Shall we let this young tender-foot run the men in, neighbor?"

"Can you?" said Rivers.

"Yes, sir; I think so," said Johnny. He turned his bright smile, not at the two elderly men who were gazing at him with extreme friendliness under their brusque business manner, but at the portrait of his father.

"Well, get busy!" said Hopkins; "have Miss Edgar in and the correspondence."

Both men looked after the young fellow as he passed out of the door on his errand.

"Favors the old man a lot," murmured Rivers.

CHAPTER XII

AS IN THE DAYS OF NOAH

There is no doubt of the advantages of the mingling of ages in social functions, the old and the young and the great middle classes of the years, making merry together; but how to win these undoubted benefits was beyond Fairport until Duplicate Whist went down the best resident streets, like scarlet fever. After that, Peggy was as likely to meet Mrs. Winter at a whist party as any of her young friends.

Mrs. Winter was a whist player of renown. She played an heretical short-suit game; but was not the less to be dreaded, since she had learned every painstaking signal of "American leads" and could read her opponents' resources while she hid her own. Were it necessary she could play as decorous and conventional a game as any one; but she was quite capable of leading a singleton, and she would sacrifice an established suit to a cross ruff, without a qualm.

"But," gently complained Miss Tina of the Miller twins, who religiously followed rules and was what is known as a "safe" partner, yet somehow never won points, "but how do you know when to do that way—or do you just guess?"

"I *count*," replied Mrs Winter; "whist strategy is only a matter of arithmetic. The long-suit game is not inspired. If I can make more tricks by a sneak I make them. That's all."

"But it's so deceiving to your partner and she might be—"

"She'll be much crosser if you come out behind in the score. Well, Miss Tina, it is time to begin."

Miss Tina was her partner, as it happened; and if ever unmerciful disaster followed fast and followed faster on imprudent advice, it did in this case; for Miss Tina, rashly emboldened, played a wild, mad, passionate game of sneaks and false cards, relentlessly forcing her partner, who had a suit of six established, and keeping her in the dark about her own good suit with three court cards at the head, all of which were squandered after trumps were exhausted in Miss Tina's mind, but unhappily, not in the adversary's hand. The slaughter was so pathetic that it is remembered to this day. But Mrs. Winter bore it with a grim and great composure. She had reason; those who had the pleasure of seeing Mrs. Winter's rendition of Miss Clementina playing the short-suit game and her final collapse were in hysterics of laughter; it was worth the five points she lost on the hand.

But poor Miss Tina went home and wept. Thenceforward and for ever, she forswore short leads in whist. "They aren't *honest!*" said Miss Tina. Nevertheless she did not think it Christian to be angry with Mrs. Winter, the cause of her woes, as she always felt; and she attended the next meeting of the Whist Club at Hazelhurst, Mrs. Winter's place, exactly the same, although with inward tremors and a heavy heart.

Mrs. Winslow was there, with Miss Margaret Rutherford, and her good fortune gave her that kind young lady for a partner. It further assisted her to remember trumps correctly, and when the first intermission came and the players were refreshed with claret cup, Miss Tina had several points to her credit. Conversation, which had been sternly suppressed before, now buzzed on all sides. Peggy leaned back in her chair and let the various streams of talk converge on an indifferent ear. She felt listless and worried and sad, that day. Quite without reason, she knew; for, of course, there was no reason to care that a few days over the usual week had elapsed since Roger Mack had heard from Johnny. Neither Peggy nor Mrs. Winslow knew of Johnny's return, as yet; for Hopkins had promised to say nothing. Peggy, therefore, did not connect Johnny with any of the perils of the strike.

The talk went on cheerfully from various quarters, its subject varying with its source.

"No, I don't belong to the Colonial Dames— though I *could*."

"I don't think much of the society, myself; nothing but social function and snippy ways—I belong to the Daughters. There is some sense to them—and real patriotism. They've put up another tablet over the river."

"Did you tell me, Mary Bee, that your cook wants a place when you go to Europe?"

"I haven't had a cook for three weeks, Elsie, and she wouldn't want a place if I had. They never seem to want places, now; they only condescend to *take* them—"

"Three yards, if you've a careful dressmaker. Three and a half is *ample*. There are some perfectly lovely taffetas down at Camden's."

"Yes, I'm on the committee. I suppose they'll take Decorative Household Art."

"Well, I think we oughtn't to educate ourselves so heavily. It's so depressing to know how impossible light oak furniture is artistically, when you've got three sets in the house, and can't afford to throw them away."

"Did you play the seven before the six? Well, I never saw it. I *beg* your pardon. I never do see trump signals."

"Oh, it was no consequence; only if you'd led out trumps I could have given you back your diamond, and that would have put us three more tricks to the good."

"Well, no, Clara, I *don't* think that when you have ace, king, queen and three small ones, you should underplay your ace!"

"She told me distinctly that they were going to have an Easter sale; and they would take orders for night-gowns. You can't buy anything you'd be willing to wear ready-made, except French, and the price is simply awful."

"Well, you know, I'm pretty busy these days, with Mabel's wedding only a month off. Did you know poor Ralph has the measles? He's nearly wild."

"Is he so ill?"

"No, he isn't even in bed; but you know they have a strike on at the Old Colony, and he can't bear to stay home. But he has to. Mr. Hopkins told him he wouldn't have him give the measles to all those colored men."

"They have negroes working?"

"Yes,—have them shut up in the shops. That new young man they have smuggled them in about three o'clock in the morning; had the train stop before it got to the depot and marched them all in before the strikers' pickets knew anything about it."

"Well, it is hard for Ralph to keep out of it at such an exciting time. He's *so* conscientious. You must often think, Mrs. Mallory, what a comfort it is when you are going to give your daughter to his keeping, that he is such an honorable, conscientious young man."

"I do feel that way. And he's good-tempered. All the family are good-tempered; I don't know as I ever knew a better-tempered woman than his mother. She was a dear woman. Do you remember the little yellow tomato preserves she used to put up? With ginger. I guess nobody had sense to get the recipe while she was alive and willing. And, now, it's too late."

"Why, no, I didn't read it. To tell the truth, all last week, I was saturated with Carlyle's *French Revolution*. You've read it, of course, Mrs. Winter. I was talking with father last night about it and he said he supposed all through those *terrible* days, the ordinary life, the buying and selling, and marrying and having your friends to dinner went on quite the same."

"Of course, it did," said Mrs. Winter. "And easy enough to understand. We have murder stalking among us at every labor conflict; do we get excited? There is a sky-scraper I was in, in Chicago, where nine men were killed and forty injured (more than in a battle) while it was building. They had strikes on every floor. Critics talk of life not being dramatic, these days, of its being *tame;* if bloodshed and murder and sacrifice and heartbreak and heroism are tame, our life is tame. Not otherwise. I drove down town yesterday, and saw the men patrolling every street near the Old Colony."

"Did they stop your carriage?"

"No; why should they? I'm not a scab. They don't stop Mr. Hopkins or Mr. Rivers. Any poor workman under them who tried to step in and earn a few dollars for his family would risk his bones if not his life; but the head man they are fighting never is molested. It is the same way with the departments that haven't been ordered out, the painters and blacksmiths and foundry men; they go by cheerfully with their dinner-pails."

"They say the strike's hurting business a great deal. And if it spreads, as the walking delegate who's running it threatens, it will be a *bad* thing. He says maybe he'll tie up the arsenal."

"Good gracious! Why? Mrs. Winter, I *will*; the claret cup is delicious."

"Oh, I don't know; they buy some things from the Old Colony or the Edgewater or whatever. These labor things are awfully mixed up in my mind."

Several ladies had drawn near the table where Mrs. Winter sat, looking her handsomest in black velvet and lace and wearing her famous rubies. There were pink ribbons in her lace cap which

matched a roseleaf flush in her delicate cheek, and
her eyes flashed like the jewels in her rings as her
hands moved in quick Southern gestures.

"They seem to be in most people's minds," said
she scornfully.

"Well, *I* believe in arbitration," explained a tall
lady with a Roman nose. "Mrs. Winter, I don't
want to criticize, but can't we women do something
to stop this fearful strike? If we add our pleadings
to those of the clergy, won't Mr. Hopkins and Mr.
Rivers listen? If *you* and Mrs. Winslow—"

"I and Mrs. Winslow?" began Mrs. Winter in a
freezing tone; then her eye took in her stately rooms
in their new Empire dressing; she bethought herself
that she was in her own house, and smiled gracious-
ly. "My dear Mrs. Weekham, you forget we are
your friends, the enemy,—the Old Colony's loss is
our loss; the Old Colony strike hits *us*."

"Ah, then, all the more, dear madam, the better
right you have to stop this most awful struggle.
There are two strikers' families live opposite us,
down in the ravine on St. Katharine Street; I don't
suppose they've had a *good* meal for a week! I send
them in skim milk every day, and in fact I tell Nan-
nie to give them anything we've left over. And
they're only two families out of how many? I'm
told the clergy went in a body to Mr. Hopkins this
morning to beg him to arbitrate."

"They did," said Mrs. Winter; "and shall I tell
you what he said? He said, 'We can't arbitrate our
contracts. The only thing to be done with a contract
is to keep it.' I suppose I'm only an unprincipled
aristocrat; but I thought that rather neat. You so-

cial reformers seem to think you can put the ten commandments to vote any time they bother you. But I disagree with you there. You can't arbitrate your word, as Mr. Hopkins says."

"Did you hear, Mrs. Winter,"—Emma Winslow spoke quietly, but every one stopped to listen—"they have fallen upon another poor man? He had nothing to do with the Old Colony, but they wouldn't believe him. They fractured his skull and kicked and beat him so the doctors think he will die. He's at St. Margaret's Hospital."

"And some people wonder at life going on at the time of the French Revolution!" said Mrs. Winter.

"But we haven't any people in whom we are interested," a young girl ventured, and instantly blushed at her boldness; "that would make all the difference. Of course it's very pitiful, the poor people suffering so, but it's not like your own—"

"Well, it will come uncommonly near my own," spoke up the mother of Mabel, who was to marry the superintendent of the Old Colony, "if things get worse and there's a fight and they bring home Ralph Holman all beaten to a pulp."

"I don't, myself," said Mrs. Winslow, "feel so absolutely secure that no harm may come to my father. You see, I am not so used to strikes. The Old Colony never had one before. My poor father used to be so proud of it."

"But I don't understand," ventured another inquirer, "what makes the men so bitter. They really haven't any special grievance, at least they hadn't at first—I understand they have injected some questions of wages and hours since—but, at first, it was simply a strike because the Old Colony sold goods to Collins, or some such name, in Chicago. Why should the men get so angry and furious about that?"

"Because they're fighting, my dear," answered Mrs. Winter; "just fight any one for three weeks and I reckon you will get bitter, however trivial the cause of the scrimmage. Besides, as I understand, the machinists' leader, Taylor—what is it, Emma? Oh, yes, Tyler. Tyler is a storm king. He throws oil on the fire. He *gets* the men to fighting. He has brass bands and meetings and processions and keeps the air full of electricity."

"Where does he get his money?"

"Oh, all the labor unions help him a little bit, some from fear, some from policy, and some from friendliness. But I think his supplies are running low. Shall we go back to the game, ladies?"

Little Miss Tina had listened eagerly, but said nothing. She turned to Peggy. "I hope Mrs. Winslow and you realize where sister and my sympathies are, Miss Rutherford. We feel as if expression—we can't quite express. And we have a—a kind of stake, I may say—I mean not holding stock so much, although sister Ally has six shares of the common, and I have sixteen, Miss Rutherford, and we always bring our proxies down *ourselves* to Mr. Hopkins. He says we needn't, but the mail isn't *always*—but I don't mean that. We know some one, the very nicest young man, sister Ally and I and cousin often say we ever knew, except—of course, poor dear Rufus Goddard, who was betrothed to Ally and died. I guess you have heard of him, a *very* promising young man—Mr. Gleason's ways so often remind us of him, though he isn't like him in physique, for Rufus was rather short and very blond, while Mr. Gleason must be six feet, and dark eyes and hair. But we certainly have grown to esteem Mr. Gleason very highly and a—a nephew couldn't be kinder. So we do feel worried about him; and sister Ally and I used to watch for his car—you feel better to know any one's safe home at night, and safe in—"

"To be sure," Peggy agreed politely, when she was sure Miss Tina had modestly abandoned her sentence. "Is Mr. Gleason in the Old Colony? I don't remember the name."

"Not regularly, Miss Rutherford, not as a general thing; he is the superintendent of the Open Hearth —isn't that, somehow, such a pleasant, hospitable sounding name, Miss Rutherford?—over at the Edgewater, but they have loaned him to the Old Colony through this strike, someway, I don't understand quite how; but they have—and we can't help feeling anxious about him, especially since he has taken to staying all night in the shops. Mrs. Delaney is frightened, too, I can see it—what say?"

"Excuse me," said Peggy, "I dropped my cards. Who is Mrs. Delaney,—Mr. Gleason's mother-in-law?"

"Oh, dear, no; he isn't married; she's no relation; indeed, although a very worthy, respectable woman, —oh, very, she is not—not at all—Mr. Gleason is very much of a gentleman. Sister and I both saw that when he was working with his hands, for he rose from the ranks; but he is an educated man; and Thyrza says he sings a Latin song. I asked her how she knew and she said she asked him if it was Italian (*Dago*, the poor child calls it; they used to live in Chicago, in rather a poor neighborhood, I infer; I know Amelia Ann said it was *fierce*)—where— oh, yes, excuse my rambling; he told her no, it was Latin. Oh, are they beginning to play?"

And the game began again.

Mrs. Winter glided up behind Peggy to watch her play. After the game was over there were coffee and chocolate and cakes, beaten biscuit and salad and hot pâtés and ice-cream; Mrs. Winter kept to her old bountiful fashion of an afternoon meal. "There isn't a quarter of them have late dinners," said she, "and your lemonade tea and hopes of a sandwich and fairy gingerbread only spoil their supper without taking the place of it,—why not give them a good meal?"

Mrs. Winter looked over the table, splendid with the Winter plate; and the great black sideboard, more resplendent still; and her eyes ran around the animated and cheerful faces. She smiled subtly to herself, and let the smile extend to Peggy, at her elbow.

"I suppose," said she, "that up on the hills there are plenty of women making a fire for supper with as little wood or coal as they can use, and wondering, maybe, where to-morrow's supper is to come from; and down below the railroad, in the saloons or at their rented headquarters, the men are plotting battle and maybe murder; and we"—she flirted upward the palms of her little, flashing hands—"well, it was so in the time of Noah, in the days before the French Revolution, in the days after; it will always be so. Life is too big to care."

"I dare say," said Peggy absently.

Mrs. Winter gave her one of the glances which Peggy nicknamed to Johnny her "circular-saw looks" because, she said, they seemed to go clear through and rip up one's innermost thoughts.

"Peggy," said Mrs. Winter, "I don't think I ever saw you play quite such a *casual* game, as you did this afternoon; I should think your mind had had a stroke!"

Peggy slipped her round, strong, young arm about the little waist and whispered:

"Oh, Cousin Rebecca, I don't care, I don't care about the days of Noah either; maybe I ought, but I don't! Cousin Rebecca, *Johnny's come back;* he's in the Old Colony; *he has come to his own again!*"

CHAPTER XIII

IN THE CAMP OF THE ENEMY

On the same afternoon that Mrs. Winter entertained the Whist Club, Mr. Walter Tyler had his feet under a table in a room of Burkholm Hall, with an open box of cigars and some schooners of beer to ease the cares of counsel, and four of the executive committee of the Old Colony strikers were grouped about him. The details of the conference the writer obtained from Billy Bates. How did he obtain them? Any frank answer to this question might imperil his sources of information. Enough that he controlled them.

When these helps from Billy allowed me to see the committee-room, Tyler was summing up the situation after three weeks' warfare.

"The pickets warming up?" said Tyler.

"They're hard propositions," was the answer; "I never saw such snowbanks. Couldn't rouse 'em worth a cent. Let one feller git 'most into the alley just because he'd some hard-luck story 'bout a sick boy he was trying to send to Colorado. I had to knock him down before I got him to see we was his true friends."

"Guess it's the same man I caught trying to sneak by as a bench molder. He's had two sons die of

425

consumption and he's kinder looney. I told him we'd give him a lift and started him with ten dollars."

The offer was like Tyler. He was always free with his money, or any one's else money on which he could lay hands, and this debonair generosity and a certain rough sympathy for distress immediately under his eyes increased his hold on his following. Now he was working at his very best, his temper well in leash, and his wits sharpened to a cutting edge. He perfectly understood the average conservative mechanic who resembles the average conservative citizen, fearing to lead, and only daring to follow in a crowd,—in short, possessing the cowardice of his opinions. Tyler had played on their fears all his life as a labor politician. He himself followed the advice which stared at Britomart from the walls of the Enchanted Palace: "Be bold! Be bold, and evermore be bold!" He knew nothing of the inner room and the final word, "Be not *too* bold!" His policy was to stir up his men to fury. Anger is a contagious passion. There were too many people about asking why were they striking, anyhow? argued Tyler. Once get the men fighting over any old thing, they would not be so captious about grievances. Grievances indeed? they had plenty; what did they want more for?

So Tyler had had meetings and parades and pickets watching the plant and turning back the workmen; and he talked at every street-corner about the power of the labor vote until the mayor could not sleep nights, and the chief of police told his men not to be too rough with the strikers; the

Old Colony was more to blame than they, importing niggers and toughs, instead of waiting. Those strike-breakers better not be too fresh! They'd arrest 'em for carrying concealed weapons.

This very thing was done. One of the strike-breakers, who had gone into town to see his sick sister, was set upon by a crowd of city hoodlums, led by a striker. He was hit by a brick and, to save his bones, pulled out a revolver, with which he held the crowd at bay, retreating all the time, until he was rescued by Johnny Winslow in Mr. Rivers' buggy. The policeman, who saw the affair, made no move to save him, but arrested him on the concealed weapon charge as soon as he was safe. The company gave bail for his appearance. Such petty annoyances were worked at every turn. And the whole power of that odious word, which working-men fear more than sin or starvation, was invoked to guard the road to the shops.

"Yes, the pickets are getting half worth something," said Tyler.

"I don't call 'em worth much yesterday night," growled one of the committee.

"How's that?"

"Why, some kind of a fakir got the boys listening to his patter and, by hell! a whole lot of fellows come a-walking down the alley six abreast with that — Gleason at the head, and they made a kind of V and just simply rushed the boys. They didn't git any show at all."

Tyler swore a minute.

"Worst is, I guess they were fellers in town, sneaking in under cover."

"The hell they were!" Tyler expressed his opinion of the workingmen of Fairport in vitriolic terms, which Billy took care, later, should come to every ear.

"I can go you one better," said another man, coming out of a cloud of smoke, "'bout that Gleason. You know this morning when those guys from the churches and the Business Men's Association went with our play for position, that arbitration offer?"

"Well?"

"He had the nerve to run in a dozen wood-workers in *hacks* with that there crowd of goozoos."

"How'd he do that? I saw the hacks come back myself," cried a man who had been on the pickets.

"Easy. The boys were all dressed up in their Sunday clothes and you took 'em for bankers. The hacks took back the real jays, and you didn't notice there were two or three instid of four in a carriage."

"Ain't he slick?" chuckled a young committeeman. He was a foolish youngster who did not know how to restrain his feelings, and was suspected to be growing lukewarm.

"He *thinks* he is," sneered Tyler; "he, maybe, won't be so satisfied with himself before he gets through."

"Billy Bates turned up yesterday," said the first speaker. "I guess that ends any chance of our gettin' the molders out *this* time."

"Damn Billy Bates!" Tyler swore savagely; "and damn that molasses-blooded president of the labor council, Harry Leroy; you'd think he was a corporation lap-dog to hear him whining about keeping the men orderly. I tell you the unions will never run the whole shooting match as they *can,* until we squeeze out such rotten snakes."

"That's right!" chanted the two satellites of Tyler on the committee.

"Who made that driveling motion not to give any strike wages to anybody with money in the savings bank?"

"I know," said the young committee-man; "it was Ellison, one of the machinists."

"I bet he got egged on to it by Bates, then."

"Well, he *was* talking to Bates."

Tyler swore vituperatively. He asked the young man why he kept such white innocence as his on earth—Heaven was his home. Couldn't he see— swinging furiously out of sarcasm into direct brutality—that if the motion had carried, which it was damn near doing, all the savings-bank men would begin kicking? "That's it! That's it!" he cried, clenching his fists, foaming and almost sobbing between rage and liquor; "you're *all* asleep! You're letting Billy, who is the very scholar of the devil for dirty, lying cowardly tricks, jest make bad blood all the time!" Thus he raged and taunted.

But he was not so wrought upon by his rage that he lost his prudence. His secret plans he kept for other ears than the committee. He and they, however, realized that the strike had reached a critical stage. Disintegration, once fairly started, gets the men into a panic which may be as contagious as the strike-fever which it cures. And disintegration was beginning.

He knew that it had been all that his influence

and his bitter tongue and the fear of him could do
to hold the men firm at the last meeting; he dared
not chance another. He knew, furthermore, that the
letters he was receiving from the higher officials of
his own union would make cheerful reading to Billy
Bates, whom he cursed for inciting them. The
others were even beginning to suspect that the Fairport end of the strike was waged to gratify private
animosities of Tyler's own. Tyler foresaw that only
success, and success at once, could save him from
being quietly pushed out of the machinists' union,
in spite of the efforts of the socialist wing.

"It's a fight to a finish, by God!" he swore. Since
the Fairport white-livered cowards wouldn't help
him, he would find his help elsewhere; but there was
nothing mean about him; he'd let the Fairport
sneaks get all the credit of doing something worth
while!

"It's up to us to do something," growled Tyler
to the man of the pickets whom he trusted most,
after he had fully collated the gallsome reports of
the week; "we have got to make a ten-strike!"

The man's mouth sagged at the corners. "How?"
said he.

"You leave that to me, Brother Finn," said Tyler.

CHAPTER XIV

Dear Roger :—

Let up a little! I didn't know what was the wisest or the kindest way to do. You know I am always too impetuous, acting in haste and repenting at leisure,—I wanted to think this over. Don't jump on a penitent sinner! And don't look me up, just yet, if you please.

    .   .   .   .   .

The poor fellow at the hospital has regained his senses enough to tell the story of his hard luck. He was attacked on his way from the train. He protested he wasn't a scab, he wasn't going to work in town at all, but a hammer fell out of his pocket, and then they nearly murdered him. Some of our men found him on the railway embankment just below the depot. You can guess who did it. But which *one,* or, rather, which two or three or four? I think I have a clue. Four of the strikers were seen on the railway. One of them was a Finn whose name no one knows, but he is called Adam Finn. He is so nicknamed because he was continually saying : "I don't like you a damn!" He is a sulky sort when sober, and a bloody maniac when drunk. And he is left-handed. The hammer wounds seem (so the doctors say) to have

431

been made by a left-handed man. As to the other
three, we'll find them.

.   .   .   .   .

We are making a sort of slogan of Hopkins'
words: "We can't arbitrate our contracts." I think
the people, generally, are getting at the real facts.
Tyler got their ear at first. The shopkeepers naturally took fright at a loss of custom. The business
men hate strikes as they hate bad crops or contagious
disease; all hurt business. They want to stamp them
all out quickly and get to making money again. And
they don't ask too many questions about the rights
of the matter. But as Billy says, "Wrong things are
almost always too expensive to be tolerated very
long." We don't find out their cost because it is in-
direct, but we pay it just the same. Formerly the
employers were tyrannical and ate up the poor as it
were bread; some of them still are—when they dare.
Thanks to the unions, they don't often dare! They
have learned it costs too much to skin their men per-
sistently. It would cost too much, anyhow, for a
man on starvation wages can't do his best; and we
want his best. But, to-day, the union is the stronger
and it often is a tyrant. I think *we* are a case in
point; so does Billy. Billy is the best ever!

.   .   .   .   .

The poor fellow at the hospital may die. The
doctors can't tell. Was there ever such irony of
fate! He isn't a machinist, but a union molder, secretary of a local in Illinois. The molders were going
to send the strikers $300, but Billy feels now that
he can't encourage such a gift until the cloud is off
the machinists' fair name; while as to striking for

such fellows, that's out of the question! Good old Billy!

Of course, Machinists' Union No. 183 met and denounced the assault as opposed to the "peaceful methods which they have always advocated." I like that, don't you? And I suppose you observed that Brother Adam Finn moved to offer a reward of $25 for the information leading to the arrest and conviction of the "miscreants." There's cold nerve for you. Tyler is sure that the assault was committed by strike-breakers in order to cast odium on the machinists' union. According to Tyler such attacks are always planned by employers to get pretexts for calling out the militia and "crushing labor."

.   .   .   .   .

The poor fellow at St. Margaret's is better; he will get well. I wish you'd ask Miss Rutherford to send him some home things. He has described his assailants, and we've got Finn nailed, I hope. Of course, he'll be bailed out.

.   .   .   .

Roger, you are quite mistaken. I run no danger. I don't go home, now. I tremble when I think of how Amelia Ann may be straining Mrs. Delaney's patience. Mark Delaney is a molder here, so far unmolested, for they don't interfere as yet with the other departments; and he says Amelia Ann has bargained with Thyrza to do her mending; in return Thyrza will be allowed to ride Ally as soon as I permit. So I hope the horse is keeping her straight.

She really is trying to be good. She made a *pie* for me yesterday, poor child! *And I ate it!* I couldn't say it was good, and I wanted to say something encouraging, so I ate the truck, cooked and uncooked (I never did like underdone pastry!), and told her she had pleased me very much, and I had eaten every crumb. But "what a tangled web we weave," and so forth. She is going to make another!

.   .   .   .   .

I assure you, my dear friend, I am cradled in Roman luxury. I have fine food—except when poor, dear Amelia Ann's affection makes a culinary spurt! I have a porcelain tub in the office. (Bless Hopkins for his passion for bathing!) Think of that! Do you know how long since I have stepped into a porcelain tub?

The darkies amuse me. They take the confinement very cheerfully. Play cards and craps. I tell them stories. And do you know what they like best? The Bible and Homer. I don't know how many Penelopes and Helens and Ajaxes and Calypsos I shall have on my conscience, when they go home to the "right new babies" they tell about. One of them is going to take Cassandra May for his. "I ben goin' to take 'Oh my' but now I'll take this heah," says he. "Oh my!" I repeated stupidly.

"Yes, boss. Doesn't you 'member dat ar ole Bible Oh my, de mudder of Rufe?" Naomi, Roger; if you please.

.   .   .   .   .

The head strike-breaker is an interesting personality (as we used to say in Harvard, where they are always discussing Personality with awe and a capital P). He is a simon-pure Vermont Yankee. He belonged to a union in some Eastern state. They went on a strike, the strike failed and the union washed its hands of him later, when he couldn't pay the dues. I don't understand. Usually they are very lenient in such cases. He had exhausted his savings in the strike. Finally he got a good job, but he didn't try to get reinstated in the union. There was trouble between him and some of the labor politicians, which ended in a fight. That was how he got his curious scar—from a cold chisel. His son tried to help him, just a mere slip of a boy, and he was killed by a chance blow. Matthew hates the unions. He is bitter, not in any vituperative fashion, he is the stillest man I ever saw; but he never lets up. I don't know how many fights he has seen. He risks his life for the fun of it, he says. He and I have funny arguments about the unions. I hope to convert him and switch him on to a better life. Tyler and he are sworn enemies. He has a funny little volume of Poe which he carries around with him and reads at intervals, and he knows Burns by heart. When he has any spare time he plays on the accordion. He has a grand one with him. And the coons flock round him like flies round molasses.

The trouble in getting food for our strike-breakers has not been so bad as Tyler wishes. He started round, betimes, to warn off butchers, bakers and candlestick makers; but we simply had the things sent in the original package style of prohibitory states to the express office, and sent an armed escort to get them, made up of our own police, special deputies, duly sworn in. The mayor *had* to let us have them. He didn't want to, crawling demagogue that he is! but we simply cowed him. We hadn't a bit of trouble. And as Tyler can't find out who sells us the stuff, he can't boycott anybody. Naturally, we sometimes take in a few men with our hams and loaves and meat and candy. Yes, candy. Tobacco, too. And sometimes kegs of beer. The darkies are as fond of candy as of beer. And they dote on trials of strength and such things. But you know all that, you Southern fire-eater. I have been surprised that they don't chafe more under their imprisonment. Our output this week is almost two-thirds what it should be. Pretty good for new hands!

.   .   .   .   .

This morning occurred a nasty thing. Some one put poison in the big well from which we get all our washing water. Since the strike we have issued strict orders that only the water out of the carboys should be drunk. This from no fear of poisoning, but because the well gets too much miscellaneous seeping in this belt of manufacturing shops. Of course, there was the usual idiot to disregard orders and drink out of a faucet. Poor fellow! he paid for it. The doctor pumped him out and he had the time of his life. It was *fierce!* After that we analyzed the water. There's no doubt of it. The well was poisoned. I don't accuse Tyler, and assuredly our old men wouldn't stoop to such a Dago trick; but the rancor runs so high that all sorts of outside riffraff have been welcomed in. Every city has its loathsome undercurrent. The fiend who tried to do this may have belonged here or been imported. Who knows? The men were less affected than you would think.

The strike-breakers took it as a part of the business, and the blacks take my word for their safety.

.   .   .   .   .

Tolstoi is a great soul, a vast soul; like Russia in both these qualities, and like Russia, furthermore, in his formlessness and his carelessness for the detail of result, once assured his principle is right. Yet it is these details, these minor things that decide whether a reform shall be successful. He has no working plan, ever. The Anglo-Saxon always strikes for a working plan first. He always demands the works without which faith is dead. I used to worship Tolstoi; I shall always admire him, love him and infinitely respect him; but I can't follow him any more. Sometimes I almost agree with Billy's irreverent and not at all refined comment— after he had conscientiously read *War and Peace* and *My Religion*—"That fellow," says Billy, "has bitten off more than he can chew."

Well, Roger, whether he's right about Tolstoi or not, he is right about a very humble young fool who is writing to you. There are some problems in this universe too big for any one man, I almost had said any one generation, to tackle. They can't be solved by machinery. They have to grow out of their tangle. All that can be done is to start the growing right and tend it patiently. You can't make a tree in a minute. But unhappily you can blow one up with dynamite and destroy it in a minute easy! To me that is the awfulest thing I know; how slow is growth and how swift destruction!

There are times when I understand how a man might go crazy merely out of self-disgust at his own asinine presumption! When I think of my own folly, I think, oh, the impudence of me! a young cub of twenty-two thinking he had the right to try to shape matters which meant happiness and misery and sin and death to human beings! What a prep trick! It's the wicked blind cruelty of it that breaks you all up; but it is the rotten, slushy, grinning conceit of it that humiliates you and makes you want to run and hide!

.   .   .   .   .

Does it seem strange to you that I should be nearer light-hearted than I have been since my mother died, here working tooth and nail against all I fervently applauded three years ago? It seems strange to me, sometimes. I am too busy to analyze, but I wonder if it isn't that I recognize that I have had what St. Paul calls a warring in my members. The Anglo-Saxon in me has conquered. And at whatever expense, I am thankful the battle is over. I believe my mother would be, too.

At least, I seem to be back to myself, in my right place. I can't tell you how good to me Mr. Hopkins and Mr. Rivers have been. I love that gnarled old Spartan!

.   .   .   .   .

Every night, before I go to bed, I write you a few words. It makes me sleep better. Some day I'll see you and tell you a lot of things. To-night I've a feeling, a presentiment you might call it. I'm going to write this, but I'll only send the first sheet. Afterward, when all this racket is over, you may have *this* to laugh over. Or if my silly presentiment comes true—it will be in my pocket for you, Peggy; Peggy, my own darling little playmate and queen, my love all my life. You see, I can't pretend any more. You won't get this if I am alive to-morrow night; and if I'm not, you will forgive me, won't you, dear, for telling you that I love you, love you, love you! There has never been anybody but you. Do you remember you promised to marry me once? You *did,* sweetheart. Our solemn troth was plighted in that little plot of grass near the japonicas. We had been talking about what we should do when we were grown up. I said (in deep confidence) that I should be a conspirator and set poor people free. You said you thought that would be very stupid. I said: "What are you going to be, Peggy?" You said: "Oh, I shall have to be a married lady, I suppose, and give balls." "Oh," I said, feeling very miserable. Then I asked you whom you would marry (I undoubtedly said *who*), and you answered: "I suppose I'll have to marry you—to keep you out of mischief!" On this I cheered up tremendously, and we arranged all the details of the wedding, and I gave you—'twas my little all—a small carnelian ring, which I had bought from a boy with my most precious alley tor. You gave me a watch-charm which my father had given you, ungraciously assuring me it was much nicer than my carnelian ring. So, my darling, you see, if I am presumptuous, I have a wee excuse. Let me be presumptuous, this once, which you will never see—if I am able to blush for my nonsense. Peggy, I have been so homesick, so infernally homesick! I longed for the hills and corn-field and the river and—oh, I longed for *you!* If I live I'll make a foothold, and *then* I'll ask you to forgive me and keep me out of mischief. Good-by, Peggy; there never was a nobler or sweeter or dearer woman in the world. There never will be for me, never. No matter how many worlds I may have to go through after this, I'll claim you at last.

Your Jo'nivan.

Billy has my insurance policy. I took it out for the children. I had to, you know. Only there's just a little for you, to whom I would love to give the whole world. And Peggy, won't you look after Amelia Ann a bit more than the others? She needs it.

Please tell Billy he was the best friend on earth to me, and give him my love; I've said it in my will, but I want *you* to tell him for me. Oh, Peggy, dear, I love you. Tell dear old Mishka it will be all right; he must take care of you. Please give my love to my stepmother.

.   .   .   .   .

When Johnny wrote this last letter he hesitated, holding the paper, as if to tear it apart. Then, with the queer smile that was like his father's, he folded it carefully and placed it in an envelope, addressing it firmly, "Miss Margaret Cary Rutherford," and after addressing, he kissed the name. "One for me, one for my mother, who loved you, my darling," he whispered. And he placed it in the pocket of his shirt, with a watch-charm which he always wore.

Then, smiling, he lay down dressed as he was, wrapped the blankets about him, and almost immediately fell asleep.

CHAPTER XV

WHEN AMELIA ANN WAS "IT"

At that very hour (it was on the stroke of midnight) Amelia Ann was groping her way over the shorn pastures blue-green with the dew. Nor was Amelia Ann's conscience in the least agog. On the contrary, it approved her, with a very rare approval. So did her self-respect. Always in all the games, Amelia Ann wanted to be "It"; now she was being "It," and enjoying the occasion, immensely.

Who can guess how tiny a hand may disarrange, may destroy wide-reaching schemes! Had Tyler passed Bloker's little daughter on the street it would never have occurred to him that she was to be the vehicle for the lame Nemesis to reach him. Yet such was the ordering of the Fates.

That afternoon, Amelia Ann had been sent to town by Mrs. Delaney to buy a certain brand of baking-powder which the worthy woman affected, and which, out of sheer perverseness, the hill grocery would not keep. Many were the injunctions given Amelia Ann to be sober, to be diligent, and to be in the constant fear of the street-cars. Silver coin to the amount of the purchase-money required, with two half-fare car tickets, were tied up in her little red-bordered handkerchief. Amelia Ann had begged for more; she had pleaded to have her little bank broken, wherein was the large treasure of sixty cents; but Mrs. Delaney was adamant. "Yous can pop corn and boil molasses when ye git back, if you're good," was her final summation; "that's better than sweeties. Run along!"

"I don't want it for candy," Amelia Ann sniffled.

"What for, then?"

"For a present for Johnny."

Mrs. Delaney indulged in no illusions regarding Amelia Ann's truthfulness; she credited or discredited the child, according to circumstances; and circumstances did not favor her to-day. Therefore, she tossed her head and retorted: "You'll wait till I help you pick out presents. And you best quit calling Mr. Gleason 'Johnny' that disrespectable way. G'wan now, and come back quick, or how'll you have biscuit for supper?"

Amelia Ann's silent obedience might have warned her guardian that some plan was brewing; but Mrs. Delaney was busy with her spring house-cleaning and her whole soul was on soft soap and scrubbing-brushes. The little girl departed, unsuspected. She bought the baking-powder, honorably, and at once carried out her plan. She entered the most pretentious saloon she could find. The saloon-keeper looked up in surprise at the neatly-dressed little girl with the red tam-o'-shanter, and legs like black slate-pencils, whose soft, childish pipe was asking: "Do you want to see me sing and dance?"

"Good lord, no, child!" snapped he, frowning. But at the same time he put a nickel in her palm.

"Can you dance?" asked another man, a tall man

with big eyes that stood out, and a wonderful diamond pin in his scarf.

"Betcher life!" returned Amelia Ann. She knew the man, although he had forgotten her. He used to come to see her papa. He was mean to Johnny.

"All right, dance!"

"For money?" inquired Amelia Ann.

Tyler (for it was he) laughed and showed a quarter.

Amelia Ann promptly laid aside her tidy little brown coat and emerged like a redbird, in her crimson frock. She knew that her dancing was good; and with some amusement she felt the change in her audience from indifferent toleration to applause. She swung, she swayed, she flung her arms out, she circled triumphantly on a single toe; light as a bird, she pirouetted over the sanded floor, caroling to her steps the song which Johnny had taught her:

> " 'Hard luck for poor old Eli,
>   Tough on the Blue;
> Now, all together, smash 'em and break through.
>   'Gainst the line of Crimson
> They can't prevail.
>   Three cheers for Harvard,
> And down with Yale!' "

The listeners did not catch the words; but the martial lilt of the air pleased them; soon they took it up, and the melody swelled out to the street. Dimes and nickels came out of pockets, with the clapping of hands. Amelia Ann was used to such triumphs; she took the silver and praise calmly. "I want it for Johnny and Ally," she explained, packing her gains in her handkerchief; and not for the first time Ally was supposed to be a human being.

"You're a nice little kid," one man said, "looking out for the young ones!"

"Don't you want me to do a dog-and-cat fight?" asked Amelia Ann kindly; she always gave her audience their money's worth. The idle listeners were ready for anything; they proposed sending for some absent "Jerry" who would like the show; and, pending his arrival, they placed Amelia Ann inside the bar in a most comfortable chair next the half-closed door of an adjoining room. Now, Amelia Ann had the ears of a hare, and when she perceived that there were two men talking, and that their voices lowered, she instantly perked up those sharp ears, understanding that something which she ought not to hear was being discussed.

She peered through the crack of the door and saw Tyler. Since she knew that Tyler was mean to Johnny, she hated him with exceeding hatred. She listened the harder. It was Tyler who spoke, first:

"All ready, then?"

"O K," replied the other man; "there'll be a big crowd from over the river. They ain't rabbits like our fellows. That miner's a whole orchestra!"

"But they don't know?"

"Oh, no. Only know there's something up. It's great. Wally, we'll clean the whole nest of damned scabs up, and do up Gleason or Winslow or whatever his name is, jest accidental."

"It'll do,"—Tyler was more moderate of accent— "if none of the outside fellers make a bungle. Write to Adam. He wanted the date."

"I sent him a postal."

"A postal! Hell!"

"Don't get giddy, Wally. I only said Twelve Nineteen, in figgers, and ran 'em together. He'll catch on all right."

"The new men understand?"

"All they need. They're to meet at twelve and git their orders."

"Which window'll they leave open?"

"Next the foundry, left side. I've marked it."

At this most exciting moment the saloon-keeper's arm beckoned. Amelia Ann must go. Her whole soul was in a tumult; but she was an artist first of all; secondly, she was a woman-child; and to both of these, acting comes like breathing. She glided forward with her chilly little stage smile on her colorless little face. The puppy and the kitty evoked shrieks of laughter. More dimes were handed to Amelia Ann. She thanked the kind gentlemen, courtesying as Johnny had taught her; but she could not be moved to repeat her exhibition.

"I got to go home now," said she; "I can't do no more stunts."

"Jest the nicest little kid going," said one man; "ain't it queer, the tricks them little innocent things will think up."

But she did not go home directly. She bought a pair of brass cuff-buttons for Johnny, and asked the baker's boy what day it was. He was rather a stupid boy, who did not read the papers. He said: "The eighteenth."

The little girl thanked him very properly. Relieved, she sought the street-car for home. She pondered much whether to tell Mrs. Delaney, but she remembered how many times and in what a forcible manner she had been forbidden to dance in public, and the remembrance tied her tongue. Johnny had been almost as outspoken as Mrs. Delaney, but, to do Amelia Ann justice, no dread of Johnny's disapproval withheld her, although a glance from him carried worse punishment to the strange little creature than all Mrs. Delaney's cuffs. But Johnny was to be over the river all the evening until late with Mr. Rivers. She knew it, because he had said so in a note to Mrs. Delaney about his clean clothes, and Mrs. Delaney had left the note on the bureau. Amelia always took her information where she found it. She had acquired the useful habit at school when "Teacher" used to pin notes to her frock for her to take home.

She rested easy on the baker boy's assurance; a big boy, in a store, must know things. Therefore she had until to-morrow morning to decide how she should get at Johnny. Her plan was simple: to go over to the Millers', who had a telephone, and call up the Old Colony and Johnny, and tell Johnny over the wire. Amelia Ann knew all about pickets and their obstructing communication—by feet; but they couldn't stop the telephone. Moreover —and this weighed with the culprit—Johnny could not scold much over the 'phone; anyhow, he couldn't *look!* Maybe she wouldn't tell him at all how she happened to overhear the talk; just say it was a "secret," and of course she couldn't tell. Amelia

Ann chuckled to herself at her own sagacity. She was placid and comfortable. She divined what the men had meant, as only a city child brought up amid strikes and rumors of strikes could have divined; old Tyler was going to try to get into the shops and drive the men out and "do up" Johnny. Oh, Amelia Ann understood. But her confidence in her one hero was boundless; to defeat "old Tyler" it merely needed that Johnny should know.

Hence, peacefully, Amelia Ann composed her mind to slumber that night in her warm little bed, with Thyrza already asleep beside her, the door open, and the flames in the base-burner of the room beyond making glowing eyes at her through its tiny mica windows. April nights were still cold sometimes, for it was a late spring, and the base-burner was not yet allowed to go out. To-night the wind was rising. To Amelia Ann, warm and comforted by biscuits and jam, the sound was delicious.

"Ain't it blowy outside! Oh, my, ain't it!" was her last waking thought. She slept a long time; when she awakened the room was dark but for the firelight. The wind was higher, and the limbs of the trees in the Millers' yard creaked and crackled. A little chill crept in by the window, which Johnny made her keep open at night. She did not feel quite so comfortable, and she could not go to sleep. She went over the events of the afternoon. Presently she began to question: was the baker's boy right about the date? She felt less confidence in a boy in a store being infallible. Why hadn't she looked in a paper? Papers always had the day of the month on

the top of the sheet; at least, the *Fairport Citizen*
had. Amelia Ann was observant,—her wits were always at the window. She hadn't the least doubt of
the meaning of the numbers on the post card; she
had known of exactly that method of conveying information being used. No, the attack would be at
twelve o'clock on the nineteenth of April. Was to-
day or to-morrow the nineteenth? Amelia Ann
knew there was a *Citizen,* for since they came to
Fairport, and Johnny got such big wages, they had
the *Fairport Citizen* every day, and Mrs. Delaney
had been reading about the strike in it that very
evening. How stupid not to have looked, then!
Well, she'd have to look now. So, very crossly,
Amelia Ann obeyed her conscience, crept out of her
warm nest and explored the kitchen, in the dark, for
the paper. Amelia Ann didn't mind prowling in the
dark; her finger-tips saw, Johnny said. She found
the paper, carried it into the light of the mica eyes—
and the number on the top of the page was nineteen!

Amelia Ann stood motionless. Through her stupid trust in a boy, Johnny might be killed! But the
child did not weep; she did not stand still, even, for
more than a second. The line of her firm little
mouth straightened, her faint, childish eyebrows
knit. Then Amelia Ann sat down and put on her
stockings. Mrs. Delaney slumbered heavily, and little Franzy less heavily, but as soundly, while the
little girl dressed herself with extraordinary swiftness. As she slipped out of the house the clock
struck twelve. She glanced over at the Miller cottage, a shadowgraph only, softly dark, with no detail

of window or door; so on, to the dark bulk of the
stable where Ally, no doubt, was sleeping, like every
one else. The idea of rousing that peaceful house
in order to telephone never so much as stirred in
Amelia Ann's mind; too carefully had Mrs. Delaney
inculcated a noiseless tread and a hushed voice if one
crossed that threshold where any noise might send
the poor lady up stairs into convulsions! No; Amelia Ann stole on tiptoe over the plank walk and
made for the stable-door, always left unlocked on
account of Miss Tina's consuming terror of fire.
Often had she said: "Ally much better be stolen
than burned alive!"

Thus no barrier met her noiseless approach. Inside the stable, she called the horse, and Ally's
friendly neigh told her she might safely enter the
stall. Once she was obliged to strike one of the
matches she had brought with her; but she blew it
out and stepped on it two times to make sure it
would stir up no harm. She put the bridle on Ally,
but she put nothing else, for by this time the little
acrobat rode like a cowboy, and it was easy enough
to leap on the horse's back from the oats box.

She had to ride carefully until she was out of
earshot of her home. Then she let Ally go, go her
best, her wildest! Down the long hill her horse's
hoofs clattered. A film of rain glistened on the
brick pavement, under the white electric lights. Ally
slipped, but she did not fall, and Amelia Ann turned
into another street with macadam paving, but she
never slackened her speed. Miss Tina would have
wrung her hands and sobbed could she have wit-

nessed that nightmare ride. Amelia Ann hadn't enjoyed herself so much since she left Chicago. To ride like that with a clear conscience was worth her numb hands and her chattering teeth.

Wakeful creatures on the road of that furious flight, nurses or mourners or toilers, heard and marveled over the pounding hoofs. They roused, for a second, many a sleeper, but ere he could harken enough to understand they were swept into silence. The pickets, patroling the side alley-way to the works, cursing the damp chill of the night air and relieving each other from their fortalice of "Oscar's Sample Rooms," had nearly let her pass out of sheer surprise. But they had been cautioned, that night, not to let a mouse go by them, and the leader shouted: "Halt!" lifting something which glinted in the street lights.

The man next him exclaimed not to shoot the child; the bar was down. The bar was a great log resting on trestles, spanning the narrow way. What the police thought of this obstruction of traffic no one knew, because they did not tell. They probably judged it one of the rights of labor.

"Whoa!" bawled the nearest picket; "whoa! you'll break your horse's neck!"

But Amelia Ann's blood was up; so was Ally's; many a time in her Kentucky youth had she leaped the pasture fence; she went over the log like a bird; she never so much as grazed it with her heels.

"Damn her! Shoot the *horse!*" screamed the first picket, who was in Tyler's secret plans. There was a shot, but it went wild. Raw marksmanship is usually uncertain at night. Amelia Ann saw the low fence, the alley between high brick walls and beyond Johnny's men and Johnny. Without an eyeblink of pausing, crouched low over Ally's neck, she put the horse to the fence; she rushed her over the litter of a foundry; she turned her so sharply that her feet slipped about in a sickening lurch, and then, while the useless fusillade still woke the echoes, she rode up to the watchman at the foundry door.

"Please let me in; I got to speak to Johnny," said Amelia Ann.

CHAPTER XVI

THE END OF THE DUEL

It was the chief strike-breaker who came out to receive the limp little form as it rolled in a heap off the trembling horse. The strike-breaker had had a little daughter of his own, who died when she was Amelia Ann's age. Very gently he carried her into the hall, through the office, to Johnny's room.

"Hurry! hurry!" she kept demanding, and the strike-breaker first walked swiftly, then more swiftly; at last he ran.

Johnny sat up in bed, fully dressed; one hand flashed out a revolver, the other turned on the electric lights.

The strike-breaker had conceived an admiration for the young fellow; he registered it justified when he heard Johnny's even tones:

"Well, Amelia Ann, what's up?"

The shivering little mite lifted undaunted eyes, and clung to the iron side of the bedstead to hold herself on her tingling, tottering feet. Her teeth chattered, but her voice was the undaunted, "sassy" voice of Amelia Ann: "Johnny, I got something terrible important to tell you, but you got to promise not to scold me first."

Johnny knew his girl; he wasted no precious minutes. "All right, I promise. Get on!" said he.

Then, Amelia Ann, with remarkable directness, for a child, blurted out her tale and its conclusion.

"I seen 'em a-comin', too, down by the river, an awful big lot! And the foundry winder's open on the alley."

"Very well," was Johnny's comment; "ring the bell, Mat,"—to the strike-breaker. "Look out for the window, first. That means we've spies inside—"

"I'll fix 'em. I'll put the man I suspect where he'll get a dose," answered the strike-breaker; "I'll see to the window and be back."

He was back before Johnny had finished telephoning Hopkins and Rivers. The strike-breaker caught his last words: "Yes, sir. Do as we agreed? Good-by; we're all right."

"You've planned this all out beforehand?" said the strike-breaker, who had been touching a bell or two, himself, sending his own prearranged signals.

"Of course,—it was such a probable thing. And you know Tyler skipped off to-day as if to Chicago —only went as far as Gillmansie. We shadowed him. So we are all ready; but it was blooming lucky the little girl gave us warning about the window; we had it boarded up and we shouldn't have given it a thought, until too late. Mr. Standish and Lossing have stiffened up the mayor—or scared him, more than Tyler can, and Company K boys are all ready to turn out for a hurry call. Mr. Hopkins will attend to that. In a minute you'll hear the bell. *There!*" He caught up the receiver. "You have?" he called; "it's all right? . . . That's good. . . . *Has* he? Ready to call the fire department if I give the signal, please! That's all right." He laid down the receiver, smiling. "Hopkins has sent in the call. He's on his way. He has called on the police, also. Now, if we can hold out twenty-odd minutes we shall send them flying." He looked at the little messenger spreading bird-like hands over the glow in his grate; his brows met, but only for an instant. "Amelia Ann," he called, and she turned. "You want to take a hand in this scrimmage?"

"Betcher life," Amelia Ann observed calmly.

"Then listen! Don't stir out of this room unless it gets afire. If it does, *skip!* But call 340 first, if you can. That's the fire department. Say: 'They need you at the Old Colony. Come a-running!' Then you get out. But don't go unless you have to. Mr. Hardy or I will tell you if you have to do anything else. Now, say it over about 340." Amelia Ann, never taking her eyes off Johnny's, repeated the message.

"Very well. Don't mind if you hear brickbats on the shutters. They're iron and bolted, and the walls are thick. Don't mind gun shots. We have guns as well as they. You're the sentry in charge. I salute you, sentinel." Gravely he lifted his hand in a military salute. Amelia Ann as gravely saluted in return. She was quite sure, now, she was "It."

"Please, Johnny, I mean Captain, kin I sing?" she asked.

"Sing away. Good night, sentinel. I'll see you later."

With the last word he turned swiftly and drew the other man out of the room. As the door closed behind them, they both paused; of a sudden, the white electric light blocked out all the upper win-

dows—below, the heavy shutters were like closed
eyelids and gave no sign—the long aisles flashed
innumerable brushes of flame over half-dressed negroes, who were making for their posts as rapidly,
and with as little excitement, as in their nightly
drills. Perhaps some of them deemed it no more,
for the white teeth shone all along the sable line.

"Guns and hose ready?" asked the young com-
mander. He had forgotten all his foreboding of the
afternoon; his veins ran the warmer for the sheer
Anglo-Saxon joy in fighting; he chuckled at poor
Holman's hard luck, sick at home with the measles;
secretly, he hoped Graves, the next in office,
wouldn't get to the spot in time. His eye was everywhere; his mind whirled through all the possibilities of attack. "Guns and hose ready?" said he. Mat
Hardy nodded.

"Water first, you know; don't shoot unless you
must, then at their legs."

"There's a tough gang from over the river," reported the strike-breaker, "not workmen, just river
scum. They'll be bound to fall in for the chance of
stealing something and the fun of scaring a nigger.
Then, some of Danbury's men are pretty hard citizens. They struck this afternoon, you know. Lot
of boys in there, too. And there are some miners
out."

"Yes, listen!"

Hardy sunk his chin on his breast with a grim
smile. He knew the sound; many a time had he
harkened to that broken, hollow murmur as of the
wind rising in the forest, as of the pounding of
muffled hammers, the marching of a mass of men,

not keeping step. The day force which slept had joined the night force which worked. Johnny and his lieutenant saw that every man was at his post. With that ominous, pounding roar in all their ears, Johnny jumped on an anvil, and smiled around the shop.

"The soldiers are coming,"—his clean-cut tones reached every man—"stand these fellows off a few minutes, and the soldiers will be here! We'll break the strike, to-night. Hot coffee and cold beer will be served as soon as the retreat is over. Three cheers for Hopkins. Now! All together!"

The men cheered, the negroes with a will, the strike-breakers rather tamely; but there was a good, steady glint in their eyes.

While the cheer yet rang, Johnny and the second in command exchanged glances. Something banged against the great arch of the foundry door. A voice demanded admission.

"What do you want here?" called Johnny back; "do you know that you are breaking and entering a house that doesn't belong to you, and that we, the lawful, legal guardians of the premises" (Johnny flung all his frail possessions in legal lore into his sentences) "that we have the right to shoot and kill you, if, being warned, you do not desist? In the name of the state of Iowa, I call upon you all to disperse!"

"Aw, go chase yourself!" a voice retorted. There rose the hideous outcry of a mob, as of a pack of wolves, heating its own fury with yells and shouts and the screaming of savage and filthy threats.

"Say, they got that there log the pickets had,"

said Mat Hardy; "they are going to make a batter-ing-ram of it, I guess."

"I don't see hardly any of our men," said Johnny; "they're all outsiders!"

Above the tumult, Tyler's voice boomed like the clang of a great bell: "Open the doors and clear out, we won't touch a hair of your heads! Stay in there, and we'll pound the —— —— scabs to rags!"

"Guess we better cool those hot heads off a bit," said Johnny; "turn on the hose."

He stood behind a window protected with heavy iron wire, and watched for the spouting streams; only two came, and Hardy reported: "That fool inside has cut the hose!"

"Do you know who he is?"

"I made a guess at it. We've a brother-in-law of Adam Finn who come in Monday, pretended he run the pickets. I got him tied up and a nigger settin' on him."

"They mean something worse than cutting hose; see that banana cart with the sacks and the spades?"

"I've seen it; the miners mean to dig holes and blow up something, most likely the shed we sleep in. That's what's the matter with the darkies; they're scared blue, 'fraid of dinnymite. Told 'em *coal* miners didn't use dinnymite; but they got it in their heads that every miner here's got his boot-legs crammed with sticks of the damn stuff and that the cart's full of bombs. Told 'em they couldn't do nothin' with sticks, if they had 'em; but you might's well reason with a mule!"

Even the two streams held the mob back a moment, and when a rashly venturesome soul got the full force in his chest and went sprawling, his own comrades screamed with laughter. But the second after, an explosion shook the windows with a crackling noise as of splintered glass, made the heavy doors chatter on their hinges, and turned the black faces a drabbled gray in their terror.

"Say, boss!" gurgled one, "I ain't aimin' to fight no dinnymite bums. I draws de line, right dar; I'll fight humans w'ile I kin stan', but dat ar's conjure work, and I *gits!*"

A groan of assent betrayed how well he spoke for his race. They were past argument. They needed a demonstration.

"Ten men to follow me!" called Johnny. "I'll finish this nonsense!"

Every strike-breaker ran forward, and half a dozen blacks. "First ten!" shouted Johnny; "no, Mat Hardy, *you* can't go! You've got to run the defense. This is *my* job! Throw the door open and shut it behind me; but be ready to pull that cart in the little door, when we get it. Now! Out of the way of the door!"

Johnny and his ten fell, like the bolt of a catapult, on the push-cart. They drenched the cart with their hose before a pick, wielded by a blackened, red-shirted fellow from the coal mines over the river, drove three or four leaks into the hose and sent the water spurting at right angles. The push-cart was wrenched from its guard and surrounded by the sallying party. Ere the assaulters quite understood the object of the sally, the cart was surrounded by drawn revolvers; until, suddenly, the small door, at

which they had not looked, swung inward and their
best weapon was inside, out of their reach, while a
child's keen, sweet high pipe cleft the uproar:

"'Gainst the line of crimson
    They can't prevail!
Three cheers for Harvard
    And down with Yale!"

"Lord!" thought Johnny; "if I only had a few of
the boys here, we'd show them!" It was strange
how the old college cries went to his head with a
kind of intoxication. He found himself yelling
"Har-vard!" as he smote, and out of his little forlorn hope, bleeding already from the missiles too
easily found in the yard, came an answering shout
of *"Yale! Yale!"* The shouter was a little strike-
breaker, whom Johnny had found out, at odds with
his people and his own foolish past, and ready for
any desperate endeavor. Johnny sent him a single
glance, and the two men knew each other.

The door had closed the instant the cart was
drawn in, as Johnny had ordered. But Tyler had
time to rush a score of men between Johnny's men
and the door. Two men had gone inside with
the push-cart; all might, perhaps, have entered, had
not one been felled by the pick of the giant in the
red shirt. He lay, with a ghastly wound in his head,
but still breathing.

"We can't leave him, boys," cried Johnny, "pull
him along with us! We can hold out for the soldiers! But push back for the door!" The men
shouted. Tyler's men yelled back, and there was a
rush; but the revolvers barked. The mob gave back.

"Aim at their legs, men! *Legs!*" commanded Johnny, who was looking a dozen ways at once. The brickbats fell about the men's heads; but so wedged into the crowd was the little hollow square that Tyler did not dare bid his own guns to fire. The best policy seemed to him to overpower the half-dozen fighters by the sheer impetus of a great mass. But there where the revolvers shot into so dense a crowd they could not miss. Half a dozen men lay on the ground; they had to be helped away, and the constant volleys from the upper windows of the factory had driven back the parties attacking the other doors. None was killed, but a score had been wounded by the riot-guns' buckshot.

Tyler drew the big fellow in the red shirt, aside. He was a man who had lost his two sons in a mine accident, caused simply and solely by the parsimony of the mine owners; he, himself, had been injured on the head and was never after wholly sane; a fight acted on him like whisky; he became a raging Berserker, absolutely reckless of life, and he hated the strike-breakers as a settler, whose family has been murdered in an Indian outbreak, hates Indians. His pick had made more than one hideous mark.

"Go for the young fellow with the light-blue shirt and the cap, right there in the middle, Luke," said Tyler. "Get *him* down, the others will run!"

"I'll *kill* him!" said Luke, "he's the boss."

"The rest of you, on this side, make for that big door! These fellows can't move, and the door's shaking; the hinges are broken. Get out that log and smash it in! They'll run like rats when they see us inside!"

It was not so bad a plan, although it did not make enough account of the riot-guns; but at this moment a shout and waving hands turned the eyes of the crowd to Shop A, the big wood-working shop, next the sheds where the shop force was sheltered. One of its second story windows was glowing blood-red and puffing smoke through every crevice of the casement. The same glance discovered a figure creeping up the fire-escape toward the glass. The creeping figure was that of a gray-haired little man, and his dried-up, wrinkled Irish face, with its stubble of gray beard, was illumined by the spouting light. Some of the mob knew him,—Dennis Fogarty, who had worked in the Old Colony for thirty years. He had a length of hose flopping clumsily after him. For a second the storm of battle was stricken dumb, and Johnny as well as Tyler caught his strained, cracked voice pleading: "Boys, turn on the water, turn it on! She's on fire! The Old Colony that's kept us all 's on fire! You wouldn't want her to burn up! I b'long to the union, I'm striking, too; but I can't let the Old Colony burn! You're burning up your *jobs*, boys!"

The hose was only a garden hose, kept in the yard, and, of course, turned on from the outside. Some one, of the few Old Colony men present, must have felt the force of the appeal and responded, for a cascade spirted up through the nozzle.

Probably the fire, with its presumable demoralization of the defenders, was part of Tyler's scheme of battle, and was started by the same hand which had ripped off the boards from the alley window and slashed the hose; Tyler may have intended but slight damage to the works; however that may be, the fire was essential to his plans; he snatched a musket from the man next him.

"Let the old man alone!" shouted Johnny; "he's one of your own men—oh, you damn mucker!" Tyler, safe beyond Johnny's reach, had taken careful aim and fired. The old man screamed. He staggered on his narrow perch; but, with a mortal effort, he jammed his hose nozzle through the window-pane, between the iron bars; then his muscles shrank, his hands opened and shut, clutching for the rounds of the ladder, his arms flew out, and he plunged downward, in a hideous bat-like dart.

"Now! he ain't looking!" cried Tyler to Luke.

But Johnny, although his face had gone white and he felt horribly sick for a second, was not off his guard. He dodged all but a graze of the terrible pick, and his left hand shot out the wickedest blow which he had ever dealt in his life; it caught the miner where it was aimed and felled him as would a hammer. As he fell, the Yale boy, whose revolver was empty, caught the pick from his hands and dealt furious blows to right and left with it, which cleared a circle, for the mob fell back beyond its swing. Adam Finn alone sprang at Johnny with his knife, got the butt of a revolver in his face, and staggered back. One of Johnny's men, who had tasted Adam's knife, already, shot his last cartridge at him; it missed, but the man smiled grimly, for it went straight to the heart of the miner in the red shirt, at that moment lifted by a comrade.

Johnny's men were fighting now for their lives. There had been no real fury, at first, in the great body of the attackers; but the combat, the ferocious hand-to-hand struggle, had roused the elemental savagery of both sides. Now, the mob fought not for their first object, which was simply to chase the strike-breakers out of the building, but out of sheer blood-hunger. Johnny's little band was dwindled to half a dozen, all bleeding from ugly wounds, two of them only keeping their feet out of their desperate determination not to fall. On the ground, which they guarded, lay two of their comrades, one of whom still gasped feebly; the other would never be disturbed by the rage about him. Adam Finn's aim had been too true. Their revolvers were empty save one shot that was still in Johnny's pistol. He was saving it for Tyler, but Tyler kept well out of range on the other side. The main body of the strikers was at the foundry door, toward which Johnny's men now wedged their way inch by inch. He could hear, to the left, the cries of the rescue party which Mat had sent in spite of orders; but they were engaged by the other wing. Tyler had sent all his guns there, but, luckily, most of them had been fired, already, in such excitement that they had done little damage, and their holders, half of them, did not know how to reload. Johnny could hear another sound. Amelia Ann's nose had not been idle; she had smelled smoke, she had seen the light; she had summoned 340, and now she screamed, "The firemen are coming! I hear them a-coming! I hear the hosses! I hear the hosses!"

Tyler ground his teeth. "Put the bar up!" he cried to Adam Finn. "Have the boys keep 'em back! Now, Bud, stand by me, it's us to the bat!"

The man addressed was an old river-rat from the southwest, thief, pirate, and cut-throat. He had come to see the fun, and found more fun than he expected.

With Bud on one side and two sure hands on the other, Tyler led his rush. Simultaneously, three men struck with their clubbed guns at the little Yale man. They believed Johnny's revolver empty, but flinging his own assailant back as if he were a sack of wheat, he sprang at Tyler. He shot and shot straight. Their eyes crossed in one flash of deadly recognition. It was the end of their long duel.

"Bud!" shrieked Tyler. And he sank against his friends. Bud responded. His knife flashed. As Johnny half wheeled, it glanced against his side, stinging only a second; at the same time, he felt a blow on his head. He had stuffed his cap with engine waste, and well the rudely armored helmet had served him; but so mighty was Adam Finn's stroke that it bore him to his knees. *"Har—vard!"* he cried, unconscious of his cry, putting all his ebbing force into one blow at the man above him, ere the crowd and the brick walls and the lights wavered, and the roar of conflict swung into the shrill cry of the fife, the roll of drums and a widening, dizzy ringing, as of bells. He knew that the soldiers were come, but come too late for him. Yet knowing it, his stiff lips smiled the smile the little boy used to give. It wouldn't be too late for the Yale boy and the others. And Bloker might forgive him now, and his father, and Peggy would know that he was some good in a Blood Feud. Then it was not only dark but still, and he was very glad to be so sound asleep.

CHAPTER XVII

JOSIAH WINSLOW'S DAY

When Johnny came out of the darkness, he was sure that he was not yet awake, for he lay in his own bed in his own room, and to his dazzled and darkling senses there was nothing incongruous in the new picture of his mother, while he remembered well the portrait of his father, whose rugged features faced him from the wall of the opposite room and seemed vaguely to welcome him. The room looked exactly as it used to look in his college vacations. There were all the old belongings of the room: the folio, the pistols, the sword of the ancient governor, the pictures which he had known from a child, the big arm-chair, the lounge at the foot of the bed, the writing-table on which Peggy and he had scratched their childish initials—Hilma had cuffed them both impartially for that same act—the samovar, which was his mother's, on her table. Through the side door, he could view the white tiles of his bath-room, and the very same old brown bath-robe of his Harvard days was flung over a chair. It was so like the old time and all so dreamlike that he wondered if he could not make his mind work more marvels, as he had made it at the hospital. Once to feel his mother's arm under his neck as he used to feel it in his childish hurts, once to hear his father's gruff whisper: "Hullo, son, feeling better?" once to see Peggy's radiant head tossed at him,—he wouldn't mind, then, having been killed, just when life meant something!

Perhaps his mind would feign images for him— yes, it was obeying him! With a thrill, he was conscious that an arm was under his pillow, that a tear splashed on his hair to roll over his forehead, that a woman's soft tones trembled on the words: "My dear boy! my *dear* boy!" Yet it was not quite, not quite *mamasa's* violin sweetness of voice. Who else, who else? Not Peggy—that was Peggy who flitted, white, silent, past the doorway down the hall! Oh, Peggy, please come back! But if not his mother, not Peggy, who could it be? It wasn't dear, strong Hilma, who was wedded and happy, and had a boy named after him; her crisp Swedish accents there would be no mistaking. And it wasn't the tall, smiling nurse in the blue and white stripes, like, yet faintly unlike, the stripes which his wandering gaze had always found at the hospital.

"He's awake," said the nurse.

The lady's voice spoke, quite changed, quite composed and cheerful: "May I give it to him, please?" Johnny sighed; he knew the voice; it was only the emotion in it which had changed it for him. "My dear boy! my dear boy!" And a tear. Could Mrs. Winslow care that he must die? He felt himself gently lifted, so gently yet so strongly; the rim of a glass touched his lips at precisely the right angle. He drank without question. "Thank you, Aunt Emma," he said and closed his eyes. It was the old name which he had given her years ago, before she took his mother's place and he had no right to be fond of her. What a mess life was! Being very pleasantly tired, however, he left it and went to sleep. The sun grew brighter while he slept. Its brightness rested on the nurse's and the doctors' faces, when he woke. He had known the older doctor ever since he was a lad, and he had seen the younger man at his father's bedside.

"Well, Johnny-Ivan," said the old doctor, "ready for something to eat?"

"Did they kill Dennis Fogarty?" said Johnny.

"By all good rights he ought to be dead, but he isn't. Not by a long shot. He'll be around by the time you get out, and from the way you're doing that will be pretty quickly."

"How did he know——"

"Oh, he's been prowling round the shops ever since he had to leave them, like a lost cat. Mr. Hopkins and Hoffman both went to see him, and it helped him more than medicine. You can rest your mind about *him*. Drink your milk!"

Obediently, Johnny quaffed the milk.

"How about the strike?" said he.

"The strike's over; most of the men back. You've saved the Old Colony Plow. Company a pretty penny, young man. Now, be quiet for half an hour."

"Then may I ask some questions?"

"Humph! yes, if you won't get excited."

"I won't. But I have to ask one more. Did Billy Bates get back from Chicago?"

"Yes, and did as much as the National Guard to quiet things."

"How many men—"

"That'll do," interrupted the young doctor, "you are not going to go over the whole strike. Shut your eyes for half an hour if you can't sleep."

Johnny shut his eyes. He only opened them once to take a thermometer in his mouth, and later watch the old doctor grin over it by the window. "Pulse down to eighty-four, temperature and respiration normal. Young man, you're doing *fine!*" called the doctor. "Mrs. Winslow, I congratulate you." He shook hands with Johnny's stepmother, who had just entered the room.

Johnny's eyes went from her quiet face to the little picture of the baby whom they had both loved, and then to his father's portrait; almost he seemed to feel his father's hand guiding his fingers to hers. He could almost hear his father's voice begging him never to quarrel with her. He turned his head and looked long and sadly at his mother's beautiful, weary features. But, at last, he faintly smiled. "You would wish it, now, I know, *maman,* dearest," he was thinking as his eyes went to Mrs. Winslow, and he held out his thin hand. "I'm glad to see you, Aunt Emma," said he.

"I'm glad to see you, Johnny," said Mrs. Winslow in her clear tones.

"Sensible woman!" one doctor hummed to the other, in the hall; "perfectly safe to leave her with him."

The sensible woman was sitting by the bedside, her head out of Johnny's range of vision, and she was very quietly wiping a tear first from one eye and then from the other, smiling all the time.

"Is Amelia Ann all right?" asked Johnny; "and I hope no harm happened to Ally."

"None at all; I think she destroyed a pattern or two by stepping on them; they put her in the foundry; but *she* is unharmed. Amelia Ann is perfectly fit and has taken a great fancy to Peggy. They had some difficulty in getting her out of the room, I understand; but she was very useful there, having summoned the fire department and done miscellaneous telephoning, to order."

"They didn't hurt the works much? The fire was put out?"

"Only a few windows broken. The fire didn't amount to anything. Dennis' hose had done good work."

"I hope they let all the men come back," said Johnny presently.

"Billy Bates interceded for them; yes, they are all back—who wanted to come."

"Was Tyler killed?"

Mrs. Winslow hesitated,—she remembered Johnny's old-time softness of heart; but Johnny read her halt in speech aright, and spoke before she could frame a subterfuge.

"I'm rather sorry," he said, but without any acute feeling; "he was a dandy fighter."

After a second, he started another line of questions. Was there a—a letter found in his inside pocket or—or any papers? But here Mrs. Winslow was prepared. "I'll see," she said glibly; "were the papers valuable?"

"Only to me, I'm afraid," said Johnny with a dry smile.

Presently he asked: "How is Michael? When can I see Michael?"

Mrs. Winslow promised that he should see Michael to-morrow.

It may be related, here, that Michael paid him the visit on the day. He made a toilet of state in his new caftan, scrubbed and polished and brushed. Every member of the household cautioned him to be cheerful, to be quiet and to say very little. Most politely, even gratefully he received the admonitions, promising obedience. When the word came to him, he tiptoed from the house-door, but lost some of the advantage of this noiseless entrance by tumbling over a chair in Johnny's room. He fell on his knees by Johnny's bed, kissed the bedclothes, kissed the pillows, kissed Johnny's hand, sniffling all the time and the tears rolling down his cheeks on either side of a smile like a gargoyle's, which he never allowed to fade. To every question he answered *gospodi, batyushka,* quite regardless of its import, and he stayed until he was led away by the scandalized nurse, whose hand he insisted on kissing. She had intended to tell him he could not come again for a week, but after this tribute of a humble and loyal heart, she relented to the limit of three days. Such things are women!

But this was to-morrow; to-day Johnny was skirting the desire of his heart. He asked (carelessly) how was Miss Rutherford. Rather tired, but very well, Mrs. Winslow told him; as soon as he was a little stronger he should see her.

"You wouldn't mind asking her just to step by the door, would you, Aunt Emma?" asked Johnny in his old wheedling voice, which made Mrs. Winslow want to kiss him. "I won't say one word to her, not *one.*"

So Peggy did pass by the door and throw one bewildering, lovely glance as she passed, and that was all Johnny saw of her until the next day. The next day he found her sitting in the room, in a far corner. He was quite content merely to look at her, happily. "When you are stronger you can speak to her," the nurse promised. He grew stronger, fast; so fast that one day, after he was sitting every day in the big chair, he began to talk business. He had thought it all out in his mind. He had even mentioned something of it to Billy, who came among the earliest admitted, and announced on his second visit, with simulated ease, but a glowing face, that he was going to be a married man.

"And I'll tell you who helped me to it," said he. "Roger Mack! Bless that boy! You listen. *You* can't talk. I went to Darrell's after Roger Mack, too. I suspected a nigger in that wood-pile, too. The worst was, one day, after you were hurt, I was looking over your traps a bit and I came across all Roger Mack's letters. There was one on the top written,—most of them were typed. Of course, I didn't read a word. But, Ivan, I *wanted* to, like the devil! I *did.* Because, you see, that handwriting I knew; it was the handwriting of—of a young lady—a friend of mine. Johnny, I felt awfully queer and mean. Because, you see, I had rather sized it up in my mind that Roger Mack was Miss Rutherford; but if it was Miss Martin, my friend, why, that supposition would fit all the facts of the case just about as well, and I was sure if—if any girl got letters from you I wouldn't have a ghost of a show. I oughtn't to have, either—"

"Billy, you old chump, it wasn't—and you're a better—"

"I'm not and I know it; but you keep cool. I went to my friend, and I opened the subject. In five minutes she put me wise: I found out she had never read a letter from you, and only written half a dozen and—and—then—Johnny, I don't know how I ever did it, but I blurted out how I had set my heart on her ever since I was a gawky boy; I got excited, I forgot the speech I had been making up for years, I'm awfully afraid I forgot to speak good grammar, but"—Billy was on his feet, swinging his arms—"my God, wasn't it wonderful! She didn't mind, she said—she said she preferred me to any man—Say, Johnny, how 'm I ever going to be half as big a man as she thinks I am?"

One can understand that this conversation gave Johnny a pleasant half-hour; but he told Billy that he had no use for such an irrationally ecstatic being as he was, for a business adviser. There was only one other person whom he could consult, namely, Mrs. Winter, who came in with her very best cards, and recommended Penelope's Web as a light yet engrossing solace for the sick-room. Certain obvious reasons restrained his tongue with her; not until he had spoken to Mrs. Winslow could he take a decisive step. Therefore, one day, he plunged into the matter in his direct fashion. "Aunt Emma, I'm thinking of buying some Old Colony stock. Aunty Winter is willing to lend me some money, and I think, between my salary and the dividends, I can pay for it in time. But I wanted to tell you first."

"Thank you, Johnny," said Mrs. Winslow—she seemed to have a curious difficulty in speaking; but her voice was as serene as usual, when she did speak —"I think it would be a good thing if—if you needed to borrow money. But you don't. You have plenty of your own."

"How, Aunt Emma?" said Johnny very quietly. He did not think anything; he felt of a sudden a curious awe and surprise, the sense of something coming which would move him, but what it was he did not in the least know. "How, Aunt Emma?" he said.

She rose and went out of the room. She did not speak, and he understood that the reason was that she couldn't, for the moment, speak calmly. In a moment she returned, carrying a letter in her hand. She had regained her usual composure, but her face was paler than Johnny's.

"Johnny," she said, "I want you to remember when you read the letter that if we—your father and I—have made mistakes in our dealing with you, they were made out of love. And I do not think your father did make a mistake; he felt that you must see for yourself that which he could not see for you. But he loved you, always, more than you can understand. And his last word, his last thought, was of you. You won't let your pride defeat his lifelong hopes, now, will you?"

She laid the letter in his hand and turned; but even as she turned, she yielded to her feelings and came back to give him the first caress she had dared to give him openly since he was a little child. She kissed him lightly on his dark curls where they touched his forehead, saying again and in the same tone: "My dear boy! My dear boy!"

After she left him it was minutes before he opened the letter; he was standing again by his father's bed; he felt the touch of the nerveless hands which had been so strong, and he heard his father's voice: "There, there, little Johnny, let papa help you climb!" With a long difficult sigh, he opened the letter. This is what he read:

My dear Son:

When you read my will, you will think I might be more fatherly, maybe. Maybe—I hope not, you are a pretty fair-minded chap, Johnny—you will be unjust to my wife. But here is the cause. I have been going over it for years, trying to find a way out of it without hurting you. I can't find it. There isn't any. The only way for you to find that the ground is hard, is to get a fall. You won't take my word for it. I don't blame you. A man has to do what he believes is right, whatever it costs him. You believe a lot of rotten nonsense, in my opinion, but that you've got to find out, yourself. All I can do is to prevent your squandering all your fortune in finding it out. A hundred thousand is a good deal of money to pay for discovering there is no short cut to the millennium; but I don't believe less would satisfy you. My only worry, son, is that you'll get some knocks on your heart and your conscience which no money is worth. I can't help you, there.

All I can do is to save you the money, so you can help other people in the only true, sensible, American way, by giving them a show to help themselves. I leave the fortune you would have had to your stepmother, who loves you truly, and whom you will truly love some day, *in trust*. So soon as she is convinced that you can manage the money and the business (or any business—but I somehow feel you'll want to run the Old Colony, *and you can do it!*) she will give you a hundred thousand. That hundred thousand I feel sure you won't lose; so you will inherit your fortune all right, in five years. Try again, Johnny. You'll make it this time. If in your business plans you should need more, she'll give you more. I trust you, my son; you are going to be a better business man than I was. You've got my head; but head is not going to be all the great business man of the future needs; he will have to have a heart or he can't understand and manage his men; you have your mother's heart, and you will have learned to know the best fellow in the world, the American workingman; you'll know him and respect him and you won't be fooled about him. And you can help him and he will help you better than I ever could manage.

Johnny, son, I expect before very long I shall see your mother. I hope she will forgive me; whatever I have to forgive her, I forgave, long ago. You will have to make up for any mistakes we have made. All our lives we both tried to win you. I guess in the end we'll both succeed, and be reconciled.

Your affectionate father,
Josiah C. Winslow.

P. S. I don't believe I ever told you, son, how glad I was you were so fond of your little sister; I'll give her your love, shan't I? Somehow, I guess I'll meet them all, and I think a good deal about it. I get a great deal of comfort out of it, too. There's another thing. Your stepmother has a notion that you will marry Peggy. That's right. She's the girl I should pick out for you, myself. But maybe it will be another girl. Whoever it is, you can trust Emma Winslow to do the right thing by her and by little Peggy, too. It has been a big comfort to me, somehow, writing this letter. Big. Be good to your stepmother, Johnny, won't you? I hope I can manage to get around to see you when you read this. Don't feel too bad about your nonsense, after you get over it; you're a fine fellow, Johnny; I am proud of you.

As Johnny's wet eyes made out the last word through their blur, he lifted them and was aware of Peggy in the doorway. If she had meant to go at the sight of his tears, the arms he unconsciously extended were enough; she came straight to him, and, still holding his father's letter, he clasped her tightly while they cried together, comforting each other, as they had comforted each other in their childish griefs. It was Peggy who spoke first:

"I got the letter, Jo'nivan."

"And you'll help me, Peggy?"

"Of course, Jo'nivan."

"And speak to me again?"

"I reckon I'll have to if—if I'm—"

"Going to marry me? I reckon you will, dear. Oh, Peggy!"

"Jo'nivan, you'll do awful things to yourself if you try to—to be so ridiculous. Put your arms down this minute. Oh, Jo'nivan, look!"

She pointed with her slim, white hand. The glory of sunlight reflected from the river flooded the portrait on the wall of his mother's writing-room where he sat, flooded almost equally the delicate and beautiful face on the wall of the chamber beyond.

"Oh, Jo'nivan," whispered Peggy in a voice of tender awe, "they are both smiling!"

THE END

A LIST *of* IMPORTANT FICTION
THE BOBBS-MERRILL COMPANY

HEARTS, GOLD AND SPECULATION

BLACK FRIDAY

By FREDERIC S. ISHAM
Author of The Strollers and Under the Rose

There is much energy, much spirit, in this romance of the gold corner. Distinctly an opulent and animated tale. *New York Sun*

Black Friday fascinates by its compelling force and grips by its human intensity. No better or more absorbing novel has been published in a decade. *Newark Advertiser*

The love story is handled with infinite skill. The pictures of "the street" and its thrilling, pulsating life are given with rare power.

Boston Herald

Illustrated by Harrison Fisher
12mo, cloth, price, $1.50

The Bobbs-Merrill Company, *Indianapolis*

WANTED:
A COOK

By ALAN DALE

An uproariously funny comedy-novel of a self-conscious couple in contact with the servant question. Their ludicrous predicaments with their cooks are described with a light, farcial quality and a satire that never fail to entertain.

"A good story well told. In every sentence a hearty laugh and many an irrepressible chuckle of mirth." *New York American*

Bound in decorated cloth, 12mo, $1.50

The Bobbs-Merrill Company, *Indianapolis*